TEN BIG ONES

"Stephanie Plum is a bounty hunter with a great sense of humor that balances out her attitude and worse luck... [Stephanie Plum] is like Dorothy Parker with a lousy job and a Jersey accent."

—Time

"Evanovich's series is as addictive as Fritos—and, 10 books in, not losing any of its salty crunch... colorful characters... Evanovich serves up consistently craveable goodies—and needless to say, they're always perfect for the beach."

—People

"Chutzpah and sheer comic inventiveness... in addition to good fun, the Evanovich/Plum books serve as a nice antidote to everything in pop fiction today."

—The Washington Post

"No less than her plotting, Evanovich's characterizations are models of screwball artistry. The intricate plot machinery of her comic capers is fueled by inventive twists."

—The New York Times

"A perfect summer read, with lots of action and snappy repartee... you don't need to read the first nine to jump into *Ten Big Ones*... one of the best in the series."

—The Oregonian (Portland, OR)

"[A] fabulous climax... as usual, [Evanovich's] characters will keep you laughing out loud."

—Times Picayune (New Orleans, LA)

"Funny, witty, and occasionally steamy . . . evolving comedy starring a sassy contemporary woman with a scene-stealing supporting cast."

—*Dallas Morning News*

"This tenth novel is a standout that zips along to its top-this finale."

—*Hartford Courant*

"[Plum's] charms are many, and they're all on display here."
—*New York Daily News*

"If you prefer your protagonists with big hair and based in Jersey, then Stephanie Plum is your crime solver of choice. Evanovich has a huge following . . . Stephanie and her sidekick, Lula, are the Lucy and Ethel of bounty hunting."

—*USA Today*

"Evanovich is possibly the only mystery writer whose extreme humor can turn what should be serious moments into boisterously funny scenes. The boundaries of good taste are deliciously stretched as Evanovich makes comedy into a kind of art."

—*South Florida Sun-Sentinel*

"A whirlwind of antic adventures . . . the characters deliver plenty . . . since Evanovich utilizes numbers instead of the alphabet to identify Plum's adventures, this series could continue forever, and what fun that would be."

—*Acadiana LifeStyle*

ELEVEN ON TOP

JANET EVANOVICH

St. Martin's Paperbacks

ELEVEN ON TOP

Copyright © 2005 by Evanovich, Inc.
Excerpt from *Twelve Sharp* copyright © 2006 by Evanovich, Inc.

All rights reserved.

For information address St. Martin's Press, 175 Fifth Avenue, New York, NY 10010.

ISBN: 0-312-98534-7
EAN: 978-0-312-98534-9

Printed in the United States of America

St. Martin's Press hardcover edition / June 2005
St. Martin's Paperbacks edition / July 2006

St. Martin's Paperbacks are published by St. Martin's Press, 175 Fifth Avenue, New York, NY 10010.

10 9 8 7

This book is a Jan-Jen production, brought to life through the extraordinary powers of SuperEditor Jen Enderlin

Thanks to Shanna Littlejohn
for suggesting the title for this book.

ELEVEN ON TOP

ONE

MY NAME IS Stephanie Plum. When I was eighteen I got a job working a hot dog stand on the boardwalk on the Jersey shore. I worked the last shift at Dave's Dogs, and I was supposed to start shutting down a half hour before closing so I could clean up for the day crew. We did chili dogs, cheese dogs, kraut dogs, and bean-topped barking dogs. We grilled them on a big grill with rotating rods. Round and round the rods went all day long, turning the dogs.

Dave Loogie owned the dog stand and came by every night to lock the stand down. He checked the garbage to make sure nothing good was thrown away, and he counted the dogs that were left on the grill.

"You gotta plan ahead," Dave told me every night. "You got more than five dogs left on the grill when we close, I'm gonna fire your ass and hire someone with bigger tits."

So every night, fifteen minutes before closing, before Dave showed up, I ate hot dogs. Not a good way to go when you're working at the shore nights and on the beach in a skimpy bathing suit by day. One night I ate fourteen hot dogs. Okay, maybe it was only nine, but it felt like fourteen. Anyway, it was *too many* hot dogs. Well hell, I needed the job.

For years Dave's Dogs took the number-one slot on my list of all-time crappy jobs held. This morning, I decided my present position had finally won the honor of replacing Dave's Dogs. I'm a bounty hunter. A bond enforcement agent, if you want to make me sound more legitimate. I work for my cousin Vinnie in his bail bonds office in the Chambersburg section of Trenton. At least I used to work for my cousin Vinnie. Thirty seconds ago, I quit. I handed in the phony badge I bought off the Net. I gave back my cuffs. And I dropped my remaining open files on Connie's desk.

Vinnie writes the bonds. Connie shuffles the paperwork. My sidekick, Lula, files when the mood strikes her. And an incredibly sexy, incredibly handsome badass named Ranger and I hunt down the morons who don't show up for trial. Until today. As of thirty seconds ago, all the morons got transferred to Ranger's list.

"Give me a break," Connie said. "You can't quit. I've got a stack of open files."

"Give them to Ranger."

"Ranger doesn't do the low bonds. He only takes the high-risk cases."

"Give them to Lula."

Lula was standing hand on hip, watching me spar with Connie. Lula's a size-sixteen black woman squashed into size-ten leopard print spandex. And the weird thing is, in her own way, Lula looks pretty good in the animal spandex.

"Hell yeah," Lula said. "I could catch them sonsabitches. I could hunt down their asses good. Only I'm gonna miss you," she said to me. "What are you gonna do if you don't work here? And what brought this on?"

"Look at me!" I said. "What do you see?"

"I see a mess," Lula said. "You should take better care of yourself."

"I went after Sam Sporky this morning."

"Melon-head Sporky?"

"Yeah. Melon-head. I chased him through three yards. A dog tore a hole in my jeans. Some crazy old lady shot at me. And I finally tackled Sporky behind the Tip Top Cafe."

"Looks like it was garbage day," Lula said. "You don't smell too good. And you got something looks like mustard all over your ass. Least I hope that's mustard."

"There were a bunch of garbage bags at the curb and Melon-head rolled me into them. We made sort of a mess. And then when I finally got him in cuffs, he spit on me!"

"I imagine that's the glob of something stuck in your hair?"

"No. He spit on my shoe. Is there something in my hair?"

Lula gave an involuntary shiver.

"Sounds like a normal day," Connie said. "Hard to believe you're quitting because of Melon-head."

Truth is, I don't exactly know why I was quitting. My stomach feels icky when I get up in the morning. And I go to bed at night wondering where my life is heading.

I've been working as a bounty hunter for a while now and I'm not the world's best. I barely make enough money to cover my rent each month. I've been stalked by crazed killers, taunted by naked fat men, firebombed, shot at, spat at, cussed at, chased by humping dogs, attacked by a flock of Canadian honkers, rolled in garbage, and my cars get destroyed at an alarming rate.

And maybe the two men in my life add to the icky feeling in my stomach. They're both Mr. Right. And they're both Mr. Wrong. They're both a little scary. I wasn't sure if I wanted a relationship with either of them. And I hadn't a clue how to choose between them. One wanted to marry me, sometimes. His name was Joe Morelli and he was a Trenton cop. Ranger was the other guy, and I wasn't sure what he wanted to do with me beyond get me naked and put a smile on my face.

Plus, there was the note that got slipped under my door two days ago. I'M BACK. What the heck did that mean? And the follow-up note tacked to my windshield. DID YOU THINK I WAS DEAD?

My life is too weird. It's time for a change. Time to get a more sensible job and sort out my future.

Connie and Lula shifted their attention from me to the front door. The bonds office is located on Hamilton Avenue. It's a small two-room storefront setup with a cluttered storage area in the back, behind a bank of file cabinets. I didn't hear the door open. And I didn't hear footsteps. So either Connie and Lula were hallucinating or else Ranger was in the room.

Ranger is the mystery man. He's a half head taller than me, moves like a cat, kicks ass all day long, only wears black, smells warm and sexy, and is 100 percent pure perfectly toned muscle. He gets his dark complexion and liquid brown eyes from Cuban ancestors. He was Special Forces, and that's about all anyone knows about Ranger. Well hell, when you smell *that* good and look *that* good, who cares about anything else, anyway?

I can usually feel Ranger standing behind me. Ranger doesn't ordinarily leave any space between us. Today, Ranger was keeping his distance. He reached around me and dropped a file and a body receipt on Connie's desk.

"I brought Angel Robbie in last night," he said to Connie. "You can mail the check to RangeMan."

RangeMan is Ranger's company. It's located in an office building in center city and specializes in security systems and fugitive apprehension.

"I got big news," Lula said to Ranger. "I've been promoted to bounty hunter on account of Stephanie just quit."

Ranger picked a couple strands of sauerkraut off my shirt and pitched them into Connie's wastebasket. "Is that true?"

"Yes," I said. "I quit. I'm done fighting crime. I've rolled in garbage for the last time."

"Hard to believe," Ranger said.

"I'm thinking of getting a job at the button factory," I told him. "I hear they're hiring."

"I don't have a lot of domestic instincts," Ranger said to me, his attention fixing on the unidentifiable glob of goo in my hair, "but I have a real strong urge to take you home and hose you down."

I went dry mouthed. Connie bit into her lower lip, and Lula fanned herself with a file.

"I appreciate the offer," I told him. "Maybe some other time."

"Babe," Ranger said on a smile. He nodded to Lula and Connie and left the office.

No one said anything until he drove off in his shiny black Porsche Turbo.

"I think I wet my pants," Lula said. "Was that one of them double entendres?"

I DROVE BACK to my apartment, took a shower all by myself, and got dressed up in a stretchy white tank top and a tailored black suit with a short skirt. I stepped into four-inch black heels, fluffed up my almost shoulder-length curly brown hair, and added one last layer to my mascara and lipstick.

I'd taken a couple minutes to print out a résumé on my computer. It was pathetically short. Graduated with mediocre grades from Douglass College. Worked as a lingerie buyer for a cheap department store for a bunch of years. Got fired. Tracked down scumbags for my cousin Vinnie. Seeking management position in a classy company. Of course, this was Jersey and classy here might not be the national standard.

I grabbed my big black leather shoulder bag and yelled good-bye to my roomie, Rex-the-hamster. Rex lives in a glass aquarium on the kitchen counter. Rex is pretty much nocturnal so we're sort of like ships passing in the night. As an extra treat, once in a while I drop a Cheez Doodle into his cage and he emerges from his soup can home to retrieve the Doodle. That's about as complicated as our relationship gets.

I live on the second floor of a blocky, no-frills, three-story apartment building. My apartment looks out over the parking lot, which is fine by me. Most of the residents in my building are seniors. They're home in front of their televisions before the sun goes down, so the lot side is quiet at night.

I exited my apartment and locked up behind myself. I took the elevator to the small ground-floor lobby, pushed through the double glass doors, and crossed the lot to my car. I was driving a dark green Saturn SL2. The Saturn had been the special of the day at Generous George's Used Car Emporium. I'd actually wanted a Lexus SC 430, but Generous George thought the Saturn was more in line with my budget constraints.

I slid behind the wheel and cranked the engine over. I was heading off to apply for a job at the button factory and I was feeling down about it. I was telling myself it was a new beginning, but truth is, it felt more like a sad ending. I turned onto Hamilton and drove a couple blocks to Tasty Pastry Bakery, thinking a doughnut would be just the thing to brighten my mood.

Five minutes later, I was on the sidewalk in front of the bakery, doughnut bag in hand, and I was face-to-face with Morelli. He was wearing jeans and scuffed boots and a black V-neck sweater over a black T-shirt. Morelli is six feet of lean, hard muscle and hot Italian libido. He's Jersey guy smart, and he's not a man you'd want to annoy . . . unless you're me. I've been annoying Morelli all my life.

"I was driving by and saw you go in," Morelli said. He was standing close, smiling down at me, eyeing the bakery bag. "Boston creams?" he asked, already knowing the answer.

"I needed happy food."

"You should have called me," he said, hooking his finger into the neckline of my white tank, pulling the neck out to take a look inside. "I have just the thing to make you happy."

I've cohabitated with Morelli from time to time and I knew this to be true. "I have stuff to do this afternoon and doughnuts take less time."

"Cupcake, I haven't seen you in weeks. I could set a new land speed record for getting happy."

"Yeah, but that would be *your* happiness," I said, opening the bag, sharing the doughnuts with Morelli. "What about mine?"

"Your happiness would be top priority."

I took a bite of doughnut. "Tempting, but no. I have a job interview at the button factory. I'm done with bond enforcement."

"When did this happen?"

"About an hour ago," I said. "Okay, I don't actually have an interview *appointment*, but Karen Slobodsky works in the personnel office, and she said I should look her up if I ever wanted a job."

"I could give you a job," Morelli said. "The pay wouldn't be great but the benefits would be pretty decent."

"Gee," I said, "that's the second scariest offer I've had today."

"And the scariest offer would be?"

I didn't think it was smart to tell Morelli about

Ranger's offer of a hosing down. Morelli was wearing a gun on his hip, and Ranger wore guns on multiple parts of his body. Seemed like a bad idea to say something that might ratchet up the competition between them.

I leaned into Morelli and kissed him lightly on the mouth. "It's too scary to share," I told him. He felt nice against me, and he tasted like doughnut. I ran the tip of my tongue along his lower lip. "Yum," I said.

Morelli's fingers curled into the back of my jacket. "*Yum* is a little mild for what I'm feeling. And what I'm feeling shouldn't be happening on the sidewalk in front of the bakery. Maybe we could get together tonight."

"For pizza?"

"Yeah, that too."

I'd been taking a time-out from Morelli and Ranger, hoping to get a better grip on my feelings, but I wasn't making much progress. It was like choosing between birthday cake and a big-boy margarita. How could I possibly decide? And probably I'd be better off without either, but jeez, that wouldn't be any fun.

"Okay," I said. "I'll meet you at Pino's."

"I was thinking my house. The Mets are playing and Bob misses you."

Bob is Morelli's dog. Bob is a big, orange, incredibly huggable shaggy-haired monster with an eating disorder. Bob eats *everything*.

"No fair," I said. "You're using Bob to lure me to your house."

"Yeah," Morelli said. "So?"

I blew out a sigh. "I'll be over around six."

♦ ♦ ♦

I DROVE A couple blocks down Hamilton and left-turned onto Olden. The button factory is just beyond the city limits of north Trenton. At four in the morning, it's a ten-minute drive from my apartment. At all other hours, the drive time is unpredictable. I stopped for a red light at the corner of Olden and State and just as the light flashed green I heard the pop of gunshot behind me and the *zing, zing, zing* of three rounds tearing into metal and fiberglass. I was pretty sure it was *my* metal and fiberglass, so I floored the Saturn and sailed across the intersection. I crossed North Clinton and kept going, checking my rearview mirror. Hard to tell in traffic, but I didn't think anyone was following me. My heart was racing, and I was telling myself to chill. No reason to believe this was anything more than a random shooting. Probably just some gang guy having fun, practicing his sniping. You've got to practice somewhere, right?

I fished my cell phone out of my purse and called Morelli. "Someone's taking potshots at cars on the corner of Olden and State," I told him. "You might want to send someone over to check things out."

"Are you okay?"

"I'd be better if I had that second doughnut." Okay, so this was my best try at bravado. My hands were white-knuckled gripping the wheel and my foot was shaking on the gas pedal. I sucked in some air and told myself I was just a little excited. Not panicked. Not terrified. Just a little excited. All I had to do was calm down and take a couple more deep breaths and I'd be fine.

Ten minutes later, I pulled the Saturn into the button factory parking lot. The entire factory was housed in a mammoth three-story redbrick building. The bricks were dark with age, the old-fashioned double-hung windows were grimy, and the landscaping was lunar. Dickens would have loved it. I wasn't so sure it was my thing. But then, *my thing* wasn't clearly defined anymore.

I got out and walked to the rear of the car, hoping I'd been wrong about the gunshot. I felt another dump of adrenaline when I saw the damage. I'd taken three hits. Two rounds were embedded in the back panel and one had destroyed a rear light.

No one had followed me into the lot, and I didn't see any cars lingering on the road. Wrong place, wrong time, I told myself. And I would have believed it entirely if it hadn't been for my lousy previous job and the two notes. As it was, I had to back-burner some paranoia so as not to be in a terror-induced cold sweat while trying to talk some guy into hiring me.

I crossed the lot to the large glass double doors leading to the offices, and I sashayed through the doors into the lobby. The lobby was small with a chipped tile floor and seasick green walls. Somewhere, not far off, I could hear machines stamping out buttons. Phones rang in another part of the building. I approached the reception desk and asked for Karen Slobodsky.

"Sorry," the woman said. "You're two hours too late. She just quit. Stormed out of here like hurricane Slobodsky, yelling something about sexual harassment."

"So there's a job opening?" I asked, thinking my day was finally turning lucky.

"Sure looks that way. I'll buzz her boss, Jimmy Alizzi."

Ten minutes later, I was in Alizzi's office, sitting across from him. He was at his desk and his slight frame was dwarfed by his massive furniture. He looked to be in his late thirties to early forties. He had slicked-back black hair and an accent and skin tone that had me thinking Indian.

"I will tell you now that I am not Indian," Alizzi said. "Everyone thinks I am Indian, but that is a false assumption. I come from a very small island country off the coast of India."

"Sri Lanka?"

"No, no, no," he said, wagging his bony finger at me. "Not Sri Lanka. My country is even smaller. We are a very proud people, so you must be careful not to make ethnic slurs."

"Sure. You want to tell me the name of this country?"

"Latorran."

"Never heard of it."

"You see, already you are treading in very dangerous waters."

I squelched a grimace.

"So, you were a bounty hunter," he said, skimming over my résumé, eyebrows raised. "That is a quite exciting job. Why would you want to quit such a job?"

"I'm looking for something that has more potential for advancement."

"Oh dear, that would be *my* job you would eventually be seeking."

"Yes, well I'm sure it would take years, and then

who knows . . . you might be president of the company by then."

"You are an outrageous flatterer," he said. "I like that. And what would you do if I were to ask you for sexual favors? Would you threaten to sue me?"

"No. I guess I'd ignore you. Unless you got physical. Then I'd have to kick you in a place that hurt a lot and you probably wouldn't be able to father any children."

"That sounds fair," he said. "It happens that I have an immediate position to fill, so you're hired. You can start tomorrow, promptly at eight o'clock. Do not be late."

Wonderful. I have a real job in a nice clean office where no one will shoot at me. I should be happy, yes? This was what I wanted, wasn't it? Then why do I feel so depressed?

I dragged myself down the stairs to the lobby and out to the parking lot. I found my car and the depression deepened. I hated my car. Not that it was a bad car. It just wasn't the *right* car. Not to mention, it would be great to have a car that didn't have three bullet holes in it.

Maybe I needed another doughnut.

A HALF HOUR later, I was back in my apartment. I'd stopped in at Tasty Pastry and left with a day-old birthday cake. The cake said HAPPY BIRTHDAY LARRY. I don't know how Larry celebrated his birthday, but apparently it was without cake. Larry's loss was my gain. If you want to get happy, birthday cake is the way to go. This was a yellow cake with thick, disgusting white frosting made with lard and artificial butter and artificial vanilla and a truckload of sugar. It was decorated with big gunky roses made out of pink and yellow and purple frosting. It was three layers thick with lemon cream between the layers. And it was designed to serve eight people, so it was just the right size.

I dropped my clothes on the floor and dug into the cake. I gave a chunk of cake to Rex, and I worked on the rest. I ate all the pieces with the big pink roses. I was starting to feel nauseous, but I pressed on. I ate all the pieces with the big yellow roses. I had a purple rose and a couple roseless pieces left. I couldn't do it. I couldn't eat any more cake. I staggered into my bedroom. I needed a nap.

I dropped a T-shirt over my head and pulled on a pair of Scooby-Doo boxers with an elastic waist. God, don't you love clothes with elastic? I had one knee on the bed when I saw the note pinned to my pillowcase. BE AFRAID. BE VERY AFRAID. NEXT TIME I'LL AIM HIGHER.

I thought I'd be more afraid if I hadn't just eaten five pieces of birthday cake. As it was, I was mostly afraid of throwing up. I looked under the bed, behind the shower curtain, and in all the closets. No knuckle-dragging monsters anywhere. I slid the bolt home on the front door and shuffled back to the bedroom.

Now, here's the thing. This isn't the first time someone's broken into my apartment. In fact, people regularly break in. Ranger slides in like smoke. Morelli has a key. And various bad guys and psychos have managed to breach the three locks I keep on the door. Some have even left threatening messages. So I wasn't as freaked out as I might have been prior to my career in bounty huntering. My immediate feelings ran more toward numb despair. I wanted all the scary things to go away. I was tired of scary. I'd quit my scary job, and now I wanted the scary people out of my life. I didn't want to be kidnapped ever again. I didn't want to be held at knifepoint or gunpoint. I didn't want to be threatened, stalked, or run off the road by a homicidal maniac.

I crawled under the covers and pulled the quilt over my head. I was almost asleep when the quilt was yanked back. I let out a shriek and stared up at Ranger.

"What the heck are you doing?" I yelled at him, grabbing at the quilt.

"Visiting, Babe."

"Did you ever think about ringing a doorbell?"

Ranger smiled down at me. "That would take all the fun out of it."

"I didn't know you were interested in fun."

He sat on the side of the bed and the smile widened. "You smell good enough to eat," Ranger said. "You smell like a party."

"It's birthday cake breath. And are we looking at another double entendre?"

"Yeah," Ranger said, "but it's not going anywhere. I have to get back to work. Tank's waiting for me with the motor running. I just wanted to find out if you're serious about quitting."

"I got a job at the button factory. I start tomorrow."

He reached across and removed the note from the pillowcase next to me. "New boyfriend?"

"Someone broke in while I was out. And I guess he shot at me this afternoon."

Ranger stood. "You should discourage people from doing that. Do you need help?"

"Not yet."

"Babe," Ranger said. And he left.

I listened carefully, but I didn't hear the front door open or close. I got up and tiptoed through the apartment. No Ranger. All the locks were locked and the bolt was in place. I suppose he could have gone out the living room window, but he would have had to climb down the side of the building like Spider-Man.

The phone rang, and I waited to see the number pop up on my caller ID. It was Lula. "Yo," I said.

"Yo, your ass. You got some nerve sticking me with this job."

"You volunteered."

"I must've had sunstroke. A person has to be nuts to want this job."

"Something go wrong?"

"Hell, yes. *Everything's* wrong. I could use some assistance here. I'm trying to snag Willie Martin, and he's not cooperating."

"How uncooperative is he?"

"He hauled his nasty ass out of his apartment and left me handcuffed to his big stupid bed."

"That's pretty uncooperative."

"Yeah, and it gets worse. I sort of don't have any clothes on."

"Omigod! Did he attack you?"

"It's a little more complicated than that. He was in the shower when I busted in. You ever see Willie Martin naked? He is *fine*. He used to play pro ball until he made a mess of his knee and had to turn to boosting cars."

"Un hunh."

"Well, one thing led to another and here I am chained to his hunk-of-junk bed. Hell, it's not like I get it regular, you know. I'm real picky about my men. And besides, anybody would've jumped those bones. He's got muscles on muscles and a butt you want to sink your teeth into."

The mental image had me considering turning vegetarian.

WILLIE MARTIN LIVED in a third-floor loft in a graffiti-riddled warehouse that contained a ground-floor chop shop. It was located on the seven-hundred block of Stark Street, an area of urban decay that rivaled Iraqi bomb sites.

I parked behind Lula's red Firebird and transferred my five-shot Smith & Wesson from my purse to my jacket pocket. I'm not much of a gun person and almost never carry one, but I was sufficiently creeped out by the shooting and the notes that I didn't want to venture onto Stark Street unarmed. I locked the car, bypassed the rickety open-cage service elevator on the ground floor, and trudged up two flights of stairs. The stairwell opened to a small grimy foyer and a door with a size-nine high-heeled boot print on it. I guess Willie hadn't answered on the first knock and Lula got impatient.

I tried the doorknob, and the door swung open.

Thank God for small favors because I'd never had any success at kicking in a door. I tentatively stuck my head in and called "Hello."

"Hello, yourself," Lula said. "And don't say no more. I'm not in a good mood. Just unlock these piece-of-crap handcuffs and stand back because I need fries. I need a whole *shitload* of fries. I'm having a fast-food emergency."

Lula was across the room, wrapped in a sheet, one hand cuffed to the iron headboard of the bed, the other hand holding the sheet together.

I pulled the universal handcuff key out of my pocket and looked around the room. "Where are your clothes?"

"He took them. Do you believe that? Said he was going to teach me a lesson not to go after him. I tell you, you can't trust a man. They get what they want and then next thing they got their tighty whities in their pocket and they're out the door. I don't know what he was so upset about, anyway. I was just doing my job. He said, 'Was that good for you?' And I said, 'Oh yeah, baby, it was real good.' And then I tried to cuff him. Hell, truth is it wasn't all that good, and besides, I'm a professional bounty hunter now. Bring 'em back dead or alive, with or without their pants, right? I had an obligation to cuff him."

"Yeah, well next time put your clothes on *before* you try to cuff a guy."

Lula unlocked the cuffs and tied a knot in the sheet to hold it closed. "That's good advice. I'm gonna remember that. That's the kind of advice I need to be a first-class bounty hunter. At least he forgot to take my

purse. I'd be really annoyed if he'd taken my purse."
She went to a chest on the far wall, pulled out one of
Willie's T-shirts and a pair of gym shorts, and put them
on. Then she scooped the rest of the clothes out of the
chest, carried them to the window, and threw them out.

"Okay," Lula said, "I'm starting to feel better now.
Thanks for coming here to help me. And good news, it
looks like no one's stolen your car. I saw it still sitting
at the curb." Lula went to the closet and scooped up
more clothes. Suits, shoes, and jackets. All went out
the window. "I'm on a roll now," she said, looking
around the loft. "What else we got that can go out the
window? You think we can fit his big-ass TV out the
window? Hey, how about some kitchen appliances? Go
get me his toaster." She crossed the room, grabbed a
table lamp, and brought it to the window. "Hey!" she
yelled, head out the window, eyes focused on the street.
"Get away from that car. Willie, is that you? What the
hell are you doing?"

I ran to the window and looked out. Willie Martin
was whaling away at my car with a sledgehammer.

"I'll show you to throw my clothes outta the window,"
he said, taking a swing at the right rear quarter panel.

"You dumb premature ejaculator," Lula shouted at
him. "You dumb-ass moron! That's not my car."

"Oh. Oops," Willie said. "Which one's *your* car?"

Lula hauled a Glock out of her purse, squeezed off
two rounds in Willie's direction, and Willie left the
scene. One of the rounds pinged off my car roof. And
the other round made a small hole in my windshield.

"Must be something wrong with the sight on this
gun," Lula said to me. "Sorry about that."

I trudged down the stairs and stood on the sidewalk examining my car. Deep scratch in roof from misplaced bullet. Hole in windshield plus embedded bullet in passenger seat. Bashed-in right rear quarter panel and right passenger-side door from sledgehammer. Previous damage from creepy gun attack by insane stalker. And someone had spray painted EAT ME on the driver's side door.

"Your car's a mess," Lula said. "I don't know what it is with you and cars."

TWO

MORELLI DRIVES AN SUV. He used to own a 4×4 truck, but he traded it in so Bob could ride around with him and be more comfortable. This isn't normal behavior for Morelli men. Morelli men are known for being charming but worthless drunks who rarely care about the comfort of their wife and kids, much less the dog. How Joe escaped the Morelli Man syndrome is a mystery. For a while he seemed destined to follow in his father's footsteps, but somewhere in his late twenties, Joe stopped chasing women and fighting in bars and started working at being a good cop. He inherited his house from his Aunt Rose. He adopted Bob. And he decided, after years of hit-and-run sex, he was in love with me. Go figure that. Joseph Morelli with a house, a dog, a steady job, and an SUV. And on *odd* days of the month he woke up wanting to marry me. It turns out I only want to marry him on *even* days of the month, so to date we've been spared commitment.

When I arrived at Morelli's house his SUV was

parked curbside and Morelli and Bob were sitting on Morelli's tiny front porch. Usually Bob goes gonzo when he sees me, jumping around all smiley face. Today Bob was sitting there drooling, looking sad.

"What's with Bob?" I asked Morelli.

"I don't think he feels good. He was like this when I came home."

Bob stood and hunched. *"Gak,"* Bob said. And he hacked up a sock and a lot of Bob slime. He looked down at the sock. And then he looked up at me. And then he got happy. He jumped around, doing his goofy dance. I gave him a hug and he wandered off, tail wagging, into the house.

"Guess we can go in now," Morelli said. He got to his feet, slid his arm around my shoulders, and hugged me to him for a friendly kiss. He broke from the kiss and his eyes strayed to my car. "I don't suppose you'd want to tell me about the body damage?"

"Sledgehammer."

"Of course."

"You're pretty calm about all this," I said to him.

"I'm a calm kind of guy."

"No, you're not. You go nuts over this stuff. You always yell when people go after me with a sledgehammer."

"Yeah, but in the past you haven't liked that. I'm thinking if I start yelling it might screw up my chances of getting you naked. And I'm desperate. I really need to get you naked. Besides, you quit the bonds office, right? Maybe your life will settle down now. How'd the interview go?"

"I got the job. I start tomorrow."

I was wearing a T-shirt and jeans. Morelli grinned down at me and slid his hands under my T-shirt. "We should celebrate."

His hands felt nice against my skin, but I was starving and I didn't want to encourage any further celebrating until I got my pizza. He pulled me close and kissed his way up my neck. His lips moved to my ear and my temple and by the time he got to my mouth I was thinking the pizza could wait.

And then we heard it . . . the pizza delivery car coming down the street, stopping at the curb.

Morelli cut his eyes to the kid getting out of the car. "Maybe if we ignore him he'll go away."

The steaming extra-large, extra cheese, green peppers, pepperoni pizza smell oozed from the box the kid was carrying. The smell rushed over the porch and into the house. Bob's toenails clattered on the polished wood hall floor as he took off from the kitchen and galloped for all he was worth at the kid.

Morelli stepped back from me and snagged Bob by the collar just as he was about to catapult himself off the porch.

"*Ulk,*" Bob said, stopping abruptly, tongue out, eyes bugged, feet off the ground.

"Minor setback with the celebration plan," Morelli said.

"No rush," I told him. "We have all night."

Morelli's eyes got soft and dark and dreamy. Sort of the way Bob's eyes got when he ate Tastykake Butterscotch Krimpets and then someone rubbed his belly. "All right," Morelli said. "I like the way that sounds."

Two minutes later, we were on the couch in

Morelli's living room, watching the pregame show, eating pizza, and drinking beer.

"I heard you were working on the Barroni case," I said to Morelli. "Having any luck with it?"

Morelli took a second piece of pizza. "I have a lot out on it. So far nothing's come in."

Michael Barroni mysteriously disappeared eight days ago. He was sixty-two years old and in good health when he vanished. He owned a nice house in the heart of the Burg on Roebling and a hardware store on the corner of Rudd and Liberty Street. He left behind a wife, two dogs, and three adult sons. One of the Barroni boys graduated with me, and one graduated two years earlier with Morelli.

There aren't a lot of secrets in the Burg and according to Burg gossip Michael Barroni didn't have a girlfriend, didn't play the numbers, and didn't have mob ties. His hardware store was running in the black. He didn't suffer from depression. He didn't do a lot of drinking, and he wasn't hooked on Levitra.

Barroni was last seen closing and locking the back door to the hardware store at the end of the day. He got into his car, drove away . . . and *poof*. No more Michael Barroni.

"Did you ever find Barroni's car?" I asked Morelli.

"No. No car. No body. No sign of struggle. He was alone when Sol Rosen saw him lock up and take off. Sol said he was putting out trash from his diner and he saw Barroni leave. He said Barroni looked normal. Maybe distracted. Sol said Barroni waved but didn't say anything."

"Do you think it's a random crime? Barroni was in the wrong place at the wrong time?"

"No. Barroni lived four blocks from his store. Every day he went straight home from work. Four blocks through the Burg. If something had gone down on Barroni's usual route home someone would have heard or seen something. The day Barroni disappeared he went someplace else. He didn't take his usual route home."

"Maybe he just got tired of it all. Maybe he started driving west and didn't stop until he got to Flagstaff."

Morelli fed his pizza crust to Bob. "I'm going to tell you something that's just between us. We've had two other guys disappear on the exact same day as Barroni. They were both from Stark Street, and a missing person on Stark Street isn't big news, so no one's paid much attention. I ran across them when I checked Barroni's missing-person status.

"Both these guys owned their own businesses. They both locked up at the end of the day and were never seen again. One of the men was real stable. He had a wife and kids. He went to church. He ran a bar on Stark Street, but he was clean. The other guy, Benny Gorman, owned a garage. Probably a chump-change chop shop. He'd done time for armed robbery and grand theft auto. And two months ago he was charged with assault with a deadly weapon. Took a tire iron to a guy and almost killed him. He was supposed to go to trial last week but failed to appear. Ordinarily I'd say he skipped because of the charge but I'm not so sure on this one."

"Did Vinnie bond Gorman out?"

"Yeah. I talked to Connie. She handed Gorman off to Ranger."

"And you think the three guys are connected?"

A commercial came on and Morelli channel surfed through a bunch of stations. "Don't know. I just have a feeling. It's too strong a coincidence."

I gave Bob the last piece of pizza and snuggled closer to Morelli.

"I have feelings about other things, too," Morelli said, sliding an arm around my shoulders, his fingertips skimming along my neck and down my arm. "Would you like me to tell you about my other feelings?"

My toes curled in my shoes and I got warm in a bunch of private places. And that was the last we saw of the game.

MORELLI IS AN early riser in many ways. I had a memory of him kissing my bare shoulder, whispering an obscene suggestion, and leaving the bed. He returned a short time later with his hair still damp from the shower. He kissed me again and wished me luck with my new job. And then he was gone . . . off on his mission to rid Trenton of bad guys.

It was still dark in Morelli's bedroom. The bed was warm and comfy. Bob was sprawled on Morelli's side of the bed, snuffling into Morelli's pillow. I burrowed under the quilt, and when I reawakened the sunlight was pouring into the room through a break in the curtain. I had a moment of absolute delicious satisfaction immediately followed by panic. According to the bedside clock it was nine o'clock. I was massively late for my first day at the button factory!

I scrambled out of bed, gathered my clothes up off the floor, and tugged them on. I didn't bother with makeup or hair. No time. I took the stairs at a run, grabbed my purse and my car keys, and bolted out of the house.

I skirted traffic as best I could, pulled into the button factory parking lot on two wheels, parked, jumped out of the car, and hit the pavement running. The time was nine-thirty. I was an hour and a half late.

I took the stairs to save time and I was sweating by the time I skidded to a stop in Alizzi's office.

"You are late," Alizzi said.

"Yes, but . . ."

He wagged his finger at me. "This is not a good thing. I told you that you must be on time. And look at you. You are in a T-shirt. If you are going to be late you should at least wear something that is revealing and shows me your breasts. You are fired. Go away."

"No! Give me another chance. Just one more chance. If you give me another chance I'll wear something revealing tomorrow."

"Will you perform a lewd act?"

"What kind of lewd act?"

"Something very, very, very lewd. There would have to be nakedness and body fluids."

"*Ick*. No!"

"Well then, you are still fired."

"That's horrible. I'm going to report you for sexual harassment."

"It will only serve to enhance my reputation."

Unh. Mental head slap.

"Okay. Fine," I said. "I didn't want this job anyway."

I turned on my heel and flounced out of Alizzi's office, down the stairs, through the lobby, and crossed the lot to my bashed-in, bullet-riddled, spray-painted car. I gave the door a vicious kick, wrenched it open, and slid behind the wheel. I punched Metallica into the sound system, cranked it up until the fillings in my teeth were vibrating, and motored across town.

By the time I got to Hamilton I was feeling pretty decent. I had the whole day to myself. True, I wasn't making any money, but there was always tomorrow, right? I stopped at Tasty Pastry, bought a bag of doughnuts, and drove three blocks into the Burg to Mary Lou Stankovic's house. Mary Lou was my best friend all through school. She's married now and has a bunch of kids. We're still friends but our paths don't cross as much as they used to.

I walked an obstacle course from my car to Mary Lou's front door, around bikes, dismembered action figures, soccer balls, remote-control cars, beheaded Barbie dolls, and plastic guns that looked frighteningly real.

"Omigod," Mary Lou said when she opened the door. "It's the angel of mercy. Are those doughnuts?"

"Do you need some?"

"I need a new life, but I'll make do with doughnuts."

I handed the doughnuts off to Mary Lou and followed her into the kitchen. "You have a good life. You like your life."

"Not today. I have three kids home sick with colds.

The dog has diarrhea. And I think there was a hole in the condom we used last night."

"Aren't you on the pill?"

"Gives me water retention."

I could hear the kids in the living room, coughing at the television, whining at each other. Mary Lou's kids were cute when they were asleep and for the first fifteen minutes after they'd had a bath. All other times the kids were a screaming advertisement for birth control. It wasn't that they were bad kids. Okay, so they dismembered every doll that came through the door, but they hadn't yet barbecued the dog. That was a good sign, right? It was more that Mary Lou's kids had an excess of energy. Mary Lou said it came from the Stankovic side of the family. I thought it might be coming from the bakery. That's where I got *my* energy.

Mary Lou opened the doughnut bag and the kids came rushing into the kitchen.

"They can hear a bakery bag crinkle a mile away," Mary Lou said.

I'd brought four doughnuts so we gave one to each kid and Mary Lou and I shared a doughnut over coffee.

"What's new?" Mary Lou wanted to know.

"I quit my job at the bonds office."

"Any special reason?"

"No. My reasoning was sort of vague. I got a job at the button factory, but I spent the night with Joe to celebrate and then I overslept this morning and was late for my first day and got fired."

Mary Lou took a sip of coffee and waggled her eyebrows at me. "Was it worth it?"

I took a moment to consider. "Yeah."

Mary Lou gave her head a small shake. "He's been making trouble worthwhile for you since you were six years old. I don't know why you don't marry him."

My reasoning was sort of vague on that one, too.

IT WAS LATE morning when I left Mary Lou. I cut over two blocks to High Street and parked in front of my parents' house. It was a small house on a small lot. It had three bedrooms and bath up and a living room, dining room, kitchen down. It shared a common wall with a mirror image owned by Mabel Markowitz. Mabel was old beyond imagining. Her husband had passed on and her kids were off on their own, so she lived alone in the house, baking coffee cakes and watching television. Her half of the house is painted lime green because the paint had been on clearance when she'd needed it. My parents' house is painted Gulden mustard yellow and dark brown. I'm not sure which house is worse. In the fall my mom puts pumpkins on the front porch and it all seems to work. In the spring the paint scheme is depressing as hell.

Since it was the end of September, the pumpkins were on display and a cardboard witch on a broomstick was stuck to the front door. Halloween was just four weeks away, and the Burg is big on holidays.

Grandma Mazur was at the front door when I set foot on the porch. Grandma moved in with my parents when my Grandpa Mazur got a hot pass to heaven compliments of more than a half century of bacon fat and butter cookies.

"We heard you quit your job," Grandma said.

"We've been calling and calling, but you haven't been answering your phone. I need to know the details. I got a beauty parlor appointment this afternoon and I gotta get the story straight."

"Not much of a story," I said, following Grandma into the hallway foyer. "I just thought it was time for a change."

"That's it? Time for a change? I can't tell people that story. It's boring. I need something better. How about we tell them you're pregnant? Or maybe we could say you got a rare blood disease. Or there was a big contract put on your head unless you gave up being a bounty hunter."

"Sorry," I said. "None of those things are true."

"Yeah, but that don't matter. Everybody knows you can't believe everything you hear."

My mother was at the dining room table with a bunch of round pieces of paper spread out in front of her. My sister, Valerie, was getting married in a week, and my mother was still working on the seating arrangements.

"I can't make this work," my mother said. "These round tables don't hold the right number of people. I'm going to have to seat the Krugers at two different tables. And no one gets along with old Mrs. Kruger."

"You should do away with the seating chart," Grandma said. "Just open the doors to the hall and let them fight for their seats."

I love my sister, but I'd deport her to Bosnia if I thought I could get away with it and it'd get me out of her wedding. I'm supposed to be her maid of honor and somehow through my lack of participation and a fabric swatch inaccuracy I've been ordered a gown that makes me look like a giant eggplant.

"We heard you quit your job," my mother said to me. "Thank goodness. I can finally sleep at night knowing you're not running around the worst parts of town chasing after criminals. And I understand you have a wonderful job at the button factory. Marjorie Kuzak called yesterday and told us all about it. Her daughter works in the employment office."

"Actually, I sort of got fired from that job," I said.

"Already? How could you possibly get fired on your first day?"

"It's complicated. I don't suppose you know anybody who's hiring?"

"What kind of job are you looking for?" Grandma asked.

"Professional. Something with career advancement potential."

"I saw a sign up at the cleaners," Grandma said. "I don't know about career advancement, but they do a lot of professional pressing. I see a lot of people taking their business suits there."

"I was hoping for something a little more challenging."

"Dry cleaning's challenging," Grandma said. "It's not easy getting all them spots out. And you gotta have people skills. I heard them talking behind the counter about how hard it was to find someone with people skills."

"And no one would shoot at you," my mother said. "No one ever robs a dry cleaner."

I had to admit, that part appealed to me. It would be

nice not to have to worry about getting shot. Maybe working at the dry cleaners would be an okay temporary job until the right thing came along.

I got myself a cup of coffee and poked through the refrigerator, searching for food. I settled on a piece of apple pie and carted the coffee and pie back to the dining room, where my mom was still arranging the paper tables.

"What's going on in the Burg?" I asked her.

"Harry Farstein died yesterday. Heart attack. He's at Stiva's."

"He's gonna have a viewing tonight," Grandma said. "It's gonna be a good one, too. His lodge will be there. And Lydia Farstein is the drama queen of the Burg. She'll be carrying on something awful. If you haven't got anything better to do, you should come to the viewing with me. I could use a ride."

Grandma loved going to viewings. Stiva's Funeral Home was the social center of the Burg. I thought having my thumb amputated would be a preferred activity.

"And everyone's going to be talking about the Barroni thing," Grandma said. "I can't believe he hasn't turned up. It's like he was abducted by Martians."

Okay, now this interested me. Morelli was working on the Barroni disappearance. And Ranger was working on the Gorman disappearance, which might be connected to the Barroni disappearance. I was glad I wasn't working on either of those cases, but on the other hand, I felt a smidgeon left out. So sue me, I'm nosy.

"Sure," I said. "I'll pick you up at seven o'clock."

"Your father got gravy on his gray slacks," my mother said. "If you're going to apply for a job at the cleaner, would you mind taking the slacks with you? It would save me a trip."

A half hour later, I had a job with Kan Klean. The hours were seven to three. They were open seven days a week, and I agreed to work weekends. The pay wasn't great, but I could wear jeans and a T-shirt to work, and they confirmed my mother's suspicion that they'd never been held up and that to date none of their employees had been shot while on the job. I handed over the gravy-stained slacks and agreed to show up at seven the next morning.

I didn't feel quite as nauseated as I had after getting the button factory job. So I was making progress, right?

I drove three blocks down Hamilton and stopped at the bonds office to say hello.

"Look what the wind blew in," Lula said when she saw me. "I heard you got the job at the button factory. How come you're not working?"

"I spent the night with Morelli and overslept. So I was late rolling in to work."

"And?"

"And I got fired."

"That was fast," Lula said. "You're good. It takes most people a couple days to get fired."

"Maybe it all worked out for the best. I got another job already at Kan Klean."

"Do you get a discount?" Lula wanted to know. "I got some dry cleaning to send out. You could pick it up tomorrow here at the office on your way to work."

"Sure," I said. "Why not." I shuffled through the

small stack of files on Connie's desk. "Anything fun come in?"

"Yeah, it's all fun," Connie said. "We got a rapist. We got a guy who beat up his girlfriend. We got a couple pushers."

"I'm doing the DV this afternoon," Lula said.

"DV?"

"Domestic violence. My time's real valuable now that I'm a bounty hunter. I gotta use abbreviations. Like I'm doing the DV in the PM."

I heard Vinnie growl from his inner office. "Jesus H. Christmas," he said. "Who would have thought my life would come to this?"

"Hey, Vinnie," I yelled to him. "How's it going?"

Vinnie poked his head out his door. "I gave you a job when you needed one and now you desert me. Where's the gratitude?"

Vinnie is a couple inches taller than me and has the slim, boneless body of a ferret. His coloring is Mediterranean. His hair looks like it's slicked back with olive oil. He wears pointy-toed shoes and a lot of gold. He's the family pervert. He's married to Harry-the-Hammer's daughter. And in spite of his personality shortcomings (or maybe because of them) he's an okay bail bondsman. Vinnie understands the criminal mind.

"You didn't *give* me the job," I said to Vinnie. "I blackmailed you into it. And I got good numbers when I was working for you. My apprehension rate was close to ninety percent."

"You were lucky," Vinnie said.

This was true.

Lula took her big black leather purse from the bottom file drawer and stuffed it under her arm. "I'm going out. I'm gonna get that DV and I'm gonna kick his ass all the way back to jail."

"No!" Vinnie said. "You're *not* gonna kick his ass *anywhere*. Ass kicking is not entirely legal. You will introduce yourself and you will cuff him. And then you will escort him to the station in a civilized manner."

"Sure," Lula said. "I knew that."

"Maybe you want to go with her," Vinnie said to me. "Since it looks like you don't have anything better to do."

"I start a new job tomorrow. I got a job at Kan Klean."

Vinnie's eyes lit up. "Do you get a discount? I got a shitload of dry cleaning."

"I wouldn't mind if you rode along," Lula said. "This guy's gonna be slam bam, thank you, ma'am. And then we drop his sorry behind off at the police station and go get some burgers."

"I don't want to get involved," I told her.

"You can stay in the Firebird. It'll only take me a minute to cuff this guy and drag . . . I mean, *escort* him out to the car."

"Okay," I said, "but I *really* don't want to get involved."

A half hour later we were at the public housing project on the other side of town and Lula was motoring the Firebird down Carter Street, looking for 2475A.

"Here's the plan," Lula said. "You just sit tight and I'll go get this guy. I got pepper spray, a stun gun, a head-bashing flashlight, two pairs of cuffs, and the BP in my purse."

"BP?"

"Big Persuader. That's what I call my Glock." She pulled to the curb and jerked her thumb at the apartment building. "This here's the building. I'll be back in a minute."

"Try to keep your clothes on," I said to her.

"Hunh," Lula said. "Funny."

Lula walked to the door and knocked. The door opened. Lula disappeared inside the house and the door closed behind her. I looked at my watch and decided I'd give her ten minutes. After ten minutes I'd do something, but I wasn't sure what it would be. I could call the police. I could call Vinnie. I could run around the outside of the building yelling *fire!* Or I could do the least appealing of all the options—I could go in after her.

I didn't have to make the decision because the front door opened after just two minutes. Lula tumbled out the door, rolled off the stoop, landed on a patch of hard packed dirt that would have been lawn in a more prosperous neighborhood, and the door slammed shut behind her. Lula scrambled to her feet, tugged her spandex lime green miniskirt back down over her ass, and marched up to the door.

"Open this door!" she yelled. "You open this door right now or there's gonna be big trouble." She tried the doorknob. She rang the bell. She kicked the door with her Via Spigas. The door didn't open. Lula turned and looked over at me. "Don't worry," she said. "This here's just a minor setback. They don't understand the severity of the situation."

I slid lower in my seat and became engrossed in the mechanics of my seat belt.

"I'm giving you one more chance to open this door and then I'm going to take action," Lula yelled at the house.

The door didn't open.

"Hunh," Lula said. She backed off from the door and cut over to a front window. Curtains had been drawn across the window, but the flicker of a television screen could faintly be seen through the sheers. Lula stood on tiptoes and tried to open the window, but the window wouldn't budge. "I'm starting to get annoyed now," Lula said. "You know what I think? I think this here's an accident waiting to happen."

Lula pulled her big Maglite out of her purse, set her purse on the ground, and smashed the window with the Maglite. She bent to retrieve her purse, and what remained of the window was blown out with a shotgun blast from inside. If Lula hadn't bent down to get her purse, the surgeon of the day at St. Francis would have spent the rest of his afternoon picking pellets out of her.

"What the F!" Lula said. And Lula did a fast sprint to the car. She wrenched the driver's-side door open, crammed herself behind the wheel, and there was a second shotgun blast through the apartment window. "That dumb son of a bitch shot at me!" Lula said.

"Yeah," I said. "I saw. I was impressed you could run like that in those heels."

"I wasn't expecting him to shoot at me. He had no call to do that."

"You broke his window."

"It was an accident."

"It wasn't an accident. I saw you do it with the Maglite."

"That guy's nuts," Lula said, taking off from the curb, leaving a couple inches of rubber on the road. "He should be reported to somebody. He should be arrested."

"*You* were supposed to arrest him."

"I was supposed to *escort* him. Vinnie made that real clear. *Escort him*. And I could escort the hell out of him except I'm hungry. I gotta get something to eat," Lula said. "I work better on a happy stomach. I could take that woman-beating moron in anytime I want, so what's the rush, right? Might as well get a burger first, that's what I think. And anyway, he might be more Ranger's speed. I wouldn't want to step on Ranger's toes. You know how Ranger likes all that shooting stuff."

"I thought you liked the shooting stuff."

"I don't want to hog it."

"Considerate of you."

"Yeah, I'm real considerate," Lula said, turning into a Cluck-in-a-Bucket drive-thru. "I'm seriously thinking of giving this case to Ranger."

"What if Ranger doesn't want it?"

"You think he'd turn down a good case like this?"

"Yeah."

"Hunh," Lula said. "Wouldn't that be a bitch?"

She got a Cluck Burger with cheese, a large side of fries, a chocolate shake, and an Apple Clucky Pie. I wasn't in a Cluck-in-a-Bucket mood so I passed. Lula finished off the last piece of the pie and looked at her watch. "I'd go back and root out that nutso loser, but it's getting late. Don't you think it's late?"

"Almost three o'clock."

"Practically quitting time."

Especially for me, since I quit yesterday.

THREE

I'M NOT THE world's best cook, but I have some specialties, and almost all of them include peanut butter. You can't go wrong with peanut butter. Today I was having a peanut butter and olive and potato chip sandwich for dinner. Very efficient since it combines legumes and vegetables plus some worthless white bread carbohydrates all in one tidy package. I was standing in the kitchen, washing the sandwich down with a cold Corona, and Morelli called.

"What are you doing?" he asked.

"Eating."

"Why aren't you eating in my house?"

"I don't live in your house."

"You were living in my house last night."

"I was *visiting* your house last night. That's different from living. Living involves commitment and closet allocation."

"We don't seem to be all that good at commitment, but I'd be happy to give up a couple closets in exchange for wild gorilla sex at least five days out of seven."

"Good grief."

"Okay, four days out of seven, but that's my best offer. How's the new job at the button factory going?"

"Got fired. And it was your fault. I was late for work on my first day."

I could feel Morelli smile at the other end of the line. "Am I good, or what?"

"I got a job at Kan Klean. I start tomorrow."

"We should celebrate."

"No celebrating! That's what lost me the button factory job. Don't you want to ask me if I can get you discount cleaning?"

"I don't clean my clothes. I wear them until they fall apart and then I throw them away."

I finished the sandwich and chugged the beer. "I've got to go," I told Morelli. "I told Grandma I'd pick her up at seven. We're going to Harry Farstein's viewing at Stiva's."

"I can't compete with that," Morelli said.

GRANDMA WAS WAITING at the door when I drove up. She was dressed in powder blue slacks, a matching floral-print blouse, a white cotton cardigan, and white tennis shoes. She had her big black patent-leather purse in the crook of her arm. Her gray hair was freshly set in tight little baloney curls that marched across her pink skull. Her nails were newly manicured and painted fire-engine red. Her lipstick matched her nails.

"I'm ready to go," she said, hurrying over to the car. "We don't get a move on, we're not gonna get a good seat. There's gonna be a crowd tonight and ever since Spiro took off, Stiva hasn't been all that good with organization. Spiro was a nasty little cockroach but he could organize a crowd like no one else."

Spiro was Constantine Stiva's kid. I went to school with Spiro and near the end I guess I inadvertently helped him disappear. He was a miserable excuse for a human being, involved in running guns and God knows what else. He tried to kill Grandma and me, there was a shoot-out and a spectacular fire at the funeral home, and somehow, in the confusion, Spiro vanished into thin air.

When I got the notes saying I'M BACK and DID YOU THINK I WAS DEAD? Spiro was one of the potential psychos who came to mind. Sad to say, he was just one name among many. And he wasn't the most likely candidate. Spiro had been a lot of things . . . dumb wasn't one of them. Plus I couldn't see Spiro being obsessed with revenge. Spiro had wanted money and power.

The funeral home was on Hamilton, a couple blocks down from the bail bonds office. It had been rebuilt after the fire and was now a jumble of new brick construction and old Victorian mansion. The two-story front half of the house was white aluminum siding with black shutters. A large porch wrapped around the front and south side of the house. Some of the viewing rooms and all of the embalming rooms were located in the new brick addition at the rear. The preferred viewing rooms were in the front and Stiva had given them names: the Blue Salon, the Rest in Peace Salon, and the Executive Slumber Salon.

It was a five-minute drive from my parents' house to Stiva's. I dropped Grandma at the door and found street parking half a block away. When I got to the funeral home Grandma was waiting for me at the entrance to the Executive Slumber Salon.

"I don't know why they call this the Executive Salon," she said. "It's not like Stiva's laying a lot of executives to rest. Think it's just a big phony-baloney name."

The Executive Slumber Salon was the largest of the viewing rooms and was already packed with people. Lydia Farstein was at the far end, one hand dramatically touching the open casket. She was in her seventies and looked surprisingly happy for a woman who had just lost her husband of fifty-odd years.

"Looks like Lydia's been hitting the sauce," Grandma said. "Last time I saw her that happy was . . . never. I'm going back to give her my condolences and take a look at Harry."

Looking at dead people wasn't high on my list of favorite activities, so I separated from Grandma and wandered to the far side of the entrance hall, where complimentary cookies had been set out.

I scarfed down a couple sugar cookies and a couple spice cookies and I felt a prickling sensation at the back of my neck. I turned and looked across the room and saw Morelli's Grandma Bella glaring at me. Grandma Bella is a white-haired old lady who dresses in black and looks like an extra out of a *Godfather* flashback. She has visions, and she puts spells on people. And she scares the crap out of me.

Bitsy Mullen was standing next to me at the cookie

table. "Omigod," Bitsy said. "I hope she's glaring at you and not me. Last week she put the eye on Francine Blainey, and Francine got a bunch of big herpes sores all over her face."

The eye is like Grandma Bella voodoo. She puts her finger to her eye and she mumbles something and whatever calamity happens to you after that you can pin on the eye. I guess it's a little like believing in hell. You hope it's bogus, but you never really know for sure, do you?

"I'm betting Francine got herpes from her worthless boyfriend," I said to Bitsy.

"I'm not taking any chances," Bitsy said. "I'm going to hide in the ladies' room until the viewing is over. Oh no! Omigod. Here she comes. What should I do? I can't breathe. I'm gonna faint."

"Probably she just wants a cookie," I said to Bitsy. Not that I believed it. Grandma Bella had her beady eyes fixed on me. I'd seen the look before and it wasn't good.

"You!" Grandma Bella said, pointing her finger at me. "You broke my Joseph's heart."

"No way," I said. "Swear to God."

"Is there a ring on your finger?"

"N-N-No."

"It's a scandal," she said. "You've brought disgrace to my house. A respectable woman would be married and have children by now. You go to his house and tempt him with your body and then you leave. Shame on you. Shame. Shame. I should put the eye on you. Make your teeth fall out of your head. Turn your hair gray. Cause your female parts to shrink away until there's nothing left of them."

Grandma Mazur elbowed her way through the crush of people around the cookie table. "What's going on here?" she asked. "What'd I miss about female parts?"

"Your granddaughter is a Jezebel," Grandma Bella said. "Jumping in and out of my Joseph's bed."

"Half the women in the Burg have been in and out of his bed," Grandma Mazur said. "Heck, half the women in the state . . ."

"Not lately," I said. "He's different now."

"I'm going to put the eye on her," Grandma Bella said. "I'm going to make her female parts turn to dust."

"Over my dead body," Grandma Mazur said.

Bella scrunched up her face. "That could be arranged."

"You better watch it, sister," Grandma Mazur said. "You don't want to get me mad. I'm a holy terror when I'm mad."

"Hah, you don't scare me," Bella said. "Stand back. I'm going to give the eye."

Grandma Mazur pulled a .45 long barrel out of her big black patent-leather purse and pointed it at Bella. "You put your finger to your eye and I'll put a hole in your head that's so big you could push a potato through it."

Bella's eyes rolled around in her head. "I'm having a vision. I'm having a vision."

I grabbed the gun from Grandma and shoved it back into her bag. "No shooting! She's just a crazy old lady."

Bella snapped to attention. "Crazy old lady? Crazy old lady? I'll show you crazy old lady. I'll give you a thrashing. Someone get me a stick. I'll put the eye on everyone if someone doesn't give me a stick."

"No one thrashes my granddaughter," Grandma Mazur said. "And besides, look around. Do you see any sticks? It's not like you're in the woods. You know what your problem is? You gotta learn how to chill."

Bella grabbed Grandma Mazur by the nose. She was so fast Grandma never saw it coming. "You're a demon woman!" Bella shouted.

Grandma Mazur clocked Bella on the side of the head with the big patent-leather purse, but Bella had a death grip on Grandma Mazur. Grandma hit her a second time and Bella hunkered in. Bella scrunched up her face and held tight to the nose.

I was in the mix, trying to wrestle Bella away. Grandma accidentally caught me with a roundhouse swing of the purse that knocked me off my feet.

Bitsy Mullen was jumping around, wringing her hands and shrieking. "Help! Stop! Someone do something!"

Mrs. Lubchek was behind Bitsy, at the cookie table, watching the whole thing. "Oh, for the love of God," Mrs. Lubchek said with an eyeroll. And Mrs. Lubchek grabbed the pitcher of iced tea off the cookie table and dumped it on Grandma Bella and Grandma Mazur.

Grandma Bella released Grandma Mazur's nose and looked down at herself. "I'm wet. What is this?"

"Iced tea," Mrs. Lubchek said. "I poured iced tea on you."

"I'll turn you into an artichoke."

"You need to take a pill," Mrs. Lubchek said. "You're nutsy cuckoo."

Stiva hurried across the room with Joe's mother close on his heels.

"We're out of iced tea," Mrs. Lubchek said to Stiva.

"I'm having a vision," Grandma Bella said, her eyes rolling around in her head. "I see fire. A terrible fire. I see rats escaping, running from the fire. Big, ugly, sick rats. And one of the rats has come back." Bella's eyes snapped open and focused on me. "He's come back to get *you*."

"Omigod," Bitsy said. "Omigod. Omigod!"

"I need to lay down now. I always get tired after I have a vision," Bella said.

"Wait," I said to her. "What kind of a vision is that? A rat? Are you sure about this vision thing?"

"Yeah, and what do you mean the rat's sick?" Grandma Mazur wanted to know. "Does it have rabies?"

"That's all I'm going to say," Bella said. "It's a vision. A vision is a vision. I'm going home."

Bella whirled on her heel and walked to the door with her back ramrod straight and Joe's mom behind her, scurrying to keep up.

Grandma Mazur turned to the cookie tray and picked through the cookies, looking for a chocolate chip. "I tell you a person's gotta get here early or there's only leftovers."

We were both dripping iced tea. And Grandma Mazur's nose was red and swollen.

"We should go home," I said to Grandma Mazur. "I have to get out of this shirt."

"Yeah," Grandma Mazur said. "I guess I could go. I

paid my respects to the deceased and this cookie tray's a big disappointment."

"Did you hear anything about Michael Barroni?"

Grandma dabbed at her shirt with a napkin. "Only that he's still missing. The boys are running the store, but Emma Wilson tells me they're not getting along. Emma works there part-time. She said the young one is a trial."

"Anthony."

"That's the one. He was always a troublemaker. Remember there was that business with Mary Jane Roman."

"Date rape."

"Nothing ever came of that," Grandma said. "But I never doubted Mary Jane. There was always something off about Anthony."

We'd walked out of the funeral home and down the street to the car. I looked inside the car and saw a note on the driver's seat.

"How'd that get in there?" Grandma wanted to know. "Don't you lock your car?"

"I stopped locking it. I'm hoping someone will steal it."

Grandma took a good look at the car. "That makes sense."

We both got in and I read the note. YOUR TURN TO BURN, BITCH.

"Such language," Grandma said. "I tell you, the world's going to heck in a handbasket."

Grandma was upset about the language. I was upset about the threat. I wasn't exactly sure what it meant, but it didn't feel good. It was crazy and scary. Who *was* this person, anyway?

I pulled away from the curb and headed for my parents' house.

"I can't get that dumb note out of my head," Grandma said when we were half a block from home. "I could swear I even smell smoke."

Now that she mentioned it . . .

I glanced in the rearview mirror and saw flames licking up the backseat. I raced the half block to my parents' house, careened into the driveway, and jerked to a stop.

"Get out," I yelled. "The backseat's on fire."

Grandma turned and looked. "Danged if it isn't."

I ran into the house, told my mother to call the fire department, grabbed the fire extinguisher that was kept in the kitchen under the sink, and ran back to the car. I broke the seal on the extinguisher and sprayed the flaming backseat. My father appeared with the garden hose and between the two of us we got the fire under control.

A half hour later, the backseat of the Saturn was pronounced dead and flame free by the fire department. The fire truck rumbled away down the street, and the crowd of curious neighbors dispersed. The sun had set, but the Saturn could be seen in the ambient light from the house. Water dripped from the undercarriage and pooled on the cement driveway in grease-slicked puddles. The stench of cooked upholstery hung in the air.

Morelli had arrived seconds behind the fire truck. He was now standing in my parents' front yard with his hands in his pockets, wearing his unreadable cop face.

"So," I said to him. "What's up?"

"Where's the note?"

"What note?"

His eyes narrowed ever so slightly.

"How do you know there was a note?" I asked.

"Just another one of those feelings."

I took the note from my pocket and handed it over.

"Do you think this has something to do with the rat?" Grandma asked me. "Remember how Bella had that vision about the fire and the rat? And she said the rat was gonna get you. Well, I bet it was the rat that wrote the note and started the fire."

"Rats can't write," I said.

"What about human rats?" Grandma wanted to know. "What about big mutant human rats?"

Morelli cut his eyes to me. "Do I want to know about this vision?"

"No," I told him. "And you also don't want to know about the fight in the funeral home between Bella and Grandma Mazur when Grandma tried to stop Bella from putting a curse on me for breaking your heart."

Morelli smiled. "I've always been her favorite."

"I didn't break your heart."

"Cupcake, you've been breaking my heart for as long as I've known you."

"How did you know about the fire?" I asked Morelli.

"Dispatch called me. They always call me when your car explodes or goes up in flames."

"I'm surprised Ranger isn't here."

"He got me on my cell. I told him you were okay."

I moved closer to the Saturn and peered inside. Most of the water and fire damage was confined to the backseat.

Morelli had his hand at the nape of my neck. "You're not thinking of driving this, are you?"

"It doesn't look so bad. It probably runs fine."

"The backseat is completely gutted and there's a big hole in the floorboard."

"Yeah, but other than that it's okay, right?"

Morelli looked at me for a couple beats. Probably trying to decide if this was worth a fight.

"It's too dark to get a really good assessment of the damage," he finally said. "Why don't we go home and come back in the morning and take another look? You don't want to drive it tonight anyway. You want to open the windows and let it air out."

He was right about the airing out part. The car reeked. And I knew he was also right about looking at the car when the light was better. Problem was, this was the only car I had. The only thing worse than driving this car would be borrowing the '53 Buick Grandma Mazur inherited from my Great Uncle Sandor. Been there, done that, don't want to do it again.

And the danger involved in driving this car seemed to me to be hardly worth mentioning compared to the threat I was facing from the criminally insane stalker who set the fire.

"I'm more worried about the arsonist than I am about the car," I said to Morelli.

"I haven't got a grip on the arsonist," Morelli said. "I don't know what to do about him. The car I have some control over. Let me give you a ride home."

Five minutes later we were parked in front of Morelli's house.

"Let me guess," I said to Morelli. "Bob still misses me."

Morelli ran a finger along the line of my jaw. "Bob

could care less. I'm the one who misses you. And I miss you bad."

"How bad?"

Morelli kissed me. "Painfully bad."

AT SIX-FIFTEEN I dragged myself out of Morelli's bed and into the shower. I'd thrown my clothes in the washer and dryer the night before, and Morelli had them in the bathroom, waiting for me. I did a half-assed job of drying my hair, swiped some mascara on my lashes, and followed my nose to the kitchen, where Morelli had coffee brewing.

Both of the men in my life looked great in the morning. They woke up clear-eyed and alert, ready to save the world. I was a befuddled mess in the morning, stumbling around until I got my caffeine fix.

"We're running late," Morelli said, handing me a travel mug of coffee and a toasted bagel. "I'll drop you off at the cleaner. You can check the car out after work."

"No. I have time. This will only take a minute. I'm sure the car is fine."

"I'm sure the car *isn't* fine," Morelli said, nudging me out of the kitchen and down the hall to the front door. He locked the door behind us and beeped his SUV open with the remote.

Minutes later we were at my parents' house, arguing on the front lawn.

"You're not driving this car," Morelli said.

"Excuse me? Did I hear you give me an order?"

"Cut me some slack here. You and I both know this car isn't drivable."

"I don't know any such thing. Okay, it's got some problems, but they're all cosmetic. I'm sure the engine is fine." I slid behind the wheel and proved my point by rolling the engine over. "See?" I said.

"Get out of this wreck and let me drive you to work."

"No."

"In twenty seconds I'm going to *drag* you out and reignite the fire until there's nothing left of this death trap but a smoking cinder."

"I hate when you do the macho-man thing."

"I hate when you're stubborn."

I hit the door locks and automatic windows, put the car into reverse, and screeched out of the driveway into the road. I changed gears and roared away, gagging on the odor of wet barbecued car. He was right, of course. The car was a death trap, and I was being stubborn. Problem was, I couldn't help myself. Morelli brought out the stubborn in me.

KAN KLEAN WAS a small mom-and-pop dry cleaners that had been operating in the Burg for as long as I can remember. The Macaroni family owned Kan Klean. Mama Macaroni, Mario Macaroni, and Gina Macaroni were the principals, and a bunch of miscellaneous Macaronis helped out when needed.

Mama Macaroni was a contemporary of Grandma Bella and Grandma Mazur. Mama Macaroni's fierce raptor eyes took the world in under drooping folds of parchment-thin skin. Her shrunken body, wrapped in layers of black, curved over her cane and conjured up images of mummified larvae. She had a boulder of a mole set into the roadmap of her face somewhere in the vicinity of Atlanta. Three hairs grew out of the mole. The mole was horrifying and compelling. It was the dermatological equivalent of a seven-car crash with blood and guts spread all over the highway.

I'd never been to Kan Klean when Mama Macaroni wasn't sitting on a stool behind the counter. Mama nodded to customers but seldom spoke. Mama only spoke when there was a problem. Mama Macaroni was the problem solver. Her son Mario supervised the day-to-day operation. Her daughter-in-law, Gina, kept the books and ran day care for the hordes of grandchildren produced by her four daughters and two sons.

"It's not difficult," Gina said to me. "You'll be working the register. You take the clothes from the customer and you do a count. Then you fill out the order form and give a copy to the customer. You put a copy in the bag with the clothes and you put the third copy in the box by the register. Then you put the bag in one of the rolling bins. One bin is laundry and one bin is dry cleaning. That's the way we do it. When a customer comes in to pick up his cleaned clothes you search for the clothes by the number on the top of his receipt. Make sure you always take a count so the customer gets all his clothes."

Mama Macaroni mumbled something in Italian and slid her dentures around in her mouth.

"Mama says you should be careful. She says she's keeping her eye on you," Gina said.

I smiled at Mama Macaroni and gave her a thumbs-up. Mama Macaroni responded with a death glare.

"When you have time between customers you can tag the clothes," Gina said. "Every single garment must get tagged. We have a machine that you use, and you have to make sure that the number on the tag is the same as the number on the customer's receipt."

By noon I'd completely lost the use of my right thumb from using the tagging machine.

"You got to go faster," Mama Macaroni said to me from her stool. "I see you slow down. You think we pay for nothing?"

A man hurried through the front door and approached the counter. He was mid-forties and dressed in a suit and tie. "I picked my dry cleaning up yesterday," he said, "and all the buttons are broken off my shirt."

Mama Macaroni got off her stool and caned her way to the counter. "What?" she said.

"The buttons are broken."

She shook her head. "I no understand."

He showed her the shirt. "The buttons are all broken."

"Yes," Mama Macaroni said.

"You broke them."

"No," Mama said. "Impossible."

"The buttons were fine when I brought the shirt in. I picked the shirt up and the buttons were all broken."

"I no understand."

"What don't you understand?"

"English. My English no good."

The man looked at me. "Do you speak English?"

"What?" I said.

The man whipped the shirt off the counter and left the store.

"Maybe you not so slow," Mama Macaroni said to me. "But don't get any ideas about taking it easy. We don't pay you good money to stand around doing nothing."

I started watching the clock at one o'clock. By three o'clock I was sure I'd been tagging clothes for at least five days without a break. My thumb was throbbing, my feet ached from standing for eight hours, and I had a nervous twitch in my eye from Mama Macaroni's constant scrutiny.

I took my bag from under the counter and I looked over at Mama Macaroni. "See you tomorrow."

"What you mean, *See you tomorrow*? Where you think you going?"

"Home. It's three o'clock. My shift is over."

"Look at little miss clock watcher here. Three o'clock on the dot. *Bing*. The bell rings and you out the door." She threw her parchment hands into the air. "Go! Go home. Who needs you? And don't be late tomorrow. Sunday is big day. We the only cleaner open on Sunday."

"Okay," I said. "And have a nice mole." *Shit!* Did I just say that? "Have a nice *day!*" I yelled. Crap.

I'd parked the Saturn in the small lot adjacent to Kan Klean. I left the building and circled the car. I didn't see any notes. I didn't smell anything burning. No one shot at me. Guess my stalker was taking a day off.

I got into the car, turned my cell phone on, and scrolled to messages.

First message. "Stephanie." That was the whole message. It was from Morelli at seven-ten this morning. It sounded like it had been said through clenched teeth.

Second message. Morelli breathing at seven-thirty.

Third message. "Call me when you turn your phone on." Morelli again.

Fourth message. "It's two-thirty and we just found Barroni's car. Call me."

Barroni's car! I dialed in Joe's cell number.

"It's me," I said. "I just got off work. I had to turn my phone off because Mama Macaroni said it was giving her brain cancer. Not that it would matter."

"Where are you?"

"I'm on the road. I'm going home to take a nap. I'm all done in."

"The car . . ."

"The car is okay," I told Morelli.

"The car is *not* okay."

"Give up on the car. What about Barroni?"

"I lied about Barroni. I figured that was the only way you'd call."

I put my finger to my eye to stop the twitching, disconnected Morelli, and cruised into my lot.

Old Mr. Ginzler was walking to his Buick when I pulled in. "That's some lookin' car you got there, chicky," Mr. Ginzler said. "And it stinks."

"I paid extra for the smell," I told Mr. Ginzler.

"Smart-ass kid," Mr. Ginzler said. But he smiled when he said it. Mr. Ginzler liked me. I was almost sure of it.

Rex was snoozing in his soup can when I let myself into my apartment. There were no messages on my machine. Most people called my cell these days. Even my mother called my cell. I shuffled into the bedroom, kicked my shoes off, and crawled under the covers.

The best I could say about today was that it was marginally better than yesterday. At least I hadn't gotten fired. Problem was, it was hard to tell if not getting fired from Kan Klean was a good thing or a bad thing. I closed my eyes and willed myself to sleep, telling myself when I woke up my life would be great. Okay, it was sort of a fib, but it kept me from bursting into tears or smashing all my dishes.

A couple hours later I was still awake and I was thinking less about breaking something and more about eating something. I strolled out to the kitchen and took stock. I could construct another peanut butter sandwich. I could mooch dinner off my mother. I could take myself off to search for fast food. The last two choices meant I'd have to get back into the Saturn. Not an appealing prospect, but still better than another peanut butter sandwich.

I laced up my sneakers, ran a brush through my hair, and applied lip gloss. The natural look. Acceptable in Jersey only if you've had your boobs enhanced to the point where no one looked beyond them. I hadn't had my boobs enhanced, and most people found it easy to look beyond them, but I didn't care a whole lot today.

I took the stairs debating the merits of a chicken quesadilla against the satisfaction of a dozen doughnuts. I was still undecided when I pushed through the lobby door and crossed the lot to my car. Turns out it wasn't a decision I needed to make because my car was wearing a police boot.

I ripped my cell phone out of my bag and punched in Morelli's number.

"There's a police boot on my car," I said to him. "Did you put it on?"

"Not personally."

"I want it off."

"I'm crimes against persons. I'm not traffic."

"Fine. I want to report a crime against a person. Some jerk booted my car."

Morelli blew out a sigh and disconnected.

I dialed Ranger. "I have a problem," I said to Ranger.

"And?"

"I was hoping you could solve it."

"Give me a hint."

"My car's been booted."

"And?"

"I need to get the boot off."

"Anything else?"

"I could use some doughnuts. I haven't had dinner."

"Where are you?"

"My apartment."

"Babe," Ranger said, and the connection went dead.

Ten minutes later, Ranger's Porsche rolled to a stop next to the Saturn. Ranger got out and handed me a bag. Ranger was in his usual black. Black T-shirt that looked like it was painted onto his biceps and clung to his washboard stomach. Black cargo pants that had lots of pockets for Ranger's goodies, although clearly not all his goodies were relegated to the pockets. His hair was medium cut and silky straight, falling across his forehead.

"Doughnuts?" I asked.

"Turkey club. Doughnuts will kill you."

"And?"

Ranger almost smiled at me. "If I had to drive this Saturn I'd want to die, too."

FOUR

"CAN YOU GET the boot off?" I asked Ranger.

Ranger toed the big chunk of metal that was wrapped around my tire. "Tank's on his way with the equipment. How'd you manage to get booted in the lot?"

"Morelli. He thinks the car's unsafe."

"And?"

"Okay, so it's got some cosmetic problems."

"Babe, it's got a twelve-inch hole in the floor."

"Yeah, but the hole's in the back and I can't even see it when I'm in the front. And if I leave the back windows open the fumes get sucked out before they get to me."

"Good to know you've thought this through."

"Are you laughing at me?"

"Do I look like I'm laughing?"

"I thought I saw your mouth twitch."

"How'd this happen?"

I took the turkey club out of the bag and unwrapped it. "It was the note guy. I took Grandma to a viewing at

Stiva's, and when we left, there was a note in the car. It said it was my turn to burn . . . and then the backseat caught fire on the way to my parents' house." I took a bite of the sandwich. "I have a feeling about the note guy. I think the note guy is Stiva's kid. Spiro. Joe's Grandma Bella told me she had a vision about rats running away from a fire. And one of the rats was sick and it came back to get me."

"And you think that rat is Spiro?"

"Do you remember Spiro? Beady rat eyes. No chin. Bad overbite. Mousy brown hair."

"Bella's a little crazy, Babe."

I finished the turkey club. "A guy named Michael Barroni disappeared ten days ago. Sixty-two years old. Upstanding citizen. Had a house on Roebling. Owned the hardware store on Rudd and Liberty. Locked the store up at the end of the day and disappeared off the face of the earth. Morelli punched Barroni into missing persons and found there were two other similar cases. Benny Gorman and Louis Lazar. Connie said you're looking for Gorman."

"Yeah, and he feels like a dead end."

"Maybe it's a dead end because he's dead."

"It's crossed my mind."

I crumpled the sandwich bag and tossed it into the back of the Saturn. It bounced off the charred backseat and fell through the hole in the floor, onto the pavement, under the car.

Ranger gave a single, barely visible shake to his head. Hard to tell if he was amused or if he was appalled.

"Did you know Barroni?" Ranger asked me.

"I went to school with his youngest son, Anthony.

Here's the thing about Michael Barroni. There's no obvious reason why he disappeared. No gambling debts. No drinking or drug problems. No health problems. No secret sex life. He just locked up the store, got into his car, and drove off into the sunset. He did this on the same day and at the same time Lazar and Gorman drove off into the sunset. It was like they were all going to a meeting."

"I made the Lazar connection," Ranger said. "I didn't know there was a third."

"That's because you're the Stark Street expert and I'm the Burg expert."

"You handed your cuffs and fake badge over to Connie," Ranger said. "Why the interest in Barroni and Lazar and Gorman?"

"In the beginning, Barroni was just Burg gossip and cop talk. Now I'm thinking Spiro's gone psycho and he's back in town and stalking me. And Barroni might be connected to Spiro. I know that sounds like a stretch, but Spiro makes bad things happen. And he drags his friends into the muck with him. All through school, Spiro hung out with Anthony Barroni. Suppose Spiro's back and he's got something bad going on. Suppose Anthony's involved and somehow his dad got in the way."

"That's a lot of supposing. Have you talked to Morelli about this?"

"No. I'm not talking to Morelli about *anything*. He booted my car. I'm doing all my talking to you."

"His loss is my gain?"

"This is your lucky day," I said to Ranger.

Ranger curled his fingers into the front of my jean

jacket and pulled me close. "How much luck are we talking about?"

"Not that much luck."

Ranger brushed a light kiss over my lips. "Someday," he said.

And he was probably right. Ranger and I have a strange relationship. He's my mentor and protector and friend. He's also hot and mysterious and oozes testosterone. A while ago, he was my lover for a single spectacular night. We both walked away wanting more, but to date, my practical Burg upbringing plus strong survival instincts have kept Ranger out of my bed. This is in direct contrast to Ranger's instincts. His instincts run more to keeping his eye on the prize while he enjoys the chase and waits for his chance to move in for the kill. He is, after all, a hunter of men ... and women.

Ranger released my jacket. "I'm going to take a look at Barroni's house and store. Do you want to ride along?"

"Okay, but it's just to keep you company. It's not like I'm involved. I'm done with all that fugitive apprehension stuff."

"Still my lucky day," Ranger said.

My apartment is only a couple miles from the store, but it was after six by the time we got to Rudd and Liberty, and the store was closed. We cruised past the front, turned the corner, and took the service road at the rear. Ranger drove the Porsche down the road and paused at Barroni's back door. There was a black Corvette parked in the small lot.

"Someone's working late," Ranger said. "Do you know the car?"

"No, but I'm guessing it belongs to Anthony. His two older brothers are married and have kids, and I can't see them finding money for a toy like this."

Ranger continued on, turned the corner, and pulled to the curb. There'd been heavy cloud cover all day and now it was drizzling. Streetlights stood out in the gloom and red brake lights traced across Ranger's rain-streaked windshield.

After five minutes, the Corvette rolled past us with Anthony driving. Ranger put the Porsche in gear and followed Anthony at a distance. Anthony wandered through the Burg and stopped at Pino's Pizza. He was inside Pino's for a couple minutes and returned to his car carrying two large pizza boxes. He found his way to Hamilton Avenue, crossed Hamilton, and after two blocks he pulled into a driveway that belonged to a two-story town house. The town house had an attached garage, but Anthony didn't use it. Anthony parked in the driveway and hustled to the small front porch. He fumbled with his keys, got the door open, and rushed inside.

"That's a lot of pizza for a single guy," Ranger said. "And he has something occupying space in his garage. It's raining, and he has his hands full of pizza boxes, and he parked in the driveway."

"Maybe Spiro's in there. Maybe he's got his car parked in Anthony's garage."

"I can see that possibility turns you on," Ranger said.

"It would be nice to find Spiro and put an end to the harassment."

Shades were drawn on all the windows. Ranger idled for a few minutes in front of the town house and moved on. He retraced the route to the hardware store and had me take him from the store to Michael Barroni's house on Roebling.

It was a large house by Burg standards. Maybe two thousand square feet. Upstairs and downstairs. Detached garage. The front of the house was gray fake stone. The other three sides were white vinyl siding. It had a full front porch and a postage-stamp front yard. There was a plaster statue of the Virgin Mary in the front yard. A small basket of plastic flowers had been placed at her feet. Shades were up in the Barroni house and it was easy to look from one end to the other. A lone woman moved in the house. Carla Barroni, Michael Barroni's wife. She settled herself in front of the television in the living room and lost herself to the evening news.

I was spellbound, watching Carla. "It must be awful not to know," I said to Ranger. "To have someone you love disappear. Not to know if he was murdered and buried in a shallow grave, or if you drove him away, or if he was sick and couldn't find his way home. It makes my problems seem trivial."

"Being on the receiving end of threatening letters isn't trivial," Ranger said.

Everything's relative, I thought. The threatening letters weren't nearly as frightening as the prospect of spending another eight hours with Mama-the-Mole Macaroni. And the problems I was thinking about were personal. My life had no clear direction. My goals were small and immediate. Pay the rent. Get a better car. Make a dinner decision. I didn't have a career. I didn't have a husband. I didn't have any special talents. I didn't have a consuming passion. I didn't have a hobby. Even my pet was small . . . a hamster. I liked Rex a lot, but he didn't exactly make a big statement.

Ranger broke into my moment. "Babe, I get the feeling you're standing on a ledge, looking down."

"Just thinking."

Ranger put the Porsche into gear and headed across town. We checked out Louis Lazar's house and bar. Then we went four blocks north on Stark and parked in front of Gorman's garage. The garage was dark. No sign of life inside. A CLOSED sign hung on the office door.

"Gorman's manager kept the garage going for a week on his own and then cut out," Ranger said. "Gorman isn't married. He was living with a woman, but she has no claim to his property. He has a pack of kids, all with different mothers. The kids are too young to run the business. The rest of Gorman's relatives are in South Carolina. I did a South Carolina search, and it came back negative. From what I can tell the business was operating in the black. Gorman had a mean streak, but he wasn't stupid. He would have made arrangements to keep the garage running if he was going FTA. I can't see him just walking away. Usually I pick up a vibe from someone . . . mother, girlfriend, coworker. I'm not getting anything on this."

We cut back two blocks and parked in front of a run-down apartment building.

"This was Gorman's last known address," Ranger said. "His girlfriend didn't wait as long as his manager. The girlfriend had a new guy hanging his clothes in her closet on day five. If she knew Gorman's location, she'd have given him up for a pass to the multiplex."

"No one saw him after he drove away from the garage?"

Ranger watched the building. "No. All I know is he drove north on Stark. Consistent with Lazar."

North on Stark didn't mean much. Stark Street deteriorated as it went north. Eventually Stark got so bad even the gangs abandoned it. At the very edge of the city line Stark was a deserted war zone of fire-gutted brick buildings with boarded-up windows. It was a graveyard for stolen, stripped-down cars and used-up heroin addicts. It was a do-it-yourself garbage dump. North on Stark also led to Route 1 and Route 1 led to the entire rest of the country.

Ranger's pager buzzed, he checked the message, and pulled away from the curb, into the stream of traffic. Ranger is hot, but he has a few personality quirks that drive me nuts. He doesn't eat dessert, he has an overdeveloped sense of secret, and unless he's trying to seduce me or instruct me in the finer points of bounty huntering, conversation can be nonexistent.

"Hey," I finally said, "Man of Mystery . . . what's with the pager?"

"Business."

"And?"

Ranger slid a glance my way.

"It's no wonder you aren't married," I said to him. "You have a lot to learn about social skills."

Ranger smiled at me. Ranger thought I was amusing.

"That was my office," Ranger said. "Elroy Dish

went FTA two days ago. I've been waiting for him to show up at Blue Fish, and he just walked in."

Vinnie's bonded out three generations of Dishes. Elroy is the youngest. His specialties are armed robbery and domestic violence, but Elroy is capable of most anything. When Elroy's drunk or drugged he's fearless and wicked crazy. When he's clean and sober he's just plain mean.

Blue Fish is a bar on lower Stark, dead center in Dish country. No point to breaking down a door and attempting to drag a Dish out of his rat-trap apartment when you can just wait for him to waltz into Blue Fish for a cold one.

Ranger brought the Porsche to the curb two doors from Blue Fish, cut the motor and the lights. Three minutes later, a black SUV rolled down the street and parked in front of us. Tank and Hal, dressed in RangeMan black, got out of the SUV and strapped on utility belts. Tank is Ranger's shadow. He watches Ranger's back, and he's second in the line of command at RangeMan. His name is self-explanatory. Hal is newer to the game. He's not the sharpest tack on the corkboard, but he tries hard. He's just slightly smaller than Tank and reminds me of a big lumbering dinosaur. He's a Halosaurus.

Ranger reached behind him and grabbed a flak vest from the small backseat. "Stay here," he said. "This will only take a couple minutes and then I'll drive you home."

Ranger angled out of the Porsche, nodded to Tank and Hal, and the three of them disappeared inside Blue

Fish. I checked my watch, and I stared at the door to the bar. Ranger didn't waste time when he made an apprehension. He identified his quarry, clapped the cuffs on, and turned the guy over to Tank and Hal for the forced march to the SUV.

I was feeling a little left out, but I was telling myself it was much better this way. No more danger. No more mess. No more embarrassing screw-ups. I was focused on the door to the bar, not paying a lot of attention to the street, and suddenly the driver's-side door to the Porsche was wrenched open and a guy slid in next to me. He was in his twenties, wearing a ball cap sideways and about sixty pounds of gold chains around his neck. He had a diamond chip implanted into his front tooth and the two teeth next to the chip were missing. He smiled at me and pressed the barrel of a gleaming silver-plated monster gun into my temple.

"Yo, bitch," he said. "How about you get your ass out of my car."

In my mind I saw myself out of the car and running, but the reality of the situation was that all systems were down. I couldn't breathe. I couldn't move. I couldn't speak. I stared openmouthed and glassy-eyed at the guy with the diamond dental chip. Somewhere deep in my brain the word *carjack* was struggling to rise to the surface.

Diamond dental chip turned the key in the Porsche's ignition and revved the engine. "Out of the car," he yelled, pushing the gun barrel against my head. "I'm giving you one second and then I'm gonna blow your brains all over this motherfucker. Now get your *fat ass* out of the car."

The mind works in weird ways, and it's strange how something dumb can push a button. I was willing to overlook the use of the MF word, but getting called a fat ass really pissed me off.

"Fat ass?" I said, feeling my eyes narrow. "Excuse me? Fat ass?"

"I haven't got time for this shit," he said. And he rammed the car into gear, mashed the gas to the floor, and the Porsche jumped away from the curb.

He was driving with his left hand and holding the gun and shifting with his right. There was light traffic on Stark, and he was weaving around cars and running lights. He came up fast behind a Lincoln Navigator and hit the brake hard. He moved to shift, and I knocked the gun out of his hand. The gun hit the console and fell to the floor on the driver's side.

"Fuck," he said. "Fucking fuck. Fucking bitch."

He leaned forward and reached for the gun, and I punched him in the ear as hard as I could. His head bounced off the wheel, the wheel jerked hard to the left, and we cut across oncoming traffic. The Porsche jumped the curb, plowed through a stack of black plastic garbage bags, and crashed through the plate glass window of a small delicatessen that was closed for the night.

The front airbags inflated with a *bang,* and I was momentarily stunned. I fought my way through the bag, somehow got the door open, and rolled out onto the deli floor. I was on my hands and knees in the dark, and it was wet under my hand. Blood, I thought. Get outside and get help.

A leg came into my field of vision. Black cargo

pants, black boots. Hands under my armpits, lifting me to my feet. And then I was face-to-face with Ranger.

"Are you okay?" he asked.

"I must be bleeding. The floor was wet and sticky."

He looked at my hand. "I don't see any blood on you." He put my hand to his mouth and touched his tongue to my palm, giving me a rush that went from my toes to the roots of my hair. "Dill," he said. He looked beyond me, to the crumpled hood of the Porsche. "You crashed into the counter and smashed the pickle barrel."

"I'm sorry about your Porsche."

"I can replace the Porsche. I can't replace you. You need to be more careful."

"I was just sitting in your car!"

"Babe, you're a magnet for disaster."

Tank had the carjacker in cuffs. He shoved him across the floor to the door, the carjacker slid in the pickle juice and went down to one knee, and I heard Tank's boot connect with solid body. "Accident," Tank said. "Didn't see you down there in the dark." And then he yanked the carjacker to his feet and threw him into a wall. "Another accident," Tank said, grabbing the carjacker, jerking him to his feet again.

Ranger cut his eyes to Tank. "Stop playing with him."

Tank grinned at Ranger and dragged the carjacker out to the SUV.

We followed Tank out, and Ranger looked at me under the streetlight. "You're a mess," he said, picking noodles and wilted lettuce out of my hair. "You're covered in garbage again."

"We hit the bags on the curb on the way into the

store. And I guess we dragged some of it with us. I probably rolled in it when I fell out of the car."

A smile hung at the corners of Ranger's mouth. "I can always count on you to brighten my day."

A shiny black Ford truck angled to a stop in front of us, and one of Ranger's men got out and handed Ranger the keys. I could see a police car turn onto Stark, two blocks away.

"Tank and Hal and Woody can take care of this," Ranger said. "We can leave."

"You have a guy named Woody?"

Ranger opened the passenger-side door to the truck for me. "Do you want me to explain it?"

"Not necessary."

I WAS IN the Saturn, parked next to Kan Klean. It was Sunday. It was the start of a new day, it was one minute to seven, and Morelli was on my cell.

"I'm in your lot," he said. "I stopped by to take you to work. Where are you? And where's your car?"

"I'm at Kan Klean. I drove."

"What happened to the boot?"

"I don't know. It disappeared."

There was a full sixty seconds of silence while I knew Morelli was doing deep breathing, working at not getting nuts. I looked at my watch, and my stomach clenched.

Mama Macaroni appeared at car side and stuck her face in my open window, her monster mole just inches from my face, her demon eyes narrowed, her thin lips drawn tight against her dentures.

"What you doing out here?" Mama yelled. "You think we pay for talking on the phone? We got work to do. You kids . . . you think you get money for doing nothing."

"Jesus," Morelli said. "What the hell is that?"

"Mama Macaroni."

"She has a voice like fingernails on a chalkboard."

I NEEDED A pill really bad. It was noon and I had a fireball behind my right eye and Mama Macaroni screeching into my left ear.

"The pink tag's for dry cleaning and the green tag's for laundry," Mama shrieked at me. "You mixing them up. You make a mess of everything. You ruin our business. We gonna be out on the street."

The tinkle bell attached to the front door jangled, and I looked up to see Lula walk in.

"Hey, girlfriend," Lula said to me. "What's shakin'? What's hangin'? What's the word?"

Lula's hair was gold today and styled in ringlets, like Shirley Temple at age five. Lula was wearing black high-heeled ankle boots, a tight orange spandex skirt that came to about three inches below her ass, and a matching orange top that was stretched tight across her boobs and belly. And Lula's belly was about as big as her boobs.

"What word?" Mama Macaroni asked. "Wadda you mean word? Who is this big orange person?"

"This is my friend Lula," I said.

"You friend? No. No friends. Wadda you think, this is a party?"

"Hey, chill," Lula said to Mama. "I came to pick up my dry cleaning. I'm a legitimate customer."

I had the merry-go-round in motion, looking for Lula's cleaning. The motor whirred, and plastic-sleeved, hangered orders swished by me, carried along on an overhead system of tracks.

"I'll take Vinnie's and Connie's too," Lula said.

Mama was off her stool. "You no take anything until I say so. Let me see the slip. Where's the slip?"

I had Lula's cleaning in hand and Mama stepped in front of me. "What's this on the slip? What's this discount?"

"You said I got a discount," I told her, trying hard not to stare at the mole, not having a lot of luck at it.

"*You* get a discount. This big pumpkin don't get no discount."

"Hey, hold on here," Lula said, lower lip stuck out, hands on hips. "Who you calling a pumpkin?"

"I'm calling *you* a pumpkin," Mama Macaroni said. "Look at you. You a big fat pumpkin. And you don't get no pumpkin discount." Mama turned on me. "You try to pull a fast one. Give everybody a discount. Like we run a charity here. A charity for pumpkins. Maybe you get the kickback. You think you make some money on the side."

"I don't like to disrespect old people," Lula said. "And you're about as old as they get. You're as old as dirt, but that don't mean you can insult my friend. I don't put up with that. I don't take that bus. You see what I'm saying?"

The pain was radiating out from my eye into all parts of my head, and little men in pointy hats and

spiky shoes were running around in my stomach. I had
to get Lula out of the store. If Mama Macaroni called
Lula a pumpkin one more time, Lula was going to
squash Mama Macaroni, and Mama Macaroni was going to be Mama Pancake.

I shoved Lula's clothes at her, but Mama got to them
first. "Gimme those clothes," Mama said. "She can't
have them until she pays full price. Maybe I don't give
them to her at all. Maybe I keep them for evidence that
you steal from us."

"I need that red sweater," Lula said. "That's my
most flattering sweater."

"Too bad for you," Mama said. "You should think of
this before you steal from us."

"That does it," Lula said. "I didn't steal from you.
And I don't like your attitude. And I'm a bounty hunter
now, and I don't got time for this like when I was a file
clerk."

Lula got a knee up on the counter and lunged for
Mama Macaroni and the dry cleaning.

"Help! Police!" Mama shrieked.

"Police, my patoot," Lula said. And she was over the
counter, going for Mama Macaroni.

Mama jumped away and scrambled around a clothes
bin, hugging the dry cleaning to her chest. Gina Macaroni and three other women, all shouting in Italian,
came running from the back room.

Gina was wielding a broom like a baseball bat.
"What's going on?" Gina wanted to know.

"Thieves. Robbers," Mama said. "They trying to
steal from us. Hit them with the broom. Hit them good.
Knock their heads off."

"This old woman's nuts," Lula said. "I just want my dry cleaning. I'd've paid for it fair and square." Lula pulled her Glock out of her handbag, and all the women shrieked and dropped to the floor. Except for Mama Macaroni. Mama Macaroni flipped Lula the bird.

"You should give her the dry cleaning," I said to Mama Macaroni. "She's real dangerous. She's shot a lot of people." That was sort of a fib. Lula's shot *at* a lot of people. I don't know that she's ever connected.

"She don't scare me," Mama said. And Mama reached underneath her long black skirt, pulled out a semiautomatic, and started shooting. She was shooting wild, taking out light fixtures and chunks of plaster from the ceiling, but that didn't make it any less terrifying . . . or for that matter, any less dangerous.

Lula and I dove for the front of the store, rolled out the door, and scrambled to the Firebird. Lula jumped behind the wheel, and we roared off.

"Do you frickin' believe that?" Lula yelled. "That crazy old lady shot at us! She could have killed us. You know what she needs?"

I looked expectantly at Lula.

"A dermatologist," Lula said. "Did you see that mole? It should be illegal to have a mole like that. That was a mutant mole. I didn't even bring it up in the conversation either. I was being real polite. Even when she was a meanie, I was still polite."

"You told her she was as old as dirt."

Lula pulled into the Cluck-in-a-Bucket lot. "Yeah, but that was a fact. You can't count a fact. How long do you get for lunch? We might as well have lunch as long as we're out."

"I don't think lunch is an issue. My employer just called me a thief and shot at me. That would lead me to believe I'm unemployed."

"I wouldn't be so sure of that. It's hard to get good help these days. That dry cleaner's lucky to have you. And I didn't hear anybody fire you. The old lady wasn't shooting at you and saying *you're fired*. The old lady was just Anna Banana probably on account of she has that mole."

We went inside, placed our order, and waited for our food to be assembled.

"Well okay, now that I think about it, probably you're fired," Lula said. "It was a nasty job anyway. You had to look at that mole all day. And I'm sorry, that's no normal mole."

"It's the mole from hell."

"Friggin' A," Lula said. "And you shouldn't worry about getting another job. You could get a better job than that. You could even get a job here. Look at the sign by the register. It says they're hiring. And there'd be advantages to working here. I bet you get free chicken and fries." Lula went back to the counter. "We want to see the manager," she said. "My friend's interested in having a job here. I'm not interested myself because I'm a kick-ass bounty hunter, but Stephanie over there just got unemployed."

I had Lula by the arm, and I was trying to drag her away from the counter. "No!" I whispered to Lula. "I don't want to work here. I'd have to wear one of those awful uniforms."

"Yeah, but you wouldn't ruin any of your real clothes that way," Lula said. "Probably you get a lot of grease stains here. And I don't think the uniform's so bad. Besides, your skinny little ass makes everything look good."

"The *hat*!"

"Okay, I see what you're saying about the hat. Suppose the hat had an accident? Suppose the hat fell into the french fry machine first thing? I bet it would take days to get a new hat."

A little guy came up behind me. He was half a head shorter than me, and he looked like a chubby pink pig in pants. His cheeks were round and pink. His hands were pink sausages. His belly jiggled when he moved. His mouth was round and his lips were pink . . . and best not to think about the pig part the mouth most resembled, but it could be found under the curly pig tail.

"I'm the manager," he said. "Milton Mann."

"This here's Stephanie Plum," Lula said. "She's looking for a job."

"Minimum wage," Mann said. "We need someone for the three-to-eleven shift."

"How about food?" Lula wanted to know. "Does she eat free? And what about takeout?"

"There's no eating on the job, but she can eat for free on her dinner break. Takeout gets a twenty percent discount."

"That sounds fair," Lula said. "She'll take the job."

"Come in a half hour early tomorrow," Mann said to me. "I'll give you your uniform and you can fill out the paperwork."

"Look at that," Lula said, claiming her tray of food, steering me back to the table. "See how easy it is to get a job? There's jobs everywhere."

"Yeah, but I don't want this job. I don't want to work here."

"Twenty percent off on takeout," Lula said. "You can't beat that. You can feed your family . . . *and friends*."

I took a piece of fried chicken from the bucket on the tray. "My car is back at the dry cleaner."

"And I didn't get my sweater. That was my favorite sweater, too. It was just the right shade of red to flatter my skin tone."

I finished my piece of chicken. "Are you going back to get your sweater?"

"Damn skippy I'm going back. Only thing is I'm waiting until they're closed and it's nice and dark out." Lula looked over my shoulder and her eyes focused on the front door. "Uh oh," Lula said. "Here comes Officer Hottie, and he don't look happy."

Morelli moved behind me and curled his fingers into the back of my jacket collar. "I need to talk to you . . . outside."

"I wouldn't go if I was you," Lula said to me. "He's wearing his mad cop face. At least you should make him leave his gun here."

Morelli shot Lula a look, and she buried her head in the chicken bucket.

When we got outside Morelli dragged me to the far side of the building, away from the big plate glass windows. He still had a grip on my jacket, and he still had the don't-mess-with-me cop face. He held tight to my jacket, and he stared at his shoes, head down.

"Practicing anger management?" I asked.

He shook his head and bit into his lower lip. "No,"

he said. "I'm trying not to laugh. That crazy old lady shot at you and I don't want to trivialize it, but I totally lost it at Kan Klean. And I wasn't the only one. I was there with three uniforms who responded to the call, and we all had to go around to the back of the building to compose ourselves. Your friend Eddie Gazarra was laughing so hard he wet his uniform. Was there really a shoot-out between the old lady and Lula?"

"Yeah, but Mama Macaroni did all the shooting. She trashed the place. Lula and I were lucky to get out alive. How'd you know where to find me?"

"I did a drive-by on all the doughnut shops and fast-food places in the area. And by the way, Mama Macaroni said to tell you that you're fired." Morelli leaned into me and nuzzled my neck. "We should celebrate."

"You wanted to celebrate when I got the job. Now you want to celebrate because I've lost the job?"

"I like to celebrate."

Sometimes I had a hard time keeping up with Morelli's libido. "I'm not talking to you," I told Morelli.

"Yeah, but we could still celebrate, right?"

"Wrong. And I need to get back inside before Lula eats all the food."

Morelli pulled me to him and kissed me with a lot of tongue. "I *really* need to celebrate," he said. And he was gone, off to file a report on my shoot-out.

Lula was finishing her half gallon of soda when I returned to the table. "How'd that go?" she wanted to know.

"Average." I looked in the chicken bucket. One wing left.

"I'm in a real mean mood after that whole cleaning incident," Lula said. "I figure I might as well make the most of it and go after my DV. When I was a file clerk I didn't usually work on Sunday, unless I was helping you. But now that I'm a bounty hunter I'm on the job twenty-four/seven. You see what I'm saying? And I know how you're missing being a bounty hunter and all, so I'm gonna let you ride with me again."

"I don't miss being a bounty hunter. And I don't want to ride with you."

"Please?" Lula said. "Pretty please with sugar on it? I'm your friend, right? And we do things together, right? Like, look at how we just shared lunch together."

"You ate all the chicken."

"Not *all* the chicken. I left you a wing. 'Course, it's true I don't particularly like wings, but that's not the point. Anyways, I kept you from putting a lot of ugly fat on your skinny ass. You aren't gonna be getting any from Officer Hottie if you get all fat and dimply. And I know you need to be getting some on a regular basis because I remember when you weren't getting *any* and you were a real cranky pants."

"Stop!" I said. "I'll go with you."

FIVE

IT TOOK US a half hour to get to the public housing projects and work our way through the grid of streets that led to Emanuel Lowe, also known as the DV. Lula had the Firebird parked across the street from Lowe's apartment, and we were both watching the apartment door, and we were both wishing we were at Macy's shopping for shoes.

"We need a better plan this time," Lula said. "Last time, I did the direct approach and that didn't work out. We gotta be sneaky this time. And we can't use me on account of everybody here knows me now. So I'm thinking it's going to have to be you to go snatch the DV."

"Not in a million years."

"Yeah, but they don't know you. And there's hardly anybody sneakier than you. I'd even cut you in. I'd give you ten bucks if you collected him for me."

I did raised eyebrows at Lula. "Ten dollars? I used to pay you fifty and up."

"I figure it goes by the pound and a little bitty thing like you isn't worth as much as a full-figured woman like me." Lula took a couple beats. "Well okay, I guess that don't fly. It was worth a try though, right?"

"Maybe you should just sit here and wait for him to come out and then you can run over him with your Firebird."

"That's sarcasm, isn't it? I know sarcasm when I hear it. And it's not attractive on you. You don't usually do sarcasm. You got some Jersey attitude going, don't you?"

I slumped lower in my seat. "I'm depressed."

"You know what would get you out of that depression? An apprehension. You need to kick some butt. You need to get yourself empowered. I bet you'd feel real good if you snagged yourself an Emanuel Lowe."

"*Fine*. Okay. I'll get Lowe for you. The day's already in the toilet. Might as well finish it off right." I unbuckled my seat belt. "Give me your gun and your cuffs."

"You haven't got your own gun?"

"I didn't think I needed to carry a gun because I didn't think I was going to be doing this anymore. When I left the house this morning I thought I was going to be working at the dry cleaners."

Lula handed me her gun and a pair of cuffs. "You always gotta have a gun. It's like wearing undies. You wouldn't go out of the house without undies, would you? Same thing with a gun. Boy, for being a bounty hunter all that time, you sure don't know much."

I grabbed the gun from Lula and marched up to Lowe's front door. I knocked twice, Lowe opened the door, and I pointed the gun at him. "On the ground," I said. "*Now.*"

Lowe gave a bark of laughter. "You not gonna shoot me. I'm a unarmed man. You get twenty years for shooting me."

I aimed high, squeezed a round off, and took out a ceiling fixture.

"Crazy bitch," he said. "This here's public housing. You costing the taxpayer money. I got a mind to report you."

"I'm not in a good mood," I said to Lowe.

"I can see that. How you like me to improve your mood? Maybe you need a man to make you feel special."

Emanuel Lowe was five foot nine and rail thin. He had no ass, no teeth, and I was guessing no deodorant, no shower, no mouthwash. He was wearing a wife-beater T-shirt that had yellowed with age, and baggy homeboy-style brown pants precariously perched on his bony hips. And he was offering himself up to me. This was the state of my life. Maybe I should just shoot *myself*.

I leveled the barrel at his head. "On the floor, on your stomach, hands behind your back."

"Tell you what. I'll get on the floor if you show me some pussy. It gotta be good pussy, too. The full show. You aren't bald down there, are you? I don't know what white bitches thinking of, waxing all the bush off. Gives me the willies. It's like bonin' supermarket chicken."

So I shot him. I did it for women worldwide. It was a public service.

"Yow!" he said. "What the fuck you do that for? We just talking, having some fun."

"*I* wasn't having any fun," I said.

I'd shot him in the foot, and now he was hopping around, howling, dripping blood. From what I could see, I'd nicked him somewhere in the vicinity of the little toe.

"If you aren't down on the floor, hands behind your back, in three seconds, I'm going to shoot you again," I said.

Lowe dropped to the floor. "I'm dying. I'm gonna bleed to death."

I cuffed him and stood back. "I just tagged your toe. You'll be fine."

Lula poked her head in. "What's going on? Was that gunshot?" She walked over to Lowe and stood hands on hips, staring down at Lowe's foot. "Damn," Lula said. "I hate when I have to take bleeders in my Firebird. I just got new floor mats, too."

"How bad is it?" Lowe wanted to know. "It feels real bad."

"She just ripped a chunk out of the side of your foot," Lula said. "Looks to me like you got all your toes and everything."

I ran to the kitchen and got a kitchen towel and a plastic garbage bag. I wrapped Lowe's foot in the towel and pulled the plastic bag over the foot and the towel and tied it at the ankle. "That's the best I can do," I said to Lula. "You're going to have to deal with it."

We got him to the curb, and Lula looked down at Lowe's foot. "Hold on here," she said. "We ripped a hole in the Baggie when we dragged him out here, and he's bleeding through the towel. He's gonna have to hang his leg out the window."

"I'm not hanging my leg outta the window," Lowe said. "How's that gonna look?"

"It's gonna look like you're on the way to the hospital," Lula said. "How else you think you're gonna get to the hospital and get that foot stitched up? You gonna sit here and wait for an ambulance? You think they're gonna rush to come get *your* sorry behind?"

"You got a point," Lowe said. "Just hurry up. I'm not feeling all that good. It wasn't right of her to shoot me. She had no call to do that."

"The hell she didn't," Lula said. "You gotta learn to cooperate with women. My opinion is she should have shot higher and rearranged your nasty."

Lula rolled the rear side window down, and Lowe got in and hung his legs out the window.

"I feel like a damn fool," Lowe said. "And this here's uncomfortable. My foot's throbbing like a bitch."

Lula walked around to the driver's side. "I saw a picture of what he did to his girlfriend," Lula said. "She had a broken nose and two cracked ribs, and she was in the hospital for three days. My thinking is he deserves some pain, so I'm gonna drive real slow, and I might even get lost on the way to the emergency room."

"Don't get too lost. Wouldn't want him to bleed to death since I was the one who shot him."

"I didn't see you shoot him," Lula said. "I especially didn't see you shoot him with my gun that might not be registered on account of I got it from a guy on a street corner at one in the morning. Anyways, I figured Lowe was running away and tore himself up on a broken bottle of hooch. You know how these guys always have broken bottles of hooch laying around." Lula muscled herself behind the wheel. "You coming with me or you staying behind to tidy up?"

I gave Lula her gun. "I'm staying behind."

"Later," Lula said. And she drove off with Lowe's legs hanging out her rear side window, the plastic bag rattling in the breeze.

I went into Lowe's apartment and prowled through the kitchen. I found a screwdriver and a mostly empty bottle of Gordon's gin. I used the screwdriver to dig the bullet out of Lowe's floor. I pocketed the round and the casing. Then I dropped the bottle of gin on the bloodiest part of the floor and smashed it with the screwdriver. I went back to the kitchen and washed the screwdriver, washed my hands, and threw the screwdriver into a pile of garbage that had collected in the corner of the kitchen. Discarded pizza boxes, empty soda bottles, fast-food bags, crumpled beer cans, and stuff I preferred not to identify.

"I hate this," I said to the empty apartment. I pulled my cell phone out of my bag and called my dad. A couple years ago my dad retired from his job at the post office, and now he drives a cab part-time.

"Hey," I said when he answered. "It's me. I need a cab."

I locked the doors and secured the windows while I waited for my dad. Not that there was much to steal from Lowe's apartment. Most of the furniture looked like Lowe had shopped at the local Dumpster. Still, it was his and I felt an obligation to be a professional.

Probably should have thought about my professional obligation before shooting Lowe in the foot.

I called Ranger. "I just shot a guy in the foot," I told him.

"Did he deserve it?"

"That's sort of a tough moral question. I thought so at the time, but now I'm not so sure."

"Did you destroy the evidence? Were there witnesses? Did you come up with a good lie?"

"Yes. No. Yes."

"Move on," Ranger said. "Anything else?"

"No. That's about it."

"One last word of advice. Stay away from the doughnuts." And he disconnected.

Great.

Twenty minutes later, my father rolled to a stop at curbside. "I thought you were working at the button factory," he said.

My father's body showed up at the dinner table every evening. His mind was usually somewhere else. I suppose that was the secret to my parents' marital success. That plus the deal that my father made money and my mother made meatloaf and the division of labor was clear and never challenged. In some ways, life was simple in the Burg.

"The button factory job didn't work out," I told my father. "I helped Lula with an apprehension today and ended up here."

"You're like your Uncle Peppy. Went from one job to the next. Wasn't that he was dumb, either. Was just that he didn't have a direction. He didn't have a passion, you know? It didn't look like he had any special talent. Like take me. I was good at sorting mail. Now, I know that doesn't seem like a big deal, but it was something I was good at. Of course, I got replaced by a machine. But that doesn't take away that I was good at something. Your Uncle Peppy was forty-two before he found out he could do latch hook rugs."

"Uncle Peppy's doing time at Rahway for arson."

"Yeah, but he's doing latch hook there. When he gets out he can make a good living with rugs. You should see some of his rugs. He made a rug that had a tiger head in it. You ask me, he's better hooking rugs than arson. He never got the hang of arson. Okay, so he set a couple good fires, but he didn't have the touch like Sol Razzi. Sol could set a fire and no one ever knew how it started. Now, *that's* arson."

Jersey's one of the few places where arson is a profession.

"Where are we going?" my father wanted to know.

"What's Mom making for supper?"

"Meatballs with spaghetti. And I saw a chocolate cake in the kitchen."

"I'll go home with you."

THERE WERE TWO cars parked in front of my parents' house. One belonged to my sister. And one belonged to a friend of mine who was helping my mom plan my sister's wedding. My father paused at the driveway entrance and stared at the cars with his eyes narrowed.

"If you smash into them your insurance will go up," I said.

My father gave a sigh, pulled forward, and parked.

When my father blew out the candles on his birthday cake I suspect he wished my grandmother would go far away. He'd wish my sister into another state, and my friend Sally Sweet, a.k.a. the Wedding Planner, into another universe. I'm not sure what he wanted to do with me. Maybe ride along on a bust. Don't get me wrong. My dad isn't a mean guy. He wouldn't want my grandmother to suffer, but I think he wouldn't be too upset if she suddenly died in her sleep. Personally, I think Grandma's a hoot. Of course, I don't have to live with her.

All through school my sister, Valerie, looked like the Virgin Mary. Brown hair simply styled, skin like alabaster, beatific smile. And she had a personality to match. Serene. Smooth. Little Miss Perfect. The exact opposite of her sister, Stephanie, who was Miss Disaster. Valerie graduated college in the top 10 percent of her class and married a perfectly nice guy. They followed his job to L.A. They had two girls. Valerie morphed into Meg Ryan. And one day the perfectly nice guy ran off to Tahiti with the baby-sitter. No reflection on Meg. It was just that time in his life. So Valerie moved back home with her girls. Angie is the firstborn and a near perfect clone of Valerie the Virgin. Mary Alice is two years behind Angie. And Mary Alice thinks she's a horse.

It's a little over a year now since Valerie returned, and she's since gained sixty pounds, had a baby out of wedlock, and gotten engaged to her boss, Albert Kloughn, who also happens to be the baby's father. The baby's name is Lisa, but most often she's called The Baby. We're not sure who The Baby is yet, but from the amount of gas she produces I think she's got a lot of Kloughn in her.

Valerie and Sally were huddled at the dining room table, studying the seating chart for the wedding reception.

"Hey, girlfriend," Sally said to me. "Long time no see."

Sally drove a school bus during the week, and weekends he played in a band in full drag. He was six foot five inches tall, had roses tattooed on his biceps, hair everywhere, a large hook nose, and he was lanky in a guitar-playing-maniac kind of way. Today Sally was wearing a big wooden cross on a chain and six strands of love beads over a black Metallica T-shirt, black hightop Chucks, and washed-out baggy jeans.

Okay, not your average wedding planner, but he'd sort of adopted us, and he was free. He'd become one of the family with my mom and grandma and they endured his eccentricities with the same eyerolling tolerance that they endured mine. I guess a pothead wedding planner seems respectable when you have a daughter who shoots people.

Angie was doing her homework across from Valerie. The Baby was in a sling attached to Valerie's chest, and Mary Alice was galloping around the table, whinnying. My father went straight to his chair in the living room and remoted the television. I went to the kitchen.

My mother was at the stove, stirring the red sauce. "Emily Restler's daughter got a pin for ten years' service at the bank," my mother said. "Ten years and she was never once in a shoot-out. I have a daughter who works one day at a dry cleaners and turns it into the gunfight at the O.K. Corral. And on a Sunday, too. The Lord's Day."

"It wasn't me. I didn't even have a gun. It was Mama Macaroni. And she wouldn't give Lula her dry cleaning."

Grandma was at the small kitchen table. "I hate to think you couldn't take down Mama Macaroni. If I'd been there you would have got the dry cleaning. In fact, I got a mind to go over there and get it for you."

"*No,*" my mother and I said in unison.

I got a soda from the fridge and eyed the cake on the counter.

"It's for supper," my mother said. "No snitching. It's got to be nice. The wedding planner is eating with us."

Sally is one of my favorite people, but Sally didn't care a lot about what went in his mouth unless it was inhaled from a bong or rolled in wacky tobacky paper.

"Sally wouldn't notice if there were roaches in the icing," I told my mom.

"It has nothing to do with Sally," my mom said. "My water glasses don't have spots. There's no dust on the furniture. And I don't serve guests half-eaten cake at my dinner table."

I didn't serve guests half-eaten cake either. To begin with, I never had guests, unless it was Joe or Ranger. And neither of them was interested in my cake. Okay, maybe Joe would want cake . . . but it wouldn't be the first thing on his mind, and he wouldn't care if it was half-eaten.

I grated parmesan for my mother, and I sliced some

cucumbers and tomatoes. In the dining room, Valerie and Sally were yelling at each other, competing with the television and the galloping horse.

"Is there any news about Michael Barroni?" I asked.

"Still missing," Grandma said. "And they haven't found his car, either. I hear he only had it for a day. It was brand-new right out of the showroom."

"I saw Anthony yesterday. He was driving a Corvette that looked new."

Grandma got dishes from the cupboard. "Mabel Such says Anthony's spending money like water. She don't know where he's getting it from. She says he doesn't make all that much at the store. She says he was on a salary just like everybody else. Michael Barroni came up the hard way, and he wasn't a man to give money away. Not even to his sons."

I got silverware and napkins, and Grandma and I set the table around Valerie and Sally and Angie.

"You can stare at that seating chart all you want," Grandma said to Valerie. "It's never gonna get perfect. Nobody wants to sit next to Biddie Schmidt. Everybody wants to sit next to Peggy Linehart. And nobody's going to be happy sitting at table number six, next to the restrooms."

My mother brought the meatballs and sauce to the table and went back for the spaghetti. My father moved from his living room chair to his dining room chair and helped himself to the first meatball. Everyone sat except Mary Alice. Mary Alice was still galloping.

"Horses got to eat," Grandma said. "You better sit down."

"There's no hay," Mary Alice said.

"Sure there is," Grandma said. "See that big bowl of spaghetti? It's people hay, but horses can eat it, too."

Mary Alice plunged her face into the spaghetti and snarfed it up.

"That's disgusting," Grandma said.

"It's the way horses eat," Mary Alice told her. "They stick their whole face in the feed bag. I saw it on television."

The front door opened and Albert Kloughn walked in. "Am I late? I'm sorry I'm late. I didn't mean to be late. I had a client."

Everyone stopped what they were doing and looked at Kloughn. Kloughn didn't get a lot of clients. He's a lawyer and his business has been slow to take off. Partly the problem is that he's a sweetie-pie guy . . . and who wants a sweetie-pie lawyer? In Jersey you want a lawyer who's a shark, a sonuvabitch, a first-class jerk. And partly the problem is Kloughn's appearance. Kloughn looks like a soft, chubby, not-entirely-with-the-program fourteen-year-old boy.

"What kind of client?" Grandma asked.

Kloughn took his place at the table. "It was a woman from the Laundromat next to my office. She was doing her whites, and she saw my sign and the light on in my office. I went in to do some filing, but I was actually playing poker on my computer. Anyway, she came over for advice." Kloughn helped himself to spaghetti. "Her husband took off on her, and she didn't know what to do. Sounded like she didn't mind him leaving. She said they'd been having problems. It was that he took their car, and she was stuck with the payments. It was a brand-new car, too."

I felt the skin prickle at the nape of my neck. "When did this guy disappear?"

"A couple weeks ago." Kloughn scooped a meatball onto the big serving spoon. The meatball rolled off the spoon, slid down Kloughn's shirt, and ski jumped off his belly into his lap. "I knew that was going to happen," Kloughn said. "This always happens with meatballs. Does it happen with chicken? Does it happen with ham? Okay, sometimes it happens with chicken and ham, but not as much as meatballs. If it was me, I wouldn't make meatballs round. Round things roll, right? Am I right? What if you made meatballs square? Did anybody think of that?"

"That would be meat*loaf*," Grandma said.

"Did this woman report her missing husband to the police?" I asked Kloughn.

"No. It was just one of those personal things. She said she knew he was going to leave her. I guess he was fooling around on the side and things weren't working out for them." Kloughn retrieved the meatball and set it on top of his spaghetti. He dabbed at his shirt with his napkin, but the smear of red sauce only got worse. "I felt sorry for her with the car payment and all, but boy, can you imagine being that dumb? Here she is living with this guy and all of a sudden he just up and leaves her. And it turns out she has nothing but bills. They had two mortgages that she didn't even know about. The bank account was empty. What a dope."

My mother, father, and Grandma and I all sucked in some air and slid our eyes to Valerie. This was exactly what happened to Valerie. This was like calling *Valerie* a dope.

"You think this woman is a dope because her husband managed to swindle her out of everything?" Valerie asked Kloughn.

"Well yeah. I mean, duh. She was probably too lazy to keep track of things and got what she deserved."

The color rose from Valerie's neck clear to the roots of her hair. I swear I could see her scalp glowing like hot coals.

"Oh boy," Grandma said.

Sally inched his chair away from Valerie.

Kloughn was working at the stain on his shirt and not looking at Valerie, and I was guessing he hadn't a clue what he'd just said. Somehow the words got put together into sentences and fell out of his mouth. This happened a lot with Kloughn. Kloughn looked up from his shirt to dead silence. Only a slight sizzle where Valerie's scalp was steaming.

"What?" Kloughn said. He searched the faces in the room. Something was wrong, and he'd missed it. He focused on Valerie, and you could see his mind working backward. And then it hit him. *Kaboom.*

"You were different," he said to Valerie. "I mean, you had a reason for being a dope. Well, not a dope actually. I don't mean to say you were a dope. Okay, you might have been a little dop*ey*. No, wait, I don't mean that either. Not dopey or dope or any of those things. Okay, okay, just a teensy bit dopey, but in a good way, right? Dopey can be good. Like dumb blond dopey. No, I don't mean that either. I don't know where that came from. Did I say that? I didn't say that, did I?"

Kloughn stopped talking because Valerie had gotten to her feet with the fourteen-inch bread knife in her hand.

"You don't want to do anything silly here," I said to Val. "You aren't thinking of stabbing him, are you? Stabbing is messy."

"Fine. Give me your gun, and I'll shoot him."

"It's not good to shoot people," I said. "The police don't like it."

"You shoot people all the time."

"Not *all* the time."

"I'll give you my gun," Grandma said.

My mother glared at my grandmother. "You told me you got rid of that gun."

"I meant I'd give her my gun if I had one," Grandma said.

"Great," Valerie said, flapping her arms, her voice up an octave. "Now I'm dopey. I'm fat, and I'm dopey. I'm a big fat dope."

"I didn't say you were fat," Kloughn said. "You're not fat. You're just . . . chubby, like me."

Valerie went wild-eyed. "*Chubby?* Chubby is awful! I used to be perfect. I used to be serene. And now look at me! I'm a wreck. I'm a big, fat, dopey, chubby wreck. And I look like a white whale in my stupid wedding gown. A big, huge *white whale*!" She narrowed her eyes and leaned across the table at Kloughn. "You think I'm dopey and lazy and chubby, and that I got what I deserved from my philandering husband!"

"No. I swear. I was under stress," Kloughn said. "It was the meatball. I never think. You know I never think."

"I never want to see you again," Valerie said. "The wedding is off." And Valerie gathered up her three kids, her diaper bag, her sling thing, her kids' backpacks, and the collapsible stroller. She went to the kitchen and took the chocolate cake. And she left.

"Dudes," Sally said. "I did the best I could with the dress."

"We're not blaming you," Grandma said. "But she *does* look like a white whale."

Kloughn turned to me. "What happened?"

I looked over at him. "She took the cake."

I CAUGHT A ride home with Sally, and I was parked in front of my television when my doorbell rang at nine o'clock. It was Lula, and she was dressed in black from head to toe, including a black ski mask.

"Are you ready?" Lula wanted to know.

"Ready for what?"

"To get my cleaning. What do you think?"

"I think we should give up on the cleaning and send out for a pizza. Aren't you hot in that ski mask?"

"That Mama Macaroni got my favorite sweater. I need that sweater. And on top of that it's the principle of the thing. It's just not right. I was a hundred percent in the right. I'm surprised at you wanting to let this go. Where's your crusading spirit? I bet Ranger wouldn't let it go. And you got to get your car, anyway. How're you gonna get over there to get your car if you don't go with me?"

My car. Mental head slap. I'd forgotten about the car.

Ten minutes later, we were idling across the street from Kan Klean. "It's nice and dark tonight," Lula said. "We got some cloud cover. Not a star in the sky and it looks like someone already took out the streetlight."

I looked at Lula and grimaced.

"Hey, don't give me that grimace. I expected you'd compliment me on my shooting. I actually hit that freaking lightbulb!"

"How many shots did it take?"

"I emptied a whole clip at it." Lula cut the engine and pulled her ski mask back over her head. "Come on. Time to rock and roll."

Oh boy.

We got out of the Firebird and waited for an SUV to pass before crossing the street. The SUV driver caught a glance at Lula in the ski mask and almost jumped the curb.

"If you can't drive, you shouldn't be on the road," Lula yelled after him.

"It was the mask," I said. "You scared the crap out of him."

"Hunh," Lula said.

We got to the store and Lula tried the front door. Locked. "How many other doors are there?" she asked.

"Just one. It's in back. But it's a fire door. You'll never get through it. There aren't any windows back there either. Just a couple big exhaust fans."

"Then we got to go in through the front," Lula said. "And I don't mind doing it because I'm justified. This here's a righteous cause. It's not every day I can find a sweater like that." She turned to me. "You go ahead and pick the lock."

"I don't know how to pick a lock."

"Hell, you were the big bounty hunter. How could you be the big bounty hunter without knowing how to pick a lock? How'd you ever get in anywhere?" She stood back and looked at the store. "Ordinarily I'd just break a window, but they got one big-ass window here. It's just about the whole front of the place. It might look suspicious if I broke the window."

Lula ran across the street to the Firebird and came back with a tire iron. "Maybe we can pry the door open." She put the tire iron to the doorjamb and another car drove by. The car slowed as it passed us and then took off.

"Maybe we should try the back door," Lula said.

SIX

WE WENT AROUND to the back and Lula tried to wedge the tire iron under the bolt. "Don't fit," she said. "This door's sealed up tight." Lula gave the door a whack with the tire iron and the door swung open. "Will you look at this," Lula said. "Have we got some luck, or what?"

"I don't like it. They always lock up and set the alarm."

"They must have just forgot. It was a traumatic day."

"I think we should leave. This doesn't feel right."

"I'm not leaving without my sweater. I'm close now. I can hear my sweater calling to me. Soon's we get inside I'll switch on my Maglite, and you can work that gizmo that makes the clothes go around, and before you know it we'll be outta here."

We both took two steps forward, the door closed behind us, and Lula hit the button on the Maglite. We cautiously walked past the commercial washers and dryers and the large canvas bins that held the clothes.

We stopped and listened for sirens, for someone else breathing, for the beeping of an alarm system ready to activate.

"Feels okay to me," Lula said.

It didn't feel okay to me. All the little hairs on my arm were standing at attention, and my heart was thumping in my chest.

"We got the counter right in front of us," Lula said. "You switch on the whirly clothes thing."

I reached for the switch and every light in the store suddenly went on. It was as bright as day. And there was Mama Macaroni, perched on her chair, a hideous crone dressed in a black shroud, sighting us down the barrel of a gun, her mole hairs glinting under the fluorescent light.

"Holy crap," Lula said. "Holy Jesus. Holy cow."

Mama Macaroni held the gun in one hand and Lula's dry cleaning in the other. "I knew you'd be back," she said. "Your kind has no honor. All you know is stealing and whoring."

"I quit whoring," Lula said. "Okay, maybe I do a little recreational whoring once in a while . . ."

"Trash," Mama Macaroni said. "Cheap trash. Both of you." She turned to me. "I never want to hire you. I tell them anything that come from your family is bad. Hungarians!" And she spat on the floor. "That's what I think of Hungarians."

"I'm not Hungarian," Lula said. "How about giving me my dry cleaning?"

"When hell freezes. And that's where you should be," Mama Macaroni said. "I put a curse on you. I send you to hell."

Lula looked at me. "She can't do that, can she?"

"You never get this sweater," Mama Macaroni said. "*Never*. I take this sweater to the grave with me."

Lula looked at me like she wouldn't mind arranging that to happen.

"It'd be expensive," I said to Lula. "Be cheaper just to buy a new sweater."

"And *you*," Mama Macaroni said to me. "You never gonna see that car again. That *my* car now. You leave it in my lot and that make it mine." She squinted down the barrel at me, leveling it at forehead level. "Give me the key."

"You don't suppose she'd actually shoot you, do you?" Lula asked.

There was no doubt in my mind. Mama Macaroni would shoot me, and I'd be dead, dead, dead. I pulled the car key out of my pocket and gingerly handed it over to Mama.

"I'm gonna leave now," Mama said. "I got a TV show I like to watch. And you gonna stay here." She backed away from us, past the washers and dryers to the rear door. She set the alarm and scuttled through the fire door. The door closed after her, and I could hear her throw the bolt.

I immediately went to the front of the store and stood behind the counter so I could look out the window. "We'll wait until we see her drive away, and then we'll leave," I said to Lula. "We'll trip the alarm when we open the door, but we'll be long gone before the police get here."

I heard the Saturn engine catch, and then there was an explosion that rocked the building. The explosion blew the fire door off its hinges, shattered the big front window, and knocked Lula and me to our knees.

"Fudge!" Lula said.

My instinct was to leave the building. I didn't know what caused the explosion, but I wanted to get out before it happened again. And I didn't know if the building was structurally sound. I grabbed Lula and got her to her feet and pulled her to the front door. We were walking carefully, crunching over glass shards. Lucky we'd been behind the counter when the explosion occurred. The door had been blown open, and Lula and I picked our way through the debris, onto the sidewalk.

Kan Klean was in a mixed neighborhood of small businesses and small homes, and people were coming out of their houses, looking around for the source of the explosion.

"What the heck was that?" Lula said. "And why's there a tire in the middle of the sidewalk?"

I looked at Lula and Lula looked at me, and we knew why there was a tire in the middle of the sidewalk.

"Car bomb," Lula said.

We ran around to the parking lot on the side of the building and stopped short. The Saturn was a blackened skeleton of smoking, twisted metal. Difficult to see details in the dark. Chunks of shredded fiberglass body, upholstered cushion, and odds and ends of car parts were scattered over the lot.

Lula had her flashlight out, playing it across the disaster. She momentarily held the light on a segment of steering wheel. Part of a hand still gripped the wheel. A ragged shred of black cloth was attached to the hand.

"Uh oh," Lula said. "It don't look good for my dry cleaning."

I felt a wave of nausea slide through my stomach. "We should secure this area until the police get here."

Fifteen minutes later, the entire block was cordoned. Yellow police tape stretched everywhere and fire trucks and emergency vehicles were angled between police cars, lights flashing. Banks of portable lights were going up to better see the scene. Macaronis from all parts of the Burg were gathered in a knot to one side of the lot.

Morelli arrived shortly after the first blue-and-white, and he immediately whisked me away, lest I be torn limb from limb by Macaronis. He got the story, and then he stuffed me into his SUV with police escort. Forty-five minutes later, he returned and slid behind the wheel.

"Tell me again how this happened," Morelli said.

"Lula and I were driving by and I saw the light on, so I thought I'd go in and try to get Lula's dry cleaning. Mama Macaroni was alone in the store, she pulled a gun on me, demanded the keys to the Saturn, and left through the back door. Moments later, I heard the explosion."

"Good," Morelli said. "Now tell me what really happened."

"Lula and I broke in through the back door so we could steal her dry cleaning. Mama Macaroni was waiting for us, and the rest of the story is the same."

"Definitely go with the first version," Morelli said.

"Did they find the rest of Mama Macaroni?"

"Most of her. They're still looking through the bushes. Mama Macaroni covered a lot of ground." Morelli turned the key in the ignition. "Do you want to go home with me?"

"Yeah. I'm a little creeped out."

"I was hoping you'd want to go home with me because I'm smart and sexy and fun."

"That, too. And I like your dog."

"That car bomb was meant for you," Morelli said.

"I thought my life would get better if I stopped chasing after bad guys."

"You've made some enemies."

"It's Spiro," I told him.

Morelli stopped for a light and looked at me. "Spiro Stiva? Constantine's kid? Do you know this for sure?"

"No. It's just a gut feeling. The notes sound like him. And he was friends with Anthony Barroni. And now Barroni's dad is missing, and people say Anthony is spending money he shouldn't have."

"So you think something's going on with Anthony Barroni and Spiro Stiva?"

"Maybe. And maybe Spiro's whacko and decided I ruined his life and now he's going to end mine."

Morelli thought about it for a moment and shrugged. "It's not much, but it's as good as anything I've got. How do the other two disappearances fit in?"

"I don't know, but I think there might be one more." And I told him about Kloughn's client. "And there's something else. Kloughn's client's husband disappeared in their brand-new car. Michael Barroni also disappeared in a brand-new car."

Morelli slid a sideways look at me.

"Okay, so I know lots of people have new cars. Still, it's something they had in common."

"Barroni, Gorman, and Lazar were the same age within two years, and they all owned small businesses. Does Kloughn's client fit that profile?"

"I don't know."

Morelli turned a corner, drove two blocks, and parked in front of his house. "You'd think someone would have seen Spiro if he was back. The Burg's not good at keeping a secret."

"Maybe he's hiding."

My mother called on my cell phone. "People are saying you blew up Mama Macaroni."

"She was in my car, and she accidentally blew herself up. *I* did not blow her up."

"How can someone accidentally blow herself up? Are you okay?"

"I'm fine. I'm going home with Joe."

IT WAS EARLY morning, and I was sitting on the side of the bed, watching Morelli get dressed. He was wearing black jeans, cool black shoes with a thick Vibram sole, and a long-sleeved blue button-down shirt. He looked like a movie star playing an Italian cop.

"Very sexy," I said to Morelli.

He strapped his watch on and looked over at me. "Say it again and the clothes come off."

"You'll be late."

Morelli's eyes darkened, and I knew he was weighing pleasure against responsibility. There was a time in Morelli's life when pleasure would have won, no contest. I'd been attracted to that Morelli, but I hadn't especially liked him. The moment passed and Morelli's eyes regained focus. The guy part was under control. Not to give him more credit than he deserved, I suspected this was made possible by the two orgasms he'd had last night and the one he'd had about a half hour ago.

"I can't be late today. I have an early meeting, and I'm way behind on my paperwork." He kissed the top of my head. "Will you be here when I come home tonight?"

"No. I'm working the three-to-eleven shift at Cluck-in-a-Bucket."

"You're kidding."

"It was one of those impulse things."

Morelli grinned down at me. "You must need money real bad."

"Bad enough."

I followed him down the stairs and closed the door after him. "Just you and me," I said to Bob.

Bob had already eaten his breakfast and gone for a walk, so Bob was feeling mellow. He wandered away, into the living room where bars of sunshine were slanting through the window onto the carpet. Bob turned three times and flopped down onto the sun spot.

I shuffled out to the kitchen, got a mug of coffee, and took it upstairs to Morelli's office. The room was small and cluttered with boxes of income tax files, a red plastic milk carton filled with old tennis balls collected during dog walks in the park, a baseball bat, a stack of phone books, gloves and wraps for a speed bag, a giant blue denim dog bed, a well-oiled baseball glove, a power screwdriver, roles of duct tape, a dead plant in a clay pot, and a plastic watering can that had obviously never been used. He had a computer and a desktop printer on a big wood desk that had been bought used. And he had a phone.

I sat at the desk, and I took a pen and a yellow legal pad from the top drawer. I had the morning free, and I was going to use it to do some sleuthing. Someone wanted me dead, and I didn't feel comfortable sitting around doing nothing, waiting for it to happen.

First on my list was a call to Kloughn.

"She wouldn't let me in the house," he said. "I had to sleep here in the office. It wasn't so bad since I have a couch, and the Laundromat is next door. I got up early and did some laundry. What should I do? Should I call? Should I go over there? I had this terrible nightmare last night. Valerie was floating over top of me in the wedding gown except she was a whale. I bet it was because she kept saying how she was a whale in the wedding gown. Anyway, there she was in my dream . . . a big huge whale all dressed up in the white wedding gown. And then all of a sudden she dropped out of the sky, and I was squashed under her, and I couldn't breathe. Good thing I woke up, hunh?"

"Good thing. I need to know your client's name," I told him. "The one with the missing husband."

"Terry Runion. Her husband's name is Jimmy Runion."

"Do you know what kind of car he just bought?"

"Ford Taurus. He got it at that big dealership on Route One. Shiller Ford."

"His age?"

"I don't know his exact age, but his wife looks like she's late fifties."

"What about his job? Did he quit his job when he disappeared?"

"He didn't have a job. He used to work for some computer company, but he took early retirement. About Valerie . . ."

"I'll talk to Valerie for you," I said. And I hung up.

Valerie answered on the second ring. "Yuh," she said.

"I just talked to Albert. He said he slept in his office."

"He said I was fat."

"He said you were chubby."

"Do you think I'm chubby?" Val asked.

"No," I told her. "I think you're fat."

"Oh God," Valerie wailed. "*Oh God!* How did this happen? How did I get *fat*?"

"You ate everything. And you ate it with gravy."

"I did it for the baby."

"Well, something went wrong because only seven pounds went to the baby, and you got the rest."

"I don't know how to get rid of it. I've never been fat before."

"You should talk to Lula. She's good at losing weight."

"If she's so good at losing weight, why is she so big?"

"She's also good at *gaining* weight. She gains it. She loses it. She gains it. She loses it."

"The wedding is on Saturday. If I really worked at it, do you think I could lose sixty pounds between now and Saturday?"

"I guess you could have it sucked out, but I hear that's real painful and you get a lot of bruising."

"I hate my life," Val said.

"Really?"

"No. I just hate being fat."

"That doesn't mean you should hate Albert. He didn't make you fat."

"I know. I've been awful to him, and he's such an adorable oogie woogams."

"I think it's great that you're in love, Val. And I'm happy for you . . . I really am. But the baby talk cuddle umpkins oogie woogams thing is making me a little barfy warfy. What about the Virgin Mary, Val? Remember when everyone said you were just like the Virgin Mary? You were cool and serene like the Virgin Mary, like a big pink plaster statue of the Virgin. Would the Virgin refer to God as her cuddle umpkins? I don't think so."

The next call was to my cousin Linda at the DMV. "I need some information," I said to Linda. "Benny Gorman, Michael Barroni, Louis Lazar. I want to know if they got a new car in the last three months and what kind?"

"I heard you quit working for Vinnie. So what's up with the names?"

"Part-time job. Routine credit check for CBNJ." I had no idea what CBNJ stood for, but it sounded good, right?

I could hear Linda type the names into her computer. "Here's Barroni," she said. "He bought a Honda Accord two weeks ago. Nothing on Gorman. And nothing's coming up on Lazar."

"Thanks. I appreciate it."

"Boy, the wedding's almost here. I guess everyone's real excited."

"Yeah. Valerie's a wreck."

"That's the way it is with weddings," Linda said.

I disconnected and took a moment to enjoy my coffee. I liked sitting in Morelli's office. It wasn't especially pretty, but it felt nice because it was filled with all the bits and pieces of Morelli's life. I didn't have an office in my apartment. And maybe that was a good thing because I was afraid if I had an office it might be empty. I didn't have a hobby. I didn't play sports. I had a family, but I never got around to framing pictures. I wasn't learning a foreign language, or learning to play the cello, or learning to be a gourmet cook.

Well hell, I thought. I could just pick one of those things. There's no reason why I can't be interesting and have an office filled with stuff. I can collect tennis balls in the park. And I can get a plant and let it die. And I can play the damn cello. In fact, I could probably be a terrific cello player.

I took my coffee mug downstairs and put it in the dishwasher. I grabbed my bag and my jacket. I yelled good-bye to Bob as I was going out the door. And I set off on foot for my parents' house. I was going to borrow Uncle Sandor's Buick. Again. I had no other option. I needed a car. Good thing it was a long walk to my parents' house and I was getting all this exercise because I was going to need a doughnut after taking possession of the Buick.

Grandma was at the door when I strolled down the

street. "It's Stephanie!" Grandma yelled to my mother.

Grandma loved when I blew up cars. Blowing up Mama Macaroni would be icing on the cake for Grandma. My mother didn't share Grandma's enthusiasm for death and disaster. My mother longed for normalcy. Dollars to doughnuts, my mother was in the kitchen ironing. Some people popped pills when things turned sour. Some hit the bottle. My mother's drug of choice was ironing. My mother ironed away life's frustrations.

Grandma opened the door for me, and I stepped into the house and dropped my bag on the hall table.

"Is she ironing?" I asked Grandma Mazur.

"Yep," Grandma said. "She's been ironing since first thing this morning. Probably would have started last night but she couldn't get off the phone. I swear, half the Burg called about you last night. Finally we disconnected the phone."

I went to the kitchen and poured myself a cup of coffee. I sat down at the little kitchen table and looked over at my mother's ironing basket. It was empty. "How many times have you ironed that shirt you've got on the board?" I asked my mother.

"Seven times," my mother said.

"Usually you calm down by the time the basket's empty."

"Somebody blew up Mama Macaroni," my mother said. "That doesn't bother me. She had it coming. What bothers me is that it was supposed to be you. It was your car."

"I'm being careful. And it's not certain that it was a bomb. It could have been an accident. You know how it is with my cars. They catch on fire, and they explode."

My mother made a strangled sound in her throat, and her eyes sort of glazed over. "That's true," she said. "Hideously true."

"Marilyn Rugach said Stiva's got most of Mama Macaroni at the funeral parlor," Grandma said. "Marilyn works there part-time doing bookkeeping. I talked to Marilyn this morning, and she said they brought the deceased to the home in a zippered bag. She said there was still some parts missing, but she wouldn't say if they found the mole. Do you think there's any chance that they'll have an open casket at the viewing? Stiva's pretty good at patching people up, and I sure would like to see what he'd do with that mole."

My mother made the sign of the cross, a hysterical giggle gurgled out of her, and she clapped a hand over her mouth.

"You should give up on the ironing and have a snort," Grandma said to my mother.

"I don't need a snort," my mother said. "I need some sanity in my life."

"You got a lot of sanity," Grandma said. "You got a real stable lifestyle. You got this house and you got a husband . . . sort of. And you got daughters and granddaughters. And you got the Church."

"I have a daughter who blows things up. Cars, trucks, funeral parlors, people."

"That only happens once in a while," I said. "I do lots of other things besides that."

My mother and grandmother looked at me. I had their full attention. They wanted to know what other things I did besides blowing up cars and trucks and funeral parlors and people.

I searched my mind and came up with nothing. I did a mental replay of yesterday. What did I do? I blew up a car and an old lady. Not personally but I was somewhere in the mix. What else? I made love to Morelli. A lot. My mother wouldn't want to hear about that. I got fired. I shot a guy in the foot. She wouldn't want to hear that either.

"I can play the cello," I said. I don't know where it came from. It just flew out of my mouth.

My mother and grandmother stood frozen in open-mouthed shock.

"Don't that beat all," Grandma finally said. "Who would have thought you could play the cello?"

"I had no idea," my mother said. "You never mentioned it before. Why didn't you tell us?"

"I was . . . shy. It's one of those personal hobbies. Personal cello playing."

"I bet you're real good," Grandma said.

My mother and grandmother looked at me expectantly. They wanted me to be good.

"Yep," I said. "I'm pretty good."

Stephanie, Stephanie, Stephanie, I said to myself. What are you doing? You are such a goofus. You don't even know what a cello looks like. Sure I do, I answered. It's a big violin, right?

"How long have you been taking lessons?" Grandma wanted to know.

"A while." I looked at my watch. "Gee, I'd like to stay, but I have things to do. I was hoping I could borrow Uncle Sandor's Buick."

Grandma took a set of keys out of a kitchen drawer. "Big Blue will be happy to see you," she said. "He doesn't get driven around too much."

Big Blue corners like a refrigerator on wheels. It has power brakes but no power steering. It guzzles gas. It's impossible to park. And it's powder blue. It has a shiny white top, powder blue body, silver-rimmed portholes, fat whitewall tires, and big gleaming chrome bumpers.

"I guess you need a big car like Blue so you can carry that cello around with you," Grandma said.

"It's a perfect fit for the backseat," I told her.

I took the keys and waved myself out of the house. I walked to the garage, opened the door, and there it was . . . Big Blue. I could feel the vibes coming off the car. The air hummed around me. Men loved Big Blue. It was a muscle car. It rode on a sweaty mix of high-octane gas and testosterone. Step on the gas and hear me roar, the car whispered. Not the growl of a Porsche. Not the *vroooom* of a Ferrari. This car was a bull walrus. This car had cojones that hung to its hubcaps.

Personally, I prefer cojones that sit a little higher, but hey, that's just me. I climbed aboard, rammed the key in, and cranked Blue over. The car came to life and vibrated under me. I took a deep breath, told myself I'd own a Lexus someday, and slowly backed out of the garage.

Grandma trotted over to the car with a brown grocery bag. "Your mother wants you to drop this off at Valerie's house. Valerie forgot to take it last night."

Valerie was renting a small house at the edge of the Burg, about a half mile away. Until yesterday, she was sharing the house with Albert Kloughn. And since she was back to calling him her oogie woogams, I suppose he was about to return.

I wound through a maze of streets, brought Big Blue to the curb in front of Val's house, and stared at the car parked in front of me. It was Lula's red Firebird. Two possibilities. One was that Valerie had skipped out on a bond. The other was that she'd taken my smart-mouth advice and called Lula for diet tips. I rolled out of the Buick and got on with the brown-bag delivery.

Val opened the door before I reached the porch. "Grandma called and said you were on your way."

"Looks like Lula's here. Are you FTA?"

"No. I'm F-A-T. So I called Lula like you suggested. And she came right over."

"I take other people's dieting seriously," Lula said to Valerie. "I'm gonna have you skinny in no time. This might even turn out to be a second career for me. Of course, now that I'm a bounty hunter I've got a lot of demands on my time. I've got a real nasty case that I'm working on. I should be out tracking this guy down right now, only I figured I could take a break from it and help you out."

"What kind of case is it?" Val asked.

"He's wanted for AR and PT," Lula said. "That's bounty hunter shorthand for armed robbery and public tinkling. He held up a liquor store and then took a leak in the domestic table wines section. I bet Stephanie here is gonna be so happy I'm helping you that she's gonna ride along and help out with the apprehension."

"Not likely," I said. "I have to be at work at three."

"Yeah, but at the rate you're going, you'll be fired by

five," Lula said. "I just hope you last through dinner-time, because I was planning on coming in for a bucket of extra crispy."

"Is that on *my* diet?" Val asked.

"Hell no," Lula said. "Ain't nothing on your diet. You want to lose weight, you gotta starve. You gotta eat a bunch of plain-ass carrots and shit."

"What about that no-carb diet? I hear you can eat bacon and steak and lobster."

"You didn't tell me what kind of diet you wanted to do. I just figured you wanted the starvation diet on account of it's the easiest and the most economical. You don't have to weigh anything. And you don't have to cook anything. You just don't eat anything." Lula motored off to the kitchen. "Let's check out your cupboards and see if you got *good* food or *bad* food." Lula poked around. "Uh oh, this don't look like skinny food. You got chips in here. Boy, I sure would like some of these chips. I'm not gonna eat them, though, 'cause I got willpower."

"Me, too," Valerie said. "I'm not going to eat them either."

"I bet you eat them when we leave," Lula said.

Valerie bit into her lower lip. Of course she'd eat them. She was human, wasn't she? And this was Jersey. And the *Burg,* for crissake. We ate chips in the Burg. We ate *everything*.

"Maybe I should take those chips," Lula said. "It would be okay if *I* ate the chips later being that *I'm* currently not in my weight-losing mode. I'm currently in my weight-*gaining* mode."

Valerie pulled all the bags of chips out of the cupboard and dumped them into a big black plastic garbage bag. She threw boxes of cookies and bags of candy into the bag. She added the junk-sugar-loaded cereals, the toaster waffles, the salted nuts. She handed the bag over to Lula. "And I'm only going to eat one pork chop tonight. And I'm not going to smother it in gravy."

"Good for you," Lula said. "You're gonna be skinny in no time with an attitude like that."

Valerie turned to me. "Grandma was all excited when she called. She said they just found out you've been playing the cello all these years."

Lula's eyes bugged out. "Are you shitting me? I didn't know you played a musical instrument. And the cello! That's real fancy-pants. That's fuckin' classy. How come you never said anything?"

Small tendrils of panic curled through my stomach. This was getting out of control. "It's no big thing," I said. "I'm not very good. And I hardly ever play. In fact, I can't remember the last time I celloed."

"I don't ever remember seeing a cello in your apartment," Valerie said.

"I keep it in the closet," I told her. *I was such a good fibber!* It had been my one real usable talent as a bounty hunter. I made a show of checking my watch. "Boy, look at the time. I have to go."

"Me, too," Lula said. "I gotta go get that stupid AR." She wrapped her arms around the bag of junk food and lugged it out to her car. "It would be like old times if you rode with me on this one," Lula said to me. "It wouldn't take us long to round up Mr. Pisser, and then we could eat all this shit."

"I have to go home and take a shower and get dressed for work. And I have to feed Rex. And I don't want to do bond enforcement anymore."

"Okay," Lula said. "I guess I could understand all that."

Lula roared off in her Firebird. And I slowly accelerated in the Buick. The Buick was like a freight train. Takes a while to get a full head of steam, but once it gets going it'll plow through anything.

I stopped at Giovichinni's Meat Market on the way home. I idled in front of the store and looked through the large front window. Bonnie Sue Giovichinni was working the register. I dialed Bonnie Sue and asked her if there were any Macaronis in the store.

"Nope," Bonnie Sue said. "The coast is clear."

I scurried around, gathering the bare essentials. A loaf of bread, some sliced provolone, a half pound of sliced ham, a small tub of chocolate ice cream, a quart of skim milk, and a handful of fresh green beans for Rex. I added a couple Tastykakes to my basket and lined up behind Mrs. Krepler at the checkout.

"I just talked to Ruby Beck," Mrs. Krepler said. "Ruby tells me you've left the bonds office so you can play cello with a symphony orchestra. How exciting!"

I was speechless.

"And have you heard if they found the mole yet?" Mrs. Krepler asked.

I paid for my groceries and hurried out of the store. The cello-playing thing was going through the Burg like wildfire. You'd think with something as good as Mama Macaroni getting blown to bits there wouldn't be time to care about my cello playing. I swear, I can't catch a break here.

I drove home and docked the boat in a spot close to the back door. I figured the closer to the door, the less chance of a bomb getting planted. I wasn't sure the theory held water, but it made me feel better. I took the stairs and opened the door to my apartment cautiously. I stuck my head in and listened. Just the sound of Rex running on his wheel in his cage in the kitchen. I locked and bolted the door behind me and retrieved my gun from the cookie jar. The gun wasn't loaded because I'd forgotten to buy bullets, but I crept through the apartment, looking in closets and under the bed with the gun drawn anyway. I couldn't shoot anyone, but at least I looked like I could kick ass.

I took a shower and got dressed in jeans and a T-shirt. I didn't spend a lot of time on my hair since I'd be wearing the dorky Cluck hat. I lined my eyes and slathered on mascara to make up for the hair. I gave Rex a couple beans, and I made myself a ham and cheese sandwich. I glanced at my gun while I ate my sandwich. The gun was loaded. I went to the cookie jar and looked inside. There was a RangeMan business card in the bottom of the jar. A single word was hand-written on the card. BABE!

I had a momentary hot flash and briefly considered checking out my underwear drawer for more business cards. "He's trying to protect me," I said to Rex. "He does that a lot."

I got the tub of ice cream from the freezer and took it to the dining room table, along with a pad. I sat at the table and ate the ice cream and made notes for myself. I had four guys who were all about the same age. They all had a small business at one time or another. Two bought new cars. They all disappeared on the same day at about the same time. None of their cars was ever retrieved. That was all I knew.

My hunch about Anthony and Spiro didn't really amount to much. Probably I was trying to make a connection where none existed. One thing was certain. Someone was stalking me, trying to scare me. And now it looked like that person was trying to kill me. Not a happy thought.

I'd eaten about a third of the tub of ice cream. I put the lid on the tub and walked it back to the freezer. I put all the food away and wiped down the countertop. I wasn't much of a housekeeper, but I didn't want to be killed and have my mother discover my kitchen was a mess.

SEVEN

I LEFT MY apartment at two-ten and gingerly circled the Buick, looking for signs of tampering. I looked in the window. I crouched down and looked under the car. Finally I put the key in the lock, squinched my eyes closed, and opened the door. No explosion. I slid behind the wheel, took a deep breath, and turned the engine over. No explosion. I thought this was good news and bad news. If it had exploded I'd be dead, and that would be bad. On the other hand, I wouldn't have to wear the awful Cluck hat, and that would be very good.

Twenty minutes later, I was standing in front of Milton Mann, receiving instructions.

"We're going to start you off at the register," he said. "It's all computerized so it's super simple. You just punch in the order and the computer sends the order to the crew in the back and tells you how much to charge the customer. You have to be real friendly and polite. And when you give the customer their change you say, 'Thank you for visiting Cluck-in-a-Bucket. Have a

clucky day.' And always remember to wear your hat.
It's our special trademark."

The hat was egg-yolk yellow and rooster-comb red.
It had a bill like a ball cap, except the bill was shaped
like a beak, and the rest of the hat was a huge chicken
head, topped off with the big floppy red comb. Red
chicken legs with red chicken toes hung from either
side of the bottom of the hat. The rest of the uniform
consisted of an egg-yolk yellow short-sleeve shirt and
elastic-waist pants that had the Cluck-in-a-Bucket
chicken logo imprinted everywhere in red. The shirt
and pants looked like pajamas designed for the criminally insane.

"You'll do a two-hour shift at the register and then
we'll rotate you to the chicken fryer," Mann said.

If it was in the cards that the bomber was going to
succeed in killing me, I prayed that it happened before
I got to the chicken fryer.

It turns out the three-to-five shift at the register is
light. Some after-school traffic and some construction
workers.

A woman and her kid stepped up to the counter.

"Tell the chicken what you want," the woman said.

"It's not a chicken," the kid said. "It's a girl in a stupid chicken hat."

"Yes, but she can cluck like a chicken," the woman
said. "Go ahead," she said to me. "Cluck like a chicken
for Emily."

I looked at the woman.

"Last time we were here the chicken clucked," the
woman said.

I looked down at Emily. "Cluck."

"She's no good," Emily said. "The other chicken was *way* better. The other chicken flapped her arms."

I took a deep breath, stuffed my fists under my armpits, and did some chicken-wing flapping. "Cluck, cluck, cluck, cluck, clu-u-u-u-ck," I said.

"I want french fries and a chocolate shake," Emily said.

The next guy in line weighed three hundred pounds and was wearing a torn T-shirt and a hard hat. "You gonna cluck for me?" he asked. "How about I want you to do something besides cluck?"

"How about I shove my foot so far up your ass your nuts get stuck in your throat?"

"Not my idea of a good time," he said. "Get me a bucket of extra crispy and a Diet Coke."

At five o'clock I was marched back to the fryer.

"It's a no-brainer," Mann said. "It's all automated. When the green light goes on the oil is right for frying, so you dump the chicken in."

Mann pulled a huge plastic tub of chicken parts out of the big commercial refrigerator. He took the lid off the tub, and I almost passed out at the site of slick pink muscle and naked flesh and cracked bone.

"As you can see, we have three stainless-steel tanks," Mann said. "One is the fryer and one is the drainer and one is the breader. It's the breader that sets us apart from all the other chicken places. We coat our chicken with the specially seasoned secret breading glop right here in the store." Mann dumped a load of chicken into a wire basket and lowered it into the breader. He swished the basket around, raised it, and gently set it into the hot oil. "When you put the chicken into the oil you push the Start button and the machine times the chicken. When the bell rings you take the chicken out and set the basket in the drainer. Easy, right?"

I could feel sweat prickle at my scalp under my hat. It was about two hundred degrees in front of the fryer, and the air was oil saturated. I could smell the hot oil. I could taste the hot oil. I could feel it soaking into my pores.

"How do I know how much chicken to fry?" I asked him.

"You just keep frying. This is our busy time of day. You go from one basket to the next and keep the hot chicken rolling out."

A half hour later, Eugene was yelling at me from the bagging table. "We need extra-spicy. All you're doing is extra-crispy. And there's all wings here. You gotta give us some backs and some thighs. People are bitchin' about the friggin' wings. If they wanted all wings, they'd order all wings."

At precisely seven o'clock, Mann appeared at my side. "You get a half-hour dinner break now, and then we're going to rotate you to the drive-thru window until closing time at eleven."

My muscles ached from lifting the chicken baskets. My uniform was blotched with grease stains. My hair felt like it had been soaked in oil. My arms were covered with splatter burns. I had thirty minutes to eat, but I didn't think I could gag down fried chicken. I shuffled off to the ladies' room and sat on the toilet with my head down. I think I fell asleep like that because next thing I knew, Mann was knocking on the ladies' room door, calling my name.

I followed Mann to the drive-thru window. The plan was that I remove my Cluck hat, put the headset on, and put the Cluck hat back over the headset. Problem was, after tending the fryer, my hair was slick with grease and the headset kept sliding off.

"Ordinarily I don't put people in the drive-thru after the fryer just for this problem," Mann said, "but Darlene went home sick and you're all I got." He disappeared into the storeroom and came back with a roll of black electrical tape. "Necessity is the mother of invention," he said, holding the headset to my head, wrapping my head with a couple loops of tape. "Now you can put your hat on and get clucky, and that headset isn't going anywhere."

"Welcome to Cluck-in-a-Bucket," I said to the first car.

"I wanna crchhtra skraapyy, two orders of fries, and a large crchhhk."

Mann was standing behind me. "That's extra crispy chicken, two fries, and a large Coke." He gave me a pat on the shoulder. "You'll get the hang of it after a couple cars. Anyway, all you have to do is ring them up, take their money, and give them their order. Fred is in back filling the order." And he left.

"Seven-fifty," I said. "Please drive up."

"What?"

"Seven-fifty. Please drive up."

"Speak English. I can't understand a friggin' thing you're saying."

"*Seven-fifty!*"

The car pulled to the window. I took money from the driver, and I handed him the bag. He looked into the bag and shook his head. "There's only one fries in here."

"Fred," I yelled into my mouthpiece, "you shorted them a fries."

Fred ran over with the fries. "Sorry, sir," he said to the guy in the car. "Have a clucky day."

Fred was a couple inches taller than me and a couple pounds lighter. He had pasty white skin that was splotched with grease burns, pale blue eyes, and red dreads that stuck out from his hat, making him look a little like the straw man in *The Wizard of Oz.* I put him at eighteen or nineteen.

"Cluck you," the guy said to Fred, and drove off.

"Thank you, sir," Fred yelled after him. "Have a nice day. Go cluck yourself." Fred turned to me. "You gotta go faster. We have about forty cars in line. They're getting nasty."

After a half hour I was hoarse from yelling into the microphone. "Seven-twenty," I croaked. "Please drive up."

"What?"

I took a sip of the gallon-size Coke I had next to my register. "Seven-twenty."

"What?"

"Seven fucking twenty."

An SUV pulled up to the window, I reached for the money, and I found myself staring into Spiro Stiva's glittering rat eyes. The lighting was bad, but I could see that his face had obviously been badly burned in the funeral home fire. I stood rooted to the spot, unable to move, unable to speak.

His mouth had become a small slash in the scarred face. The mouth smiled at me, but the smile was tight and joyless. He handed me a ten. His hand shook, and the skin on his hand was mottled and glazed from burn scars.

Fred gave me a bag, and I automatically passed it through to Spiro.

"Keep the change," Spiro said. And he tossed a medium-size box wrapped in Scooby-Doo paper and tied with a red ribbon through the drive-thru window. And he drove away.

The box bounced off the small service counter and landed on the floor between Fred and me. Fred picked the box up and examined it. "There's a gift tag attached. It says 'Time is ticking away.' What's that supposed to mean? Hey, and you know what else? I think this thing is ticking. Do you know that guy?"

"Yeah, I know him." I took the box and turned to throw it out the drive-thru window. No good. Another car had already pulled up.

"What's the deal?" Fred asked.

"I need to take this outside."

"No way. There are a bazillion cars lined up. Mann will have a cow." Fred reached for the box. "Give it to me. I'll put it in the back room for you."

"No! This might be a bomb. I want you to *very quietly* call the police while I take this outside."

"Are you shitting me?"

"Just call the police, okay?"

"Holy crap! You're serious. That guy gave you a bomb?"

"Maybe . . ."

"Put it under water," Fred said. "I saw a show on television and they put the bomb under water."

Fred ripped the box out of my hand and dumped it into the chicken fryer. The boiling oil bubbled up and spilled over the sides of the fryer. The oil slick carried to the grill, there was a sound like *phuunf*, and suddenly the grill was covered in blue flame.

Fred's eyes went wide. "Fire!" he shrieked. He grabbed a super-size cup and scooped water from the rinse sink.

"No!" I yelled. "Get the chemical extinguisher."

Too late. Fred threw the water at the grill fire, a whoosh of steam rose in the air, and fire raced up the wall to the ceiling.

I pushed Fred to the front of the store and went back to make sure no one was left in the kitchen area. Flames were running down the walls and along the counters and the overhead sprinkler system was shooting foam. When I was sure the prep area was empty I left through a side door.

Sirens were screaming in the distance and the flash of emergency-vehicle strobes could be seen blocks away. Black smoke billowed high in the sky and flames licked out windows and doors and climbed up the stucco exterior.

Customers and employees stood in the parking lot, gawking at the spectacle.

"It wasn't my fault," I said to no one in particular.

Carl Costanza was the first cop on the scene. He

locked eyes with me and smiled wide. He said something to Dispatch on his two-way, and I knew Morelli would be getting a call. Fire trucks and EMT trucks roared into the parking lot. More cop cars. The crowd of spectators was growing. They spilled onto the street and clogged the sidewalk. The evening news van pulled up. I moved away from the building to stand by the Buick at the outermost perimeter of the lot. I would have driven home, but the keys were in my bag, and my bag was barbecued.

The flashing strobes and the glare of headlights made it difficult to see into the jumble of parked cars and emergency trucks. Fire hoses snaked across the lot and silhouettes of men moved against the glare. Two men walked toward me, away from the pack. The silhouettes were familiar. Morelli and Ranger. They had a strange alliance. They were two very different men with similar goals. They were teammates of a sort. And they were competitors. They were both smiling when they reached me. I'd like to think it was because they were happy to see me alive. But probably it was because I was my usual wreck. I was grease stained and smoke smudged. I still had the headset taped to my head. I was still wearing the awful chicken hat and Cluck pajamas. And globs of pink foam hung from the hat and clung to my shirt.

They both stood hands on hips when they reached me. They were smiling, but there was a grim set to their mouths.

Morelli reached over and swiped at the pink gunk on my hat.

"Fire extinguisher foam," I said. "It wasn't my fault."

"Costanza told me the fire was started with a bomb."

"I guess that might be true . . . indirectly. I was working the drive-thru window, and Spiro pulled up. He tossed a gift-wrapped box at me and drove away. The box was ticking, and Fred got all excited and dumped the box in the vat of boiling oil. The oil bubbled over onto the grill and next thing the place was toast."

"Are you sure it was Spiro?"

"Positive. His face and hands are scarred, but I'm sure it was him. The card on the box said 'Time is ticking away.' "

Morelli took a quarter from his pocket and flipped it into the air. "Call it," he said to Ranger.

"Heads."

Morelli caught the quarter and slapped it over. "Heads. You win. I guess I have to clean her up."

"Good luck," Ranger said. And he left.

I was too exhausted to get totally irate, but I managed to muster some half-assed outrage. I glared at Morelli. "I don't believe you tossed for me."

"Cupcake, you should be happy I lost. He would have put you through the car wash at the corner of Hamilton and Market." He took my hand and tugged me forward. "Let's go home."

"Will Big Blue be safe here?"

"Big Blue is safe *everywhere*. That car is indestructible."

MORELLI WAS IN the shower with me. "Okay," he said. "There's some bad news, and then there's some bad news. The bad news is that it would seem some clumps of hair got yanked out of your head when we ripped the electrician's tape off. The other bad news is that you still smell like fried chicken, and it's making me hungry. Why don't we towel you off and send out for food?"

I put my hand to my hair. "How bad is it?"

"Hard to tell with all that oil in it. It's sort of clumping together."

"I shampooed three times!"

"I don't think shampoo is going to cut it. Maybe you need something stronger . . . like paint stripper."

I grabbed a towel, stepped out of the shower, and looked at myself in the mirror over the sink. He was right. Shampoo wasn't working, and I had bald spots at the side of my head where the tape had been bound to me.

"I'm not going to cry," I said to him.

"Thank God. I hate when you cry. It makes me feel really shitty."

A tear slid down my cheek.

"Oh crap," Morelli said.

I wiped my nose with the back of my hand. "It's been a long day."

"We'll figure this out tomorrow," Morelli said. He took the cap off a tube of aloe ointment and carefully dabbed the ointment on my chicken-fryer burns. "I bet if you go to that guy at the mall, Mr. Whatshisname . . ."

"Mr. Alexander."

"Yeah, he's the one. I bet he'll be able to fix your hair." Morelli recapped the tube and reached for his cell phone. "I'm calling Pino. What do you want to eat?"

"Anything but chicken."

◆ ◆ ◆

I WOKE UP thinking Morelli was licking me, but it turned out to be Bob. My face was wet with Bob slurpies, and he was gnawing on my hair. I made a sound that was halfway between laughing and crying, and Morelli opened an eye and batted Bob away.

"It's not his fault," Morelli said. "You still smell like fried chicken."

"Great."

"Could be worse," Morelli said. "You could still smell like cooked car."

I rolled out of bed and shuffled into the bathroom. I soaped myself in the shower until there was no more hot water. I got out and sniffed at my arm. Fried chicken. I returned to the bedroom and checked out the bed. Empty. Large grease stain on my pillowcase. I borrowed some sweats from Morelli's closet and followed the coffee smell to the kitchen.

Bob was sprawled on the floor next to his empty food bowl. Morelli was at the table, reading the paper.

I poured out a mug of coffee and sat across from Morelli. "I'm not going to cry."

"Yeah, I've heard that before," Morelli said. He put the paper aside and slid a bakery bag over to me. "Bob and I went to the bakery while you were in the shower. We thought you might need happy food."

I looked inside the bag. Two Boston cream doughnuts. "That's so nice of you," I said. And I burst into tears.

Morelli looked pained.

"My emotions are a little close to the surface," I told

him. I blew my nose in a paper napkin and took a doughnut. "Any word on the fire?"

"Yeah. First, some good news. Cluck-in-a-Bucket is closed indefinitely, so you don't have to go back to work there. Second, some mixed news. Big Blue is parked at the curb in front of my house. I'm assuming this is Ranger's handiwork. Unfortunately, unless you have an extra key you're not going to be driving it until you get a locksmith out here. And now for the interesting stuff. They were able to retrieve the gift box from the chicken fryer."

I pulled the second doughnut out of the bag. "And?"

"It was a clock. No evidence that it was a bomb."

"Is that for sure?"

"That's what the lab guys said. I also got a report back on the car bomb. It was detonated from an outside source."

"What does that mean?"

"It means it didn't go off when Mama Macaroni stepped on the gas or turned the key in the ignition. Someone pushed the button on Mama Macaroni when they saw her get into the car. We'll assume it was Spiro since he gave you the box. Hard to believe he'd mistake Mama Macaroni for you, so I have to think he blew her away for giggles."

"Yikes."

Bob lumbered over and sniffed at the empty doughnut bag. Morelli crumpled the bag and threw it across the room, and Bob bounded after it and tore it to shreds.

"I'm guessing Spiro was waiting for you and when Mama Macaroni showed up he couldn't resist blowing her to smithereens. Hell, I'm not sure *I* could resist."

Morelli took a sip of my coffee. "Anyway, it looks like he isn't trying to kill you . . . yet."

I drank a second cup of coffee. I called Mr. Alexander and made an appointment for eleven o'clock. I stood to leave and realized I had nothing. No key to the Buick. No key to my apartment. No credit cards. No money. No shoes. No underwear. We'd thrown all my clothes, including my shoes, into the trash last night.

"Help," I said to Morelli.

Morelli smiled at me. "Barefoot and desperate. Just the way I like you."

"Unless you also like me with a greasy head you'd better find a way to get me dressed and out to the mall."

"No problemo. I have a key to your apartment. And I have the day off. I'm ready to roll anytime you are."

"HOW DID THIS happen?" Mr. Alexander asked, studying my hair. "No. On second thought, don't tell me. I'm sure it's something awful. It's *always awful*!" He leaned over me and sniffed. "Have you been eating fried chicken?"

Morelli was slouched in a chair, hiding behind a copy of *GQ*. He was armed, he was hungry, and he was hoping for a nooner. From time to time, women walked in and checked Morelli out, starting with the hip work boots, going to the long legs in professionally faded jeans, pausing at the nicely packaged goods. He didn't have a ring on his left hand. He didn't have a diamond stud in his ear. He didn't look civilized enough to be gay. He also didn't return the interest. If he looked beyond the magazine it was to assess the progress Mr.

Alexander was making. If he locked eyes with an ogling woman his message wasn't friendly and the woman hurried on her way. I suspected the unfriendly disinterest was more a reflection of Morelli's impatience than of his single-minded love for me.

"I'm done!" Mr. Alexander said, whipping the cape off me. "This is the best I can do to cover up the bald spots. And we've gotten all the oil out." He looked over at Morelli. "Do you want me to tame the barbarian?"

"Hey, Joe," I yelled to him. "Do you need a haircut?"

Morelli *always* needed a haircut. Ten minutes after he got a haircut he still needed a haircut.

"I just got a haircut," Morelli said, getting to his feet.

"It would look wonderful if we took a smidgeon more off the sides," Mr. Alexander said to Morelli. "And we could put the tiniest bit of gel in the top."

Morelli stood hands on hips, his jacket flared, his gun obvious on his hip.

"But then maybe not," Mr. Alexander said. "Maybe it's perfect just as it is."

Morelli's cell phone rang. He answered the phone and passed it over to me. "Your mother."

"I've been calling and calling you," my mother said. "Why don't you answer your cell phone?"

"My phone was in my bag and my bag was in Cluck-in-a-Bucket when it burned down."

"Omigod, it's true! People have been calling night and day, and I thought they were joking. Since when do you work at Cluck-in-a-Bucket?"

"Actually, I don't work there anymore."

"Where are you? You're with Joseph. Are you in jail?"

"No. I'm at the mall."

"Four days to your sister's wedding and you're burning down the Burg. You have to stop exploding things and burning things. I need help. Someone has to check on the cake. Someone has to pick up the decorations for the cars. And the flowers for the church."

"Albert is in charge of the flowers."

"Have you seen Albert lately? Albert is drinking. Albert is locked away in his office having conversations with Walter Cronkite."

"I'll talk to him."

"No! No talking. It's better he's drunk. If he gets sober he might back out. And leave him in the office. The less time spent with Valerie the more likely he is to marry her."

I could see Morelli losing patience. He wasn't much of a mall person. He was more a bedroom and bar and playing-football-in-the-park person.

My grandmother was yelling in the background. "I gotta go to a viewing tonight. Stiva's laying out Mama Mac. I need a ride."

"Are you insane?" my mother said to my grandmother. "The place will be filled with Macaronis. They'll tear you to pieces."

MORELLI PARKED THE SUV in front of my parents' house and looked over at me. "Don't get any ideas about your powers of persuasion. I'm only doing this for the meatloaf."

"And later you're going to play detective with me."

"Maybe."

"You promised."

"The promise doesn't count. We were in bed. I would have promised *anything*."

"Spiro's going to make an appearance, one way or another. I know it. He's going to have to see his handiwork. He's going to want to be part of the process."

"He won't see any of his handiwork tonight. The lid will be nailed down. I know Stiva's good, but trust me, all the king's horses and all the king's men couldn't put Mama Macaroni together again."

Morelli and I got out of the SUV and watched a car creep down the street toward us. It was a blue Honda Civic. It was Kloughn's car. Kloughn hit the curb and eased one tire over before coming to a complete stop. He looked through the windshield at us and waved with just the tips of his fingers.

"Snockered," I said to Morelli.

"I should arrest him," Morelli said.

"You can't arrest him. He's Valerie's cuddle umpkins."

Morelli closed the distance, opened the door for Kloughn, and Kloughn fell out of the car. Morelli dragged Kloughn to his feet and propped him against the Civic.

"You shouldn't be driving," Morelli said to Kloughn.

"I know," Kloughn said. "I tried walking, but I was too drunk. It's okay. I was driving very slooooowly and 'sponsibly."

Kloughn started to sink to the ground, and Morelli grabbed him by the back of his coat. "What do you want me to do with him?" Morelli asked.

Here's the thing. I like Albert Kloughn. I wouldn't marry him. And I wouldn't hire him to defend me if I was accused of murder. I might not even trust him to baby-sit Rex. Kloughn sort of falls into the Bob Dog category. Kloughn inspires maternal pet instincts in me.

"Bring him inside," I told Morelli. "We'll put him to bed and let him sleep it off."

Morelli carted Kloughn into the house and up the stairs with Grandma trotting behind.

"Put him in the third bedroom," Grandma said to Morelli. "And then let's get to the table. Dinner's almost ready, and I don't want to get a late start on the meatloaf. I gotta get to the viewing."

"Over my dead body," my mother yelled from the bottom of the stairs.

My father was already at the table. He had his fork in his hand, and he was watching the kitchen door, as if the food would come marching out to him without my mother's help.

A car pulled up outside. Car doors opened and slammed shut, and then there was chaos. Valerie, Angie, The Baby, and the horse were in the house, and the house suddenly got very small.

Grandma bustled down the stairs and took the diaper bag off Valerie's shoulder. "Everybody sit," Grandma said. "The meatloaf's done. We got meatloaf and gravy and mashed potatoes. And we got pineapple upside-down cake for dessert. And we put lots of whipped cream on the cake." Grandma eyed Mary Alice. "And only horses who sit at the table and eat their vegetables and meatloaf are gonna get any of the whipped cream and cake."

"Where's my oogie woogie bear?" Valerie wanted to know. "I saw his car on the curb."

"He's upstairs drunk as a skunk," Grandma said. "I just hope his liver don't explode before we get you married off. You should make sure he's got life insurance."

My mother brought the meatloaf and green beans to the table. Grandma brought the red cabbage and a bowl of mashed potatoes. I pushed my chair back and went to the kitchen to fetch the gravy and get milk for the girls.

Dinner at my parents' house is survival of the fastest. We all sit down at the table. We all put napkins on our laps. And that's where the civility ends and the action heats up. Food is passed, shoveled onto plates, and consumed at warp speed. To date, no one has been stabbed with a fork for taking the last dinner roll, but that's only because we all understand the rules. Get there first and fast. So we were all a little stunned when Valerie put five green beans on her big empty plate and angrily stabbed them with her fork. *Thunk, thunk, thunk.*

"What's with you?" Grandma said to Valerie.

"I'm on a diet. All I get to eat are these beans. Five boring hideous beans." The grip on her fork was white-knuckled, her lips were pressed tightly together, and her eyes glittered feverishly as she took in Joe's plate directly across from her. Joe had a mountain of creamy mashed potatoes and four thick slabs of meatloaf, all drenched in gravy.

"Maybe this isn't a good time to be on a diet, what with all the stress over the wedding and all," Grandma said.

"It's *because* of the wedding that I have to diet," Valerie said, teeth clenched.

Mary Alice forked up a piece of meatloaf. "Mommy's a blimp."

Valerie made a growling sound that had me worrying her head was going to start doing full rotations on her neck.

"Maybe I should check on Albert," Morelli said to me.

I narrowed my eyes and looked at him sideways. "You're going to sneak out, aren't you?"

"No way. Honest to God." He blew out a sigh. "Okay, yeah, I was going to sneak out."

"I had a good idea today," Grandma said, ignoring the possibility that Valerie might be possessed. "I thought it would be special if we could have Stephanie play the cello at Valerie's wedding. She could play it at the church while the people are coming in. Myra Sklar had a guitar player at her wedding, and it worked out real good."

My mother's face brightened. "That's a wonderful idea!"

Morelli turned to me. "You play the cello?"

"You bet she does," Grandma said. "She's good, too."

"No, really, I'm not that good. And I don't think it would work if I played at the church. I'm in the wedding party. I have to be with Valerie."

Valerie was momentarily distracted from her green-bean stabbing. "It would just be while the people are walking in," Valerie said. "And then you can put the cello aside and take your place in line."

Morelli was smiling. He knew I didn't play the cello. "I think you should do it," Morelli said. "You wouldn't want all those years of cello lessons to go to waste, would you?"

I shot him a warning look. "You are *so toast*."

EIGHT

"THIS IS GOING to be a humdinger of a wedding," Grandma said, returning her attention to her meatloaf and potatoes. "And it's going to be smooth sailing because we got a wedding planner."

Morelli and I exchanged glances. The Kloughn wedding was going to be a disaster of epic proportions.

We heard some scuffling and mumbling from the second floor. There was a moment of silence. And then Kloughn rolled down the stairs and landed at the bottom with a good solid thud. We all pushed back from the table and went to assess the damage.

Kloughn was spread-eagled on his back. His face was white and his eyes were wide. "I had the nightmare again," he said to me. "The one I told you about. It was awful. I couldn't breathe. I was suffocating. Every time I go to sleep I get the nightmare."

"What nightmare is he talking about?" Valerie wanted to know.

I didn't want to tell Valerie about the whale. It

wasn't the sort of recurring dream a bride could get all gushy about. Especially since Val had almost gone into cardiac arrest when Mary Alice had called her a blimp. "It's a nightmare about an elevator," I said. "He's in this elevator, and all the air gets sucked out, and he can't breathe."

"All that white," Kloughn said, sweat popping out on his forehead. "It was all I could see. I could only see white. And then I couldn't breathe."

"It was a white elevator," I said to Valerie. "You know how dreams can get weird, right?"

Morelli had Kloughn on his feet, holding him up by the back of his jacket again. "Now what?" Morelli said. "Where do you want him this time?"

"We should lock him up someplace safe where he can't get away," Grandma said. "Someplace like jail. Maybe you should bust him."

"What's in his jacket pocket?" Valerie asked, patting the pocket. "It's a candy bar!" She ran her fingers over it. "It feels like a Snickers."

Some people can read Braille . . . my sister can feel up a candy bar in a pocket and identify it.

"I need that candy bar," Valerie said.

"It wouldn't be good for your diet," I told her.

"Yeah," Grandma said. "Go eat another green bean."

"I *need* that candy bar," Valerie said, eyes narrowed. "I *really need* it."

Kloughn pulled the candy bar out of his pocket, the candy bar slipped through his fingers, flew through the air, and bounced off Valerie's forehead.

Valerie blinked twice and burst into tears. "You hit me," she wailed.

"You're a nutso bride," Grandma said, retrieving the candy bar, tucking it into the zippered pocket of her warm-up suit jacket. "You're imagining things. Just look at Snoogie Boogie here. Does he look like he could hit someone? He don't know the time of day."

"I don't feel so good," Kloughn said. "I want to lie down."

"Put him on the couch," my mother said to Morelli. "He'll be safer there. He's lucky he didn't break his neck when he fell down the stairs."

We went back to the table and everybody dug in again.

"Maybe I don't want to get married," Valerie said.

"Of course you want to get married," Grandma told her. "How could you pass up Snogle Wogle out there? It'll be his job to take the garbage out on garbage day. And he'll get the oil changed in the car. You want to do those things all by yourself? And after we get you married off we gotta work on Stephanie." Grandma fixed an eye on Morelli. "How come you don't marry her?"

"Not my fault," Morelli said. "She won't marry *me*."

"Of course it's your fault," Grandma said. "You must be doing something wrong, if you know what I mean. Maybe you need to buy a book that tells you how to do it. I hear there are books out there with pictures and everything. I saw one in the store the other day. It was called *A Sex Guide for Dummies*."

Morelli paused with a chunk of meatloaf halfway to his mouth. No one had ever questioned his expertise in the sack before. His sexual history was legend in the Burg.

My sister gave a bark of laughter and quickly

clapped a hand over her mouth. My mother went pale. And my father kept his head down, not wanting to lose the fork-to-mouth rhythm he had going.

Morelli sat frozen in his seat for a long moment and then obviously decided no answer was the way to go. He gave me a small tight smile and got on with his meal. Things quieted down after that until Grandma started checking her watch halfway through dessert.

"No," my mother said to her. "Don't even think it."

"Think what?" Grandma asked.

"You know what. You're not going to the viewing. It would be in terrible taste. The Macaronis have suffered enough without us adding to their grief."

"The Macaronis are probably dancing in their socks," Grandma said. "Susan Mifflin saw them eating at Artie's Seafood House the day after the accident. She said they were going at the all-you-can-eat crab legs like it was a party."

When the only thing left of the pineapple upside-down cake was a smudge of whipped cream on the cake plate, I helped my mother clear the table. I promised I'd get the decorations for the cars. And I made a mental note that in the future I would avoid weddings, mine or anyone else's. And while I was making my never-again list, I might add never have another dinner at my parents' house . . . although it was pretty funny when Grandma suggested Morelli get a *Dummies'* guide to good sex.

Ten minutes later, Morelli and I were parked on Hamilton, across from the funeral home.

"Tell me again why we're doing this," Morelli said.

"The bad guy always returns to the scene of the crime. Everybody knows that."

"This isn't the scene of the crime."

"Work with me here, okay? It's close enough. Spiro seems like the kind of guy who would hate to be left out. I think he'd want to watch the spectacle."

We sat for a couple minutes in silence and Morelli turned to me. "You're smiling," Morelli said. "It's making me uneasy. Anyone in their right mind wouldn't be smiling after that dinner."

"I thought there were some good moments."

Morelli was dividing his attention between the people arriving for the viewing and me. "Like when your grandmother suggested I get a book?"

"That was the *best* moment."

It was deep twilight. Light pooled on the sidewalk and road from overhead halogens, and Stiva's front porch was glowing. Stiva didn't want the old folks falling down the stairs after visiting with the deceased.

Morelli reached out to me in the darkened car. His fingertips traced along my hairline. "Do you want to throw out a comment here? Was your grandmother right? Is that why we're not married?"

"You're fishing for compliments."

That got Morelli smiling. "Busted."

Someone rapped on the driver's-side window, and we both flinched. Morelli rolled the window down a crack, and Grandma squinted in at us.

"I thought I recognized the car," Grandma said.

"What are you doing here?" I asked Grandma. "I thought it was settled that you'd stay away."

"I know your mother means well, but sometimes she can be a real pain in the patoot. This viewing will be the talk of the town. How can I go to the beauty parlor tomorrow if I don't know anything about the viewing? What will I say to people? I got a reputation to uphold. People expect me to know the dirt. So I sneaked out when your mother went to the bathroom. I was lucky to be able to hitch a ride with Mabel from next door."

"We can't let Grandma go to that viewing," I said to Morelli. "She'll be nothing but a grease spot on Stiva's carpet after the Macaronis get done with her."

"You really shouldn't go to the viewing," he said to Grandma. "Why don't you get in the car, and we'll go to a bar and get wasted?"

"Not a bad offer," Grandma said. "But no can do. I can't take a chance on them having the lid up."

"There's no chance they'll have the lid up," Morelli said. "I saw them collecting the pieces, and they're not going to fit together."

Grandma slid her dentures around in her mouth while she weighed her choices. "Don't seem right not to pay my respects," she finally said.

"Here's the deal," Morelli said. "I'll go in and scope things out. If the lid is up I'll come get you. If the lid is down I'll drive you home."

"I guess that sounds reasonable," Grandma said. "I don't want to get torn limb from limb by the Macaronis for no good cause. I'll wait here."

"And ask Constantine if he's seen Spiro," I told Morelli.

Morelli got out, and Grandma took his place behind the wheel. We watched Morelli walk into the funeral home.

"He's a keeper," Grandma said. "He's turned into a real nice young man. And he's nice looking, too. Not as hot as that Ranger but pretty darn close."

Cars rolled past us on Hamilton. People parked in the lot next to Stiva's and made their way to the big front porch. A group of men stood just outside the door. They were smoking and talking and occasionally there'd be a bark of laughter.

"I guess you're unemployed again," Grandma said. "You have any ideas where you'll go next?"

"I hear they're hiring at the sanitary products plant."

"That might work out. That plant is way down Route One and they might not have heard about you yet."

The light changed at the end of the block and cars began moving again. An SUV slid by us going in the opposite direction . . . and Spiro was behind the wheel.

I started climbing over the console. "Get out of the car," I yelled. "I need to follow that SUV."

"No way. I'm not missing out on this. I can catch him," Grandma said. "Buckle your seat belt."

I opened my mouth to say no, but Grandma already had the car in gear. She shot back and rammed the car behind us, knocking him back a couple feet.

"That's better," Grandma said. "Now I got room to get out." She wheeled Morelli's SUV into traffic, stopped short, laid on the horn, and cut into the stream of oncoming cars.

Grandma learned to drive a couple years ago. She immediately racked up points for speeding and lost her license. She wasn't all that good a driver back then, and she wasn't any better now. I tightened my seat belt and started making deals with God. I'll be a better person, I told God. I swear I will. I'll even go to church. Okay, maybe that's not going to happen. I'll go to church on holidays. Just don't let Grandma kill us both.

"I'm coming up on him," Grandma said. "He's just two cars ahead of us."

"Keep the two cars between us," I told her. "I don't want him to see us."

The light changed at the corner. Spiro went through on the yellow, and we were stopped behind the two cars. Grandma yanked the wheel to the right, jumped the curb, and drove on the sidewalk to the intersection. She leaned on the horn, smashed her foot to the floor, and rocketed across two lanes of traffic. I had my feet braced against the dash and my eyes closed.

"I have a better idea," I said. "Why don't we go back to the funeral home? You wouldn't want to miss hearing that the lid was up. And maybe it would be a good idea to pull over and let me drive, since you don't have a license."

"I got him in my sights," Grandma said, hunched over the wheel, eyes narrowed.

Spiro turned right and Grandma raced to the corner and took it on two wheels. One block ahead of us we saw Spiro right-turn again. Grandma stuck with him, and two turns later we found ourselves back on Hamilton, heading for the funeral home. Spiro was going to make another pass.

"This is convenient," Grandma said. "We can see if Joseph is waiting for us."

"Not good," I said. "He won't be happy to see you behind the wheel. He's a cop, remember? He arrests people who drive without a license."

"He can't arrest me. I'm an old lady. I got rights. And besides, he's practically family."

Was that true? Was Morelli practically family? Had I become accidentally married?

My attention returned to Spiro, and I realized Grandma had closed the gap, and we were one car behind him. We sailed past the funeral home, past Morelli standing at the side of the road, hands on hips. He gave his head a small shake as we whizzed by. Probably best not to second-guess his thoughts . . . they didn't look happy.

"I know I should have stopped to find out about the viewing," Grandma said, "but I hate to lose this guy. I don't know why I'm following him, but I can't seem to quit."

Spiro drove three blocks and did another loop, taking himself back down Hamilton. We lost the single-car buffer, and Grandma got on Spiro's bumper just as he came up to the funeral home. Spiro flashed his right-turn signal and after that it was all horror and panic and life in slow motion, because Spiro jumped the curb and plowed into a group of men on the sidewalk. He hit two men I'd never seen before and Morelli. One of the men was knocked aside. One was pitched off the hood. And Morelli spiraled off the right front fender of Spiro's SUV and was thrown to the ground.

Probably I should have gone after Spiro, but I acted without thought. I was out of the car and running to

Morelli before Grandma had come to a complete stop. He was on his back, his eyes open, his face white.

"Are you okay?" I asked, dropping to my knees.

"Do I look okay?"

"No. You look like you've just been run over by an SUV."

"Last time this happened I got to look up your skirt," he said. And then he passed out.

IT WAS CLOSE to midnight when I was told Morelli was out of surgery. His leg had been broken in two places but aside from that he was fine. I'd taken Grandma home, and I was alone in the hospital. A bunch of cops had stopped by earlier. Eddie Gazarra and Carl Costanza had offered to stay with me, but I'd assured them it wasn't necessary. I'd already been informed Morelli's injuries weren't life threatening. The two other guys that were mowed down by Spiro were going to be okay, too. One had been sent home with scrapes and bruises. The other was being kept overnight with a concussion and broken collarbone.

I was allowed to see Morelli for a moment when he was brought up to his room. He was hooked to an IV drip, his leg was elevated on the bed, and he was still groggy. He was half a day beyond a five o'clock shadow. He had a bruise on his cheek. His eyes were partly closed, and his dark lashes shaded his eyes.

I brushed a light kiss across his lips. "You're okay," I told him.

"Good to know," he said. And then the drugs dragged him back into sleep.

I walked the short distance to the parking garage and found a blue-and-white parked next to Morelli's SUV. Gazarra was at the wheel.

"I had late shift and this is as good a place as any to hang," he said. "Lock the car in Morelli's garage tonight. I wouldn't want to see you in the room next to Mama Mac tomorrow."

I left the garage and followed Gazarra's instructions. It was a dark moonless night with a chill in the air that ordinarily would have me thinking about pumpkins and winter clothes and football games. As it was, I had a hard time pushing the anger and fear generated by Spiro into the background. Hard to think about anything other than the pain he'd caused Morelli.

Morelli's garage was detached from his house and at the rear of his property. Bob was waiting for me when I let myself into the house through the back door. He was sleepy-eyed and lethargic, resting his big shaggy orange head against my leg. I scratched him behind his ear and gave him a dog biscuit from the cookie jar on the counter.

"Do you have to tinkle?" I asked Bob.

Bob didn't look especially interested in tinkling.

"Maybe you should try," I told him. "I'm going to sleep late tomorrow."

I opened the back door, Bob picked his head up, his nose twitched, his eyes got wide, and he bolted through the door and took off into the night. Shit! I could hear Bob galloping two yards over, and then there was nothing but the sound of distant cars and the whir of Morelli's refrigerator in defrost cycle behind me.

Great job, Stephanie. Things aren't bad enough,

now you've lost Morelli's dog. I got a flashlight, pocketed the house key, and locked up behind me. I crossed through two yards and stopped and listened. Nothing. I kept walking through yards, occasionally sweeping the area with the light. At the very end of the block I found Bob munching his way through a big black plastic garbage bag. He'd torn a hole in the bag and had pulled out chicken remains, wads of paper towels, empty soup cans, lunch-meat wrappers, and God knows what else.

I grabbed Bob by the collar and dragged him away from the mess. Probably I should clean up the garbage, but I was in no mood. With any luck, a herd of crows would descend on the carnage and cart everything off to Crowland.

I dragged Bob all the way home. When I got to the house there was a piece of notebook paper tacked to the back door. A smiley face was drawn on the paper. ISN'T THIS FUN? was printed under the smiley face.

I got Bob inside and threw the bolt. And then as a double precaution I locked us into Morelli's bedroom.

IT WAS A little after nine, and I had the phone cradled between my ear and shoulder as I scoured Morelli's kitchen floor, cleaning up the chicken bones Bob had hacked up.

"I can come home," Morelli said. "I need some shorts and a ride."

"I'll be there as soon as I finish cleaning the kitchen." I disconnected and looked over at Bob. "Are you done?"

Bob didn't say anything, but he didn't look happy. His eyes cut to the back door.

I hooked a leash to Bob and took him into the yard. Bob hunched over and pooped out a red lace thong. I was going to have to check upstairs to be sure, but I strongly suspected it was mine.

MORELLI WAS ON the couch with his foot propped up on a pillow on the coffee table. He had the television remote, a bowl of popcorn, his cell phone, a six-pack of soda, crutches, a week's supply of pills for pain, an Xbox remote, his iPod with headset, a box of dog biscuits, and a gun, all within reach. Bob was sprawled on the floor in front of the television.

"Is there anything else before I go?" I asked him.

"Do you have to go?"

"Yes! I promised my mother I'd get the decorations for the cars. I need to check in on Valerie. We have no food in the house. I used up all the paper towels cleaning up Bob barf. And I need to stop at the personal products plant and get a job application."

"I think you should stay home and play with me. I'll let you write dirty suggestions on my cast."

"Appealing, but no. Your mother and your grandmother are going to show up. They're going to need to see for themselves that you're okay. They're going to bring a casserole and a cake, because that's what they always do. And if I'm here they're going to grill us about getting married, because that's what they always do. And then Bella is going to have a vision that involves my uterus, because that's also a constant. Better to take the coward's way out and run errands." Plus, I wanted to drop in at the funeral home and talk to Constantine Stiva about his son.

"What if I fall and I can't get up?"

"Nice try, but I've got it covered. I've got a baby-sitter for you. Someone who will attend to your every need while I'm gone."

There was a sharp rap on the front door, and Lula barged in. "Here I am, ready to baby-sit your ass," she said to Morelli. "Don't you worry about a thing. Lula's here to take care of you."

Morelli looked over at me. "You're kidding."

"I wanted to make sure you were safe."

And that was true. I was worried about Spiro returning and setting the house on fire. Spiro was nuts.

Lula set her bag in the hall and walked to the curb with me. Big Blue was soaking up sun on the street, ready to spring into action. I had an extra car key from Grandma. I'd gotten an extra apartment key from my building super, Dillon Ruddick. I had Morelli's credit card for the food. I was ready to roll. It was early afternoon, and if I didn't hit too much traffic on Route 1 I'd be home to feed Morelli dinner.

"We'll be fine," Lula said. "I brought some videos to watch. And I got the whole bag of tricks with me if anything nasty goes down. I even got a Taser. It's brand-new. Never been used. I bet I could give a guy the runs with that Taser."

"I should be back in a couple hours," I told her. I slid behind the wheel and turned the key in the ignition. Something under the car went *phunnnf*, and flames shot out on all sides and the car instantly died. I got out, and Lula and I got on our hands and knees and checked the undercarriage.

"Guess that was a bomb," Lula said.

Little black dots floated in front of my eyes, and there was a lot of clanging in my head. When the clanging stopped, I stood and brushed road gravel off my knees, using the activity to get myself under control. I was freaking out deep inside, and that wasn't a good thing. I needed to be brave. I needed to think clearly. I needed to be Ranger. Get a grip, I said to myself. Don't give in to the panic. Don't let this bastard run your life and make you afraid.

"You're starting to scare me," Lula said. "You look like you're having a whole conversation with someone and it isn't me."

"Giving myself a pep talk," I said. "Tell Morelli about the bomb. I'm taking his SUV."

"You're whiter than usual," Lula said.

"Yeah, but I didn't totally faint or throw up, so I'm doing good, right?"

I backed Morelli's car out of the garage and hit the first stop on my list. A party store on Route 33 in Hamilton Township. Valerie had, at last count, three bridesmaids, one maid of honor (me), and two flower girls (Angie and Mary Alice). We were riding in six cars. The party store had dolls in fancy gowns for the hood, bows for all the door handles, and streaming ribbons that got attached to the back of each car. Everything corresponded to the color of the gown inside the car. Mine was eggplant. Could it get any worse? I was going to look like the attendant to the dead.

"I'm here to pick up the car decorations for the Plum wedding," I said to the girl at the counter.

"We have them right here, ready to go," she said, "but there's a problem with one of them. I don't know what happened. The woman who makes these is always so careful. One of the dolls looks like . . . an eggplant."

"It's a vegetarian wedding," I told her. "New Age."

I lugged the six boxes out to the car and drove them to my parents' house. I left the SUV idling at the curb, ran in with the boxes, dumped them on the kitchen table, and turned to leave.

"Where are you going so fast?" Grandma wanted to know. "Don't you want a sandwich? We have olive loaf."

"No time. Lots of errands today. And I need to get back to Morelli." Also I didn't want to leave the car unattended long enough for Spiro to set another bomb.

My mother was at the stove, stirring a pot of vanilla pudding. "I hope Joseph is feeling better. That was a terrible thing last night."

"He's on the couch, watching television. His leg is achy, but he's going to be okay." I looked over at Grandma Mazur. "He said to tell you the lid was down, and rumor has it Mama Mac went to the hereafter without the mole. Morelli said the medical examiner thinks the mole is still in the parking lot somewhere, but there might not be a lot left of it due to all the foot traffic around the scene."

"I get a chill just thinking about it," Grandma said. "Someone could be walking around with Mama Mac's mole on the bottom of their shoe."

From the corner of my eye I saw my mother take a

bottle out of a cupboard, pour two fingers of whisky into a juice glass, and knock it back. Guess the ironing wasn't doing it for her anymore.

"Gotta go," I said. "If you need me I'll be staying with Morelli. He needs help getting around."

"The organist at the church would like to know if you want her to accompany you when you play the cello," Grandma said. "I saw her at the market this morning."

I smacked my forehead with the heel of my hand. "With all the excitement I forgot to tell you. I don't have a cello anymore. I gave it away. It was taking up too much space in my closet. You know how it is when you live in an apartment. Never enough closet space."

"But you loved your cello," Grandma said.

I tried to plaster an appropriate expression of remorse on my face. "That's the way it goes. A girl has to have priorities."

"Who got the cello?"

"Who?" My mind was racing. Who got the cello? "My cello teacher," I said. "I gave it to my cello teacher."

"Do we know her?"

"Nope. She lived in New Hope. But she's moved. She moved to South Carolina. That's another reason I stopped playing. My cello teacher moved, and I didn't feel like finding a new cello teacher. So I gave the cello back to her. It was originally hers, anyway." Sometimes I was really impressed with my ability to come up with this shit. Once I got going, it just rolled out of me. I could compose a whole parallel universe for myself in a matter of seconds.

I glanced down at my watch. "Look at the time! I'm late."

I snatched a couple cookies off the plate on the kitchen table and ran through the house to the car. I jumped in the SUV and roared away. Next stop was Valerie. I didn't have any real reason to visit Valerie. It was just that I was her sister and her maid of honor and Val wasn't entirely together these days. I thought it wouldn't hurt to check on her once in a while until she made it through the wedding.

The first thing I noticed when I got to her house was the absence of Kloughn's car. Not surprising since this was a workday. Sort of surprising that he was able to get himself up and out on the road with a raging hangover.

"What?" Val yelled when she opened the door to me.

"I just stopped by to say hello."

"Oh. Sorry I yelled at you. I'm having a problem with volume control. It turns out when you're starving to death you do a lot of yelling."

"Where's Albert? I thought he'd still be in bed with a hangover."

"He decided he was better off at the office. He couldn't stand the galloping and whinnying. You might want to see how he's doing. He left in his pajamas."

"You know, Val, not everyone's cut out to have a big wedding. Maybe you should reconsider the eloping option."

"I wish I'd never started this wedding thing," Val wailed. "What was I thinking?"

"It's not too late to bail."

"It is. And I'm too chicken. Everybody's made all these plans!"

"Yeah, but it's your wedding. It shouldn't be some horrible stressful thing. It should be something you enjoy." Not to mention, if Valerie eloped I wouldn't have to wear the hideous eggplant getup.

I left Valerie and drove to Kloughn's office. There was a CLOSED sign on his door and when I looked in the window I could see Kloughn was stretched out on the floor in his pajamas with a wet towel over his face. I didn't want to make him get up, so I tiptoed away and headed down Route 1 to the personal products plant. I parked in a visitor slot, ran in, and got a job application from the personnel office. I had no illusions of getting an office job here. I had no references and few skills. I'd be lucky if I could get a job on the line. I'd bring the application back tomorrow and wait for a phone call for an interview.

I slid to a stop in front of Giovichinni's Market and didn't bother to call to check on Macaronis. I figured I had bigger problems than Macaronis. I was being stalked by a homicidal maniac. Spiro was officially over the edge.

I ran through the store gathering together some basic foods. Bread, cheese, Tastykakes, peanut butter, cereal, milk, Tastykakes, eggs, frozen pizza, Tastykakes, orange juice, apples, lunch meat, and Tastykakes. I checked out and muscled my way through the door with bags in my arms.

Ranger was leaning against the SUV, waiting for me. He pushed off, took the bags, and put them in the car. "Looks like you're playing house," he said.

"More like nurse. Morelli needs some help."

"Is that your job application on the front seat?"

"Yep."

"Personal products plant?"

"It's halfway to New Brunswick. I'm hoping they won't have heard about me. That's Grandma's line, but it's true."

"Babe," Ranger said. He was smiling, but there was a quality to his voice that told me it wasn't actually funny. We both knew that my life wasn't going in the carefree direction I'd hoped for.

NINE

"I HAVE AN office position open," Ranger said. "Are you interested in working for RangeMan?"

"Oh great. A pity position."

"If I gave you a pity position it wouldn't be in the office."

This got a burst of laughter out of me because I knew he was taking a zing at my sex life with Morelli. For the most part, Ranger had a consistent personality. He wasn't a guy who wasted a lot of unnecessary energy and effort. He moved and he spoke with an efficient ease that was more animal than human. And he didn't telegraph his emotions. Unless Ranger had his tongue in my mouth it was usually impossible to tell what he was thinking. But every now and then, Ranger would step out of the box, and like a little treat that was doled out on special occasions, he would make an entirely outrageous sexual statement. At least it would be outrageous coming from an ordinary guy . . . from Ranger it seemed on the mark.

"I didn't think you hired women," I said to him. "The only woman you have working for you is your housekeeper."

"I hire people who have the skills I need. Right now I could use someone in the building who can do phone work and paperwork. You'd be an easy hire. You already know the drill. Nine to five, five days a week. You can discuss salary with my business manager. You should consider it. The garage is secure. You wouldn't have to worry about getting blown up when you leave at the end of the day."

Ranger owns a small seven-story office building in downtown Trenton. The building is unspectacular on the outside. Well maintained but not architecturally interesting. The interior of the building is high tech and slick, equipped with a state-of-the-art control center, offices, a gym, studio apartments for some of Ranger's crew, plus an apartment for Ranger on the top floor. I'd stayed in Ranger's apartment for a short time on a non-conjugal basis not long ago. It had been equal parts pleasure and terror. Terror because it was Ranger's apartment and Ranger could sometimes be a scary guy. Pleasure because he lives well.

The job offer was tempting. My car would be safe. I'd be safe. I'd be able to pay my rent. And the chances of rolling in garbage were slim.

"Okay," I said. "I'll take the job."

"Use the intercom at the gate when you come in tomorrow. Dress in black. You'll be working on the fifth floor."

"Any leads on Benny Gorman?"

"No. That's one of the things I want you to do. I want you to see what you can turn up."

Ranger's pager buzzed, and he checked the readout. "Elroy Dish is back at Blue Fish. Do you want to ride along?"

"No thanks. Been there, done that."

"Be careful."

And he was gone.

I looked at my watch. Almost five. Perfect. Stiva would be between afternoon and evening viewings. I drove the short distance up Hamilton and parked on the street. I found Stiva in his office just off the large entrance foyer. I rapped on the doorjamb, and he looked up from his computer.

"Stephanie," he said. "Always nice to see you."

I appreciated the greeting, but I knew it was a big fat lie. Stiva was the consummate undertaker. He was an island of professional calm in an ocean of chaos. And he never alienated a future customer. The ugly truth is, Stiva would rather shove a sharp stick in his eye than see Grandma or me alive on his doorstep. Dead would be something else.

"I hope this visit isn't due to bad news," Stiva said.

"I wanted to talk to you about Spiro. Have you seen him since the fire?"

"No."

"Spoken to him?"

"No. Why do you ask?"

"He was driving the car that ran over Morelli."

Stiva went as still as stone, and his pale vanilla custard cheeks flushed pink. "Are you serious?"

"Unfortunately, yes. I'm sorry. I saw him clearly."

"How does he look?" Stiva asked.

I felt my heart constrict at his response. He was a concerned parent, anxious to hear word of his missing son. What on earth could I say to Stiva?

"I only saw him briefly," I said. "He seemed healthy. Maybe some scars on his face from the fire."

"He must have been driving by and lost control of his car," Stiva said. "At least I know he's alive. Thank you for coming in to tell me."

"I thought you'd want to know."

No point to saying more. Stiva didn't have information to share, and I didn't want to tell him the whole story. I left the funeral home and returned to the SUV. I drove two blocks to Pino's and got two meatball subs, a tub of coleslaw, and a tub of potato salad. Morelli was going to be in a bad mood after spending the afternoon with Lula. I figured I'd try to mellow him out with the sub before I dropped the news about my new job. Morelli wasn't going to be happy to hear I was working for Ranger.

I went out of my way on the trip home to drive by Anthony Barroni's house. I had no real basis for believing he was involved with Spiro and the missing men. Just a gut feeling. Maybe it was desperation. I wanted to think I had a grip on the problem. The grip loosened when I got to Barroni's house. No lights shining. Curtains drawn. Garage door closed. No car in driveway.

I turned at the corner and wound my way through the Burg to Chambers Street. I crossed Chambers and two blocks later I pulled the SUV into Morelli's garage. Big Blue and Lula's Firebird were still at the curb. I made sure the garage door was locked, and I carted the bags in through the back door.

"Is that Stephanie Plum coming through the back door?" Lula yelled. "'Cause if it's some maniac pervert I'm gonna kick his ass."

"It's me," I yelled back. "Sorry you don't get to do any ass kicking."

I put the bags on the counter and went into the living room to see Lula and Morelli. Morelli was still on the couch. Bob was still on the floor. And Lula was packing up.

"This wasn't so bad," Lula said. "We played poker and I won three dollars and fifty-seven cents. I would have won more, but your boyfriend fell asleep."

"It's the drugs," Morelli said. "You're a sucky poker player. I would have won if I wasn't all drugged up. You took advantage."

"I won fair and square," Lula said. "Anytime you want to get even you let me know. I can always use extra cash."

"Any other fun things happen that I should know about?"

"Yeah," Lula said. "His mother and grandmother came over. And they're nuts. The old lady said she was putting the eye on me. I told her she better not pull any of that voodoo shit with me or I'll beat her like a piñata."

"I bet that went over big."

"They left after that. They brought a casserole, and I put it in the refrigerator. I didn't think it looked all that good."

"No cake?"

"Oh yeah, the cake. I ate the cake."

"All of it?"

"Bob had some. I would have given some to Morelli, but he was sleeping." She had her bag over her shoulder and her car keys in her hand. "I walked Bob about an hour ago, and he pooped twelve times, so he should be good for the night. I didn't feed him, but he ate one of Morelli's sneakers around three o'clock. You might want to go light on the dog crunchies until he horks the sneaker up."

Morelli waited until he heard Lula's car drive off before speaking again. "Another fifteen minutes and I would have shot her. I would have gone to jail for the rest of my life, and it would have been worth it."

I brought out the subs and the coleslaw and the potato salad. "Don't you want to know how my day went?"

He unwrapped his sub. "How did your day go?"

"I didn't get blown up."

"Speaking of getting blown up, the lab took a look at your Buick. The bomb was very similar to the bomb that killed Mama Mac. The difference being that this bomb was detonated when you turned the key in the ignition, and it was much smaller. It wasn't intended to kill."

"Spiro is still playing with me."

"You're sure it's Spiro?"

"Yes. I stopped in to see Stiva. He had no idea Spiro was back. Said he hasn't heard from him since the fire."

"You believed him?"

"Yeah."

"I talked to Ryan Laski today. He's been working the Barroni case with me. I told him about Spiro, and I asked him to keep an eye on Anthony Barroni. And I asked my mother about Spiro. So far as I can tell, you're the only one who's seen him. There's no gossip on Spiro circulating in the Burg."

AT TEN O'CLOCK Morelli and I were still on the couch. We'd watched the news while we ate our subs. And then we watched some sitcom reruns. And then we watched a ball game. And now Morelli was getting *that look*.

"You have a cast on your leg, and you're full of painkillers," I said to him. "One would think it would slow you down."

"What can I say . . . I'm Italian. And that part of me isn't broken."

"There are some logistical things involved here. Can you get up to the bedroom?"

"I might need motivation to get through the pain . . . like, seeing you naked and gyrating at the top of the stairs."

"And what about a shower?"

"Can't take a shower," Morelli said. "I'm going to have to lie on the bed and let you wash me . . . everywhere."

"I can see you've given this some thought."

"Yeah. That's why it's not just my cast that's hard."

Okay, so this might not be so bad. I thought I could probably get into the naked gyrating and the washing. And it seemed to me I'd pick up some perks from the injury. Morelli wasn't going to be especially mobile with that heavy cast. Once I got him on his back he was going to stay there, and I'd have the top all to myself.

I'D SET THE alarm for 7:00 A.M. I didn't have to be at work until 9:00, but I had to shower and do the hair and makeup thing, walk and feed Bob, get Morelli set for the day, and make a fast trip back to my apartment in search of black clothes. And I needed to get Rex. He didn't require a lot of care, but I didn't like to leave him alone for more than a couple days.

Morelli threw an arm over me when the alarm went off. "Did you set it for sex?" he asked.

"No, I set it for *get up*."

"We don't have to get up early this morning."

I slipped out from under the arm and rolled out of bed. "*You* don't have to get up early. I have lots of things to do."

"Again? You're not going to bring Lula back, are you?"

"No. Based on your performance last night, I'd say you're not in the least impaired."

I didn't want to give details on the day's activities, so I hurried off to the bathroom. I showered, did the blow-dry thing, slathered on some makeup, and bumped into Morelli when I opened the bathroom door.

"Sorry," I said. "Are you waiting to use the bathroom?"

"No, I'm waiting to talk to you."

"Jeez, I'm in kind of a hurry. Maybe we can talk after I walk Bob."

Morelli pinned me to the wall. "Let's talk now. Where are you going today?"

"I need to go back to my apartment for clothes."

"And?"

"And I have a job."

"I hate to ask. Your jobs have been getting progressively worse. I can't imagine who would hire you after the Cluck-in-a-Bucket fiasco. Is it the personal products plant?"

"It's Ranger."

"That makes sense," Morelli said. "I should have guessed. I can hardly wait to hear your job description."

"It's a good job. I'm doing phone work from the office. Nothing in the field. And I get to park in the RangeMan garage, so my car will be secure. Is this where you start yelling?"

Morelli released me. "Hard to believe, but I'm actually relieved. I was afraid you were going to be out there trying to find Spiro today."

Go figure this. "You love me," I said to Morelli.

"Yeah. I love you." He looked at me expectantly. "And?"

"I . . . l-l-like you, too." *Shit.*

"Jesus," Morelli said.

I did a grimace. "I feel it. I just can't say it."

Bob padded out of the bedroom. *"Gak,"* Bob said, and he barfed out a slimy mess on the hall carpet.

"Guess that's what's left of my sneaker," Morelli said.

I PARKED MORELLI'S SUV in my lot and ran upstairs to change my clothes. I unlocked my apartment door, rushed inside, and almost stepped on a small, gift-wrapped box. Same wrapping paper Spiro had used for the clock. Same little ribbon bow.

I stared down at the box for a full minute without breathing. I didn't have a gun. I didn't have pepper spray. I didn't have a stun gun. My toys had all gone up in smoke at Cluck-in-a-Bucket.

"Anyone here?" I called out.

No one answered. I knew I should call Ranger and have him go through the apartment, but that felt wimpy. So I backed out, closed the door to my apartment, and called Lula.

Ten minutes later, Lula was standing alongside me in front of the door.

"Okay, open it," Lula said, gun in hand, Taser on her hip, pepper spray stuck into her pocket, bludgeoning flashlight shoved under the waistband of her rhinestone-studded spandex jeans, flak vest stretched to the max over her basketball boobs.

I opened the door and we both peeked inside.

"One of us should go through and check for bad guys," Lula said.

"You've got the gun."

"Yeah, but it's your apartment. I could check, but I don't want to be intrusive. It's not that I'm chicken or anything, I just don't want to deprive you of checking."

I rolled my eyes at her.

"Don't you roll eyes at me," Lula said. "I'm being considerate. I'm giving you the opportunity to get shot before me."

"Gee, thanks. Can I at least have the gun?"

"Damn skippy. It's loaded and everything."

I was 99 percent sure the apartment was empty. Still, why take a chance with the 1 percent, right? I crept through the apartment with Lula three steps behind me. We looked in closets, under the bed, behind the shower curtain. No spooky Spiro. We returned to the front door and stared down at the box.

"I guess you should open it," Lula said.

"Suppose it's a bomb?"

"Then I guess you should open it far away from me."

I cut a look to her.

"Well, if it's a bomb it's a little bitty one," Lula said. "Anyway, maybe it's not a bomb. Maybe it's a diamond bracelet."

"You think Spiro's sending me a diamond bracelet?"

"It would be a long shot," Lula said.

I blew out a sigh and gingerly picked the box up. It wasn't heavy. It wasn't ticking. I shook it. It didn't rattle. I carefully unwrapped the box. I lifted the lid and looked inside.

Lula looked over my shoulder. "What the hell is that?" Lula asked. "It's got hairs growing out of it. *Holy fuck!* Is that what I think it is?"

It was Mama Mac's mole. I dropped the box and ran into the bathroom and threw up. When I came out of the bathroom, Lula was on the couch, flipping through television channels.

"I scooped the mole up and put it back in the box," Lula said. "And then I put it in a plastic Baggie. It doesn't smell all that great. It's on the counter in the kitchen."

"I have to change clothes. I took a job working for Ranger, and I need to wear black."

"Does this job involve fancy underwear? Oral sex? Lap dancing?"

"No. It involves phone investigation."

Lula remoted the television off and stood to leave. "I bet it'll work its way around to one of those other things. You'd tell me, right?"

"You'll be the first to know."

I bolted the door after Lula and got dressed in black jeans, black Puma sneakers, and a stretchy black V-neck T-shirt. I took Mama's mole, shrugged into my denim jacket, and looked out the window at Morelli's SUV. No one lurking around, planting bombs. Hooray. I grabbed Rex's cage and vacated the apartment, locking up after me. Lot of good that did. Everybody and their brother broke into my apartment.

I drove the mole to Morelli's house, handed it over, and took Rex into the kitchen.

"This is disgusting," Morelli said, opening the box, checking the mole out. "This is sick."

"Yeah. You'd better call Grandma and let her come over to have a look before you turn it in. Grandma will never forgive you if you don't let her see the mole."

Morelli looked at the packet of painkillers on his coffee table. "I need more drugs," he said. "If I have to have your grandmother over here examining the mole I definitely need more drugs."

I gave him a fast kiss and ran back to the SUV. If I got all the lights right I might make work on time.

I PARKED IN the underground garage and took the elevator to the fifth floor. I already knew most of the guys who worked for Ranger. No one looked surprised to see me when I came onto the floor of the control room. Everyone was dressed in black jeans or cargo pants and black T-shirts. Ranger and I were the only ones without RANGEMAN embroidered on the front of the shirt. Ranger had been slouched in a chair, watching a monitor, when I stepped out of the elevator. He came to my side and walked me station to station.

"As you can see there are two banks of monitors," Ranger said. "Hal's watching the cameras in the building and listening to police scanners. He also watches the GPS screen that tracks RangeMan vehicles. Woody and Vince are monitoring private security systems. RangeMan provides personal, commercial and residential security to select clients. It's not a large operation in the world of security specialists, but the profit margin is good. I have similar operations in Boston, Miami, and Atlanta. I'm in the middle of a sellout to my Atlanta partner, and I'll probably sell Boston. I like being out on the street. I'm not crazy about running a national empire. Too difficult to control quality.

"I'm going to give you the cubby on the far side of the room. It's the area we set aside for investigation. Silvio has been doing this job, but he's transferring to the Miami office on Monday. He has family there. He'll sit with you today and make sure you know how to get into the search programs. Initially, I want you to concentrate on Benny Gorman. We've already run him through the system. Silvio will give you the file. I want you to read the file and then start over.

"The gym is open to you. Unfortunately, the locker room is men only. I'm sure they'd be happy to share, but I don't think it's a good idea. If you need to change clothes or shower you can use my apartment. Tank will issue you a key fob similar to mine. It'll get you into the building and into my apartment. My housekeeper, Ella, keeps food in the kitchen at the end of the hall. It's for staff use. There are always sandwiches, raw vegetables, and fruit. You're going to have to bring your own Cheez Doodles and Tastykakes. My business manager will stop by later this morning to discuss salary and benefits. I'll have Ella order some Range-Man shirts for you. If you decide to go back to Vinnie you can keep the shirts." Ranger almost smiled. "I like the idea of you wearing my name on your breast." He had his hand at the back of my waist, and he guided me into the cubby. "Make yourself comfortable. I'll send Silvio in to you. I'll be out of the office all day, but you can reach me on my cell if there's a problem. Are there any new disasters you want to share with me before I take off?"

"Spiro sent me Mama Mac's mole."

"Her mole?"

"Yeah, she had this horrible mutant mole on her face that the crime lab was never able to find. Spiro left it for me in my apartment. He had it all gift wrapped in a little box."

"Walk me through this."

"I went back to my apartment this morning to find something black to wear to work. I opened my locked door and the little gift-wrapped package was on the floor in the foyer. I was worried Spiro might still be in the apartment, so I called Lula and we went through together."

"Why didn't you call me?"

"It felt wimpy."

"Do you honestly think Lula would protect you against Spiro?"

"She had a gun."

There was an awkward pause while Ranger came to terms with the possibility that I didn't have my own gun.

"My gun melted down in the Cluck-in-a-Bucket fire," I told him. Not nearly so much of a loss as my lip gloss.

"Tank will also outfit you with a gun," Ranger said. "I expect you to carry it. And I expect it to be loaded. We have a practice range in the basement. Once a week I expect you to visit the practice range."

I snapped him a salute. "Aye, aye, sir!"

"Don't let the rest of the men see you being a smart-ass," Ranger said. "They're not allowed."

"I'm allowed?"

"I have no illusions over my ability to control you. Just try to keep the power play private, so you don't undermine my authority with my men."

"You're assuming we'll have private time?"

"It would be nice." The almost smile turned into a for-sure smile. "Are you flirting with me?"

"I don't think so. Did it feel like flirting?" Of course I was flirting with him. I was a horrible person. Morelli was home with a broken leg and a mutant mole, and I was flirting with Ranger. God, I was such a slut.

"Finish walking me through your latest disaster."

"Okay, so Lula and I went through the apartment and there was no Spiro. So we went back to the box, and I opened it."

"You weren't worried that it was a bomb?"

"It would have been a little bomb."

Ranger looked like he was trying hard not to grimace. "What happened after you opened it?"

"I threw up."

"Babe," Ranger said.

"Anyway, I gave the mole to Morelli. I figured he'd know what to do with it."

"Good thinking. Anything else you want to share?"

"Maybe later."

"You're flirting again," Ranger said.

And he left.

I saw him stop to talk to Tank on his way out. Tank nodded and looked my way. I gave Tank a little finger wave and both men smiled.

The cubby walls were corkboard. Good for deadening sound, and also good for posting notes. I could see holes where Silvio had tacked messages and whatever, but the messages had all been removed, and only the pushpins remained. I had a workstation desk, a comfy-looking leather desk chair, a computer that could probably e-mail Mars, a phone that had too many buttons, a headset to go with the phone, file cabinets, in/out baskets that were empty, a second chair for guests, and a printer.

I sat in my chair and swiveled around. If I leaned back I could see out of the cubby, into the control room. The computer was different from the one I had at home. I hadn't a clue how to work the darn thing. Ditto the multiline phone. Maybe I shouldn't throw the personal products plant application away. Maybe overseeing the boxing machine was more my speed. I looked in the desk drawers. Pens, sticky-note pads, tape, stapler, lined pads, Advil. The Advil might not be a good sign. I was dying to go to the kitchen for coffee, but I didn't want to leave my cubby. It felt safe in the cubby. I didn't have to make eye contact with any of the guys. Some of Ranger's men looked like they should be wearing orange jumpsuits and ankle monitors.

Five minutes after Ranger left, Tank came into my cubicle with a small box. He set the box on my desk and removed the contents. Key fob for the garage and Ranger's apartment, Sig Sauer 9 with extra mag, stun gun, cell phone, laminated photo ID on a neck chain identifying me as a RangeMan employee. I hadn't posed for the photo and decided not to ask how it was obtained.

"I don't know how to work this kind of gun," I told Tank. "I use a revolver."

"Ranger has practice time reserved for you tomorrow at ten A.M. You're required to carry the gun, the phone, and the ID with you at all times. You don't have to wear the ID. It's for fieldwork. It's a good idea to keep it on you in case you're questioned about the gun."

Silvio arrived with a cup of coffee, and Tank disappeared. "I brought you cream, no sugar," he said, setting the coffee on the desk in front of me. "If you want sugar there are some packets in the left-hand drawer." He pulled the extra chair next to mine. "Okay," he said. "Let's see what you know about computers."

Oh boy.

BY NOON I had the phone figured out, and I could navigate the Net. I was already familiar with most of the search programs used by RangeMan. I'd used them from time to time on Connie's computer. Beyond the standard search programs that Connie used, Range-Man had a few extra that were frighteningly invasive. Just for the heck of it, I typed my name in on one of the super searchers and blanched at what appeared on my screen. I had no secrets. The file stopped just short of a Webcam view of my last gyn exam.

I followed Silvio to the kitchen and took a food survey. Fresh fruit and vegetables, cut and washed. Turkey, roast beef, tuna sandwiches on seven-grain bread. Low-fat yogurt. Energy bars. Juice. Skim milk. Bottles of water.

"No Tastykakes," I said to Silvio.

"Ella used to set out trays of cookies and brownie bars, but we started to get fat, so Ranger banned them."

"He's a hard man."

"Tell me about it," Silvio said. "He scares the crap out of me."

I took a turkey sandwich and a bottle of water and returned to my cubicle. Hal, Woody, and Vince were watching their screens. Silvio went off to clean out his locker. So I was now officially Miz Computer Wiz. Three requests for security searches were sitting in my in-box. Mental note. Never leave cubby. Work appears when cubby is left unattended. I looked at the name requesting the search requests. Frederick Rodriguez. Didn't know him. Didn't see him out and about in the control room. There was another floor of offices. I guessed Frederick Rodriguez was in one of those offices.

I called my mom on my new cell phone and gave

her the number. I could hear my grandmother yelling in the background.

"Is that Stephanie?" Grandma Mazur hollered. "Tell her the Macaroni funeral is tomorrow morning, and I need a ride."

"You're not going to the funeral," my mother said to Grandma Mazur.

"It's gonna be the big event of the year," Grandma said. "I have to go."

"Joseph let you see the mole before he gave it over to the police," my mother said. "You're going to have to be satisfied with that." My mother's attention swung back to me. "If you take her to that funeral there's no more pineapple upside-down cake for the rest of your life."

I disconnected from my mother, ate my sandwich, and ran the first name. It was close to three by the time I was done running the second name. I set the third request aside and paged through the Gorman file. Then I did as Ranger suggested and ran Gorman through all the searches again. I called Morelli to make sure he was okay and to tell him I might be late. There was a stretch of silence while he wrestled with trust, and then he put in a request for a six-pack of Bud and two chili dogs.

"And by the way," Morelli said. "The lab guy called and told me the mole was made out of mortician's putty."

"Don't tell Grandma," I said. "It'll ruin everything for her."

TEN

I PRINTED THE Gorman search, and then I searched Louis Lazar. Both men yielded volumes of information. Date of birth, medical history, history of employment, military history, credit history, history of residence, class standings through high school. Neither man attended college. Personal history included photos, wives, kids, assorted relatives.

I printed Lazar and moved to Michael Barroni. Most of this information I already knew. Some was new and felt embarrassingly intrusive. His wife had miscarried two children. He'd gotten psychiatric counseling a year ago for anxiety. He'd had a hernia operation when he was thirty-six. He'd been asked to repeat the third grade.

I'd just started a credit check on Barroni when my cell rang.

"I'm hungry," Morelli said. "It's seven o'clock. When are you coming home?"

"Sorry. I lost track of the time."

"Bob is standing by the door."

"*Okay!* I'll be right there."

I put the Barroni search on hold and dropped the Lazar file and the Gorman file into my top desk drawer. I grabbed my bag and my jacket and dashed out of my cubby. There was an entirely new crew in the control room. Ranger ran the control room in eight-hour shifts around the clock. A guy named Ram was at one of the monitor banks. Two other men were at large.

I crossed the room at a run, barreled through the door to take the stairs, and crashed into Ranger. We lost balance and rolled tangled together to the fourth-floor landing. We lay there for a moment, stunned and breathless. Ranger was flat on his back, and I was on top of him.

"Oh my God," I said. "I'm so sorry! Are you okay?"

"Yeah, but next time it's my turn to have the top."

The door opened above us and Ram stuck his head out. "I heard a crash . . . oh, excuse me," he said. And he pulled his head back and closed the door.

"I wish this was as bad as it looks," Ranger said. He got to his feet, scooping me up with him. He held me at arm's length and looked me over. "You're a wreck. Did I do all this damage?"

I had some scratches on my arm, the knee had gotten torn on my jeans, and there was a rip in my T-shirt. Ranger was perfect. Ranger was like Big Blue. Nothing ever touched Ranger.

"Don't worry about it," I said. "I'm fine. I'm late. Gotta go." And I took off, down the rest of the stairs and out the door to the garage.

I crossed town and stopped at Mike the Greek's deli

for the hot dogs and beer. Five minutes later, I had the SUV locked up in Morelli's garage. I took his back porch steps two at a time, opened the back door, and Bob rushed past me and tinkled in the middle of Morelli's backyard.

The instant the last drop hit grass, Bob bolted off into the night. I rustled the hot dog bag, pulled out a hot dog, and waved it in Bob's direction. I heard Bob stop galloping two houses down, there was a moment of silence, and then he came thundering back. Bob can smell a hot dog a mile away.

I lured him into the house with the hot dog and locked up. Morelli was still on the couch with his foot on the coffee table. The room was trashed around him. Empty soda cans, newspapers, a crumpled fast-food bag, a half-empty potato chip bag, an empty doughnut box, a sock (probably Bob ate the mate), assorted sports and girlie magazines.

"This room is a Dumpster," I said to him. "Where'd all this stuff come from?"

"Some of the guys visited me."

I doled out the hot dogs. Two to Morelli, two to Bob, two to me. Morelli and I got a Bud. Bob got a bowl of water. I kicked through the clutter, brushed potato chip crumbs off a chair, and sat down. "You need to clean up."

"I can't clean up. I'm supposed to stay off my leg."

"You weren't worrying about your leg last night."

"That was different. That was an emergency. And anyway, I wasn't on my leg. I was on my back. And what's with the scratches on your arm and the torn clothes? What the hell were you doing? I thought you were supposed to be working in the office."

"I fell down the stairs."

"At RangeMan?"

"Yep. Do you want another beer? Ice cream?"

"I want to know how you managed to fall down the stairs."

"I was rushing to leave, and I sort of crashed into Ranger, and we fell down the stairs."

Morelli stared at me with his unreadable cop face. I was ready for him to morph into the jealous Italian boyfriend with a lot of arm flapping and yelling, but he gave his head a small shake and took another pull on his Bud. "Poor dumb bastard," he said. "I hope he's got insurance on that building."

I was pretty sure I'd just been insulted, but I thought it was best to let it slide.

Morelli leaned back into the couch and smiled at me. "And before I forget, your cello is in the front hall."

"My cello?"

"Yeah, every great cello player needs a cello, right?"

I ran to the hall and gaped at the big bulbous black case leaning against the wall. I dragged the case into the living room and opened it. There was a large violin sort of thing in it. I supposed it was a cello.

"How did this get here?" I asked Morelli.

"Your mother rented it for you. She said you gave yours away, and she knew how much you were looking forward to playing at Valerie's wedding, so she rented a cello for you. I swear to God, those were her exact words."

I guess the panic showed on my face because Morelli stopped smiling.

"Maybe you should fill me in on your musical accomplishments," Morelli said.

I plunked down on the couch beside him. "I don't have any musical accomplishments. I don't have any accomplishments of any kind. I'm stupid and boring. I don't have any hobbies. I don't play sports. I don't write poetry. I don't travel to interesting places. I don't even have a good job."

"That doesn't make you stupid and boring," Morelli said.

"Well, I *feel* stupid and boring. And I wanted to feel interesting. And somehow, someone told my mother and grandmother that I played the cello. I guess it was me . . . only it was like some foreign entity took possession of my body. I heard the words coming out of my mouth, but I'm sure they originated in some other brain. And it was so simple at first. One small mention. And then it took on a life of its own. And next thing, *everyone* knew."

"And you can't play the cello."

"I'm not even sure this *is* a cello."

Morelli went back to smiling. "And you think you're boring? No way, Cupcake."

"What about the stupid part?"

Morelli threw his arm around me. "Sometimes that's a tough call."

"My mother expects me to play at Valerie's wedding."

"You can fake it," Morelli said. "How hard can it be? You just make a couple passes with the bow and then you faint or pretend you broke your finger or something."

"That might work," I said. "I'm good at faking it."

This led to a couple moments of uncomfortable silence from both of us.

"You didn't mean . . . ?" Morelli asked.

"No. Of course not."

"Never?"

"Maybe once."

His eyes narrowed. "Once?"

"It's all that comes to mind. It was the time we were late for your Uncle Spud's birthday party."

"I remember that. That was great. You're telling me you faked it?"

"We were late! I couldn't concentrate. It seemed like the best way to go."

Morelli took his arm away and started flipping through channels with the remote.

"You're mad," I said.

"I'm working on it. Don't push me."

I got up and closed the cello case and kicked it to the side of the room. "Men!"

"At least we don't fake it."

"Listen, it was *your* uncle. And we were *late,* remember? So I made the sacrifice and got us there in time for dessert. You should be thanking me."

Morelli's mouth was open slightly and his face was registering a mixture of astonished disbelief and wounded, pissed-off male pride.

Okay, it wasn't that much of a sacrifice at the time, and I knew he shouldn't be thanking me, but give me a break here . . . this wasn't famine in Ethiopia. And it wasn't as if I hadn't *tried* to have an orgasm. And it wasn't as if we didn't fib to each other from time to time.

"I should be thanking you," Morelli repeated,

sounding like he was making a gigantic but futile effort to understand the female mind.

"All right, I'll concede the *thanking* thing. How about if you're just happy I got you to the party in time for dessert?"

Morelli cut me a sideways look. He wasn't having any of it. He returned his attention to the television and settled on a ball game.

This is the reason I live with a hamster, I thought.

MORELLI WAS STILL on the couch watching television when I went downstairs to take Bob for his morning walk. I was wearing sweats that I'd found in Morelli's dresser, and I'd borrowed his Mets hat. I clipped the leash on Bob, and Morelli glanced over at me. "What's with the clothes? Trying to fake being me?"

"Get a grip," I said to Morelli.

Bob was dancing around, looking desperate, so I hurried him out the front door. He took a big tinkle on Morelli's sidewalk and then he got all smiley and ready to walk. I like walking Bob at night when it's dark and no one can see where he poops. At night Bob and I are the phantom poopers, leaving it where it falls. By day, I have to carry plastic pooper bags. I don't actually mind scooping the poop. It's carrying it around for the rest of the walk that I hate. It's hard to look hot when you're carrying a bag of dog poop.

I walked Bob for almost an hour. We returned to the house. I fed Bob. I made coffee. I brought Morelli coffee, juice, his paper, and a bowl of raisin bran. I ran upstairs, took a shower, did some makeup and hair magic, got dressed in my black clothes, and came downstairs ready for work.

"Is there anything you need before I leave?" I asked Morelli.

Morelli gave me a full body scan. "Dressing sexy for Ranger?"

I was wearing black jeans, black Chucks, and a stretchy V-neck black T-shirt that didn't show any cleavage. "Is that sarcasm?" I asked.

"No. It's an observation."

"This is *not* sexy."

"That shirt is too skimpy."

"I've worn this shirt a million times. You've never objected to it before."

"That's because it was worn for me. You need to change that shirt."

"Okay," I said, arms in air, nostrils flaring. "You want me to change my shirt. I'll change my shirt." And I stomped up the stairs and stripped off all my clothes. I'd brought every piece of black I owned to Morelli's house, so I pawed through my wardrobe and came up with skintight black spandex workout pants that rode low and were worn commando. I changed my shoes to black Pumas. And I wriggled into a black spandex wrap shirt that didn't quite meet the top of the workout pants and showed *a lot* of cleavage . . . at least as much as I could manage without implants. I stomped back down the stairs and paraded into the living room to show Morelli.

"Is this better?" I asked.

Morelli narrowed his eyes and reached for me, but he couldn't move far without his crutches. I beat him to the crutches and ran to the kitchen with them. I hustled out of the house, backed Morelli's SUV out of the garage, and motored off to work.

I used my new key fob to get into the underground garage and parked in the area reserved for noncompany cars. I took the elevator to the fifth floor, stepped into the control room, and six sets of eyes looked up from the screens and locked onto me. Halfway to work, I'd pulled Morelli's sweatshirt out of my shoulder bag and put it on over my little stretchy top. It was a nice, big shapeless thing that came well below my ass and gave me a safe unisex look. I smiled at the six men on deck. They all smiled back and returned to their work.

I was a half hour early and for the first time in a long time I was excited to get to work. I wanted to finish the Barroni search, and then I wanted to move on to Jimmy Runion. I still had one file left to search for Frederick Rodriguez. I decided to do it first and get it off my desk. I was still working on the Rodriguez file when Ranger appeared in my cubby entrance.

"We have a date," Ranger said. "You're scheduled for ten o'clock practice downstairs."

Here's the thing about guns. I hate them. I don't even like them when they're not loaded. "I'm in the middle of something," I said. "Maybe we could reschedule for some other time." Like never.

"We're doing this now," Ranger said. "This is important. And I don't want to find your gun in your desk drawer when you leave. If you work for me, you carry a gun."

"I don't have permission to carry concealed."

Ranger shoved my chair with his foot and rolled me back from the computer. "Then you carry exposed."

"I can't do that. I'll feel like Annie Oakley."

Ranger pulled me out of the chair. "You'll figure it out. Get your gun. We have the range for an hour."

I took the gun out of the desk drawer, shoved it into my sweatshirt pocket, and followed Ranger to the elevator. We exited into the garage and walked to the rear. Ranger unlocked the door to the range and switched the light on. The room was windowless and appeared to stretch the length of the building. There were two lanes for shooters. Remote-controlled targets at the far end. Shelves and a thick bulletproof glass partition that separated the shooters at the head of each lane.

"With a little effort you could turn this into a bowling alley," I said to Ranger.

"This is more fun," Ranger said. "And I'm having a hard time seeing you in bowling shoes."

"It's not fun. I don't like guns."

"You don't have to like them, but if you work for me you have to feel comfortable with them and know how to use them and be safe."

Ranger took two headsets and a box of ammo and put them on my shelf. "We'll start with basics. You have a nine-millimeter Sig Sauer. It's a semiautomatic." Ranger removed the magazine, showed it to me, and shoved it back into the gun. "Now you do it," he said.

I removed the magazine and reloaded. I did it ten times. Ranger did a step-by-step demonstration on firing. He gave the gun back to me, and I went through the process ten times. I was nervous, and it felt stuffy in the narrow room, and I was starting to sweat. I put the gun on the shelf, and I took off Morelli's sweatshirt.

"Babe," Ranger said. And he pulled his key fob out of his pocket and hit a button.

"What did you just do?" I asked him.

"I scrambled the security camera in this room. Hal will fall out of his seat upstairs if he sees you in this outfit."

"You don't want to know the long story, but the short story is I wore it to annoy Morelli."

"I'm in favor of anything that annoys Morelli," Ranger said. He moved in close and looked down at me. "This wouldn't be my first choice as a work uniform, but I like it." He ran a finger across the slash of stomach not covered by clothing, and I felt heat rush into private places. He splayed his hand at my hip and turned his interest to my workout pants. "I especially like these pants. What do you wear under them?"

And here's where I made my mistake. I was hot and flustered and a flip answer seemed in order. Problem was, the answer that popped out of my mouth was a tad flirty.

"There are some things a man should find out for himself," I said.

Ranger reached for the waistband on the spandex pants, and I shrieked and jumped back.

"Babe," Ranger said, smiling. I was amusing him, again.

I glanced at my watch. "Actually, I need to leave the building for a while."

"Looking for another job?"

"No. This is personal."

Ranger pushed the button to unscramble the surveillance camera. "Wear the sweatshirt when you're on deck in the control room."

"Deal."

A HALF HOUR later, I was idling across the street from Stiva's. The hearse and the flower cars were in place at the side entrance. Three black Town Cars lined up behind the flower cars. I sat and watched the casket come out. Macaronis followed. The flower cars were already loaded. The cars slowly moved out and drove the short distance to the church. I saw no sign of Spiro. I followed at a distance and parked half a block from the church. I had a clear view of the parking lot and the front of the church. I settled back to wait. This would take a while. The Macaronis would want Mass. The parking lot was full and the surrounding streets were bumper-to-bumper cars. The entire Burg had turned out.

An hour later, I was worrying about my cubicle sitting empty. I was getting paid to do computer searches, not hang out at funerals. And then, just as I was thinking about leaving and returning to work, the doors to the church opened and people began to file out. I caught a glimpse of the casket being rolled out a side door to the waiting hearse. Engines caught up and down the street. Stiva's assistants were out, lining up cars, attaching flags to antennae. I was intently watching the crowd at the church and jumped when Ranger rapped on my side window.

"Have you seen Spiro?"

"No."

"I'm right behind you. Lock up and we'll take my car."

Ranger was driving a black Porsche Cayenne. I slid onto the passenger seat and buckled up. "How did you find me?"

"Woody picked you up on the screen, realized you were following the funeral, and told me."

"It'll be ugly if Morelli finds out you're tracking his SUV."

"I'll remove the transponder when you stop using the car."

"I don't suppose there's any way I can get you to stop tracking *me*?"

"You don't want me to stop tracking you, Babe. I'm keeping you safe."

He was right. And I was sufficiently freaked out by Spiro to tolerate the intrusion.

"This isn't personal leave time," Ranger said. "This is work. You should have run it by me. We had to scramble to coordinate this."

"Sorry. It was a last-minute decision . . . as you can see from my clothes. My mother will need a pill after she starts getting the reports back on my cemetery appearance."

"We're wearing black," Ranger said. "We're in the ballpark. Just keep your sweatshirt zipped, so the men don't accidentally fall into the grave."

Cars were moving around in front of the church, jockeying for position. The hearse pulled into the street and the procession followed, single file, lights on. Ranger waited for the last car to go by before he fell into line. There'd been no sign of Spiro, but then I hadn't expected him to show up at church, shaking hands and chatting. I'd expected him to do another drive-by or maybe hang in a shadow somewhere. Or maybe he'd be hidden at some distance, waiting for the graveside ceremony, using binoculars to see the results of his insanity.

"Tank's already at the cemetery," Ranger said. "He's watching the perimeter. He's got Slick and Eddie working with him."

It was a slow drive to Mama Mac's final resting place. Ranger wasn't famous for making small talk, so it was also a quiet drive. We parked and got out of the Cayenne. The sky was overcast, and the air was unusually cool for the time of year. I was happy to have the sweatshirt. We'd been the last to arrive, and that meant we had the longest walk. By the time we made it to the grave site, the principals were seated and the large crowd had closed around them. This was perfect for our purpose. We were able to stand at a distance and keep watch.

Ranger and I were shoulder to shoulder. Two professionals, doing a job. Problem was, one of the professionals didn't do well at funerals. I was a funeral basket case. Possibly the only thing I hated more than a gun was a funeral. They made me sad. *Really sad*. And the sadness had nothing to do with the deceased. I got weepy over perfect strangers.

The priest stood and repeated the Lord's Prayer and I felt my eyes well with tears. I concentrated on counting blades of grass at my feet, but the words intruded. I blinked the tears back and swung my thoughts to Bob. I tried to envision Bob hunching. He was going to hork up a sock. The tears ran down my cheeks. It was no good. Bob thoughts couldn't compete with the smell of fresh-turned earth and funeral flowers. "Shit," I whispered. And I sniffed back some snot.

Ranger turned to me. His brown eyes were curious and the corners of his mouth were tipped up ever so slightly. "Are you okay?" he asked.

I found a tissue in one of the sweatshirt pockets, and I blew my nose. "I'm fine. I just have this reaction to funerals!"

Several people on the outermost ring of mourners glanced our way.

Ranger put his arm around me. "You didn't like Mama Mac. You hardly knew her."

"It doesn't m-m-matter," I sobbed.

Ranger drew me closer. "Babe, we're starting to attract a lot of attention. Could you drop the sobbing down a level?"

"Ashes to ashes . . ." the priest said.

And I totally lost it. I slumped against Ranger and cried. He was wearing a windbreaker, and he wrapped me in the open windbreaker, hugging me in to him, his face pressed to the side of my head, shielding me as best he could from people turning to see the sobbing idiot. I was burrowed into him, trying to muffle the sobs, and I could feel him shaking with silent laughter.

"You're despicable," I hissed, giving him a punch in the chest. "Stop laughing. This is s-s-s-sad."

Several people turned and shushed me.

"It's okay," Ranger said, still silently laughing, arms wrapped tight around me. "Don't pay any attention to them. Just let it all out."

I hiccupped back a couple small sobs, and I wiped my nose with my sleeve. "This is nothing. You should see me at a parade when the drums and the flag go by."

Ranger cradled my face in his hands, using his thumbs to wipe the tears from my eyes. "The ceremony is over. Can you make it back to the car?"

I nodded. "I'm okay now. Am I red and blotchy from crying?"

"Yes," Ranger said, brushing a kiss across my forehead. "I love you anyway."

"There's all kinds of love," I said.

Ranger took me by the hand and led me back to the SUV. "This is the kind that doesn't call for a ring. But a condom might come in handy."

"That's not love," I told him. "That's lust."

He was scanning the crowd as we walked and talked, watching for Spiro, watching for anything unusual. "In this case, there's some of both."

"Just not the marrying type?"

We'd reached the car, and Ranger remoted it open. "Look at me, Babe. I'm carrying two guns and a knife. At this point in my life, I'm not exactly family material."

"Do you think that will change?"

Ranger opened the door for me. "Not anytime soon."

No surprise there. Still, it was a teeny, tiny bit of a downer. How scary is that?

"And there are things you don't know about me," Ranger said.

"What kind of things?"

"Things you don't *want* to know." Ranger rolled the

engine over and called Tank. "We're heading back," he said. "Anything on your end?"

The answer was obviously negative because Ranger disconnected and pulled into the stream of traffic. "Tank didn't see any bad guys, but it wasn't a total wash," Ranger said, handing his cell phone over to me. "I managed to take a picture for you while you were tucked into my jacket."

Ranger had a picture phone, exactly like the one I'd been issued. I went to the album option and brought up four photos of Anthony Barroni. The images were small. I chose one and waited while it filled the screen. Anthony appeared to be talking on his phone. Hold on, he wasn't talking . . . he was taking a picture. "Anthony's taking photos with his phone," I said. "Omigod, that's so creepy."

"Yeah," Ranger said. "Either Anthony's really into dead people or else he's sending photos to someone not fortunate enough to have a front-row seat."

"Spiro." Maybe.

Most of the cars left the cemetery and turned toward the Burg. The wake at Gina Macaroni's house would be packed. Anthony Barroni peeled away from the herd at Chambers Street. Ranger stuck to him, and we followed him to the store. He parked his Vette in the rear and sauntered inside.

"You should go talk to him," Ranger said. "Ask him if he had a good time."

"You're serious."

"Time to stir things up," Ranger said. "Let's raise the stakes for Anthony. Let him know he's blown his cover. See if anything happens."

I chewed on my lower lip. I didn't want to face Anthony. I didn't want to do this stuff anymore. "I'm an office worker," I said. "I think *you* should talk to him."

Ranger parked the SUV in front of the store. "We'll both talk to Anthony. Last time I left you alone in my car someone stole you."

It was early afternoon on a weekday, and there wasn't a lot of activity in the store. There was an old guy behind the counter, waiting on a woman who was buying a sponge mop. No other customers. Two of the Barroni brothers were working together, labeling a carton of nails in aisle four. Anthony was on his cell phone to the rear of the store. He was shuffling around, nodding his head and laughing.

I always enjoy watching Ranger stalk prey. He moves with single-minded purpose, his body relaxed, his gait even, his eyes unswerving and fixed on his quarry. The eye of the tiger.

I was one step behind Ranger, and I was thinking this wasn't a good idea. We could be wrong and look like idiots. Ranger never worried about that, but I worried about it constantly. Or we could be right, and we could set Anthony and Spiro off on a killing spree.

Anthony saw us approaching. He closed his phone and slipped it into his pants pocket. He looked to Ranger and then to me.

"Stephanie," he said, grinning. "Man, you were really bawling at the cemetery. Guess you got real broken up having Mama Melanoma blown to bits in your car."

"It was a touching ceremony," I said.

"Yeah," Anthony said, snorting and laughing. "The Lord's Prayer always gets to me, too."

Ranger extended his hand. "Carlos Manoso," he said. "I don't believe we've met."

Anthony shook Ranger's hand. "Anthony Barroni. What can I do for you? Need a plunger?"

Ranger gave him a small cordial smile. "We thought we'd stop by to say hello and see if Spiro liked the pictures."

"Waddaya mean?"

"It's too bad he couldn't have been there in person," Ranger said. "So much is lost in a photograph."

"I don't know what you're talking about."

"Sure you do," Ranger said. "You made a bad choice. And you're going to die because of it. You might want to talk to someone while there's still time."

"Someone?"

"The police," Ranger said. "They might be able to cut you a deal."

"I don't need a deal," Anthony said.

"He'll turn on you," Ranger said. "You made a bad choice for a partner."

"You should talk. Look who you've got for a partner. Little Miss Cry-Her-Eyes-Out." Anthony rubbed his eyes like he was crying. "Boohoohoo."

"This is embarrassing," I said. "I *hate* when I cry at funerals."

"Boohoo-ooo."

"Stop. That's enough," I said. "It's not funny."

"Boohoo boohoo boohoo."

So I punched him. It was one of those bypass-the-brain impulse actions. And it was a real sucker punch. Anthony never saw it coming. He had his hands to his eyes doing the boohoo thing, and I guess I threw all my fear and frustration into the punch. I heard his face crunch under my fist, and blood spurted out of his nose. I was so horrified I froze on the spot.

Ranger gave a bark of laughter and dragged me away so I didn't get splattered.

Anthony's eyes were wide, his mouth open, his hands clapped over his nose.

Ranger shoved a business card into Anthony's shirt pocket. "Call me if you want to talk."

We left the store and buckled ourselves into the Cayenne. Ranger turned the engine over and slid a glance my way. "I usually spar with Tank. Maybe next time I should get in the ring with you."

"It was a lucky punch."

Ranger had the full-on smile and there were little laugh lines at the corners of his eyes. "You're a fun date."

"Do you really think Spiro and Anthony are partners?"

"I think it's unlikely."

ELEVEN

I LEFT RANGER in the control room and hurried into my cubicle, anxious to finish running the check on Barroni. I came to a skidding stop when I saw my in-box. Seven new requests for computer background searches. All from Frederick Rodriguez.

I stuck my head out of my cubicle and yelled at Ranger. "Hey, who's this Frederick Rodriguez guy? He keeps filling up my in-box."

"He's in sales," Ranger said. "Let them sit. Work on Gorman."

I finished Barroni, printed his entire file, and dropped it into the drawer with Gorman and Lazar. I entered Jimmy Runion into the first search program and watched as information rushed onto my screen. I'd been scanning the searches as they appeared, taking notes, trying to find the one thing that bound them together in life and probably in death. So far, nothing had jumped out at me. There were a few things that were common to the men, but nothing significant. They were all approximately the same age. They had all owned small businesses. They were all married. When I finished Runion I'd take all the files and read through them more carefully.

I was halfway through Runion when my mom called on my cell.

"Where are you?" she wanted to know.

"I'm at work."

"It's five-thirty. We're supposed to be at the church for rehearsal. You were going to stop here first, and then we were all going over to the church. We've been waiting and waiting."

Crap! "I forgot."

"How could you forget? Your sister's getting married tomorrow. How could you forget?"

"I'm on my way. Give me twenty minutes."

"I'll take your grandmother with me. You can meet us at the church. You just bring Joseph and the cello."

"Joseph and the cello," I dumbly repeated.

"Everyone's waiting to hear you play."

"I might be late. There might not be time."

"We don't have to be at Marsillio's for the rehearsal dinner until seven-thirty. I'm sure there'll be time for you to practice your cello piece."

Crap. *Crap*. And *double crap!*

I grabbed my bag and took off, across the control room, down the stairs, into the garage. Ranger had just pulled in. He was getting out of his car as I ran to Morelli's SUV.

"I'm late!" I yelled to him. "I'm frigging late!"

"Of course you are," Ranger said, smiling.

◆ ◆ ◆

IT TOOK ME twelve minutes to get across town to the Burg and then into Morelli's neighborhood. I'd had to drive on the sidewalk once when there was traffic at a light. And I'd saved two blocks by using Mr. Fedorka's driveway and cutting through his backyard to the alley that led to Morelli's house.

I locked the SUV in the garage, ran into the house, into the living room.

"The wedding rehearsal is tonight," I yelled at Morelli. "The wedding rehearsal!"

Morelli was working his way through a bag of chips. "And?"

"And we have to be there. We're in the wedding party. It's my sister. I'm the maid of honor. You're the best man."

Morelli set the chips aside. "Tell me those aren't blood splatters on your shoes."

"I sort of punched Anthony Barroni in the nose."

"Anthony Barroni was at RangeMan?"

"It's a long story. I haven't time to go into it all. And you don't want to hear it anyway. It's . . . embarrassing." I had Bob clipped to his leash. "I'm taking Bob out, and then I'm going to help you get dressed." I dragged Bob out the back door and walked him around Morelli's yard. "Do you have to go, Bob?" I said. "Gotta tinkle? Gotta poop?"

Bob didn't want to tinkle or poop in Morelli's yard. Bob needed variety. Bob wanted to tinkle on Mrs. Rosario's hydrangea bush, two doors down.

"This is it!" I yelled at Bob. "You don't go here and you're holding it in until I get back from the stupid rehearsal dinner."

Bob wandered around a little and tinkled. I could tell he didn't have his heart in it, but it was good enough, so I dragged Bob inside, fed him some dog crunchies for dinner, and gave him some fresh water. I ran upstairs and got clothes for Morelli. Slacks, belt, button-down shirt. I ran back downstairs and shoved him into the shirt, and then realized he couldn't get the slacks over the cast. He was wearing gray sweatpants with one leg cut at thigh level.

"Okay," I said, "the sweats are good enough." I took a closer look. Pizza sauce on the long leg. Not good enough.

I ran upstairs and rummaged through Morelli's closet. Nothing I could use. I rifled his drawers. Nothing there. I went through the dirty clothes basket, found a pair of khaki shorts, and ran downstairs with them.

"Ta-*dah!*" I announced. "Shorts. And they're almost clean." I had Morelli out of his sweatpants in one fast swoop. I tugged the shorts up and zipped them.

"Jeez," Morelli said. "I can zip my own shorts."

"You weren't fast enough!" I looked at my watch. It was almost six o'clock! *Yikes*. "Put your foot on the coffee table, and I'll get shoes on you."

Morelli put his foot on the coffee table, and I stared up his shorts at Mr. Happy.

"Omigod," I said. "You're wearing boxers. I can see up your shorts."

"Do you like what you see?"

"Yes, but I don't want the world seeing it!"

"Don't worry about it," Morelli said. "I'll be careful."

I pulled a sock on Morelli's casted foot, and I laced a sneaker on the other. I raced upstairs, and I changed into a skirt and short-sleeved sweater. I threw my jean jacket over the sweater, grabbed my bag, got Morelli up on his crutches, and maneuvered him to the kitchen door.

"I hate to bring this up," Morelli said. "But aren't you supposed to take the cello?"

The cello. I squinched my eyes closed, and I rapped my head on the wall. *Thunk, thunk, thunk.* I took a second to breathe. I can do this, I told myself. Probably I can play a little something. How hard can it be? You just do the bowing thing back and forth and sounds come out. I might even turn out to be good at it. Heck, maybe I should take some lessons. Maybe I'm a natural talent and I don't even *need* lessons. The more I thought about it, the more logical it sounded. Maybe I was always meant to play the cello, and I'd just gotten sidetracked, and this was God's way of turning me in the direction of my true calling.

"Wait here," I said to Morelli. "I'll put the cello in the car, and I'll come back to get you."

I ran into the living room and hefted the cello. I carted it into the kitchen, past Morelli, out the door, and crossed the yard with it. I opened the garage door, rammed the cello into the back of the SUV, dropped my purse onto the driver's seat, and returned to the kitchen for Morelli. I realized he was just wearing a cotton shirt. No sweater on him. No jacket. And it was cold out. I ran upstairs and got a jacket. I helped him into the jacket, stuffed the crutches back under his arms, and helped him navigate through the back door and down the stairs.

We started to cross the yard, and the garage exploded with enough force to rattle the windows in Morelli's house.

The garage was wood with an asbestos-shingle roof. It hadn't been in the best of shape, and Morelli seldom used it. I'd been using it to keep the SUV bomb-free, but I now saw the flaw in the plan. It was an old garage without an automatic door opener. So to make things easier, I'd left the garage open when not in use. Easy to pull in and park. Also easy to sneak in and plant a bomb.

Morelli and I stood there, dumbstruck. His garage had gone up like fireworks and had come down like confetti. Splintered boards, shingles, and assorted car parts fell out of the sky into Morelli's yard. It was Mama Mac all over again. Almost nothing was left of the garage. Morelli's SUV was a fireball. His yard was littered with smoldering junk.

"Omigod!" I said. "The cello was in your SUV." I pumped my fist into the air and did a little dance. "*Yes!* Way to go! *Woohoo!* There is a God and He loves me. It's good-bye cello."

Morelli gave his head a shake. "You're a very strange woman."

"You're just trying to flatter me."

"Honey, my garage just blew up, and I don't think it was insured. We're supposed to be upset."

"Sorry. I'll try to look serious now."

Morelli glanced over at me. "You're still smiling."

"I can't help it. I'm trying to be scared and depressed, but it's just not working. I'm just so frigging relieved to be rid of that cello."

There were sirens screaming from all directions, and the first of the cop cars parked in the alley behind Morelli's house. I borrowed Morelli's cell phone and called my mother.

"Bad news," I said. "We're going to be late. We're having car trouble."

"How late? What's wrong with the car?"

"Real late. There's a lot wrong with the car."

"I'll send your father for you."

"Not necessary," I said. "Have the rehearsal without me, and I'll meet you at Marsillio's."

"You're the maid of honor. You have to be at the rehearsal. How will you know what to do?"

"I'll figure it out. This isn't my first wedding. I know the drill."

"But the cello . . ."

"You don't have to worry about that either." I didn't have the heart to tell her about the cello.

Two fire trucks pulled up to the garage. Emergency-vehicle strobes flashed up and down the alley, and headlights glared into Morelli's yard. The garage had been blown to smithereens, and the remaining parts had rained down over a three-house area. Some parts had smoked but none had flamed. The SUV had burned brightly but not long. So the fire had almost entirely extinguished itself before the first hose was unwound.

Ryan Laski crossed the yard and found Morelli. "I'm seeing a disturbing pattern here," Laski said. "Was anyone hurt . . . or vaporized?"

"Just property damage," Morelli said.

"I've sent some uniforms off to talk to neighbors. Hard to believe no one ever sees this guy. This isn't the sort of place where people mind their own business."

A mobile satellite truck for one of the local television stations cruised into the alley.

Laski cut his eyes to it. "This is going to be a big disappointment. I'm sure they're hoping for disintegrated bodies."

THERE'S SOMETHING HYPNOTIC about a disaster scene, and time moves in its own frame of reference, lost in a blur of sound and color. When the first fire truck rumbled away I looked at my watch and realized I had ten minutes to get to Marsillio's.

"The rehearsal dinner!" I said to Morelli. "I forgot about the rehearsal dinner."

Morelli was blankly staring at the charred remains of his garage and the blackened carcass of his SUV. "Just when you think things can't get any worse . . ."

"The rehearsal dinner won't be that bad." This was a blatant lie, but it didn't count since we both knew it was a blatant lie. "We need a car," I said. "Where's Laski? We can use his car."

"That's a department car. You can't borrow a department car to go to a rehearsal dinner."

I looked at my watch. Nine minutes! *Shit*. I didn't want to call anyone in the wedding party. I'd rather they read about this in the paper tomorrow. I didn't think Joe would be excited about getting a lift from Ranger. There was Lula, but it would take her too long to get here. I searched the crowd of people still milling around in Morelli's yard. "Help me out here, will you?" I said to Morelli. "I'm running down roads of blind panic."

"Maybe I can get someone to drop us off," Morelli said.

And then it came to me. Big Blue. "Wait a minute! I just had a brain flash. The Buick is still sitting in front of the house."

"You mean the Buick that's been sitting there unprotected? The Buick that's very likely booby-trapped?"

"Yeah, that one."

Now Morelli was seriously looking around. "I'm *sure* I can find someone . . ."

I could hear time ticking away. I looked down at my watch. Seven minutes. "I have seven minutes," I said to him.

"This is an extreme circumstance," Morelli said. "It's not every day someone blows up my garage. I'm sure your family will understand."

"They won't understand. This is an everyday occurrence for me."

"Good point," Morelli said. "But I'm not getting in the Buick. And you're not getting in it either."

"I'll be careful," I said. And I ran through the house, locking up behind myself. I got to the Buick, and I hesitated. I wasn't crazy about my life, but I wasn't ready to die. I especially didn't like the idea that my parts could be distributed over half the county. Okay, so what was stronger . . . my fear of death or my fear of not showing up at the rehearsal dinner? This one was a no-brainer. I unlocked the Buick, jumped behind the wheel, and shoved the key into the ignition. No explosion. I drove around the block, turned into the alley, and parked as close as I could to Morelli. I left the motor running and ran to retrieve him.

"You're a nut," he said.

"I looked it all over. I swear."

"You didn't. I know you didn't. You didn't have time. You just took a deep breath, closed your eyes, and got in."

"Five minutes!" I shrieked. "I've got five friggin' minutes. Are you going with me or what?"

"You're unglued."

"And?"

Morelli blew out a sigh and hobbled over to the Buick. I put the crutches in the trunk and loaded Morelli into the car with his back to the door, his casted leg stretched flat on the backseat.

"I guess you're not that unglued," Morelli said. "You just spared a few seconds to look up my pants leg again."

He was right. I'd taken a few seconds to look up his pants leg. I couldn't help myself. I liked the view.

I got behind the wheel and put my foot to the floor. When I reached the corner the Buick was rolling full-steam-ahead and I didn't want any unnecessary slowdowns, so I simply jumped the curb and cut across Mr. Jankowski's lawn. This was the hypotenuse is shorter than the sum of two sides school of driving, and the only thing I remember from high school trigonometry.

Morelli fell off the backseat when I jumped the curb, and a lot of creative cursing followed.

"Sorry," I yelled to Morelli. "We're late."

"You keep driving like this and we're going to be *dead*."

I got there with no minutes to spare. And there were no parking places. It was Friday night, and Marsillio's was packed.

"I'm dropping you off," I said.

"No."

"Yes! I'm going to have to park a mile away, and you can't walk with that cast." I double-parked, jumped out, and hauled Morelli out of the backseat. I gave him his crutches, and I left him standing on the curb while I ran inside and got Bobby V. and Alan. "Get him up the stairs and into the back room," I told them. "I'll be there in a minute."

I roared away, circling blocks, looking in vain for a place to park. I looked for five minutes and decided parking wasn't going to happen. So I parked in front of a fire hydrant. It was very close to Marsillio's, and if there was a fire I'd run out and move the car. Problem solved.

I rolled into the back room just as the antipasto was set on the table. I took my seat beside Morelli and shook out my napkin. I smiled at my mother. I smiled at Valerie. No one smiled back. I looked down the line at Kloughn. Kloughn smiled at me and waved. Kloughn was wasted. Drunk as a skunk. Grandma didn't look far behind.

Morelli leaned over and whispered in my ear. "Your ass is grass. Your mother's going to cut you off from pineapple upside-down cake."

• • •

"This is the big day," Morelli said.

I was slumped in a kitchen chair, staring at my mug of coffee. It was almost eight o'clock, and I wasn't looking forward to what lay in front of me. I was going to have to call my mom and tell her about the cello. Then I was going to have to give her the fire details. Then I was going to dress up like an eggplant and walk down the aisle in front of Valerie.

"Your big day, too," I said. "You're Albert's best man."

"Yeah, but I don't have to be a vegetable."

"You have to make sure he gets to the church."

"That could be a problem," Morelli said. "He wasn't looking good last night. I hate to be the bearer of bad news, but I don't think he's hot on marriage."

"He's confused. And he keeps having this nightmare about Valerie smothering him with her wedding gown."

Morelli was looking beyond me, out the back window to the place where he used to have a garage.

"Sorry about your garage," I said. "And your SUV."

"Tell you the truth, it wasn't much of a loss. The garage was falling apart. And the SUV was boring. Bob and I need something more fun. Maybe I'll buy a Hummer."

I couldn't see Morelli in a Hummer. I thought Morelli was more suited to his Duc. But of course, Bob couldn't ride on the Duc. "Your Ducati wasn't in the garage," I said. "Where's the Ducati?"

"Getting new pipes and custom paint. No rush now. By the time I get the cast off it'll be too cold to ride."

The phone rang and I froze. "Don't answer it."

Morelli looked at the caller ID and handed the phone over to me. "Guess who."

"Stephanie," my mother said. "I have terrible news. It's about your sister. She's gone."

"Gone? Gone where?"

"Disney World."

I covered the phone with my hand. "My mother's been drinking," I whispered to Morelli.

"I heard that," my mother said. "I haven't been drinking. For goodness sakes, it's eight o'clock in the morning."

"You have too been drinking," Grandma yelled from the background. "I saw you take a nip from the bottle in the cupboard."

"It was either that or kill myself," my mother said. "Your sister just called from the airport. She said they were all on a plane . . . Valerie, the three girls, and cuddle umpkins. And they were going to Disney World, and she had to disconnect because they were about to take off. I could hear the announcements over the phone. I sent your father over to her house, and it's all locked up."

"So there's no wedding?"

"No. She said she didn't lose enough weight. She said she was sixty pounds short. And then she said something about cuddle umpkins having an asthma attack from her wedding gown. I couldn't figure out what that was about."

"What about the reception? Is there a reception?"

"No."

"Never?"

"Never. She said if they liked Disney World they were going to live there and never return to Jersey."

"We should get the cake," I said. "Be a shame to waste the cake."

"At a time like this, you're thinking of cake? And what's wrong with your new cell phone?" my mother asked. "I tried to call you, and it's not working."

"It got blown up in Joe's garage."

"Be sure to give me your new number when you replace your phone," my mother said. "I'm sorry you didn't get to play the cello for everyone."

"Yeah, that would have been fun."

I disconnected and looked across the table at Morelli. "Valerie's going to Disney World."

"Good for her," Morelli said. "Guess that leaves the rest of the day open. It'll give you a chance to look up my pants leg again."

Here's a basic difference between Morelli and me. My first thought was always of cake. His first thought was always of sex. Don't get me wrong. I like sex . . . a lot. But it's never going to replace cake.

Morelli topped up our coffee. "What did your mother say when you told her about your cell phone?"

"She said I should tell her my new number when I got a new phone."

"That was it?"

"Pretty much. Guess your garage wasn't big news."

"Hard to top the Mama Macaroni explosion," Morelli said.

Last night, Morelli's garage had been cordoned off with crime-scene tape, and men were now carefully moving around inside the tape, gathering evidence, photographing the scene. A couple cop cars and crime-scene vans were parked in the alley. A few neighbors were standing, hands in pockets, watching at the edge of Morelli's yard.

I saw Laski cross the yard and come to the back door. Laski let himself in and put a white bakery bag on the table. "Doughnuts," he said. "You got coffee?"

Two uniforms followed Laski into the kitchen.

"Was that a bakery bag I saw come in here?" one of them asked.

I started a new pot of coffee going and excused myself. The house was going to be filled with cops today. Morelli wasn't going to need Nurse Stephanie. I took a shower, pulled my hair back into a half-assed ponytail, and dressed in black jeans, a black T-shirt, and the Pumas. I grabbed the jean jacket and the keys to the Buick and returned to the kitchen to give the good news to Morelli.

"I'm going to work," I told him. "I wasn't able to get through everything yesterday."

Our eyes held and I guess Morelli decided I was actually going in to work and not going in to boff Ranger. "Are you taking the Buick?"

"Yes."

"Let Ryan go over the car before you touch it."

That worked just fine for me. I wasn't in the mood to get exploded.

I HAD THREE complete files in front of me. Barroni, Gorman, and Lazar. I had Runion running on the first of the search programs. I had my pad half filled with notes, but so far, nothing had added up to anything resembling *a clue*.

I knew by the sudden silence that Ranger was in the control room. When the men were alone there was constant low-level chatter. When Ranger appeared there was silence. I rolled back so I could see into the room. Ranger was standing, quietly talking to Tank. He glanced my way and our eyes met. He finished his conversation with Tank, and he crossed the room to speak to me.

His hair was still damp from his shower, and when he entered my cubicle he brought the scent of warm Ranger and Bulgari shower gel with him. He leaned against my desk and looked down at me. "Aren't you supposed to be in a wedding?"

"Valerie took off for Disney World."

"Alone?"

"With Albert and the three kids. It's almost ten o'clock. Aren't you getting a late start? Have a late night?"

"I worked out this morning. I understand you had an interesting evening. You stopped sending signals abruptly at six-oh-four. We heard the fire and police request go out on the scanner at six-ten. Tank reported to me at six-twelve that there were no injuries. Next time call me, so I don't have to send a man out."

"Sorry. My phone went with the garage."

Ranger flipped my top drawer open. I'd left my gun and stun gun and pepper spray in the drawer overnight.

"I forgot to take them," I said.

"Forget them again, and you don't have a job."

"That's harsh."

"Yeah, but you can keep the key to my apartment."

TWELVE

RANGER TOOK MY pad and read through my notes. He looked over at the thick printouts on my desk. "Files on Barroni, Gorman, and Lazar?"

"Yes. I'm running Runion now. I think he fits the profile. If you haven't got anything better to do, you might go over the files for me. Maybe you'll see something I missed."

Ranger slouched in the chair next to me and started with Barroni.

I finished Runion a little after noon. I printed him out and pushed back from my station. Ranger looked over at me. He was on the third file.

"How long are you staying?" Ranger asked.

"As long as it takes. I'm going to the kitchen for a sandwich."

"Bring something back for me. I want to keep reading."

"Something?"

"Anything."

"You don't mean that. You have all these rules about eating. No fat. No sugar. No white bread."

"Babe, I don't keep things in my kitchen that I don't eat."

"You want tuna?"

"No. I don't want tuna."

"You see!"

Ranger put the file aside and stood. He crooked an arm around my neck, kissed the top of my head, and dragged me off to the kitchen. We got chicken salad on wheat, bottles of water, and a couple apples and oranges.

"No chips," I said. "Where are the chips?"

"I have chips upstairs in my apartment," Ranger said.

"Are you trying to lure me to your apartment with chips?"

Ranger smiled.

"Okay, tell me the truth. Do you really have chips?"

"There are some things a woman should find out for herself," Ranger said.

I thought that was as far as I wanted to go under the present circumstances. Going upstairs with Ranger, chips or no chips, was a complication I didn't think I could manage right now. So I returned his smile and carted my food back to the cubicle.

I was almost done rereading Runion when it hit me. The one possible thing that would tie the four men to each other. I looked over at Ranger and saw that he was watching me. Ranger had seen it, too. He was a step ahead of me.

"I haven't read Runion yet," Ranger said. "Tell me he was in the army."

"He was in the army."

"Thirty-six years ago he was stationed at Fort Dix."

"Bingo."

"A lot of people pass through Fort Dix," Ranger said. "But it feels good."

I agreed. It felt good. "I'm tired of sitting," I told him. "I think we need a field trip."

"Babe, you're not going to make me go to the mall, are you?"

"I was thinking more along the lines of doing some B and E on Anthony's house."

"I thought you were out of the B and E business."

"Here's the thing, someone keeps blowing up my cars, and it's getting old."

Ranger's cell rang. He answered it and passed it over to me. "It's Morelli," he said.

"I see you're working very closely with the boss," Morelli said.

"Don't start."

"I heard from the crime lab. The bomb was inside the garage, next to a wall, halfway to the rear. It was manually detonated."

"Like the Mama Macaroni bomb."

"Exactly. They found another interesting piece of equipment. Did you know you were being tracked?"

"Yes."

"And last but not least, your mother called and said she was having meatballs and wedding cake for dinner."

"I'll pick you up at six."

"It's amazing what you'll do for a piece of cake," Morelli said.

I gave the phone back to Ranger. "He could have killed me, but he didn't."

"Morelli?"

"The bomber. The bomb was detonated manually, like the bomb that killed Mama Macaroni."

"So this guy is still taking risks to play with you."

"I guess I can sort of understand his motivation. If he thinks I ruined his life, his face, maybe he wants to torment me."

"The notes felt real. The sniping felt real. The first car bomb made sense to me. They were all consistent with increasing harassment and intimidation. After the Mama Macaroni bombing he loses me."

"What's your theory?"

"I don't have a theory. I just think it feels off."

"Do you think there's a copy cat?"

"Possible, but you'd think the crime lab would have noticed differences in the bomb construction." Ranger slid the files into my file cabinet. "Let's roll. If we're going to break into Anthony's house we want to do it before the store closes and he comes home."

I grabbed my jean jacket and got halfway out of my cubby when I was yanked back by my ponytail.

"What did you forget?" Ranger asked.

"My orange?"

"Your gun."

I blew out a sigh, took the gun out of my desk drawer, and then didn't know what to do with it. If I carry a gun, I almost always carry it in my purse, but guess what, no purse. My purse was a cinder in what was left of Morelli's SUV.

Ranger took the gun, pulled me flat against him, and slid the gun under the waistband of my jeans, so that it was nestled at the small of my back.

"This is uncomfortable," I said. "It's going to give me a bruise."

Ranger reached around and removed the gun. And before I realized what he was doing, he had the gun tucked into the front of my jeans at my hipbone. "Is this better?"

"No, but I can't imagine where you'll put it next, so let's just leave it where it is and forget about it."

We rode the elevator to the garage, and Ranger confiscated one of the black Explorers normally set aside for his crew. "Less memorable than a Porsche," he said. "In case we set off an alarm."

We got into the Explorer, and I couldn't sit with the gun rammed into my pants. "I can't do this," I said to Ranger. "This dumb gun is too big. It's poking me."

Ranger closed his eyes and rested his forehead against the wheel. "I can't believe I hired you."

"Hey, it's not my fault. You picked out a bad gun."

"Okay," he said, swiveling to face me. "Where's it poking you?"

"It's poking me in my . . . you know."

"No. I don't know."

"My pubic area."

"Your pubic area?"

I could tell he was struggling with some sort of emotion. Either he was trying hard not to laugh or else he was trying hard not to choke me.

"Give me the gun," Ranger said.

I extracted the gun from my pants and handed it over.

Ranger held the gun in the palm of his hand and smiled. "It's warm," he said. He put the gun in the glove compartment and plugged the key into the ignition.

"Am I fired?"

"No. Any woman who can heat up a gun like that is worth keeping around."

In twenty minutes we were parked across the street and two houses down from Anthony. Ranger cut the engine and dialed Anthony's home number. No answer.

"Try the door," he said to me. "If someone opens it tell them you're selling Girl Scout cookies and keep them talking until I call you. I'm going in through the back. I'm parking one street over."

I swung out of the Explorer and watched Ranger drive away. I waited a couple minutes and then I crossed the street, marched up to Anthony's front door, and rang the bell. Nothing. I rang again and listened. I didn't hear any activity inside. No television. No footsteps. No dog barking. I was about to ring a third time when the door opened, and Ranger motioned me in. I followed him to the second floor, and we methodically worked our way through all three levels.

"I don't see any evidence of a second person living here," Ranger said when we reached the basement.

"This is a real bummer," I said. "No books on how to build a bomb. No sniper rifles. No dirty underwear with 'Spiro' embroidered on it."

We were in the kitchen and only the garage remained. We knew there was something in the garage because Anthony never parked his fancy new Vette there. Ranger drew his gun and opened the door that led to the garage, and we both looked in at wall-to-wall boxes. Never-been-opened cartons containing toaster ovens, ceiling fans, nails, duct tape, grout guns, electric screwdrivers.

"I think the little jerk is stealing from his brothers," I said to Ranger.

"I think you're right. There'd be larger quantities of single items if he was hijacking trucks or legally storing inventory. This looks like he randomly fills his trunk every night when he leaves."

We backed out and closed the garage door.

Ranger looked at his watch. "We have a little time. Let's see what he's got on his computer."

Anthony had a small office on the first floor. Cherry built-ins lined the walls, but Anthony hadn't yet filled them with books or objets d'art. The cherry desk was large and masculine. The cushy desk chair was black leather. The desktop held a phone, a computer and keyboard, and small printer.

Ranger sat in the chair and turned the computer on. A strip of icons appeared on the screen. Ranger hit one of the icons and Anthony's e-mail program opened. Ranger scrolled through new mail and sent mail and deleted mail. Not much there. Anthony didn't do a lot of e-mailing. Ranger opened Anthony's address book. No Spiro listed. Ranger closed the program and tried another icon.

"Let's see what he surfs," Ranger said. He went to the bookmarked sites. They were all porn.

Ranger closed the program and returned his attention to the icon strip. He hit iPhoto and worked his way through the photo library. There were a couple pictures of Anthony's Vette. A couple pictures of the front of his town house. And three photos from the Macaroni funeral. The quality wasn't great since they were downloaded from his phone, but the subject matter was clear. He'd been taking pictures of Carol Zambelli's hooters. Zambelli had just purchased the set, and couldn't get her coat closed at the graveside.

Ranger shut the computer down. "Time to get out of here."

We left through the back door and followed a bike path through common ground to the street. Ranger remoted the SUV open, we buckled ourselves in, and Ranger hung a U-turn and headed back to the office.

"This trip doesn't take Anthony Barroni out of the picture," Ranger said, "but it definitely back-burners him."

We pulled into the RangeMan garage at five-thirty. Ranger parked and walked me to the Buick. "You have a half hour to get to Morelli. Where are you taking him?"

"We're having dinner with my parents. They have wedding cake for two hundred."

"ISN'T THIS NICE," my mother said, glass in hand, amber liquid swirling to the rim, stopping just short of sloshing onto the white tablecloth. "It's so quiet. I hardly have a headache."

Two leaves had been taken out of the dining room table, and the small dining room seemed strangely spacious. The table had been set for five. My mother and father sat at either end, and Morelli and I sat side by side and across from Grandma, who was lost behind the massive three-tier wedding cake that had been placed in the middle of the table.

"I was looking forward to a party," Grandma said. "If it was me, I would have had the reception anyway. I bet nobody would even have noticed Valerie wasn't there. You could have just told everybody she was in the ladies' room."

Morelli and my father had their plates heaped with meatballs, but I went straight for the cake. My mother was going with a liquid diet, and I wasn't sure what Grandma was eating since I couldn't see her.

"Valerie called when they got off the plane in Orlando, and she said Albert was breathing better, and the panic attacks were not nearly as severe," my mother said.

My father smiled to himself and mumbled something that sounded like "friggin' genius."

"How'd Sally take the news?" I asked my mother. "He must have been upset."

"He was upset at first, but then he asked if he could have the wedding gown. He thought he could have it altered so he could wear it onstage. He thought it would give him a new look."

"You gotta credit him," Grandma said. "Sally's always thinking. He's a smart one."

I had the cake knife in hand. "Anyone want cake?"

"Yeah," Morelli said, shoving his plate forward. "Hit me."

"I heard your garage got blown up," Grandma said to Morelli. "Emma Rhinehart said it went up like a bottle rocket. She heard that from her son, Chester. Chester delivers pizza for that new place on Keene Street, and he was making a delivery a couple houses down from you. He said he was taking a shortcut through the alley, and all of a sudden the garage went up like a bottle rocket. Right in front of him. He said it was real scary because he almost hit this guy who was standing in the alley just past your house. He said the guy looked like his face had melted or something. Like some horror movie."

Morelli and I exchanged glances, and we were both thinking *Spiro*.

An hour later, I helped Morelli hobble down the porch stairs and cross the lawn. I'd parked the Buick in the driveway, and I'd bribed one of the neighborhood kids into baby-sitting the car. I loaded Morelli into the car, gave the kid five dollars, and ran back to the house for my share of the leftovers.

My mother had bagged some meatballs for me, and now she was standing in front of the cake. She had a cardboard box on the chair and a knife in her hand. "How much do you want?" she asked.

Grandma was standing beside my mother. "Maybe you should let me cut the cake," Grandma said. "You're tipsy."

"I'm not tipsy," my mother said, very carefully forming her words.

It was true. My mother wasn't tipsy. My mother was shit-faced.

"I tell you, we're lucky if we don't find ourselves talking to Dr. Phil one of these days," Grandma said.

"I like Dr. Phil," my mother said. "He's cute. I wouldn't mind spending some time with him, if you know what I mean."

"I know what you mean," Grandma said. "And it gives me the creeps."

"So how much of the cake do you want?" my mother asked me again. "You want the whole thing?"

"You don't want the whole thing," Grandma said to

me. "You'll give yourself the diabetes. You and your mother got no control."

"Excuse me?" my mother said. "No control? Did you say I had no control? I am the queen of control. Look at this family. I have a daughter in Disney World with oogly woogly smoochikins. I have a granddaughter who thinks she's a horse. I have a mother who thinks she's a teenager." My mother turned to me. "And you! I don't know where to begin."

"I'm not so bad," I said. "I'm taking charge of my life. I'm making changes."

"You're a walking disaster," my mother said. "And you just ate seven pieces of cake."

"I didn't!"

"You did. You're a cakeaholic."

"I don't mind thinking I'm a teenager," Grandma said. "Better than thinking I'm an old lady. Maybe I should get a boob job, and then I could wear them sex-kitten clothes."

"Good God," my mother said. And she drained her glass.

"I'm not a cakeaholic," I said. "I only eat cake on special occasions." Like Monday, Tuesday, Wednesday, Thursday . . .

"You're one of them comfort eaters," Grandma said. "I saw a show about it on television. When your mother gets stressed, she irons and tipples. When you get stressed, you eat cake. You're a cake abuser. You need to join one of them help groups, like Cake Eaters Anonymous."

My mother sliced into the cake and carved off a

chunk for herself. "Cake Eaters Anonymous," she said. "That's a good one." She took a big bite of the cake and got a smudge of icing on her nose.

"You got icing on your nose," Grandma said.

"Do not," my mother said.

"Do, too," Grandma Mazur said. "You're three sheets to the wind."

"Take that back," my mother said, swiping her finger through the frosting on the top tier and flicking a glob at Grandma Mazur. The glob hit Grandma in the forehead and slid halfway down her nose. "Now you've got icing on your nose, too," my mother said.

Grandma sucked in some air.

My mother flicked another glob at Grandma.

"That's it," Grandma said, narrowing her eyes. "Eat dirt and die!" And Grandma scooped up a wad of cake and icing and smushed it into my mother's face.

"I can't see!" my mother shrieked. "I'm blind." She was wobbling around, flailing her arms. She lost her balance and fell against the table and into the cake.

"I tell you it's pathetic," Grandma said. "I don't know how I raised a daughter that don't even know how to have a food fight. And look at this, she fell into a three-tiered wedding cake. This is gonna put a real crimp in the leftovers." She reached out to help my mother, and my mother latched on to Grandma and wrestled her onto the table.

"You're going down, old woman," my mother said to Grandma.

Grandma yelped and struggled to scramble away, but she couldn't get a grip. She was as slick as a greased pig, in lard icing up to her elbows.

"Maybe you should stop before someone falls and gets hurt," I told them.

"Maybe you should mind your own beeswax," Grandma said, mashing cake into my mother's hair.

"Hey, wait a minute," my mother said. "Stephanie didn't get her cake."

They both paused and looked over at me.

"How much cake did you want?" my mother asked. "This much?" And she threw a wad of cake at me.

I jumped to dodge the cake, but I wasn't quick enough, and it caught me in the middle of the chest. Grandma nailed me in the side of my head, and before I could move she got me a second time.

My father came in from the living room. "What the devil?" he said.

Splat, splat, splat. They got my father.

"Jesus Marie," he said. "What are you, friggin' nuts? That's good wedding cake. You know how much I paid for that cake?"

My mother threw one last piece of cake. It missed my father and hit the wall.

I had cake and icing in my hair, on my hands and arms, on my shirt, my face, my jeans. I looked over at the cake plate. It was empty. The aroma of sugar and butter and vanilla was enticing. I swiped at the cake sliding down the wall and stuck my finger in my mouth. If I'd been alone I probably would have licked the wall. My mother was right. I was a cakeaholic.

"Boy," my grandmother said to my mother. "You're fun when you've got a snootful."

My mother looked around the room. "Do you think that's how this happened?"

"Do you think you'd do this if you were sober?" Grandma asked. "I don't think so. You got a real stick up your ass when you're sober."

"That's it," my mother said. "I'm done tippling."

I caught myself licking cake off my arm. "And maybe I should cut back on the cake," I said. "I *do* feel a little addicted."

"We'll have a pact," my mother said. "No more tippling for me and no more cake for you."

We looked at Grandma.

"I'm not giving up nothing," Grandma said.

I took my bag of meatballs and went out to the car. I slid behind the wheel, turned the key in the ignition, and Morelli leaned over the seat at me.

"What the hell happened to you?" he asked.

"Food fight."

"Wedding cake?"

"Yep."

Morelli licked icing off my neck, and I accidentally jumped the driveway and backed out over my parents' front lawn.

"OKAY, LET ME get this correct," Morelli said. "You're giving up sweets."

We were sitting at Morelli's kitchen table, having a late breakfast.

"If it's got sugar on it, I'm not eating it," I told Morelli.

"What about that cereal you've got in front of you?"

"Frosted Flakes. My favorite."

"Coated with sugar."

Shit. "Maybe I got carried away last night. Maybe I was overreacting to Valerie gaining all that weight, and then Kloughn dreaming about her smothering him. And my mother said I ate seven pieces of wedding cake, but I don't actually remember eating anything. I think she must have been exaggerating."

Morelli's phone rang. He answered and passed it to me. "Your grandmother."

"Boy, that was some mess we made last night," Grandma said. "We're gonna have to put up new paper in the dining room. It was worth it, though. Your mother got up this morning and cleaned the bottles out of the cupboard. 'Course, I still got one in my closet, but that's okay on account of I can handle my liquor. I'm not one of them anxiety-ridden drunks. I just drink because I like it. Anyway, your mother's not drinking so long as you're off the sugar. You're off the sugar, right?"

"Right. Absolutely. No sugar for me."

I gave the phone back to Morelli, and I went to look in the cupboard. "Do we have cereal that's not coated with sugar?"

"We have bagels and English muffins."

I popped a bagel into the toaster and drank coffee while I waited. "Ranger thinks some of the bombings feel off."

"I agree," Morelli said. "Laski's double-checking the crime-lab reports to make sure we don't have an opportunist at work. And I left a message for him to talk to Chester Rhinehart. So far Chester's the only other person besides you to see Spiro."

"So, what's up for today? How's your leg?"

"The leg is a lot better. No pain. My foot isn't swollen."

There was a lot of loud knocking on the front door. I grabbed my bagel and went to investigate.

It was Lula, dressed in a poison green tank and spandex jeans with rhinestones running down the side seam. "I heard about the wedding," Lula said. "I bet your mama had a cow. Imagine having to call all those people and tell them they're on their own for burgers tonight. But there's some good news in all this, right? You didn't have to go parading around like a freakin' eggplant."

"It all worked out for the best," I said.

"Damn skippy. Glad you feel that way. Wouldn't want you to be in a bad mood since I need a little help."

"Oh boy."

"It's just a little help. Moral support. But you can jump in on the physical stuff if you want. Not that I expect anyone's gonna shoot at us or anything."

"No. Whatever it is . . . I'm not doing it."

"You don't mean that. I can see you don't mean that. Where's Officer Hottie? He in the kitchen?" Lula swept past me and went in search of Morelli. "Hey," she said to him. "How's it shakin'? You don't mind if I borrow Stephanie today, do you?"

"He does," I said. "We were going to do something . . ."

"Actually, it's Guy Day," Morelli said to me. "I promised the guys we could hang out today."

"You hung out with the guys yesterday. And the day before."

"Those were cop guys. These are just guy guys. My

brother Tony and my cousin Mooch. They're coming over to watch the game."

"Lucky for you I came along," Lula said to me. "You would have had to hide upstairs in your room so you didn't ruin Guy Day."

"You can stay and watch the game with us," Morelli said to me. "It's not like it's a stag party. It's just Tony and Mooch."

"Yeah," Lula said. "They probably be happy to have someone do the pizza run and open their beer bottles for them."

"Think I'll pass on Guy Day," I said to Morelli. "But thanks for inviting me." I grabbed my jacket and followed Lula out to the Firebird. "Who are we looking for?"

"I'm gonna take another shot at Willie Martin. I'm gonna keep my clothes on this time. I'm gonna nail his ass."

"He didn't leave town?"

"He's such an arrogant so-and-so. He thinks he's safe. He thinks no one can touch him. He's still in his cheap-ass apartment over the garage. My friend Lauralene made a business call on him last night. Do you believe it?"

In a former life, Lula was a 'ho, and she still has a lot of friends in the industry. "Is Lauralene still there?"

"No. Willie's too cheap to pay for a night. Willie's strictly pay by the job."

We crossed town, turned onto Stark, and Lula parked in front of the garage. We both looked up at Willie's apartment windows on the third floor.

"You got a gun?" Lula asked.

"No."

"Stun gun?"

"No."

"Cuffs?"

"Negative."

"I swear, I don't know why I brought you."

"To make sure you keep your clothes on," I said.

"Yeah, that would be it."

We got out of the Firebird and took the stairs. The air was foul, reeking of urine and stale fast-food burgers and fries. We got to the third-floor landing, and Lula started arranging her equipment. Gun shoved into the waistband of her jeans. Cuffs half out of her pocket. Stun gun rammed into her jeans at the small of her back. Pepper spray in hand.

"Where's the Taser?" I asked.

"It's in my purse." She rooted around in her big shoulder bag and found the Taser. "I haven't had a chance to test-drive this baby yet, but I think I could figure it out. How hard can it be, right?" She powered up and held on to the Taser. She motioned me to the door. "Go ahead and knock."

"Me?"

"He won't open the door if it's me. I'm gonna hide to the side, here. He see a skinny white girl like you standing at his door, he's gonna get all excited and open up."

"He'd better not get *too* excited."

"Hell, the more excited the better. Slow him down running. Make him do some pole vaulting."

I rapped on the door, and I stood where Martin could see me. The door opened, and he looked me over.

"I don't know what you're selling, but I might be willing to buy it," Willie said.

"Boy, that's real original," I said, walking into his apartment. "I bet you had a hard time coming up with that one."

"Wadda ya mean?"

I turned to face him. Was he really that dumb? I looked into his eyes and decided the answer was yes. And the frightening part is that he outsmarted Lula last time she tried to snag him. Best not to dwell on that realization. The door was still open, and I could see Lula creeping forward behind Willie Martin. She had pepper spray in one hand and the Taser in the other.

"I was actually looking for Andy Bartok," I said to Martin. "This is his apartment, right?"

"This is my apartment. There's no Andy here. Do you know who I am? You follow football?"

"No," I said, putting the couch between me and Martin. "I don't like violent sports."

"I like violent sports," Lula said. "I like the sport called kick Willie Martin in his big ugly blubber butt."

Martin turned to Lula. "You! Guess you didn't get enough of Will Martin, hunh? Guess you came back for more. And look at this here present you brought me . . . a candy-ass white woman."

"The only thing I brought you is a ticket to the lockup," Lula said. "I'm hauling your nasty blubber butt off to jail."

"I haven't got no blubber butt," Martin said. He

turned again so he could moon Lula, and he dropped his drawers to prove his point.

I was standing in front of him so I got the pole-vaulting demonstration. Lula got the rear view, and whether it was intentional or just a jerk-action reflex was hard to say, but Lula shot Martin in the ass with the Taser.

Martin went down with his pants at half-mast and flopped around on the floor, twitching on the Taser line like a fresh-caught fish.

"Get your finger off the button," I yelled to Lula. "You're going to kill him!"

"Oops," Lula said. "Guess I should have read the instruction book."

Martin was facedown, doing shallow breathing. He was about six foot five and close to three hundred pounds. I had no idea how we were going to get him to the Firebird.

"I'll cuff him, and you pull his pants up," Lula said.

"Good try, but this is your party. I'm not doing pants wrangling."

"The bounty hunter assistant is supposed to take orders," Lula said.

I cut my eyes to her.

"Of course, that don't count for you," she said. "On account of you're not an official assistant. You're the . . ."

"The friend of the bounty hunter," I said.

"Yeah, that's it. The friend of the bounty hunter. How about you cuff him, and I'll get his pants up."

I took the cuffs from Lula. "Works for me."

I cuffed Martin's hands behind his back and stepped away, and Lula straddled him and yanked the Taser leads off. By the time she got his pants up, she was sweating.

"Usually I'm taking pants *off* a man," Lula said. "It's a lot more work getting them up than down."

Especially when you're wrestling them up the equivalent of a 280-pound sandbag.

Willie had one eye open, and he was making some low-level gurgling sounds.

"He's gonna be pissed off when he comes around," Lula said. "I'm thinking we want to get him into the car before that happens."

"I'd feel a lot better about this if you had ankle shackles," I said.

"I forgot ankle shackles."

I grabbed a foot and Lula grabbed a foot, and we threw our weight into dragging Martin to the door. We got him through the door and onto the cement landing and realized we were going to have to use the rickety freight elevator.

"It's probably okay," Lula said, pushing the button.

I closed and locked Martin's door. I repeated Lula's words. It's probably okay. It's probably okay.

The elevator made a lot of grinding, clanking noises, and we could see it shudder as it rose from the bottom floor.

"It's just three floors," Lula said, more to herself than to me. "Three floors isn't a whole lot, right? Probably you could jump from three floors if you had to. Remember when you fell off that fire escape? That was three floors, right?"

"Two floors by the time I actually started free falling." And it knocked me out and hurt like hell.

The open-air car came to a lurching stop three inches below floor level. Lula struggled with the grate and finally got it half open.

"You got the least weight," Lula said. "You go in first and see if it holds you."

I gingerly got into the cage. It swayed slightly but held. "Feels okay," I said.

Lula crept in. "See, this is gonna be fine," Lula said, standing very still. "This is one sturdy-ass elevator. You give this elevator a coat of paint and it'll be like new."

The elevator groaned and dropped two inches.

"Just settling in," Lula said. "I'm sure it's fine. I could see this is a real safe elevator. Still, maybe we should get off and reconsider our options."

Lula took a step forward and the elevator went into a downslide, banging against the side of the building, groaning and screeching. It reached the second floor and the bottom dropped out from under us. Lula and I hit the ground level and lay there stunned, knocked breathless, with rust sifting down on us like fairy dust.

"Fuck," Lula said. "Take a look at me and tell me if anything's broken."

I got to my hands and knees and crawled out of the elevator. It was Sunday and the garage was closed, thank God. At least we didn't have an audience. And probably the guys who worked in the garage wouldn't be real helpful when it came to capturing Martin. Lula crawled out after me, and we slowly got to our feet.

"I feel like a truck rolled over me," Lula said. "That

was a dumb idea to take the elevator. You're supposed to stop me from acting on those dumb ideas."

I tried to dust some of the rust and elevator grit off my jeans, but it was sticking like it was glued on. "I don't know how to break this to you," I said. "But your FTA is still on the third floor."

THIRTEEN

"WE'RE JUST GONNA have to carry Willie down the stairs," Lula said. "I got him cuffed. I'm not giving up now."

"We can't carry him. He's too heavy."

"Then we'll drag him. Okay, so he might get a little bruised, but we'll say we were walking him down and he slipped. That happens, right? People fall down the stairs all the time. Look at us, we just fell down an elevator, and are we complaining?"

We were standing next to a stack of tires that were loaded onto a hand truck. "Maybe we could use this hand truck," I said. "We could strap Martin on like a refrigerator. It'll be hard to get him down the two flights of stairs, but at least we won't crack his head open."

"That's a good idea," Lula said. "I was just going to think of that idea."

We off-loaded the tires and carted the truck up the stairs. Martin was still out. He was drooling and his expression was dazed, but his breathing had normalized, and he now had both eyes open. We laid the hand truck flat and rolled Martin onto it. I'd brought about thirty feet of strapping up with the hand truck, and we wrapped Martin onto the truck until he looked like a mummy. Then we pushed and pulled until we had Martin and the truck upright.

"Now we're going to ease him down, one step at a time," I said to Lula. "We're both going to get a grip on the truck, and between the two of us we should be able to do this."

By the time we got Martin to the second-floor landing we were soaked through. The air in the stairwell was hot and stagnant, and lowering Martin down the stairs one at a time was hard work. My hands were raw from gripping the strapping and my back ached. We stopped to catch our breath, and I saw Martin's fingers twitch. Not a good sign. I didn't want him struggling to get free on the next set of stairs.

"We have to get moving," I said to Lula. "He's coming around."

"I'm coming around, too," Lula said. "I'm having a heart attack. I think I gave myself a hernia. And look . . . I broke a nail. It was my best nail, too. It was the one with the stars and stripes decal."

We shifted the hand truck into position to take the first step, and Martin turned his head and looked me in the eye.

"What the . . ." he said. And then he went nuts, yelling and struggling against the strapping. He was crazy-eyed and a vein was popped out in his forehead. I was having a hard time hanging on to the hand truck, and I was watching the strapping around his chest go loose and show signs of unraveling.

"The stun gun," I yelled to Lula. "Give him a jolt with the stun gun. I can't hang on with him struggling like this."

Lula reached around back for the stun gun and came up empty. "Must have fallen out when the elevator crashed," she said.

"Do something! The strap is unraveling. Shoot him. Zap him. Kick him in the nuts. *Do something! Anything!*"

"I got my spray!" Lula said. "Stand back, and I'll spray the snot out of him."

"No!" I shrieked. "Don't spray in the stairwell!"

"It's okay, I got plenty," Lula said.

She hit the button, and I got a faceful of pepper spray. Martin gave an enraged bellow and wrenched the hand truck away from Lula and me. I was blinded and gagging, and I could hear the hand truck banging down the stairs like a toboggan. There was some scuffling at ground level, the door opened, and then it was quiet at the bottom of the stairs. At the top of the stairs, Lula and I were gasping for breath, feeling our way down, trying to get away from the droplets that were still hanging in the torpid air on the second-floor landing.

We stumbled over the hand truck when we got to the bottom. We pushed through the door and stood bent at the waist, waiting for the mucus production to slow, eyes closed and tearing, nose running.

"Guess pepper spray wasn't a good idea," Lula finally said.

I blew my nose in my T-shirt and tried to blink my eyes clear. I didn't want to touch them with my hand in case I still had some spray left on my skin. Martin was nowhere to be seen. The wrapping was in a heap on the sidewalk.

"You don't look too good," Lula said. "You're all red and blotchy. I'm probably red and blotchy, too, but I got superior skin tone. You got that pasty white stuff that only looks good after you get a facial and put on makeup."

We were squinting, not able to fully open our eyes, my throat burned like fire, and I was a mucus factory.

"I need to wash my hands and my face," I said. "I have to get this stuff off me."

We got into Lula's Firebird, and Lula crept down Stark to Olden. She turned on Olden and somehow the Firebird found its way to a McDonald's. We parked and dragged ourselves into the ladies' room.

I stuck my entire head under the faucet. I washed my face and hair and hands as best I could, and I dried my hair under the hot-air hand dryer.

"You're a little scary," Lula said. "You got a white-woman-Afro thing going."

I didn't care. I shuffled out of the ladies' room and got a cheeseburger, fries, and a bottle of water.

Lula sat across from me. She had a mountain of food and a gallon of soda. "What's with you?" she wanted to know. "Where's your soda? Where's your pie? You gotta have a pie when you come here."

"No soda and no pie. I'm off sweets."

"What about cake? What about doughnuts?"

"No cake. No doughnuts."

"You can't do that. You need cake and doughnuts. That's your comfort food. That's your stress buster. You don't eat cake and doughnuts, and you'll get all clogged up."

"I made a deal with my mother. She's off the booze as long as I'm off the sugar."

"That's a bad deal. You're not good at that deprivation stuff. You're like a big jelly doughnut. You give it a squeeze and the jelly squishes out. You don't let it squish out where it wants and it's gotta find a new place to squish out. Remember when your love life was in the toilet and you weren't getting any? You were eating bags of candy bars. You're a compensator. Some people can hold their jelly in, but not you. Your jelly gotta squish out somewhere."

"You've got to stop talking about doughnuts. You're making me hungry."

"See, that's what I'm telling you. You're one of them hungry people. You deprive yourself of cake and you're gonna want to eat something else."

I shoved some fries into my mouth and crooked an eyebrow at Lula.

"You know what I'm saying," Lula said. "You better be careful, or you'll send Officer Hottie to the emergency room. And you're working for Ranger now. How're you gonna keep from taking a bite outta that? He's just one big hot sexy doughnut far as I'm concerned."

"What are you going to do about Willie Martin?"

"I don't know. I'm gonna have to think about it. Taking him down in his apartment doesn't seem to be working."

"Does he have a job?"

"Yeah, he works nights, stealing cars and hijacking trucks."

I drained my bottle of water and bundled my trash. "I need to go back to Morelli's house and get out of these clothes. Call me when you get a new plan for Martin."

"You mean you'd go out with me again?"

"Yeah." Go figure that. Truth is, it was getting pretty obvious that being a bounty hunter wasn't the problem. In fact, maybe being a bounty hunter was the solution. At least I'd acquired a few survival skills. When trouble followed me home I was able to cope. I was never going to be Ranger, but I wasn't Ms. Wimp either.

THERE WERE A bunch of cars parked in front of Morelli's house when Lula dropped me off.

"You sure you want to go in there?" Lula asked. "Looks like it's still Guy Day."

"I don't care what day it is. I'm beat. I want to take a shower, get into clean clothes, and turn into a couch potato."

I straggled into the house and found five guys slouched in front of the television. I knew them all. Mooch, Tony, Joe, Stanley Skulnik, and Ray Daily. There were pizza boxes, boxes of doughnuts, discarded candy bar wrappers, beer bottles, and chip bags on the coffee table. Bob was sound asleep on the floor by Morelli. He had orange Cheez Doodle dust on his nose, and a red jelly bean stuck in the fur on his ear. Everyone but Bob was eyes glued to the television. They all turned and stared at me when I walked into the room.

"How's it going?" Mooch said.

"Looking good," Stanley said.

"Yo," from Tony.

"Long time no see," Ray said.

And they turned back to the game.

I had hair from hell, I'd blown my nose in my shirt, I was covered with rust and crud, my jeans were torn, and I was holding a roll of toilet paper from McDonald's, and no one noticed. Not that I was surprised by this. After all, these guys were from the Burg, and a game was on television.

Morelli continued to stare after the others had turned away.

"Fell down an elevator shaft and got sprayed with pepper spray," I said to him. "Picked up the toilet paper at McDonald's."

"And you're okay?"

I nodded.

"Could you get me a cold one?"

I GOT INTO the shower and stood there until there was no more hot water. I got dressed in Morelli's sweats, blasted my hair with the dryer, and crawled into bed. It was close to seven when I woke up. The house was quiet. I shuffled into the bathroom, glanced in the mirror, and realized there was a note pinned to my sweatshirt.

WENT OUT TO EAT WITH MOOCH AND TONY. DIDN'T WANT TO WAKE YOU. CALL MY CELL IF YOU WANT ME TO BRING SOMETHING HOME. THERE'S LEFTOVER PIZZA IN THE FRIDGE.

Apparently Guy Day continued into Guy Night. I shuffled downstairs and ate the leftover pizza. I washed it down with a Bud. I checked out the doughnut box. Three doughnuts left in the box. I blew out a sigh. I wanted a doughnut. I paced in the kitchen. I finished off a bag of chips. I drank another Bud. I couldn't stop thinking about the doughnuts. It's only been one friggin' day, I thought. Surely I can make it through one lousy day without a doughnut. I went to the living room and remoted the television. I flipped through the channels. I couldn't concentrate. I was haunted by the doughnuts. I stormed into the kitchen space, got the doughnuts, and threw them in the garbage. I paced around, and I got the doughnuts out of the garbage. I rammed them down the garbage disposal and ran the disposal. I stared into the sink at the empty drain. No doughnuts. I couldn't believe I had to disposal the doughnuts. I was pathetic.

I went back to the living room and tried television again. Nothing held my attention. I was restless. Big Blue was at the curb, but I had nowhere to go. It was Sunday night. The mall was closed. I wasn't up to a visit with my parents. Probably I shouldn't be driving Big Blue anyway. It was sitting out there unprotected.

A couple minutes after nine, Morelli swung in on his crutches. "You're looking better," he said. "You were out like a light when I left. I guess falling down an elevator shaft is exhausting. Did you get your man?"

"No. He ran away."

Morelli grinned. "You're not supposed to let them do that."

"Did I miss anything important?"

"Yeah. I just got a call from Laski. Four bodies were found in a shallow grave in a patch of woods off upper Stark this afternoon. Some kids stumbled across it. They said they were looking for their dog, but they were probably looking for a place to smoke weed." Morelli eased himself onto the couch. "Laski said the bodies were pretty decomposed, but there were rings and belt buckles. None of the bodies has been officially identified yet, but Laski's certain one of them is Barroni. He was wearing an initialed belt buckle when he disappeared, and the wedding ring matches the description his wife, Carla, gave when she filed missing persons."

I sat next to Morelli. "That's so sad. I always hoped they'd suddenly reappear. Did Laski know how they were killed?"

"Shot. Multiple times. All in the chest, as if they'd been standing together and someone sprayed them with bullets like in an old Al Capone movie."

"What about the cars?"

"Laski said there was a dirt road going in. Most likely used by kids looking for privacy for one reason or another. So cars could have driven in there. But no cars were found with the bodies."

"I have profiles on the four missing men. I've been trying to tie them together. And I had a feeling Anthony Barroni and Spiro Stiva were involved somehow. Now I'm not so sure. Maybe Spiro came back for the sole purpose of terrorizing me and eventually killing me. Maybe he's a lone gun out there and not hanging with anyone. That would partially explain why no one's seen him."

"There's a description out on him now. There's a

corroborating witness that Spiro, or at least someone with a badly scarred face, was seen in the area when my garage went up. I don't know what to say about the men who were just found. It's pretty clear that someone called a meeting and executed them."

"They had to have known the gunman," I said. "I can't see any of these men getting in his car and driving off to a meeting on upper Stark at the request of a stranger."

"I agree, but we don't know the relationship. It could have been something impersonal, like blackmail. And the blackmailer decided to terminate."

"Do you think that's it?"

"No," Morelli said. "I think they all knew each other, and there was a fifth member of the group who had his own agenda."

"They were all in the same unit at Fort Dix."

Morelli turned and looked at me. "You found that out?"

"Yeah."

"So, not only are you hot but you're smart, too?"

"You think I'm hot?"

Morelli had his hand up my shirt, tinkering with my bra. "Cupcake, I'm not sharing my house with you because you can cook."

I cut my eyes to him. "Are you telling me I'm here just for the sex?"

Morelli was concentrating on getting me undressed and not paying attention to the tone of my voice. "Yeah, the sex has been great."

"What about the companionship, the friendship, the relationship part of this?"

Morelli paused in his effort to release the clasp on my bra. "Uh oh, did I just say something stupid?"

"Yes. You said I was just here for the sex."

"I didn't mean that."

"Yes, you did! It's all you think about with me."

"Cut me some slack," Morelli said. "I have a broken leg. I sit here all day, eating jelly beans and thinking about you naked. It's what guys do when they have a broken leg."

"You did that *before* you broke your leg."

"Oh man," Morelli said. "This isn't going to turn into one of those issue discussions, is it? I hate those discussions."

"Suppose for some reason we couldn't have sex. Would you still love me?"

"Yeah, but not as much."

"What kind of an answer is that? That's not the right answer."

Okay, so I knew his answer wasn't serious, and I didn't really think my relationship with Morelli was entirely sexual, but I couldn't seem to stop myself from getting crazy. I was on my feet, flapping my arms and yelling. This was usually Morelli's role, and here I was, working myself into a frenzy, going down a one-way street to nowhere. And I suspected it was Lula's jelly doughnut. The doughnut was bursting with jelly, and the jelly was squishing out in all the wrong places. And if that wasn't frightening enough, I was turning myself on. All the while I was yelling about Morelli wanting nothing but sex, the truth is, I could think of nothing else.

"Can we finish this upstairs?" Morelli asked. "My leg wants to go to bed."

"Sure," I said. "There are parts of me that want to go to bed, too."

I WAS SHOWERED and dressed and ready to go to work. I'd had two mugs of coffee and an English muffin. It was 8:00 A.M., and Morelli was still in bed.

"Hey," I said. "What's up with you? You're always the early riser."

"Mmmmph," Morelli said, pillow over his face. "Tired."

"How could you be tired? It's eight o'clock. It's time to get up! I'm leaving. Don't you want to kiss me good-bye?"

Nothing. No answer. I whipped the sheet off him and left him lying there in all his glorious nakedness. Morelli still didn't move.

I sat on the bed next to him. "Joe?"

"I thought you were going to work."

"You're looking very sexy ... except for Mr. Happy, who seems to be sleepy."

"He's not sleepy, Steph. He's in a coma. You woke him up every two hours and now he's dead."

"He's dead?"

"Okay, not dead, but he's not going to be up and dancing anytime soon. You might as well go to work. Did you walk Bob?"

"I walked Bob. I fed Bob. I cleaned the living room and the kitchen."

"Love you," Morelli said from under the pillow.

"I l-l-l-like you, too." *Shit.*

I went downstairs and stood at the front door, looking out at Big Blue. Probably perfectly safe, but I didn't feel comfortable taking the chance. Bob came to stand next to me. "I have no way to get to work," I said to Bob. "I could call Ranger, but lately it feels like I'm on a date when I'm in a car with Ranger, and it would be tacky to have a date pick me up here. Lula probably isn't up yet." I went to the kitchen and dialed my parents' number.

"I need a ride to work," I told my mom. "Can you or Dad take me?"

"Your father can pick you up," my mom said. "He's driving the cab today, anyway. Are you still off dessert?"

"Yes. How about you?"

"It's amazing. I don't even have the slightest need to tipple now that the wedding is behind us and Valerie's in Disney World."

Great. My mother doesn't need to tipple, and I'm so strung out with doughnut cravings I put Mr. Happy into a coma.

My dad showed up ten minutes later. "What's wrong with the Buick?" he said.

"Broken."

"I figured you were worried it was booby-trapped."

"Yep. That, too."

RANGER WAS WAITING for me when I arrived. He was in my cubby, slouched in the extra chair, reading through the files on Gorman, Lazar, Barroni, and

Runion. There was a new cell phone on my desk, plus a new key fob, and my Sig. The Sig was in a holster that clipped to a belt.

"They found them," I said.

"I heard. How'd you get in to work?"

"My dad."

"I have a bike set aside for you downstairs. If you park it exposed, be sure to look it over before getting on. It's hard to hide a bomb on a bike, but you still need to be careful. The key is on your keychain.

"As far as RangeMan is concerned, Gorman is found, and the file is closed," Ranger said. "If you still think there's a connection between the murdered men and your stalker, and you want to use this office to continue searching, you have permission to do that."

I looked at my in-box and stifled a groan. It was packed with search requests.

Ranger followed my eyes. "You're going to have to divide your time and get through some of those files. They're not just from Rodriguez. You do the searches for everyone here, including me."

He stood and brushed against me, and I had a wave of desire rush into my chest and shoot south.

"What?" Ranger said.

"I didn't say anything."

"You moaned."

"I was thinking of Butterscotch Krimpets."

Our eyes locked for a long moment. "I'll be in my office the rest of the morning," Ranger said. "Let me know if you need anything."

Oh boy.

I sorted through the requests that had come in over

the weekend. Three were from Ranger. I'd do them first. He was the boss. And he was hot. One was from someone named Alvirez. The rest were from Rodriguez.

Ranger's files were all standard searches. Nothing unusual. I had them done by noon. My plan was to get a quick lunch, run the Alvirez and two for Rodriguez, and then see what I could turn up at Fort Dix. I prowled through the kitchen, not finding anything inspiring to eat. I settled on the turkey again and took it back to my cubicle with a bottle of water. I finished lunch, finished Alvirez and Rodriguez, and started surfing Fort Dix.

I called my mother, Morelli, Lula, and Valerie and told them I had a new cell phone. Valerie was in the Magic Kingdom and said she'd be home at the end of the week. They liked Florida, but the girls missed their friends, and Albert had broken out in hives when he was approached by a six-foot-tall, four-foot-wide Pooh Bear. Lula wasn't answering. I left a message. Morelli wasn't answering. I left a message. My mother invited me for dinner, and I declined.

It was midafternoon when Ranger returned to my cubby. I was pacing, unable to focus on anything beyond my need for a cupcake.

"Babe," Ranger said. "You're looking a little strung out. Is there anything I should know?"

"I'm in sugar withdrawal. I've given up dessert, and it's all I can think about." That had been true five minutes ago. Now that Ranger was standing in front of me I was thinking a cupcake wasn't what I actually wanted.

"Maybe I can help get your mind off doughnuts," Ranger said.

My mouth dropped open, and I think some drool might have dribbled out.

"Did Silvio show you how to search the newspapers?" Ranger asked.

"No."

"Sit down and I'll show you how to get into the programs. It's tedious work, but it accesses a lot of information. You want to go to the local paper and look for something bad that happened when the four men were at Dix. An unsolved murder, a high-stakes robbery, unsolved serial crimes like multiple burglaries."

"Morelli thinks there were five men involved. Originally, I thought Anthony Barroni was the fifth guy, but now I'm not sure. Is there a way to get a list of men who were in that unit at Dix?"

"I don't have access to those records. I could get someone to hack in but I'd rather not. It would be safer to have Morelli do it."

I was hearing the words, but they weren't sticking. My brain was clogged with naked and sweaty Ranger thoughts.

"Babe," Ranger said, smiling. "You just looked me up and down like I was lunch."

"I need a doughnut," I told him. "I *really* need a doughnut."

"That would have been my second guess."

"I'll feel better tomorrow. The sugar will be out of my system. The cravings will be gone." I sat down and faced the keyboard. "How do I do this?"

Ranger pulled a chair next to me. His leg pressed against mine and when he leaned forward to get to my keyboard we were shoulder to shoulder, his arm brushing the side of my breast when he typed. He was warm and he smelled delicious. I felt my eyes glaze over, and I worried I might start panting.

"You should take notes," Ranger said. "You're going to need to remember some passwords."

Get a grip, I said to myself. It wouldn't be good to jump on him here. You'd be on television. And you haven't got a door on your cubby. And then there was Morelli. I was living with Morelli. It wouldn't be right to live with Morelli and boink Ranger. And what was wrong with me, anyway, that I needed two men? Especially when the second man was Ranger. Ever since we'd had the discussion about marriage my imagination had been running wild dredging up possibilities for his deep dark secret. I knew it had nothing to do with killing people because that was no secret. I knew he wasn't gay. I'd seen that one firsthand. The memory brought a new rush of heat, and I resisted squirming in my seat. Was he scarred by a terrible childhood? Had his heart been so badly broken he was unable to recover?

"Earth to Babe," Ranger said.

I looked at him and unconsciously licked my lips.

"I'm going to have to disconnect your cubby's security camera," Ranger said. "I just heard everyone in the control room gasp when you licked your lips. I could have a hatchet murder taking place in full monitor view on one of my accounts, and I don't think anyone would notice as long as you're sitting in here." Ranger signed off the search he'd just pulled up. He took my pad and wrote out instructions for retrieving information from newspapers. He returned the pad to my desk and stood. "Let's go on a field trip," he said. "I want to see the area where the bodies were recovered."

I thought that sounded sufficiently grim to be a good doughnut diversion. I stood and clipped my new cell phone onto the waistband of my jeans. I pocketed the key fob. And I stared at the gun. The gun was in a holster that attached to a belt, and I wasn't wearing a belt.

"No belt," I said to Ranger.

"Ella has some clothes for you upstairs in my apartment. Try them on. I'm sure she's included a belt. I'll meet you in the garage. I need to talk to Tank."

I took the elevator to the top floor and stepped out into the small marble-floored foyer. I'd lived here for a brief time not long ago, so I was familiar with the apartment. I opened the locked door with the key he'd given me and stepped inside. His apartment always felt cool and serene. His furniture was comfortable, with clean lines and earth tones, and felt masculine without being overbearing. There were fresh flowers on the sideboard by the door. I doubted Ranger ever noticed the flowers, but Ella liked them. They were part of Ella's campaign to civilize Ranger and make his life nicer.

I dropped my keys in the silver dish beside the flowers. I walked through the apartment and found my clothes stacked on a black leather upholstered bench in Ranger's dressing room. Two black shirts, two black cargo pants, a black belt, a black windbreaker, a black sweatshirt, a black ball cap. I was going to look like a mini-Ranger. I stepped into the cargo pants. Perfect fit.

Ella had remembered my size from the last time I'd stayed here. I belted the cargo pants, and I tugged the shirt over my head. It was a short-sleeved shirt, female cut with some spandex. It had a V-neck that was relatively high. RANGEMAN was embroidered on the left breast with black thread. The shirt was a good fit with the exception of being too short to tuck into the cargo pants. The shirt barely touched the top of the cargo pants waistband.

I called Ranger on his cell. "This shirt is short. I'm not sure you're going to like it on the control room floor."

"Put a jacket over it and come down to the garage."

I shrugged into the windbreaker. Black on black again, with RANGEMAN embroidered on the left breast of the jacket. I took my phone off my jeans and clipped it onto the cargo pants. I grabbed the black-on-black ball cap, and I left Ranger's apartment and rode the elevator to the garage.

Ranger was waiting by his truck. He was wearing a windbreaker exactly like mine, and the almost smile expression was fixed on his face.

"I feel like a miniature Ranger," I said to him.

Ranger unzipped the windbreaker and looked me over. "Nice, but you're no miniature Ranger." He took my Sig out of his jacket pocket and snapped it onto my belt just in front of my hip, his knuckles grazing bare skin. "There are some advantages to this short shirt," he said, sliding his hands under, fingertips stopping short of my bra.

"Okay, here's the deal," I said to him. "You know how when you squeeze a jelly doughnut and the jelly squirts out in the weakest spot of the doughnut? Well, if I'm a jelly doughnut then my weak spot is dessert. Every time I get stressed I head for the bakery. I'm trying to stop the dessert thing now, and so the jelly is squirting out someplace else."

"And?"

"And this place that it's squirting out . . . maybe squirting out isn't a good way to put this. Forget squirting out."

"You're trying to tell me something," Ranger said.

"Yes! And it would be a lot easier if you didn't have your hands under my shirt. It's hard for me to think when you've got your hands on me like this."

"Babe, has it occurred to you that you might be giving information to the enemy?"

"The thing is, I have all these excess hormones. They used to be jelly-doughnut hormones, but somehow they got switched over to sex-drive hormones. Not that sex-drive hormones are bad, it's just that my life is so complicated right now. So I'm trying to control all these stupid hormones, to keep them locked up in the doughnut. And you're going to have to help."

"Why?"

"Because you're a good guy."

"I'm not that good," Ranger said.

"So I'm in trouble?"

"Big time."

"You told Ella to get me this short shirt, didn't you?"

Ranger's fingers were slowly creeping up my breast. "No. I told her to get you something that didn't look like it was made for Tank. She probably didn't realize it was cut off at the waist."

"The hand," I said. "You have to remove the hand. You're poaching."

Ranger smiled and kissed me. Light. No tongue. The appetizer on Ranger's dinner menu. "Don't count on my help with the overactive sex drive," he said. "You're on your own with this one."

I looked up at the security camera focused on us. "Do you think Hal will sell this tape to the evening news?"

"Not if he wants to live." Ranger took a step back and opened the passenger-side door to the truck for me.

FOURTEEN

RANGER TOOK THE wheel, drove out of the garage, and headed for the patch of scrub woods east of center city where the four men had been found. Neither of us spoke. Understandable since there wasn't a lot to say after I explained my jelly doughnut dilemma, and Ranger'd declared open season on Stephanie. Still, it was good to have cleared the air, and now if I accidentally ripped his clothes off he'd understand it was one of those odd chemical things.

The crime-scene tape blocked the dirt road leading back to the crime site and covered a couple acres along the road and into the woods. Ranger parked the truck, and we got out and scooted under the yellow tape. I could see a van through the trees, and snatches of conversation carried to me. Men's voices. Two or three.

We walked the dirt road through the scrubby field and into the woods. The graves weren't far in. There was an area about the size of a two-car garage where the vegetation had been trampled over the years, leaving hard-packed dirt and some hardscrabble grass. This was the end of the road, the turnaround point. This was the place where drug deals were made, sex was sold, and kids got drunk, stoned, pregnant.

The van belonged to the state lab. The side door was open. One guy stood by the open door, writing on a pad. Two guys in shirtsleeves were working at the grave site. They were wearing disposable gloves and carrying evidence bags. They looked our way and nodded, recognizing Ranger.

"Your FTA's long gone," the guy at the van said.

"Just curious," Ranger told him. "Wanted to see what the scene looked like."

"Looks like you got a new partner. What happened to Tank?"

"It's Tank's day off," Ranger said.

"Hey, wait a minute," the guy said, smiling at me. "Aren't you Stephanie Plum?"

"Yes," I said. "And whatever you've heard . . . it isn't true."

"You two are kind of cute together," the guy said to Ranger. "I like the matching clothes. Does Celia know about this?"

"This is business," Ranger said. "Stephanie's working for RangeMan. Are you finding anything interesting?"

"Hard to say. There was a lot of trash here. Everything from left-behind panties to crack cookers. A lot of used condoms and needles. You want to watch where you walk. Be best if you stay on the road. The road's clean."

"How deep was the grave?"

"A couple feet. I'm surprised they weren't found

sooner. It's on the far perimeter of the cleared area so maybe it wasn't noticed. Or maybe no one cared. From the way the ground's settled I'd say they were here for a while. Couple weeks at least. Looks to me like they were shot here. Won't know for sure until the lab tests come back."

"Did he leave the shells?"

"Took the shells."

Ranger nodded. "Later."

"Later. Give Celia a hug for me."

We got back to the truck and Ranger shielded his eyes from the low-angled sun and studied the road we'd just walked.

"There was just barely enough room back there for five cars," Ranger said. "We know two of them were SUVs. Probably they could at least partially be seen from the main road. And that probably ensured their privacy. We know when three of the men left work and got into their cars. If they came directly here they'd arrive around six-thirty, which meant there was still daylight."

"You'd think someone would have heard gunshots. This guy didn't just pop off a couple rounds."

"It's an isolated area. And if you were a passing motorist it might be hard to tell where the shots originated. Most likely you'd just get the hell out of here."

We climbed into the truck and buckled ourselves in.

"Who's Celia?" I asked Ranger.

"My sister. Marty Sanchez, the guy by the van, went to school with Celia. They dated for a while."

"Is she your only sister?"

"I have four sisters."

"Any brothers?"

"One."

"And you have a daughter," I said.

Ranger swung the truck onto the paved road. "Not many people know about my daughter."

"Understood. Do I get to ask more questions?"

"One."

"How old are you?"

"I'm two months older than you," Ranger said.

"You know my birthday?"

"I know lots of things about you. And that was two questions."

IT WAS FIVE o'clock when we pulled into the garage.

"How's Morelli doing?" Ranger asked.

"Good. He's going back to work tomorrow. The cast won't come off for a while, so he's limited. He's on crutches, and he can't drive, and he can't walk Bob. I'm going to stay until he's more self-sufficient. Then I'll go back to my apartment."

Ranger walked me to the bike. "I don't want you going back to your apartment until we get this guy."

"You don't have to worry about me," I said. "I've got a gun."

"Would you feel comfortable using it?"

"No, but I could hit someone over the head with it."

The bike was a black Ducati Monster. I'd driven Morelli's Duc, so I was on familiar ground. I took the black full-face helmet off the grip and handed it to Ranger. I took the key out of my pocket, and I swung my leg over the bike.

Ranger was watching me, smiling. "I like the way you straddle that," he said. "Someday . . ."

I revved the engine and cut off the rest of the sentence. I didn't have to read his lips to know where he was going. I put the helmet on, Ranger remoted the gate open for me, and I wheeled out of the garage.

It felt great to be on the bike. The air was cool, and traffic was light. It was just a few minutes short of rush hour. I took it slow, getting the feel of the machine. I cut to the alley and brought the bike in through Morelli's backyard. Morelli had an empty tool shed next to his house. The shed was locked with a combination lock, and I knew the combination. I spun the dial, opened the shed, and locked the bike away.

Morelli was waiting for me in the kitchen. "Let me guess," Morelli said. "He gave you a bike. A Duc."

"Yeah. It was terrific riding over here." I went to the fridge and studied the inside. Not a lot there. "I'll take Bob out, and you can dial supper," I said.

"What do you want?"

"Anything without sugar."

"You're still on the no-sugar thing?"

"Yeah. I hope you took a nap this afternoon."

Morelli poked me with his crutch. "Where are your clothes? You weren't wearing this when you left this morning."

"I left them at work. I didn't have a way to carry them on the bike. I could use a backpack." I still had the windbreaker zipped over the shirt. I thought it was best to delay the short-shirt confrontation until after we'd eaten. I clipped Bob to his leash and took off. I got back just as the Pino's delivery kid was leaving.

"I ordered roast beef subs," Morelli said. "Hope that's okay."

I took a sub and unwrapped it and gave it to Bob. I handed a sub to Morelli, and I unwrapped the third for myself. We were in the living room, on the couch, as always. We ate, and we watched the news.

"The news is always the same," I said. "Death, destruction, blah, blah, blah. There should be a news station that only does happy news."

I collected the wrappers when we were done eating and carted them off to the kitchen. Morelli followed after me on his crutches.

"Take your jacket off," Morelli said. "I want to see the rest of the uniform."

"Later."

"Now."

"I was thinking I might go back to work just for a couple hours. I started a search and didn't get to finish it."

Morelli had me backed into a corner. "I don't think so. I have plans for tonight. Let's see the shirt."

"I don't want to hear any yelling."

"It's that bad?"

It wasn't just the shirt. It was also the gun. Morelli was going to be unhappy that I was carrying. He knew I was a moron when it came to guns.

I took the jacket off and twirled for him. "What do you think?"

"I'm going to kill him. Don't worry. I'll make it look like an accident."

"He didn't pick out the shirt. His housekeeper picked out the shirt. She's short. It probably came to her knees."

"Who picked out the gun?"

"Ranger picked out the gun."

"Is it loaded?"

"I don't know. I didn't look."

"You aren't really going to keep working for him, are you? He's a nut. Plus half his workforce has graduated from Jersey Penal," Morelli said. "And what about not wanting a dangerous job?"

"The job isn't dangerous. It's boring. I sit at a computer all day."

I HAD MORELLI up and dressed. I got him down the stairs and into the kitchen. I sat him at the table, put the coffee on, and left for a short walk with Bob. When I came back, Morelli was asleep with his head on the table. I put a mug of coffee in front of him, and he opened an eye.

"You have to open *both* eyes," I said. "You're going to work today. Laski's picking you up in five minutes."

"That gives me five minutes to sleep," Morelli said.

"No! Drink some coffee. Get some legal stimulants into your system." I danced in front of him. "Look at me. I'm wearing a gun! And look at the short shirt. Are you going to let me go to work like this?"

"Cupcake, I haven't got the energy to stop you. Anyway, maybe if you look slutty enough, Ranger will take up some of the slack in the bedroom before you make a permanent cripple out of me. Maybe you should wear that shirt with the neckline that lets your boobs hang out." Morelli squinted at me. "Why aren't you tired?"

"I don't know. I feel all energized. I always thought

I couldn't keep up with you, but maybe you've just been slowing me down all these years."

"Stephanie, I'm begging you. Eat some doughnuts. I can't keep going like this."

I poured his coffee into a travel mug and got him to his feet. I shoved the crutches under his arms and pushed him to the front door. Laski was already at the curb. I helped Morelli hobble down the stairs and maneuver himself into the car. I threw his crutches onto the backseat and handed Morelli his mug of coffee.

"Have a nice day," I said. I gave him a kiss, closed the car door, and watched as Laski motored them away, down the street.

There was a chill to the air, so I went back to the house, ran upstairs, and borrowed Morelli's leather biker jacket. I tied the RangeMan windbreaker around my waist, I gave Bob a hug, and I let myself out through the back door. I unlocked the shed and rolled the bike out, and a half hour later, I was at my desk.

I went straight into the newspaper search. I limited the search to the last three months the men were at Dix. It seemed to me that was the most likely time frame for them to do something catastrophic. I began with a name search and came up empty. None of the men were mentioned in any of the local papers. My next search was front page. I was only reading headlines, but it was still a slow process.

I stopped the Fort Dix search at nine-thirty and switched to RangeMan business, working my way through the security check requests. By noon I was questioning my ability to do the job long-term. The words were swimming on the screen, and I felt creaky from sitting. I went to the kitchen and poked at the sandwiches. Turkey, tuna, grilled vegetables, roast beef, chicken salad. I dialed Ranger on my cell phone.

"Yo," Ranger said. "Is there a problem?"

"I don't like any of these sandwiches."

There was a moment of dead phone time before Ranger answered. "Go upstairs to my apartment. I think there's some peanut butter left from last time you stayed there."

"Where are you?"

"I'm with an account. I'm inspecting a new system."

"Are you coming home for lunch?"

"No," Ranger said. "I won't be back until three. Are you still off sugar?"

"Yes."

"Maybe I can get back sooner."

"No rush," I said. "I'm happy with peanut butter."

"I'm counting on that being a lie," Ranger said.

I let myself into Ranger's apartment and went straight to the kitchen. He still had the peanut butter in his fridge, and there was a loaf of bread on the granite countertop. I made myself a sandwich and washed it down with a beer. I was tempted to take a nap in Ranger's bed, but that felt too much like Goldilocks.

I was on my way out when I got a call from Lula. "I got him trapped," she yelled into the phone. "I got Willie Martin trapped in the deli at the corner of Twenty-fifth Street and Lowman Avenue. Only I'm gonna need help to bag him. If you're at RangeMan it's just around the corner."

"Are you sure you need my help?"

"Hurry!"

I took the elevator to the first floor and went out the front door. No point taking the bike. The deli was only a block away. I jogged to Lowman, and saw Lula standing in front of Fennick's Deli.

"He's in there eating," she said to me. "I just happened on him. I was going in for sandwiches for Connie and me and there he was. He's in the back where they have some tables."

"Did he see you?"

"I don't think so. I got out right away."

"So what do you need me for?"

"I thought you could be a diversion. You could go in there and get his attention, and then I'll sneak up and zap him with the stun gun."

"Didn't we already try the zapping thing?"

"Yeah, but we'd be better this time on account of we got some practice at it."

"Okay, but you'd better not screw up. If you screw up he's going to beat the crap out of me."

"Don't worry," Lula said. "The third time's a charm. This is going to work. You'll see. You go on up to him, and I'll sneak around from the side and get him from the back."

"Have you tested the stun gun? Does it work?"

We were standing next to a bus stop with a bench. Three elderly men were sitting on the bench. One was reading a paper, and the other two were zoned out, staring blankly into space. Lula reached out and pressed the stun gun to one of the men. He gave a twitch and slumped onto the man next to him.

"Yep," Lula said. "It works."

I was speechless. My mouth was open and my eyes were wide.

"What?" Lula said.

"You just zapped that poor old man."

"It's okay. I know him. That's Gimp Whiteside. He don't do nothing all day. Might as well help us hard-working bounty hunters. Anyway, he didn't feel any pain. He's just taking a snooze now." Lula looked me over and grinned. "Look at you! You look like Range-Man Barbie. You got a gun and everything."

"Yeah, and I have to get back to work, so let's do this. I'm going to talk to Willie and see if I can get him to surrender. Give me your cuffs, and don't use the stun gun until I tell you to use it."

Lula handed her cuffs over to me. "You're taking some of the fun out of it, but I guess I could do it that way."

I walked straight back to Willie Martin. He was sitting alone at a small bistro table. He'd finished his sandwich, and he was picking at a few remaining fries. There was a second chair at his table. I slid the chair over next to him and sat down. "Remember me?" I asked him.

Willie looked at me and laughed. It was a big open-mouthed, mashed-up-french-fries-and-ketchup laugh that sounded like *haw, haw, haw*. "Yeah, I remember you," he said. "You're the dumb white bitch who came with fat-ass Lula."

He dipped a french fry into a glob of ketchup with his right hand, and I clamped a cuff onto his left.

He looked down at the cuff and grinned. "I already got a pair of these. You giving me another?"

"I'm asking you nicely to return to the courthouse with me, so we can get you rescheduled."

"I don't think so."

"It's just a formality. We'll rebond you."

"Nope."

"I have a gun."

"You gonna use it?"

"I might."

"I don't think so," Willie said. "I'm unarmed. You shoot me, and you'll do more time than I will. That's assault with a deadly weapon."

"Okay, how about this. If you don't let me cuff your other hand, and you don't quietly walk out with me and get in Lula's car, we're going to send enough electricity through you to make you mess your pants. And that's going to be an embarrassing experience. It'll probably make the papers—'Pro ball all-star Willie Martin messed his pants in Fennick's Deli yesterday . . .' "

"I didn't mess my pants last time."

"Do you want to risk it? We'd be happy to give you a few volts."

"You swear you'll rebond me?"

"I'll call Vinnie as soon as we get you into the car."

"Okay," Willie said. "I'm gonna stand and put my hands behind my back. And we'll do this real quiet so nobody notices."

Lula was a short distance away with the stun gun in hand, her eyes glued to Willie. I stood, and Willie stood, and next thing I knew I was flying through the air. He'd moved so fast and scooped me up so effortlessly, I never saw it coming. He threw me about fifteen feet, and I crash-landed on a table of four. The table gave way and I was on the floor with the burgers and shakes and soup of the day. I was flat on my back, the wind knocked out of me, dazed for a moment, the world swirling around me. I rolled to my hands and knees and crawled over smashed food and dishes to get to my feet.

Willie Martin was facedown on the floor just beyond the table debris. Lula was sitting on him, struggling with the second cuff. "Boy, you really know how to make a diversion," Lula said. "I zapped him good. He's out like a light. Only I can't get his second hand to cooperate."

I limped over and held Martin's hand behind his back while she cuffed him. "Do you have shackles in the car?"

"Yeah. Maybe you should go get them while I babysit here."

I took the key to the Firebird, got the shackles, and brought them back to Lula. We got the shackles on Martin, and a squad car pulled up outside the deli. It was my pal Carl Costanza and his partner, Big Dog.

Costanza grinned when he saw me. "We got a call that two crazy fans were on Willie like white on rice."

"That would be Lula and me," I said. "Except we're not fans. He's FTA."

"Looks like you're wearing lunch."

"Willie threw me into the table. And then he decided to take a nap."

"We'd appreciate it if you could help us drag his sorry ass out of here," Lula said. "He weighs a ton."

Big Dog got Willie under the armpits, Carl took the feet, and we hauled Willie out of the deli and dumped him into the back of Lula's Firebird.

"We need to do a property damage report," Costanza said to me. "You're wearing RangeMan clothes. Are you hunting desperadoes for Vinnie or for Ranger?"

"Vinnie."

"Works for me," Costanza said. And they disappeared inside the deli.

Lula and I looked over at the bench by the bus stop. Two of the three men were gone from the bench. The guy Lula stun-gunned was still there.

"Looks like Gimp missed his bus," Lula said. "Guess he didn't come around fast enough. Hey, Gimp," she yelled. "You want a ride? Get your bony behind over here."

"You're a big softy," I said.

"Yeah, don't tell nobody."

I walked back to RangeMan and entered through the front door. "Don't say anything," I told the guy at the desk. "I've just walked two blocks through town, and I've heard it all. And just in case you're wondering, those are noodles stuck in my hair, not worms."

I rode the elevator to the control room and had the full attention of everyone there as I crossed to my desk.

"I got tired of turkey so I went out for lunch," I told them.

I retrieved the key fob I'd left on my desk, got back into the elevator, and rode to Ranger's floor. I knocked on his door and didn't get an answer, so I let myself in. I took my shoes off in the hall and left them on the marble floor. I didn't want to trash Ranger's apartment, and the shoes were coated with chocolate milkshake and some smushed cheeseburger. I padded into Ranger's bathroom, locked the door, and dropped the rest of my clothes. I washed with his delicious shower gel and stood under the hot water until I was relaxed and no longer cared that just minutes before I'd had chicken noodle soup in my hair.

I wrapped myself in Ranger's luxuriously thick terry-cloth robe, unlocked the door, and stepped into his bedroom. Ranger was stretched out on the bed, ankles crossed, arms behind his head. He was fully clothed, and he was obviously waiting for me.

"I had a small mishap," I said.

"That's what they tell me. What happened?"

"I was helping Lula snag Willie Martin at Fennick's and next thing I knew I was airborne. He threw me about fifteen feet, into a table full of food and people."

"Are you okay?"

"Yeah, but my sneakers are history. They're covered with chocolate milkshake."

Ranger crooked a finger at me. "Come here."

"No way."

"What about the jelly-doughnut hormones and the sex-drive hormones?"

"Getting thrown across a room seems to have a calming effect on them."

"I could fix that," Ranger said.

I smiled at him. "There's no doubt in my mind, but I'd rather you didn't. I have a lot of things going on in my head right now, and you could make it a lot more confusing."

"That's promising," Ranger said. He got off the bed and crossed the room. He grabbed me by the big shawl collar on the robe and pulled me to him. "I like when you wear my robe."

"Because I'm cute in it?"

"No, because it's all you're wearing."

"You don't know that for sure," I said. "I could have clothes under this."

"Is this another one of those things I should find out for myself?"

I was skating on thin ice here. I had the jelly-doughnut hormone problem going on, and I didn't want it to get out of control. I'd spent a night with Ranger a while ago, and I knew what happened when he was encouraged. Ranger knew how to make a woman want him. Ranger was magic.

"Let's take a look at my life," I said to Ranger. "I keep rolling in garbage."

"Mind-boggling," Ranger said.

"And let's take a look at your life. You have a deep dark secret."

"Let it go," Ranger said.

"Are you sick?"

"No, I'm not sick. Not physically, anyway. I'm not so sure sometimes about the mental, emotional, and sexual."

I locked myself in Ranger's dressing room and got dressed in the second RangeMan outfit. Short black T-shirt, black cargo pants, black socks. Ella hadn't provided underwear or shoes, so I sent my soda-and-ketchup-soaked underwear and my chocolate-shake-covered shoes off to the laundry with the first RangeMan outfit. I was feeling a little strange without underwear, but a girl's gotta do what a girl's gotta do, right?

I returned to my desk, and I ignored the search requests piling up in my in-box. I picked up where I left off with the Dix search, reading the front pages. By five o'clock I had a list of crimes that I thought had potential. Nothing sensational. Just good solid crimes like a rash of unsolved burglaries, an unsolved murder, an unsolved hijacking. None of the crimes really grabbed me, and I still had lots of front pages to read, so I decided to keep searching.

I called Morelli and told him I was working late.

"How late?" he said.

"I don't know. Does it matter?"

"Only if you come home with your underwear on backwards."

I could go him one better than that. How about no underwear at all?

"Dial yourself some food," I said. "And tie Bob out back. I need to finish this project. How was your day? Is your leg okay?"

"The leg is okay. The day was long. I don't like being stuck in the building."

"Anything on Barroni and the three other guys?"

"They've all been positively identified. You were right about all of them. They were killed on-site. That's it so far."

"No one's seen Spiro?"

"No, but the pizza kid gave a good description, and it matches yours."

I STRUGGLED UP from a deep sleep and opened my eyes to Ranger.

"Babe," he said softly. "You need to wake up. You need to go home."

I had my arms crossed on my desk and my head on my arms. The screen saver was up on my computer. "What time is it?"

"It's a little after eleven. I just came back from a break-in on one of the RangeMan accounts and saw you were still here."

"I was looking for a crime."

"Did you call Morelli?"

"Earlier. He knows I'm working late."

Ranger looked down at my feet. "Have you heard anything about your shoes? Ella was going to wash them."

"Haven't heard anything."

Ranger punched Ella's extension on my phone. "Sorry to call so late," he said. "What's happening with Stephanie's shoes?"

Ranger smiled at Ella's answer. He disconnected and slung an arm around my shoulder. "Bad news on the shoes. They melted in the dryer. Looks like you're going home in your socks." He pulled me to my feet. "I'll drive you. You can't ride the bike like this."

FIFTEEN

WE TOOK THE elevator to the garage, and Ranger went to the Porsche. Of all his cars, this was my favorite. I loved the sound of the engine, and I loved the way the seat cradled me. At night, the dash looked like controls on a jet, and the car felt intimate.

I was groggy from sleep and exhausted from the events of the day. And I suspected the last two nights were catching up with me. I closed my eyes and melted into the cushy leather seat. I felt Ranger reach across and buckle my seat belt. I heard the Porsche growl to life and move up the ramp to exit the garage. I dozed on the way home and came awake when the car stopped. I looked out at the darkened neighborhood. Not a lot of lights shining in windows at this time of the night. These were hardworking people who rose early and went to bed early. We were stopped half a block from Morelli's house.

"Why are we stopped here?" I asked Ranger.

"I have a working relationship with Morelli. I think

he's a good cop, and he thinks I'm a loose cannon. Since we both carry guns, I try not to do things that would upset the balance in an insulting way. I wanted to give you a chance to wake up, so we didn't sit at the curb in front of his house like a couple teenagers adjusting their clothes." Ranger looked over at me. "You got the rest of your clothes from Ella, didn't you?"

Damn. "I forgot! I was working, and then I fell asleep. She's got my underwear."

Ranger laughed out loud, and when he looked back at me he was smiling the full-on Ranger smile. "I'm worrying about parking too long in front of Morelli's house, and I'm bringing his girlfriend home without her underwear. I'll have to put double security on the building tonight." He put the Porsche in gear, drove half a block, and parked. Lights were on in the downstairs rooms. "Are you going to be okay?" he asked.

"Morelli's a reasonable person. He'll understand." Plus he had a cast on his leg. He couldn't move fast. I'd head straight for the stairs, and I'd be changed before he could get to me.

Ranger locked eyes with me. "Just so you know, for future reference, *I* wouldn't understand. If you were living with me, and you came home without underwear, I'd go looking for the guy who had it. And it wouldn't be pretty when I found him."

"Something to remember," I said. And the truth is, Morelli wasn't so different from Ranger. And Morelli wasn't usually a reasonable person. Morelli was being uncharacteristically mellow. I wasn't sure why I was seeing the mellow, and I wasn't sure how long it would last. The main difference between Morelli and Ranger was that when Morelli got mad he got loud. And when Ranger got mad he got quiet. They were both equally scary.

I jumped out of the Porsche and ran to the house. I let myself in, called to Morelli, and ran up the stairs and into the bedroom to get clothes. I smacked into Morelli en route to the bathroom. He dropped a crutch and put an arm out to steady me.

"What are you doing up here?" I asked.

"Going to bed? I live here, remember?"

"I thought you were downstairs."

"You were wrong." He looked over at me. "Where's your bra?"

"What?"

"I know your body better than I know my own. And I know when you're not wearing a bra."

I slumped against the doorjamb. "It's in Ranger's dryer. You're not going to make a big deal about this, are you?"

"I don't know. I'm waiting to hear the whole story."

"I helped Lula capture Willie Martin this morning, and I sort of got thrown into a table filled with food and people."

"Costanza told me."

"Yeah, he responded to the call from Fennick's. Anyway, my clothes and my shoes were a mess, and I had chicken soup in my hair, so I used Ranger's shower to get cleaned up. And I put clean clothes on, except Ella hadn't gotten me any underwear or shoes." We both looked down at my feet. Black socks. No shoes. "So here I am, and I don't have any underwear."

"Was Ranger in the shower with you?"

"Nope. Just me."

"And you were actually working tonight?"

"Yep."

"If I had anyone else for a girlfriend I'd be out the door with a gun in my hand, looking for Ranger—but your life is so insane I'm willing to believe anything. Living with you is like being in one of the reality shows on television where people keep getting covered with bees and dropped off forty-story buildings into a vat of Vaseline."

"I admit it's been a little . . . hectic."

"Hectic is getting three kids to soccer practice on time. Your life is . . . there are no words for your life."

"That's what my mother says. Is this leading to something?"

"I don't know. I'm really tired right now. Let's talk about it tomorrow."

I picked Morelli's crutch up for him, and he moved toward the little guest room.

"Where are you going?" I asked him.

"I'm sleeping in the guest room, and I'm locking the door. I need a night of uninterrupted sleep. I'm running on empty. I was a mess at work. I couldn't keep my eyes open. And my guys feel like they've been run over by a truck. They need a day off."

"What about *my* guys?"

"Cupcake, you don't have guys."

"I have *something*."

"You do. And I love it. But you're on your own tonight. You're going to have to fly solo."

I ROLLED OUT of bed and crossed the hall to the little guest room. The door was open, and the room was empty. No Morelli in the bathroom or study, but Bob was sleeping in the bathtub. I crept down the stairs and walked through the house to the kitchen. There was hot coffee, and a note had been left by the coffeemaker.

SORRY ABOUT LAST NIGHT. THE GUYS MISSED YOU THIS MORNING. DON'T WORK LATE.

That sounded hopeful. I poured a mug of coffee, added milk, and took it upstairs. An hour later, I was dressed in black jeans and black T-shirt, and I was ready for work. I'd called my dad and mooched a ride. He was at the curb when I came down the stairs.

"You're doing pretty good on the new job," he said. "Almost a week. And nothing's caught fire or blown up at work."

It'd be a real challenge for Spiro to penetrate Range-Man. And that's probably the reason Morelli's garage got destroyed. Spiro went for what was available. Truth is I was beginning to be bothered by the lack of activity. The garage went five days ago and there hadn't been any threatening notes, snipings, or bombings since the Buick.

"They're holding a memorial service for Michael Barroni today," my father said. "Your mother said to tell you she's taking your grandmother. It's being held at Stiva's. Ordinarily they'd hold it at the church, but Stiva and Barroni were old friends, and I guess Stiva gave the Barronis a discount if they held the service in his chapel."

"I didn't realize Stiva and Barroni were that close."

"Yeah, me neither. I didn't see them spending a lot of time together. But then that happens when you got a big family and a business to run. You lose touch with your buddies."

I had a chill run up my spine to the roots of my hair, and my scalp was tingling like I was electric. "How'd Stiva and Barroni get to be friends?" I asked, holding my breath, my heart skipping beats.

"They were in the army together. They were both at Dix."

I might have the fifth man. I was so excited I was hyperventilating. Now here's the thing, *why was I so excited?* Ranger had his FTA, so the excitement didn't come from case closure. I barely knew Barroni and I didn't know the other three men at all, so there was nothing personal. My original long jump tying Anthony Barroni to Spiro and the missing men proved to be groundless. So why did I care? The four missing men seemed to be completely unrelated to anything I'd care about. And even if Spiro *did* turn out to have a tie to the four men, even if there *was* a crime involved, it really didn't matter to me, did it? Finding Spiro and stopping the harassment was really the only thing that mattered, right? Right. But stopping the harassment could be a problem. There were really only two ways the harassment would stop. Ranger could kill Spiro. Or Spiro could get convicted of a crime, like murdering Mama Macaroni, and get locked away. The latter was definitely the preferred. Okay, maybe I was excited about the fifth man because it might be Constantine Stiva. And if Con was involved, then Spiro might be involved. And if there wasn't evidence that convicted Spiro of the bombings, there might be evidence to convict him of the shallow grave homicides. So, was this why I couldn't wait to plug Con's name into the search program? I didn't think so. I suspected the hard reality was that it all just came down to tasteless curiosity. I was a product of the Burg. I had to know all the dirt.

My dad pulled up to the front of the building and I jumped out. "Thanks," I yelled, hitting the ground running.

I was supposed to sign in and sign out when I entered and left the building. And I was supposed to show my picture ID when I came through the first-floor lobby. I never remembered to sign in or out, and my picture ID was lost in the garage fire. Good thing everyone knew me. Being the only woman in an organization had its upside.

I waved to the guy at the desk and danced in place, waiting for the elevator. I barreled out of the elevator on the fifth floor and crossed to my cubby. I got my computer up and running and punched "Constantine Stiva" into the newspaper search program. A single article appeared. It was small and on page thirteen. I would have missed it on my front-page search.

Private First Class Constantine Stiva had been injured in his attempt to thwart a robbery. A government armored truck carrying payroll had been hijacked when it had stopped for a routine gate check at Fort Dix. Stiva had been on guard duty, along with two other men. Stiva was the only guard to survive. He'd been shot in the leg. There'd been no mention of the amount of money involved. And there weren't a lot of details on the hijacking, other than a few brief sentences that the truck had been recovered. I searched papers for two weeks following the incident but came up empty. There'd only been the one article.

I called Ranger on his cell and got a message. I left my cubby and went to the console that monitored Rangeman cars. "Where's Ranger?" I asked Hal. "He's not answering his cell, and I don't see him on the board."

"He's on a plane," Hal said. "He had to bring an FTA up from Miami. He'll be back tonight. Manny was supposed to bring the guy up on a red-eye yesterday, but he had problems with security, so Ranger had to go down this morning." Hal tapped Ranger's number into his computer and a screen changed and brought Ranger's car up. Philadelphia airport. "He should be on the ground in three hours," Hal said. "His cell will come back on then."

I went back to my cubby and I called Morelli.

"I might know the fifth guy," I told him. "It might be Constantine Stiva. He was at Dix when Barroni was there. They were army buddies."

"I can't imagine Con in the army," Morelli said. "I can't imagine him ever being anything other than a funeral director."

"It gets even stranger. He was on guard duty, and he was shot during an armored car hijacking."

"How do you know all this?"

"I've been searching newspapers. I'm going to e-mail you the article on Con. I know it's stupid, but I just have this feeling everything fits somehow. Like maybe the four missing men were involved in the armored car hijacking and Con recognized them."

"Then it would seem to me Con should be the one in the shallow grave."

"Yes, but suppose Con told Spiro and Spiro came back and was extorting money from the four men? And then when he didn't think he could get any more he shot them."

"It's a lot of supposing," Morelli said.

"And here's something else that's interesting. There's been no activity since your garage got blown up. Five days without a note, a sniping, or a bombing. Don't you think that's odd?"

"I think it's all odd."

I sent the news article to Morelli, and then I went to the kitchen, got coffee with milk, no sugar, and went back to my desk and called my mother. "Are you tippling yet?" I asked her.

"No," she said.

Damn. "Dad said you and Grandma were going to the memorial service."

"Yes. It's at one o'clock. I feel so sorry for Carla and the three boys. What a terrible thing. I might have to tipple after the service. Do you think that would be bad?"

"Everybody tipples after a memorial service," I told her. I knew it was the wrong thing to say. God help me, I was a rotten daughter, but I really needed dessert!

I disconnected and started working my way through the search requests. I called Morelli at noon.

"How's it going?"

"I talked to Con."

"Just for the heck of it."

"Yeah. Just for the heck of it. He said the army tried to keep the armored truck robbery as quiet as possible.

The two guards that Con was working with were shot and killed. Con said he was alive because he fainted when he got shot in the leg, and he supposed the hijackers thought he was dead. He couldn't identify any of the hijackers. They were all dressed in fatigues, wearing masks. For security purposes the army never released the entire death toll, but Con said it was rumored that there were three men in the truck who were killed."

"Did he say how much money was involved?"

"He didn't know."

"Did you ask him if he thought Barroni might have been involved in that hijacking?"

"Yeah. He looked at me like I was on drugs."

"Did Spiro know about the hijacking?"

"Spiro knew his dad was shot. Con said there was a time when Spiro was a kid, and he was sort of obsessed with it. Kept the newspaper article in a scrapbook."

"What does he have to say about the Spiro sightings?"

"Not much. He seemed confused more than anything else. He said he thought Spiro had perished in the fire. If he's telling the truth he's in a strange spot, not sure if he should be happy Spiro's alive or sad that Spiro blew up Mama Macaroni."

"Do you think he's telling the truth?"

"Don't know. He sounds convincing enough. The big problem for me isn't that Spiro came back to harass you. That I could easily believe, and you've actually seen him. My problem is I don't feel comfortable involving him in the Barroni murder."

"You don't think Spiro's a multitasker."

"Spiro's a rodent. You put a rodent in a maze, and he focuses on one thing, he goes for the piece of cheese."

"Then who killed Michael Barroni?"

"Don't know. If I was going on gut instinct, I'd have to say it feels like Spiro's got his finger in that pie, but there's absolutely no evidence. We don't know *why* Barroni was killed, and we have no reason to believe he was involved in the hijacking."

"Jeez, you're such a party pooper."

"Yeah, insisting on evidence is always a downer."

I hung up and went back to my searches, but I couldn't keep my mind on them. I was getting double vision from looking at the computer, and I was tired of sitting in the cubby. And even worse, I was feeling friendly. I was thinking Morelli's voice had sounded nice on the phone. I was wondering what he was wearing. And I was remembering what he looked like when he wasn't wearing anything. And I was thinking I might have to leave work early, so I could be naked by the time Morelli walked through the door at four o'clock.

I pushed away from my desk, stuffed myself into the windbreaker, and grabbed the key fob.

"I need to get some air," I told Hal. "I won't be gone long."

I rode the elevator to the garage and got on the bike. When I pushed away from my desk I didn't have a direction in mind. By the time I'd reached the garage I knew where I was going. I was going to the memorial service.

I got to Stiva's exactly at one o'clock. Latecomers were hunting parking places and hustling up to the big front porch. I zipped into the lot with the Duc and parked on a patch of grass separating the lot from the drive-thru lane for the hearse and the flower car. My mother's gray Buick was in the lot. From the location of her parking place I was guessing she'd gotten there early. Grandma always liked a seat up front.

Stiva had a chapel on the first floor to the rear of the building. When there was a large crowd he opened the doors and seated the overflow on folding chairs in the wide hallway. Today was standing room only. Since I was one of the last to arrive, I was far down the hall, catching the service over the speaker system.

I wandered away after fifteen minutes and peeked in some of the other rooms. Mr. Earls was in Slumber Salon number three. I thought he was sort of a sad sack in there all by himself while everyone else was at the service. It felt like poor Mr. Earls didn't get an invitation to the party. I snooped in the kitchen and spent a moment considering the cookie tray. I told myself they weren't that good. They were store-bought cookies, and there weren't any of my favorites on the tray. There were better things to nibble on, I told myself. Fresh doughnuts, homemade chocolate chip cookies . . . Ranger. I left the kitchen and tiptoed into Con's office. He'd left the door open. It was an announcement that he had nothing to hide. If you can't trust your undertaker, who *can* you trust, eh?

I don't ordinarily do recreational mortuary tours, and I'd absolutely believed Con when he said he hadn't seen Spiro, so I wasn't sure why I felt compelled to search the building. I guess it just wasn't adding up for me. I kept coming back to the mole. It had been made from mortician's putty. Stiva doesn't run the only funeral home in the greater Trenton area. And for that matter, you can probably order mortician's putty on the

Net. Still, this was the easiest and most logical place for Spiro to get a chunk of the stuff. I had a feeling that if I opened enough doors here, I'd find Spiro or at least some evidence that Spiro had passed through.

I went upstairs and checked out the storage room and the two additional viewing rooms Con reserved for peak periods, like the week after Christmas. I returned to the ground level, exited the side door, and looked in the garage. Two slumber coaches, waiting for the call. Two flower cars that were somber, even when filled with flowers. Two Lincoln Town Cars. And Con's black Navigator, the vehicle of choice when someone inconveniently dies during a blizzard.

I returned to the main building through the back door. The chapel was straight ahead, at the end of a short corridor. The embalming rooms were in the new wing, to my left. These rooms were added after the fire. The new structure was cinder block and the equipment supposedly was state of the art, whatever that meant.

I took a deep breath and turned left. I'd gone this far, I should finish the search. I tested the door that led to the new wing. Locked. Gee, too bad. Guess God doesn't want me to see the embalming rooms.

The basement also remained unexplored. And that's the way it was going to stay. The furnaces and meat lockers are in the basement. This is where the fire started. I've been told the basement's all rebuilt and shiny and bright, but I'd rather not see for myself. I'm afraid the ghosts are still there . . . and the memories.

Con lived in a house that sat next to the mortuary. It was a good-size Victorian, not as big as the original mortuary house, but twice the size of my parents' house. Spiro had grown up in that house. I'd never been inside. Spiro hadn't been one of my friends. Spiro had been a kid who lived in shadows, scheming and spying on the rest of the world, occasionally sucking another kid into the darkness.

I went out through the back door and followed the walkway past the garages to Con's house. It was a pretty house, well maintained, the property professionally landscaped. It was painted white with black shutters, like the mortuary. I circled the house and stepped up onto the small back porch that sheltered the kitchen door. I looked in the windows. The kitchen was dark. I could see through to the dining room. It was also dark. Nothing out of place. No dirty dishes on the counter. No cereal boxes. No sweatshirt draped over a chair. I stood very still and listened. Nothing. Just the beating of my heart, which seemed frighteningly loud.

I tried the door. Locked. I worked my way around the side of the house. No open windows. I returned to the back of the house and looked up at the second floor. An open window. People felt safe leaving windows open on the second floor. And most of the time they were safe. But not this time. This window was over the little back porch, and I was good at climbing up back porches. When I was in high school my parents' back porch had been my main escape route when I was grounded. And I was grounded a lot.

Stephanie, Stephanie, Stephanie, I said to myself. This is insane. You're obsessed with this Spiro thing. There's no good reason to believe you'll find anything helpful in Con's house. What if you get caught? How embarrassing will that be? Then the stupid Stephanie spoke up. Yes, but I won't get caught, the stupid Stephanie said. Everyone's at the memorial service and it'll go on for another half hour at least. And no one can see this side of the house. It's blocked by the garage. The smart Stephanie didn't have an answer to that, so the stupid Stephanie shimmied up the porch railing and climbed through the second-story window and dropped into the bathroom.

The bathroom was white tile, white walls, white towels, white fixtures, white shower curtain, white toilet paper. It was blindingly antiseptic. The towels were perfectly folded and lined up on the towel bar. There was no scum in the soap dish. I took a quick peek in the medicine cabinet. Just the usual over-the-counter stuff you'd expect to find.

I walked through the three upstairs bedrooms, looking in closets and drawers and under beds. I went downstairs and walked through the living room, dining room, and den. The house was eerily unlived-in. No wrinkles on the pillowcases, and all the clothes hanging in the closet and folded in the chest were perfectly pressed. Just like Con, I thought. Lifeless and perfectly pressed.

I went to the kitchen. No food in the fridge. A bottle of water and a bottle of cranberry juice. The poor man was probably anemic from starvation. No wonder he was always so pale. His complexion frequently mirrored the deceased. Not flawed by death or disease but not quite human either. I thought it was by association, but Grandma said she thought Con dabbled in the makeup tray in the prep room.

Constantine Stiva was surrounded by grieving people every night, left alone with the dead by day, and went home to this sterile house after the evening viewings. And if we're to believe him, he has a son who came back to the Burg but never stopped by to say hello. Morelli thought Spiro was a single-minded rodent. I thought Spiro was a fungus. I thought Spiro fed off a host, and his host had always been Con.

I opened the door to the cellar, switched the light on, and cautiously crept down the stairs. *Eureka.* This was the room I'd been looking for. It was a windowless basement room that had been made into a do-it-yourself apartment. There was a couch covered by a rumpled sleeping bag and pillow. A television. A comfy chair that had seen better days. A scarred coffee table. A bookshelf that had been stocked with cans of soup and boxes of crackers. At the far end someone had installed a sink and a makeshift counter. There was a hotplate on the counter. And there was a small under-the-counter refrigerator. This was the perfect hiding hole for Spiro. There was a door next to the refrigerator. Bathroom, I thought.

I opened the door and looked around the room. I'd expected to find a small bathroom. What I had in front of me was a mortician's workroom. Two long tables covered with tubes of paint, artists' brushes, a couple large plastic containers of mortician's modeling clay, wigs and hairpieces, trays of cosmetics, jars of replacement teeth. And on a chair in the corner was a jacket and hat. Spiro's.

I had my cell phone clipped to my belt alongside my gun. I unclipped the phone and went to dial. No service in the basement. I was on my way through the door when a flash of color caught my eye. It was a rubbery blob that looked a lot like uncooked bacon. I moved closer and realized it was several pieces of the material morticians used for facial reconstruction. I didn't know a lot about the mechanics of preparing the dead for their last appearance, but I'd seen shows on movie makeup, and this looked similar. I knew it was possible to transform people into animals and aliens with this stuff. It was possible to make young actors look old, and it was possible to give the appearance of health and well-being to the newly departed. Stiva was a genius when it came to reconstructing the dead. He added fullness to the cheeks, smoothed over wrinkles, tucked away excess skin. He filled in bullet holes, added teeth, covered bruises, straightened noses when necessary.

Stiva was Burg comfort food. Burg residents knew their secrets and flaws were safe in Stiva's hands. At the end of the day, Stiva would make the fat look thin and the jaundiced look healthy. He wiped away time and alcoholism and self-indulgence. He chose the most flattering lipstick shade for the ladies. He hand-selected men's ties. Even fifty-two-year-old Mickey Branchek, who had a heart attack while laboring over Mrs. Branchek and died with an enormous erection that gave new meaning to the term stiffy, looked rested and respectable for his last hoohah. Best not to consider the process used to achieve that result.

Spiro had watched his father at work and would know the same techniques. So it wasn't shocking that the mole had been made from mortician's putty. The pieces of plastic that were lying on the table were more disturbing. They reminded me of Spiro's scars, and I realized Spiro would have the ability to change his appearance. A perfectly healthy Spiro could make himself horribly disfigured. He wouldn't fool anyone up close, but I'd only seen him at a distance, in a car. And Chester Rhinehart had seen him at night. If I was, in fact, looking at a disguise, it was pretty darn creepy.

I heard movement behind me, and I turned to find Con standing in the doorway.

"What are you doing? How'd you get in here?" he asked. "The doors to the house were closed and locked."

"The back door was open." When in a jam always go with a fib. "Is the service done?"

"No. I came back here because you tripped my alarm."

"I didn't hear it."

"It rings in my office. It monitors the cellar door, among others."

"You're hiding Spiro," I said. "I recognize the coat and hat on the chair. I'm sorry. This must be awful for you."

Con looked at me, his face composed, as always, his eyes completely devoid of emotion. "You're perfect," he said. "Stupid to the end. You haven't figured it out, have you? There's no Spiro. Spiro is dead. He died in the fire. There was nothing left of him but ashes and his school ring."

"I thought he was never found. There was never a service."

"He wasn't found. There wasn't anything left of him. Just the ring. I stumbled across it and never said anything. I didn't want a service. I wanted to move on, to rebuild my business. If he'd lived he would have ruined me, anyway. He was a moron."

This was the first I'd ever heard Con speak badly of the dead. And it was of his son. I didn't know what to say. It was true. Spiro was a moron, but it was chilling to hear it from Con. And if Spiro was dead then who was tormenting me? Who blew up Mama Macaroni? I suspected the answer was standing two feet away, but I couldn't put it together. I couldn't imagine solicitous Constantine Stiva, Mr. No Personality, offing Mama Mac.

"So it wasn't Spiro who was leaving me notes and blowing up cars?"

"No."

"It was you."

"Hard to believe, isn't it?"

"Why? Why were you stalking me?"

"Why doesn't matter," Con said. "Let's just say you're serving a purpose. I guess it's just as well that you're here. I don't have to hunt you down."

I put my hand to the gun at my hip, but it was an unfamiliar act, and I was slow. Con was much faster with his weapon. He lunged forward, and I saw the glint of metal in his hand, and I barely registered *stun gun* before I went out.

I WAS IN absolute blackness when I came around. My mind was working, but my body was slow to respond, and I couldn't see. I was cuffed and shackled, and I was blindfolded. No, I thought. Back up. I wasn't blindfolded. I could open and close my eyes. It was just very, very dark. And silent. And stuffy. I was disoriented in the dark, and I was having a hard time focusing. I rocked side to side. Not much room. I tried to sit but couldn't raise my head more than a couple inches. The space around me was minimal. The realization of confinement sent a shock of panic into my chest and burned in my throat. I was in a silk-lined container. God help me. Constantine Stiva had put me in one of his caskets. My heart was pounding and my mind was in free fall. This couldn't be real. Con was the heart and soul of the Burg. No one would ever suspect Con of bad things.

My hands ached from the cuffs, and I couldn't breathe. I was suffocating. I was buried alive. Hysteria came in waves and receded. Tears slid down my cheeks and soaked into the satin lining. I had no idea of time, but I didn't think much time had passed. Maybe a half hour. An hour at most. I had a moment of calm and realized I was breathing easier. Maybe I wasn't suffocating. Maybe I was just suffering a panic attack. I didn't smell dirt. I wasn't cold. Maybe I wasn't buried. Okay, hold that thought. Did I hear a siren far off in the distance? A dog barking?

My confinement stretched on with nothing to break the monotony. My muscles were cramping and my hands were numb. I no longer knew if it was day or night. What I knew with certainty was that Ranger would be looking for me. He'd return from Florida, and he'd do what he does best . . . he'd go into tracking mode. Ranger would find me. I just hoped he'd get to me in time.

I heard a door slam and an engine catch. The casket

shifted. I was pretty sure I was being driven somewhere. I hoped it wasn't the cemetery. I strained to hear
voices. If I heard voices I'd make noise. I seemed to
have air, but I didn't want to chance depleting the oxy-
gen if I didn't hear voices. We were stopping and starting and turning corners. We stopped, and a door
opened and slammed shut, and then I was sliding and
bumping along. I'd been to a lot of funerals with
Grandma Mazur. I knew what this was. I was moving
on the casket gurney. I was out of the hearse or the
truck or whatever, and I was being taken somewhere. I
was wheeled around corners, and then the motion
stopped. Nothing happened for what seemed like years,
and finally the lid was raised, and I blinked up at Con.

"Good," he said, "you're still alive. Didn't die of
fright, eh?" He looked in at me. "Undertaker humor."

My first thought was that I wouldn't cry. I'd try to
stay smart. I'd keep him talking. I'd look for an opportunity to escape. I'd stall for time. Time was my friend.
If I had enough time, Ranger would find me.

"I need to get out of this casket," I said.

"I don't think that's a good idea."

"I need to use the bathroom . . . bad."

Con was fastidious to a fault, and he looked gen-
uinely horrified at the possibility of a woman peeing in
one of his silk-lined caskets. He cranked the gurney
down to floor level and helped me wriggle myself out
of the box.

"This is the way it will work," he said. "I don't want
you making a mess all over everything, so I'm going to
let you use the bathroom. I'm going to release one cuff,
but I'll stun-gun you if you do anything dumb."

It took a moment to get my balance, and then I very carefully shuffled into the bathroom. When I shuffled out I felt a lot better. My hands were no longer numb and the cramps in my legs had subsided. We were in a house that looked like a small '70s ranch. It was sparsely furnished with mix-and-match hand-me-downs. The kitchen linoleum was old and the paint was faded. The counters were red Formica dotted with cigarette burns. The white ceramic sink was rust stained. Some of the over-the-counter kitchen cabinets were open and I could see they were empty. The casket was in the kitchen, and I was guessing it had been wheeled in from an attached garage.

"Is this in retaliation for Spiro's death or the fire in the funeral home?" I asked Con.

"Only tangentially. It's a bonus. Although it's a very nice bonus. There've been a couple nice bonuses to this charade. I got to kill Mama Macaroni. Who wouldn't love to do that? And then I got to bury her! Life doesn't get much better. The Macaronis bought the top-of-the-line slumber bed."

I cut my eyes to *my* slumber bed.

"Sorry," Con said. "Molded plastic. Not one of my better caskets. Lined with acetate. Still, it's good quality for people who haven't set aside funeral expenses. I'd like to put your grandmother in one of these. Her death should be declared a national holiday. What is this morbid obsession she has with the dead? I have to nail the lid down when there's a closed casket. And she's never happy with the cookies. Always wanting the kind with the icing in the middle. What does she think, cookies grow on trees?" Con smiled. "Maybe

I'll nail your lid down just to annoy her. That would be fun."

"So, I guess that means you're not going to bury me alive?"

"No. If I buried you alive I'd have to put you back in the casket. And I have plans for the casket. Mary Aleski is on a table back at the mortuary, and she'll be on view in that casket tomorrow. And besides, do you have any idea how much digging is involved in burying someone in a casket? I have a better plan. I'm going to hack you up and leave you here on the kitchen floor. It's important to my plan that you're found in this house."

"Why?"

"This house belongs to Spiro. It's tied up in probate because he hasn't been pronounced dead. If Spiro killed you it would be in this house, don't you think?"

"You still haven't told me why you want to kill me."

"It's a long story."

"Are we in a rush?"

Con looked at his watch. "No. As a matter of fact, I'm ahead of schedule. I'm coordinating this with the last of the Spiro sightings. Spiro will be seen in his car around midnight, and then I'll come back here and kill you, and Spiro will disappear forever."

"I don't get the Spiro tie-in. I don't get anything."

"This is about a crime that happened a long time ago. Thirty-six years to be exact. I was stationed at Fort Dix, and I masterminded a hijacking. I had four friends who helped me. Michael Barroni, Louis Lazar, Ben Gorman, and Jim Runion."

"The four men who were found shot to death behind the farmers' market."

"Yes. An unfortunate necessity."

"I wouldn't have pegged you for a criminal mastermind."

"I have many unappreciated talents. For instance, I'm quite good as an actor. I play the role of the perfect undertaker each night. And as you know I'm a genius with makeup. All I needed was a hat and a jacket, some colored contacts and handmade scars, and I was able to fool you and that pizza delivery boy."

"You always seemed like you enjoyed being a funeral director."

"It has its moments. And I hold a certain prominence in the community. I like that."

Constantine Stiva has an ego, go figure. "So you masterminded a hijacking."

"I saw the trucks come through once a week, and I knew how easy it would be to take one of them down on that isolated back station. Lazar was a munitions expert. I learned everything I know about bombs from Lazar. Gorman had been stealing cars since he was nine. Gorman stole the tow truck we used to drag the armored truck away. Barroni had all kinds of connections to launder the money. Runion was the dumb muscle.

"Do you want to know how we did it? It was so simple. I was on guard duty with two other men. The armored truck pulled up. Runion and Lazar were directly behind it in a car. Lazar had already planted the bomb when the truck stopped for lunch. *Kaboom,* the bomb went off and disabled the truck. Runion killed the other two guards on duty and shot me in the leg. Then Gorman hooked the truck up to the tow truck and hauled it off about a quarter mile down the road into an abandoned barn. I wasn't there, of course, but they told me Lazar set a charge that opened the truck like he'd used a can opener. They killed the truck guards and in a matter of minutes were miles away and seven million dollars richer."

"And no one ever solved the crime."

"No. The army expended so much energy hushing it all up that there wasn't a lot of energy left to investigate. They didn't want anyone to know the extent of the loss. That was very big money back then."

"What happened to the money?"

"There were five of us. We each took two hundred thousand as seed money for start-up businesses when we got out. And we agreed that every ten years we'd take another two hundred thousand apiece until we hit the forty-year mark and then we'd divide up what was left."

"So?"

"We had a vault in the mortuary basement. We had a system that each of us had a number, and it took all of us to open the vault. No one knew, but over the years I'd figured out the numbers. So I borrowed from the vault from time to time. Then you and your grandmother burned my business down. The vault survived, but I didn't. I was underinsured. So I took what was left in the vault and used it to rebuild. Two months ago, Barroni found out he had colon cancer and asked for his share of the money. He wanted to make sure it went to his family. We set the meeting up in the field behind the farmers' market so we could take a vote. I knew they were going to give Barroni the money. And they were going to want their share early, too. We were all at that age. Colon cancer. Heart disease. Irritable bowel. Everyone wants to take a cruise. Live the good life. Buy a new car. They were going to go down to my basement, open the vault, find out I'd stolen the money, and then they would have killed me."

"So you killed them."

"Yes. Death isn't such a big deal when it's happening to someone else."

"How do I fit in?"

"You're my insurance policy.

"Just in case one of my comrades shared the secret with a wife and she came looking for me, maybe with the police, I would confess to telling Spiro about the crime. Of course, it would be my version of the crime and I'd be non-culpable. Easy to believe Spiro would return to extort money and then resort to mass murder. And easy to believe Spiro would be a little goofy and take to stalking you. And I'd be the poor grieving father of the little bastard."

"That's the dumbest thing I ever heard."

"*You* fell for it," Con said. "Actually my original plan was just to leave you a few notes. Then I realized you'd made so many enemies you might not consider Spiro as the stalker, so I had to get more elaborate. Probably I could have stopped after you identified me at Cluck-in-a-Bucket, but by that time I was addicted to the rush of the game. It's too bad I have to kill you. It would have been fun to blow up more cars. I really like blowing up cars. And it turns out I'm good at it."

He was crazy. He'd inhaled too much embalming fluid. "You won't get away with it," I told him.

"I think I will. Everyone loves me. Look at me. I'm above suspicion. I'm the social director of the Burg."

"You're insane. You blew up Mama Macaroni."

"I couldn't resist. Did you like my present to you? The mole? I thought that was a good touch."

"What about Joe? Why did you run him over?"

"It was an accident. I was trying to get home, and I couldn't get rid of you and your idiot grandmother. I hit the curb and lost control of the car. Too bad I didn't kill him. That was a slow week."

Shades were drawn in the house. I looked around for a clock.

"It's almost ten," Con said. "I need to have Spiro seen one last time, driving the car that will be found in this garage. Sadly, it will be my final Spiro performance. And your body will be found in the kitchen. Horribly mutilated, of course. It seems like Spiro's style. He had a flare for the dramatic. I suppose in some ways the apple didn't fall far from the tree." He held the stun gun up for me to see. "Do you want me to stun you before I put you away or will you cooperate?"

"What do you mean, put me away?"

"I want you to be freshly killed after Spiro is seen driving the car. So I'm going to have to put you on ice for a couple hours."

I cut my eyes to the casket. I really didn't want to go back in the casket.

"No," Con said. "Not the casket. I need to get that back to the mortuary. It was just an easy way to transport you." He was looking around. "I need to find something that will keep you out of sight. Something I can lock."

"Ranger will find me," I told him.

"Is that the Rambo bounty hunter? Not a chance. No one's going to find you until I point him in the right direction."

He turned and looked at me with his pale, pale eyes, I saw his hand move, I heard something sizzle in my head, and everything was black.

MY MOUTH WAS dry and my fingertips were tingling. The jerk had zapped me again and stuffed me into something. I was on my back, and I was curled up fetus style. No light. No room to stretch my legs. My arms were pinned under me and the cuffs were cutting into my wrists. No satin lining this time. I was pretty sure I was crammed into some sort of wooden box. I tried rocking side to side. No room to get any momentum and nothing gave. This wasn't as terrifying as being locked in the casket, but it was much more uncomfortable. I was taking shallow breaths against the pain in my back and arms, playing games to occupy my mind, imagining that I was a bird and could fly, that I was a fire-breathing dragon, that I could play the cello in spite of the fact that I wasn't sure what a cello sounded like.

And suddenly there was a very slim, faint sliver of light in my box. I went still and listened with every molecule in my body. Someone had turned a light on. Or maybe it was daylight. Or maybe I was going to heaven. There were muffled sounds and men's voices, and there was a lot of door banging. I opened my mouth to yell for help, but the box opened before I had the chance. I tumbled out, and fell into Ranger's arms.

He was as stunned as I was. He had a vise-like grip on my arms, holding me up. His eyes were dilated black, and the line of his mouth was tight. "I saw you folded up in there, and I thought you were dead," he said.

"I'm okay. Just cramped."

I'd been stuffed into one of the empty over-the-counter cabinets. How Con had gotten me up there was a mystery. I guess when you're motivated you find strength.

Ranger had come in with Tank and Hal. Tank was at my back with a handcuff key, and Hal was working on the shackles.

"It's not Spiro," I said. "It's Con, and he's coming back to kill me. If we hang around we can catch him."

Ranger raised my bruised and bloody wrist to his mouth and kissed it. "I'm sorry to have to do this to you, but there's no *we*. I've just had six really bad hours looking for you. I need to know you're safe. Sitting in this house waiting for a homicidal undertaker doesn't feel safe." And he clamped the handcuff back on my wrist. "You've had enough fun for one day," he said. And the other bracelet went on Tank's wrist.

"What the . . ." Tank said, caught by surprise.

"Take her back to the office and have Ella tend to her wrists and then take her to Morelli," Ranger told Tank.

I dug my heels in. "No way!"

Ranger looked at Tank. "I don't care how you do it. Pick her up. Drag her. Whatever. Just get her out of here and keep her safe. And I don't want those bracelets to come off either of you until you hand her over to Morelli."

I glared at Tank. "I'm staying."

Tank looked back at Ranger. Obviously trying to decide which of us was more to be feared.

Ranger locked eyes with me. "Please," he said.

Tank and Hal were goggle-eyed. They weren't used to "please." I wasn't used to it either. But I liked it.

"Okay," I said. "Be careful. He's insane."

HAL DROVE, AND Tank and I sat in back in the Explorer. Tank was looking uncomfortable with me as an attachment, looking like he was searching for something to say but couldn't for the life of him come up with anything. I finally decided to come to his rescue.

"How did you find me?" I asked him.

"It was Ranger."

That was it. Three words. I knew he could talk. I saw him talking to Ranger all the time.

Hal jumped in from the front seat. "It was great. Ranger dragged some old lady out of bed to open the records office and hunt down real estate. He brought her in at gunpoint."

"Omigod."

"Boy, he was intense," Hal said. "He had every RangeMan employee and twenty contract workers out looking for you. We knew you disappeared at Stiva's because I was monitoring your bike. Tank and me started looking for you before Ranger even landed. You told me you were coming back and I got worried."

"You were worried about me?"

"No," Hal said. "I was worried Ranger would kill me if I lost you." He shot me a look in the rearview mirror. "Well yeah. Maybe I was a little worried about you, too."

"I was worried," Tank said. "I like you."

Hot damn! I leaned into him and smiled, and he smiled back at me.

"We went through the funeral home, and we went through the undertaker's home," Hal said. "And then Ranger figured they might own property someplace else, so he got the old lady in the tax records to open the office. She found that little ranch house under Spiro's name. It was all tied up because Spiro was never declared dead."

FORTY MINUTES LATER, I got dropped off at Morelli's. I had my wrists bandaged, and I had some powdered-sugar siftings on my black T-shirt. Tank walked me to the door and unlocked the cuffs while Morelli waited, a crutch under one arm, his other hand hooked into Bob's collar.

"She's in your care," Tank said to Morelli. "If Ranger asks, you can tell him I unlocked the cuffs in front of you."

"Do you want me to sign for her?" Morelli asked, on a smile.

"Not necessary," Tank said. "But I'm holding you responsible."

I ruffled Bob's head and slipped past Morelli. He shut the door and looked at my T-shirt.

"Powdered sugar?" he asked.

"I *needed* a doughnut. I had Hal stop at Dunkin' Donuts on the way across town."

"Ranger called and told me you were safe and on your way here, but he wouldn't tell me anything else."

Ranger was going to take Stiva down, and he didn't want anything going wrong. He didn't want to lose Stiva. He wanted to do the takedown himself, without a lot of police muddying the water.

"I accidentally got lost trying to find the memorial service and happened to stumble into Con's personal work-room. I tripped an alarm and Con found me snooping."

"I'm guessing he wasn't happy about you snooping?"

"It turns out Spiro is dead. Con said he found Spiro's ring in the fire debris. Con needed a scapegoat and decided Spiro was the ghost for the job. So Con's been going around in mortician's makeup, looking like a scarred Spiro."

"Why did Con need a scapegoat?"

I told Morelli about the hijacking and the money missing from the vault, and I told him about the mass murder.

Morelli was grinning. "Let me get this straight," he said. "In the beginning, you basically made all the wrong assumptions about Anthony's involvement and Spiro's identity. And yet, at the end, you solved the crime."

"Yeah."

"Fucking amazing."

"Anyway, Stiva locked me up in a casket and took me somewhere to kill me. He left so he could do one last Spiro impersonation, and while he was gone Ranger found me."

"And Ranger's waiting for him to return?"

"Yep."

"He should have told me," Morelli said.

"Probably didn't want the police involved. Ranger likes to keep things simple."

"Ranger's a little psycho."

"Marches to his own drummer," I said.

"His drummers are all psycho, too."

I looked at Bob. "Has he been out?"

"Only in the yard."

"I'll take him for a short walk."

I went to the kitchen and got Bob's leash. And while I was at it I pocketed the keys to the Buick. I was feeling left out. And I was feeling pissed off. I wanted to be part of the takedown. And I wanted to release some anger on Stiva. I'd quit my job in an effort to normalize my life, and he'd sabotaged my plan. Of course, he'd done some good things, too, like blowing up Mama Macaroni and sending my cello to cello heaven. Still, it was small compensation for mowing Joe down and stuffing me into a casket. Maybe I should be feeling charitable because it appeared he was insane, but I just didn't feel charitable. I felt angry.

I snapped the leash on Bob, took him out the front door, and loaded him into the Buick. There was a slight chance we'd both be blown to smithereens, but I didn't think so. Blowing me up wasn't in Stiva's plan. I shoved the key in the ignition and listened to the Buick suck gas. Music to my ears. Morelli wouldn't be happy when he heard the Buick drive off, but I couldn't risk telling him I was going back to help Ranger. Morelli would never let me go.

I'd paid attention when we left the little ranch house

where I'd been held captive, and in fifteen minutes I was back in the neighborhood. I cruised by the house. It was dark. Half a block away I spotted the Explorer. Hal and Tank were in the house with Ranger. I backed the Buick into a dark driveway directly across from the little ranch. I sat with the motor running and my lights off. Bob was panting in the backseat, snuffling his nose against the window. Bob liked being part of an adventure.

After ten minutes, a green sedan came down the street. The car passed under a streetlight, and I could see Stiva behind the wheel. He was wearing the hat, and a splash of light illuminated his fake scars. He turned into the ranch house driveway and stopped. The garage door started to slide up. This was my moment. I stomped my foot down on the gas and roared across the street, slamming into the back of the green sedan. I caught it square, sending it crashing through the bottom half of the garage door, pushing it into the back of the garage.

Bob was barking and jumping around in the backseat. Bob probably drove NASCAR in another life. Or maybe demolition derby. Bob loved destruction.

"So what do you think?" I asked Bob. "Should we hit him again?"

"Rolf, rolf, rolf!"

I backed up and rammed the green sedan a second time.

Ranger and Tank ran out of the house, guns drawn. Hal came five steps behind them. I backed up about ten feet and got out. I inspected the Buick. Hard to get a good look in the dark, but I couldn't see any damage by the light of the moon.

Tank played a beam of light from his Mag across the green sedan. The hood was completely smashed, the roof had been partially peeled away by the garage door, and the trunk was crumple city. Steam hissed from the radiator and liquid was pooling dark and slick under the car. Stiva was fighting the airbag.

I took Bob out of the backseat and walked him around on Spiro's front lawn so he could tinkle. I was thinking I'd move back into my apartment tomorrow. And maybe I'd get a cello. Not that I needed it. I was pretty darned interesting without it. Still, a cello might be fun.

Ranger was standing, hands on hips, watching me.

"I feel better now," I said to Ranger.

"Babe."

Enjoy this Excerpt from

TWELVE SHARP

the New Stephanie Plum Novel
From Janet Evanovich—

Now Available from St. Martin's Paperbacks.

WHEN I WAS twelve years old I accidentally substituted
salt for sugar in a cake recipe. I baked the cake, iced
the cake, and served it up. It looked like a cake, but as
soon as you cut into it and took a taste, you knew something else was going on. People are like that, too.
Sometimes you just can't tell what's on the inside from
looking at the outside. Sometimes people are a big surprise, just like the salt cake. Sometimes the surprise
turns out to be good. And sometimes the surprise turns
out to be bad. And sometimes the surprise is just friggin' confusing.

Joe Morelli is one of those good surprises. He's two
years older than me, and for most of my school years,
spending time with Morelli was like a visit to the dark
side, alluring and frightening. He's a Trenton cop now,
and he's my off-again, on-again boyfriend. He used to
be the hair-raising part of my life, but my life has had a
lot of changes, and now he's the normal part. He has a
dog named Bob, and a nice little house, and a toaster.

On the outside Morelli is still street tough and dangerously alluring. On the inside Morelli is now the guy with the toaster. Go figure.

I have a hamster named Rex, a utilitarian apartment, and my toaster is broken. My name is Stephanie Plum, and I work as a bond enforcement agent, aka bounty hunter, for my cousin Vinnie. It's not a great job, but it has its moments, and if I mooch food off my parents, the job almost pays enough to get me through the month. It would pay a lot more, but the truth is, I'm not all that good at it.

Sometimes I moonlight for a guy named Ranger, who's extremely bad in an incredibly good way. He's a security expert, and a bounty hunter, and he moves like smoke. Ranger is milk chocolate on the outside . . . a delicious, tempting, forbidden pleasure. And no one knows much of what's on the inside. Ranger keeps his own counsel.

I work with two women I like a lot. Connie Rosolli is Vinnie's office manager and junk-yard dog. She's a little older than I am. A little smarter. A little tougher. A little more Italian. She's got a lot more chest, and she dresses like Betty Boop.

The other woman is my sometimes partner Lula. Lula was, at this moment, parading around in the bail-bonds office, showing Connie and me her new outfit. Lula is a way-beyond-voluptuous black woman who was currently squashed into four-inch spike heels and a sparkly gold spandex dress that had been constructed for a *much* smaller woman. The neckline was low, and the only thing keeping Lula's big boobs from popping out was the fact that the material was snagged on her nipples. The skirt was stretched tight across her ass and hung two inches below the full moon.

With Connie and Lula you get what you see.

Lula bent to take a look at the heel on her shoe, and Connie was treated to a view of the night sky.

"Crikey," Connie said. "You need to put some underwear on."

"I got underwear on," Lula said. "I'm wearing my best thong. Just 'cause I used to be a ho don't mean I'm cheap. Problem is that little thong stringy gets lost in all my derriere."

"Tell me again what you're doing in this get-up," Connie said.

"I'm gonna be a rock-and-roll singer. I got a gig singing with Sally Sweet's new band. You heard of the *Who*? Well, we're gonna be the *What*."

"You can't sing," Connie said. "I've heard you sing. You can't hold a tune to 'Happy Birthday.' "

"The hell I can't," Lula said. "I could sing your ass off. Besides, half those rock singers can't sing. They just open their big oversize mouth and yell. And you gotta admit, I look good in this here dress. Nobody gonna be paying attention to my singing when I'm wearing this dress."

"She's got a point," I said to Connie.

"No argument," Connie said.

"I'm under-realized," Lula said. "I gotta lot of untapped potential. Yesterday my horoscope said I gotta expand my horizons."

"You expand anymore in that dress, and you'll get yourself arrested," Connie said.

The bonds office is on Hamilton Avenue, a couple

blocks from Saint Frances Hospital. Handy for bonding out guys who've been shot. It's a small store front office sandwiched between a beauty parlor and a used bookstore. There's an outer room with a scarred imitation leather couch, a couple folding chairs, Connie's desk and computer and a bank of files. Vinnie's office is located in a room behind Connie's desk.

When I started working for Vinnie he used his office to talk to his bookie and set up nooners with barnyard animals, but Vinnie has recently discovered the Internet, and now he uses his office to surf porn sites and online casinos. Behind the bank of file cabinets is a storeroom filled with the nuts and bolts of the bailbonds business. Confiscated televisions, DVD players, ipods, computers, a velvet painting of Elvis, a set of cookware, blenders, kids' bikes, engagement rings, a tricked-out Hog, a bunch of George Foreman grills, and God knows what else. Vinnie had some guns and ammo back there too. Plus a box of cuffs that he got on ebay. There's a small bathroom that Connie keeps spotless and a back door in case there's a need to sneak off.

"I hate to be a party pooper," Connie said, "but we're going to have to put the fashion show on hold because we have a problem." She slid a stack of folders across her desk at me. "These are all unresolved skips. If we don't find some of these guys we're going belly up."

Here's the way bailbonds works. If you're accused of a crime and you don't want to sit and rot in jail while you're waiting for your trial to come up, you can give the court a wad of money. The court takes the money and lets you walk, and you get the money back when you show up on your trial date. If you don't have that money stashed under your mattress, a bail bondsman can give the court the money on your behalf. He'll charge you a percentage of the money (maybe ten percent), and he'll keep that percentage whether you're proven guilty or not. If the accused shows up for court, the court gives the bail bondsman his money back. If the accused doesn't show up, the court keeps the money until the bondsman finds the accused and drags his sorry butt back to jail.

So you see the problem, right? Too much money going out and not enough money going in, and Vinnie might have to refinance his house. Or worse, the insurance company that backs Vinnie could yank the plug.

"Lula and I can't keep up with the skips," I said to Connie. "There are too many of them."

"Yeah, and I'll tell you the problem," Lula said. "Ranger's not pulling his weight. Any more there's just Stephanie and me catching bad guys."

It was true. Ranger had moved most of his business toward the security side and only went into tracking mode when something came in that was over my head. There are some who might argue *everything* is over my head, but for practical purposes we've had to ignore that argument.

"I hate to say this," I told Connie, "but you need to hire another bond enforcement person."

"It's not that easy," Connie said. "Remember when we had Joyce Barnhardt working here? That was a disaster."

Joyce Barnhardt is my archenemy. I went all

through school with her, and she was a misery. And before the ink was dry on my marriage license, she was in bed with my husband, who is now my ex-husband. Thank you, Joyce.

"We could put a ad in the paper," Lula said. "That's how I got my filing job here. Look at how good that turned out."

Connie and I did eye rolls.

Lula was about the worst file clerk ever. Lula kept her job because no one else would tolerate Vinnie. The first time Vinnie made a grab at Lula, she clocked him on the side of the head with a five-pound phone book and told him she'd staple his nuts to the wall if he didn't show respect. And that was the end of sexual harassment in the bail bonds office.

Connie read the names off the files on her desk. "Lonnie Johnson, Kevin Gallager, Leon James, Dooby Biagi, Caroline Scarziolli, Melvin Pickle, Charles Chin, Bernard Brown, Mary Lee Truk, Luis Queen, John Santos. These are all current. You already have half of them. The rest came in last night. Plus we have nine outstanding that we've relegated to the 'temporarily lost cause' file. Word's getting out that we're not enforcing the bond."

When someone doesn't show up for a court appearance, we call them FTA. Failure To Appear. People fail to appear for a bunch of reasons. Hookers and pushers can make more money on the street than they can in jail, so they only show up in court when you finally stop bonding them out. All other people just don't want to go to jail.

Connie gave me the new files, and a wave of nausea

slid through my stomach. Lonnie Johnson was wanted for armed robbery. Leon James was suspected of arson and attempted murder. Kevin Gallager was wanted for grand theft auto. Mary Lee Truk had inserted a carving knife into her husband's left buttock during a domestic disturbance. And Melvin Pickle was caught with his pants down in the third row of the multiplex.

Lula was looking over my shoulder, reading along with me.

"Melvin Pickle sounds like fun," she said. "I think we should start with Melvin."

"Maybe an ad in the paper isn't such a bad idea," I said to Connie.

"Yeah," Lula said. "Just be careful how you word it. You probably want to fib a little. Like you *don't* want to say we're looking for some gun-happy lunatic to take down a bunch of scum bags."

"I'll keep that in mind when I write it up," Connie said.

"I'm going down the street," I told Lula. "I need something to settle my stomach. We'll go to work when I get back."

"You going to the drugstore?" Lula wanted to know.

"No. The bakery."

"I wouldn't mind if you brought me back one of them cream-filled doughnuts with the chocolate frosting," Lula said. "I could use to settle my stomach too."

At mid-morning the Garden State was heating up. Pavement was steaming under a cloudless sky, petrochemical plants were spewing to the north, and cars were emitting hydrocarbons statewide. By midafternoon I'd feel the toxic stew catch in the back of my throat, and I'd know it was truly summer in Jersey. For me, the stew is part of the Jersey experience. The stew has attitude. And it enhances the pull of Point Pleasant. How can you completely appreciate the Jersey shore if the air is safe to breathe in the interior parts of the state?

I swung into the bakery and went straight to the doughnut case. Marjorie Lando was behind the counter, filling cannoli for a customer. Fine by me. I could wait my turn. The bakery was always a soothing experience. My heart rate slowed in the presence of massive quantities of sugar and lard. My mind floated over the acres of cookies and cakes and doughnuts and cream pies topped with rainbow sprinkles, chocolate frosting, whipped cream and meringue.

I was in my zone, patiently contemplating my doughnut selection, when I sensed a familiar presence behind me. A hand brushed my hair back, and Ranger leaned into me and kissed me on the nape of my neck.

"I could get you to look at *me* like that if I had five minutes alone with you," Ranger said.

"I'll give you five minutes alone with me if you'll take over half my skips."

"Tempting," Ranger said, "but I'm on my way to the airport, and I'm not sure when I'll be back. Tank is in charge. Call him if you need help. And let him know if you decide to move into my apartment."

Not that long ago I needed a safe place to stay, and sort of commandeered Ranger's apartment when he was out of town. Ranger had come home and found me sleeping in his bed like Goldilocks. He'd very graciously not thrown me out the seventh-floor window. And in fact he'd allowed me to stay with a minimum of sexual harassment. Okay, maybe *minimum* isn't entirely accurate. Maybe it was a seven on a scale of ten, but he hadn't forced the issue.

"How did you know I was here?" I asked him.

"I stopped at the bonds office, and Lula told me you were on a doughnut mission."

"Where are you going?"

"Miami."

"Is this business or pleasure?"

"It's bad business."

Marjorie finished with her customer and made her way over to me. "What'll it be?" she wanted to know.

"A dozen Boston cream doughnuts."

"Babe," Ranger said.

"They're not all for me."

Ranger doesn't often smile. Mostly he thinks about smiling, and this was one of those thinking smile times. He wrapped his hand around my wrist, pulled me to him and kissed me. The kiss was warm and short. No tongue in front of the bakery lady, thank God. He turned and walked away. Tank was idling at the curb in a black SUV. Ranger got in and they drove off.

Marjorie was behind the counter with a cardboard box in her hand and her mouth dropped open. "Wow," she said.

That dragged a sigh out of me because she was right. Ranger was definitely a *wow*. He stood half a head taller than me. He was perfectly toned muscle, and he had classic Latino good looks. He always smelled great. He dressed only in black. His skin was dark. His eyes were dark. His hair was dark. His life was dark. Ranger had lots of secrets.

"It's a work relationship," I told Marjorie.

"If he was in here any longer the chocolate would have melted off the eclairs."

"I DON'T LIKE this," Lula said. "I wanted to go after the pervert. I personally think it's a bad choice to go after the guy who likes guns."

"He's got the highest bond. The fastest way to dig Vinnie out of the hole is to get the guy with the highest bond."

We were in Lula's red Firebird, sitting across the street from Lonnie Johnson's last known address. It was a small clapboard bungalow in a depressed neighborhood that backed up to the hockey arena. It was close to noon and not a great time to roust a bad guy. If he's still in bed it's because he's drunk and mean. If he's not in bed it's most likely because he's at a bar getting drunk and mean.

"What's the plan?" Lula wanted to know. "We gonna just bust in like gangsta bounty hunter and kick his ass?"

I looked at Lula. "Have we *ever* done that?"

"Don't mean we can't."

"We'd look like idiots. We're incompetent."

"That's harsh," Lula said. "And I don't think we're *completely* incompetent. I think we're closer to eighty percent incompetent. Remember the time you wrestled that naked greased-up fat guy? You did a good job with that one."

"Too early in the day to do the pizza delivery routine," I said.

"Can't do the flower delivery either. Nobody believe someone sending flowers to this dope."

"If you hadn't changed clothes you could do the hooker delivery routine," I said to Lula. "He would have opened the door to you in that gold thing."

"Maybe we pretend we're selling cookies. Like Girl Scouts. All we gotta do is go back to the 7-Eleven and get some cookies."

I looked Johnson's phone number up on the bond sheet and called him from my cell.

"Yeah?" a man said.

"Lonnie Johnson?

"What the fuck you want? Fuckin' bitch calling me at this hour. You think I got nothin' better to do than answer this phone?" And he hung up.

"Well?" Lula asked.

"He didn't feel like talking. And he's angry."

A shiny black Hummer with tinted windows and bling wheel covers rolled down the street and stopped in front of Johnson's house.

"Uh oh," Lula said. "Company."

The Hummer sat there for a moment, and then opened fire on Johnson's house. Multiple weapons. At least one was automatic, firing continuous rounds. Windows blew out and the house was drilled with shots. Gunfire was returned from the house, and I saw the nose of a rocket launcher poke out a front window.

Obviously the Hummer saw it too, because it laid rubber taking off.

"Maybe this isn't a good time," I said to Lula.

"I *told* you to go for the pervert."

MELVIN PICKLE WORKED in a shoe store. The store was part of the mall that attached to the multiplex where he'd been caught shaking hands with the devil. I didn't have a lot of enthusiasm for this capture, since I had some sympathetic feelings for Pickle. If I had to work in a shoe store all day, I might go to the multiplex to whack off once in a while, too.

"Not only is this going to be an easy catch," Lula said, parking at the food court entrance, "but we can get pizza and go shopping."

A half hour later, we were full of pizza and had taken a couple new perfumes out for a test drive. We'd moseyed down the mall and were standing in front of Pickle's shoe store, scoping out the employees. I had a photo of Pickle that had come with his bond agreement.

"That's him," Lula said, looking over my shoulder. "That's him on his knees, trying to sell that dumb woman those ugly-ass shoes."

According to Pickle's paperwork he'd just turned forty. He had sandy colored hair that looked like it had been cut in boot camp. His skin was pale, his eyes hidden behind round-rimmed glasses, his mouth accented by a big herpes sore. He was 5'7" and had an average build gone soft. His slacks and dress shirt were just short of shabby. He didn't look like he cared a whole lot if the woman bought the shoes.

I moved my cuffs from my shoulder bag to my jeans pocket. "I can manage this," I said to Lula. "You stay here in case he bolts."

"I don't think he looks like a bolter," Lula said. "I think he looks more like the walking dead."

I agreed with Lula. Pickle looked like he was two steps away from putting a bullet in his brain. I moved behind him and waited for him to stand.

"I love this shoe," the woman said. "But I need a size nine."

"I don't have a size nine," Pickle said.

"Are you sure?"

"Yeah."

"Maybe you should go back and look again."

Pickle sucked air for a couple beats and nodded. "Sure," he said.

He stood and turned and bumped into me.

"You're going to leave, aren't you?" I said. "I bet you're going to go out the back door and go home and never come back."

"It's a reoccurring fantasy," he said.

I glanced at my watch. It was twelve-thirty. "Have you had lunch?" I asked him.

"No."

"Take your lunch now and come with me, and I'll buy you a piece of pizza."

"There's something wrong with this picture," Pickle said. "Are you one of those religious nuts who wants to save me?"

"No. I'm not a religious nut." I held my hand out. "Stephanie Plum."

He automatically shook my hand. "Melvin Pickle."

"I work for Vincent Plum Bail Bonds," I said. "You missed a court date, and you need to reschedule."

"Sure," he said.

"Now."

"I can't go now. I gotta work."

"You can take your lunch break."

"I had plans for lunch."

Probably going to see a movie. I was still holding his hand, and with my other hand I clapped a bracelet on him.

He looked down at the cuff. "What's this? You can't do this. People will ask questions. And then what will I tell them? I'll have to tell them I'm a pervert!"

Two women looked over at him and raised their eyebrows.

"No one will care," I said. I turned to the women. "You don't care, right?"

"Right," they murmured and hurried out of the store.

"Just walk out into the mall quietly with me," I said. "I'll take you to court and get you rebonded."

Actually Vinnie would rebond him. Vinnie and Connie could write bond. Lula and I did the capture thing.

"Darn," Pickle said. "Darn it all."

And he took off with the cuff dangling from his wrist. Lula stepped in front of him, but he had momentum and knocked her on her ass. He faltered for a moment, got his footing and ran off, into the mall. I was ten steps behind him. I stumbled over Lula, scrambled to my feet and kept going. I chased him through the mall and up an escalator.

A hotel with an open atrium was attached to one end of the mall. Pickle ran into the hotel and barreled through the fire door into the stairwell. I chased him up five flights of stairs and thought my lungs were going to explode. He exited the stairwell, and I dragged myself, gasping to the door.

There were seven floors to the hotel. All rooms opened to a hallway that overlooked the hotel atrium. We were on the sixth floor. I staggered out of the stairwell and saw that Pickle had made it halfway around the atrium and was straddling the balcony railing.

"Don't come near me," he yelled. "I'll jump."

"Fine with me," I said. "I get my money dead or alive."

Pickle looked depressed at that fact. Or maybe Pickle just *always* looked depressed.

"You're in pretty good shape," I said, still winded. "How do you stay in such good shape?"

"My car got repossessed. I walk everywhere. And all day long I'm up and down with the shoes. At the end of the day my knees are killing me."

I was talking to him, creeping closer. "Why don't you get a different job? One that's easier on your knees."

"Are you kidding me? I'm lucky to have *this* job. Look at me. I'm a loser. And now everybody's going to know I'm a pervert. I'm a pervert loser. And I have a big herpes. I'm a pervert loser with a herpes!"

"You need to get a grip. You don't have to be a pervert loser if you don't want to be."

He sat on the railing and swung both legs over. "Easy for you to say. You aren't named Melvin Pickle. And I bet you were a baton twirler in high school. You probably had friends. You probably date."

"I don't exactly date, but I sort of have a boyfriend."

"What does *sort of* mean?"

"It means that he looks like my boyfriend, but I don't say it out loud."

"Why not?" Pickle wanted to know.

"It feels weird. I'm not sure why." Okay, I knew *why*, but I wasn't going to say *that* out loud either. I had feelings for two men, and I didn't know how to choose between them. "And I wish you wouldn't sit like that. It's creeping me out."

"Are you afraid I'll fall? I thought you didn't care. Remember dead or alive?"

My cell phone was ringing in my bag.

"For crying out loud, answer it," Pickle said. "Don't worry about me, I'm only going to kill myself."

I did an exaggerated eye-roll and answered the phone.

"Hey," Lula said. "Where are you? I been looking all over."

"I'm in the hotel at the end of the mall."

"I'm right outside of that hotel. What are you doing there? Do you have Pickle?"

"I don't exactly *have* Pickle. We're on the sixth floor and he's thinking about jumping off the balcony."

I looked over the railing and saw Lula walk into the atrium. She looked up, and I waved at her.

"I see you," Lula said. "Tell Pickle he's gonna make a big mess if he jumps. This floor's marble, and his head's gonna crack open like a fresh egg, and there's gonna be brains and blood all over the place."

I disconnected and relayed the message to Pickle.

"I have a plan," he said. "I'm going to jump feet first. That way my head won't make such an impact when I land."

Pickle was getting noticed. People were dotted around the atrium, looking up at him. The elevator opened behind me and a man in a suit stepped out.

"What's going on here?" he wanted to know.

"Don't come near me!" Pickle yelled. "If you come near me, I'll jump."

"I'm the hotel manager," the man said. "Is there something I can do?"

"Do you have a giant net?" I asked him.

"Just go away," Pickle said. "I have big problems. I'm a pervert."

"You don't look like a pervert," the manager said.

"I whacked off in the multiplex," Pickle told him.

"Everybody whacks off in the multiplex," the manager said. "I like to go when there's one of those chick flicks playing, and I wear my wife's panties and I . . ."

"Jeez," Pickles said. "Too much information."

The manager disappeared behind the elevator doors and minutes later reappeared in the lobby. He stood in a small cluster of hotel employees, everyone with their head back, their eyes glued to Pickle.

"You're making a scene," I said to Pickle.

"Yeah," Pickle said. "Pretty soon they're going to start yelling *'jump'*. The human race is lacking. Have you noticed?"

"There are some good people," I told him.

"Oh yeah? Who's the best person you know? Of all the people you know personally, is there anyone who has a sense of right and wrong and lives by it?"

This was a sticky question because it would have to be Ranger . . . but I suspected he occasionally killed people. Only *bad* people, of course, but still . . .

The crowd in the atrium was growing and now included some uniformed security guys and two Trenton cops. One of the cops was on his two-way, probably calling Morelli to tell him I was involved in yet another disaster. A cameraman and his assistant joined the crowd.

"We're on television," I told Pickle.

Pickle looked down, waved at the camera, and everyone cheered.

"This is getting too weird," I told Pickle. "I'm leaving."

"You can't leave. If you leave, I'll jump."

"I don't care, remember?"

"Of course you care. You'll be responsible for my death."

"Oh no. No, no, no." I wagged my finger at him. "That won't work with me. I grew up in the Burg. I was raised Catholic. I know guilt in and out. The first thirty years of my life were ruled by guilt. Not that guilt is an entirely bad thing. But you're not going to lay it on me. Whether you live or die is your choice. I have nothing to do with it. I'm not taking responsibility for the state of the pot roast any more."

"Pot roast?"

"Every Friday I'm expected for dinner at my parents' house. Every Friday my mom makes pot roast. If

I'm late, the pot roast cooks too long and gets dry, and it's all my fault."

"And?"

"And it's not my fault!"

"Of course it's your fault. You were late. They were nice enough to make a pot roast for you. Then they were nice enough to hold dinner for you even though it meant ruining the pot roast. Boy, you should learn some manners."

My cell phone rang again. It was my Grandma Mazur. She lives with my mom and dad. She moved in when Grandpa Mazur sailed off in a heaven-bound gravy boat.

"You're on television," she said. "I was trying to find Judge Judy, and you popped up. They said you were Breaking News. Are you trying to rescue that guy on the railing, or are you trying to get him to jump?"

"In the beginning I was trying to rescue him," I said. "But I'm starting to change my mind."

"I gotta go now," Grandma said. "I gotta call Ruth Biablocki and tell her you're on television. She's always going on about her granddaughter and how she's got that good job at the bank. Well, let's see her top this one. Her granddaughter don't get on television!"

"What are you so depressed about that you want to jump off this balcony?" I asked Pickle. "Jumping to your death is pretty severe."

"My life sucks! My wife left me and took everything, including my clothes and my dog. I got fired from my job and had to go to work in a shoe store. I have no money so I had to move back home and live with my mother. And I got caught whacking off in a multiplex. Could it possibly get any worse?"

"You have your health."

"I think I'm getting a cold. And as you can see because you're *staring*, I have a *huge oozing herpes!*"

My phone rang again.

"Cupcake," Morelli said, "I don't like finding you in a hotel with another guy."

I looked down and saw Morelli standing next to Lula.

"He's a jumper," I told Morelli.

"Yeah," Morelli said. "I can see that. What's the story?"

"He got caught whacking off in the multiplex and doesn't want to go to jail."

"He won't get a lot of jail time for that," Morelli said. "Maybe a couple weekends or community service. It's not a big deal. Everyone whacks off in the multiplex."

I relayed the message to Pickle.

"It's not just jail," Pickle said. "It's me. I'm a loser."

Morelli was still on the phone. "Now what?"

"He's a loser."

"You're on your own with that one," Morelli said. "Are you going to need help with this?"

"Maybe you need . . . vitamins," I said to Pickle.

Pickle looked at me. Hopeful. "Do you think that could be it?"

"Yeah. If you get off the railing we could go to the health food store and get some."

"You're just saying that to get me off the railing."

"True. The police will probably arrest you for being a nut. You'll have to go to the station and wait for Vinnie to get there to bond you out again."

"I can't afford to get bonded out again. I just walked off my job. I'm probably unemployed."

"Oh for the love of everything holy." I peeked at my watch. I didn't have time for this. I had other fish to fry. "How about this? We need someone to do filing at the bonds office. Maybe I can get Vinnie to hire you so you can work off the fee to get bonded out."

"Really? You'd do that for me?"

Morelli was still listening in. "Okay, so far we've promised him community service, vitamins, and a job. The only thing left that he could possibly want is gorilla sex. And if you promise that to him I'm not going to be happy."

I disconnected Morelli and put the phone back into my pocket.

"About the job," Pickle said. "Vinnie wouldn't mind that I'm a . . . you know, pervert?"

That was pretty funny. Vinnie minding that Pickle whacked off at the multiplex. "It's probably the only thing you have going for you," I told Pickle.

"Okay," he said. "But you're going to have to help me get off this railing. I'm terrified to move."

I grabbed the back of his shirt and hauled him off the railing, and we both collapsed into a heap on the floor. The crowd reaction was mixed. Some cheers and some boos. We got to our feet, I cuffed his hands behind his back and led him to the elevator.

Morelli was waiting for me when the doors opened at the atrium level. He stepped in with two uniforms, and we all rode one floor down to the parking garage where a cruiser was idling. I got Pickle into the back seat, and promised to get him rebonded.

"And the vitamins," Pickle said. "Don't forget the vitamins."

"Sure."

The cruiser took off, and I turned to Morelli. He was standing thumbs hooked into his jeans pockets, and he was smiling at me. Morelli is six foot tall and is all lean planes and angles and hard muscle. His complexion is Mediterranean. His hair is almost black and curls against his neck. His brown eyes are liquid chocolate when he's aroused.

"What?" I asked Morelli.

"I can always count on you to add some fun to the day. Did you make any more promises after you hung up on me?"

"None you want to know about."

The smile widened. "Bob misses you. He hasn't seen you in a couple days."

Bob is Morelli's big orange dog. And this is Morelli's ploy when he wants me to do a sleepover. Not that he needs a ploy.

"I'll have to call you later this afternoon," I said. "I don't know how my day will go. I'm on a mission to clean up a bunch of FTAs for Vinnie."

He curled his fingers into my T-shirt, pulled me to him and kissed me. There was a lot of tongue involved and some wandering hands. When he was done he held me at arm's length. "Be careful," he said.

"Too late," I told him.

He moved me five steps backward into the elevator, pushed the button and sent me up to the atrium where Lula was waiting.

"I'm not even going to guess what went on in that

parking garage," Lula said. "But you better wipe that goofy smile off your face, or people are gonna get the right idea."

I called Connie and told her about Pickle.

"Vinnie's out of town," she said. "I'll bond Pickle out. And before I forget, there was a woman in here asking for you. She said her name was Carmen."

Off-hand I couldn't think of anyone I knew named Carmen. "Did she say what she wanted?"

"She said it was personal. I'm guessing she was in her late twenties. Soft spoken. Pretty. And crazy."

Great. "What kind of crazy are we talking about? Crazy stressed? Crazy dressed in clown shoes with a red rubber nose? Or crazy crazy?"

"Crazy stressed and crazy crazy. She was dressed all in black. Like Ranger. Black boots, black cargo pants, black t-shirt, black hair. And she was . . . intense. She said she would track you down. And then she asked about Ranger. I guess she's looking for him too."

"We got choices to make," Lula said when I put my phone away. "We could cruise for shoes, or we could embarrass ourselves some more by pretending to be bounty hunters."

"I think we're on a roll. I say we keep pretending to be bounty hunters."

"I want to see the woman who stabbed her husband in the ass," Lula said. "Let's do her next."

"She's in the Burg," I said to Lula, pulling the file on Mary Lee Truk. "I'll call my mom and see if she knows her."

The Burg is a small chunk of Trenton just outside center city. It's a working-class neighborhood that can't keep a secret and takes care of its own. My parents live in the Burg. My best friend Mary Lou Molnar lives in the Burg. Morelli's family is in the Burg. Morelli and I have moved out . . . but we haven't moved far.

Grandma Mazur answered the phone. "Of course I know Mary Lee Truk," Grandma said. "I play Bingo with her mother."

"Does Mary Lee get along with her husband?"

"Not since she stabbed him in the behind. I understand he got real cranky about that and packed up and left."

"Why did she stab him?"

"The story is that she asked him if he thought she was putting on weight, and he said *yes,* and then she stabbed him. It was one of them spontaneous acts. Mary Lee's going through the change, and everyone knows you don't just up and tell a menopausal woman she's getting fat. I swear, some men have no brains at all.

"And by the way, I forgot to tell you before, but some woman came to the house this afternoon, looking for you. I said I didn't know exactly where you were, and she said that was okay, that she'd find you with or without anyone's help. And she was dressed like that hottie you work with, Ranger."

LULA PULLED THE Firebird into the curb, and we sat looking at the Truk house.

"I don't have a good feeling about this," Lula said.

"You were the one who wanted to do the butt stabber."

"That was before I knew the menopause story. What if she has a hot flash while we're there and goes looney tunes?"

"Just don't turn your back on her. And don't comment on her weight."

I got out of the car and walked to the door, and Lula followed. I was about to knock when the door was wrenched open, and Mary Lee glared out at me. She had short brown hair that looked like it had been styled with an electric mixer. She was fifty-two according to her bond papers. She was a couple inches shorter than me and a couple pounds heavier.

"What?" she asked.

"Yow!" Lula whispered to me.

I introduced myself and gave Mary Lee the routine about getting rebonded.

"I can't go with you," she wailed. "Look at my hair! I used to be so good with hair, but lately I can't do anything with this mess."

"I use conditioner on mine," Lula said. "Have you tried that?"

We both looked at Lula's hair. It was orangutang orange and the texture of boar bristles.

"How about a hat?" I said.

"A hat," Mary Lee sobbed. "My hair's so bad I need a hat!" Mary Lee's face got red, and she stripped her T-shirt off. "God, it's *hot* in here." She was in her bra, sweating, and fanning herself with her shirt.

Lula put her finger to the side of her head and made circles. The international sign for *bats in her belfry*.

"I saw that!" Mary Lee said, eyes narrowed. "You think I'm nuts. You think the big fatso is nuts!"

"Lady, you just took your shirt off," Lula said. "I used to do that, but I made money on it."

Mary Lee looked at the shirt in her hand. "I don't remember taking it off."

Mary Lee's face wasn't red anymore, and she'd stopped sweating, so I took the shirt and tugged it over her head. "I can help you," I said. "I know just what you need." I rummaged through my shoulder bag, found my baseball cap and clapped it onto her head and tucked most of her hair in. I did a fast walk through the house to make sure it was locked up and Mary Lee hadn't accidentally put the cat in the oven, and then Lula and I steered Mary Lee out of the house and into the car.

Five minutes later I had Mary Lee standing in front of the doughnut case at the bakery.

"Okay, take a deep breath and look over all the doughnuts," I told her. "Look at the strawberry doughnut with the rainbow sprinkles. Doesn't it make you happy?"

Mary Lee smiled at the doughnut. "Pretty."

"And the meringue that looks like a fluffy cloud. And the birthday cakes with the pink and yellow roses. And the chocolate cream pie."

"This is very relaxing," Mary Lee said.

I called Connie's cell phone. "Are you still at the courthouse?" I asked her. "I'm bringing Mary Lee Truk in and we're going to want to bond her out right away before she gets another hot flash."

"I hate to break into the moment," Marjorie Lando said. "But what'll it be?"

"A dozen assorted doughnuts to go," I told her.

◆ ◆ ◆

LULA DROPPED ME off in front of the bonds office. "That wasn't so bad," she said. "We helped two lost souls today. That's real good for my horizon expanding and positive karma stockpile. Usually we just piss people off, and that don't do me any good in the karma department. And it's only five o'clock. I got plenty of time to get to rehearsal. See you tomorrow."

"See you tomorrow," I said, and I waved Lula away and beeped my car open. I was driving a black-and-white Mini Cooper that I'd gotten from Honest Dan the Used Car Man. The interior space was a little cozy for carting bad guys off to jail, but the car had been the right price, and it was fun to drive. I slid behind the wheel, and jumped when someone knocked on the driver's side window.

It was the woman dressed in black.

I started the car and rolled the window down. I had my bag on my lap and my gun in my bag. The gun didn't have any bullets in it, but I felt sort of like a professional when I carried it, and it gave me a nice false sense of security. I was ready to pull the gun out and scare the jeepers out of the woman if she got crazy.

"You wanted to speak to me?" I asked the woman.

The woman looked in the window at me. "You're Stephanie Plum?"

"Yes. And you would be . . ."

"My name is Carmen Manoso," she said. "I'm Ranger's wife."